To: Deborah, Vanderhorst

Chester A, Wright

9/10/2009

Black Men and Blue Water

Historical Context and the Origins of the Stewards, Cooks and Messboys of the U.S. Navy

by

Chester A. Wright

authorHOUSE®

AuthorHouse™
1663 Liberty Drive, Suite 200
Bloomington, IN 47403
www.authorhouse.com
Phone: 1-800-839-8640

First published by AuthorHouse   5/12/2009

ISBN: 978-1-4343-7061-7 (sc)
ISBN: 978-1-4343-7060-0 (hc)

Printed in the United States of America
Bloomington, Indiana

This book is printed on acid-free paper.

TABLE OF CONTENTS

References and Sources.. ix

Acknowledgements xi

Introduction xiii

PART I. BLACK SAILORS IN EARLY AMERICA: FROM THE PRE-REVOLUTIONARY PERIOD TO 1775

Chapter 1:   An Inherited Naval Tradition.................................... 3

Chapter 2.   Negro Participation and Performance in the
             Revolutionary War... 37

Chapter 3.   The Aftermath of the Revolution and the War of
             1812 48

PART II. FROM THE WAR OF 1812 TO THE CIVIL WAR AND POST RECONSTRUCTION

Chapter 4.   The Negroes' Rewards for Fighting in the War of
             1812 99

Chapter 5.   The Civil War and the Post-War Reconstruction
             Period: The First Attempt at Establishment of the
             Stewards Branch Failed 105

PART III. THE POST-RECONSTRUCTION ERA NAVY

Chapter 6. The End of Reconstruction (1877) 137

Chapter 7. The Abolitionist Demise, Betrayal by the Republican Party and White Supremacy: The Emergence of Naval Policy Based Upon Racism 142

Chapter 8. Methods of Forced Submission and Exploitation: Affect Upon Navy Personnel Policy 152

Chapter 9. The Next Push Toward A Naval Policy Based Upon Race 158

Chapter 10. The Formation of the Messmen/Stewards Branch (1893) 166

PART IV. NEGROES IN THE U.S. NAVY DURING THE SPANISH-AMERICAN WAR (1898)

Chapter 11. The Intensification and the Continued Rise of Racism: It's Affect Upon Naval Personnel Policy 177

Chapter 12. The Proud History of the Steward's Branch........ 184

Chapter 13. World War I and the Final Push for a "Lily White" Navy..192

PART V. NEGROES IN THE U.S. NAVY DURING WORLD WAR II

Chapter 14. U.S. Mobilization for WWII: The Status of Negroes 209

Chapter 15. Messboys at the Naval Academy: The Lost Battalion and Bancroft Hall 221

Chapter 16. The Messboy's Required Adaptation for Naval Service.. 240

Chapter 17. Negro Performance in WWII: Stolen Honor........ 248

Chapter 18. Goals of Naval Personnel Policy: The Selection of Messboys 1932-1974...259

Chapter 19. The Effects of Executive Order #8802 Upon the Messmen's Branch.. 282

Chapter 20. The Battle Record of the Navy's Stewards in WWII... 306

Chapter 21. Changes in U.S. Naval Policy Between WWII and the "Korean Conflict"... 327

Chapter 22. Racism Retards Navy's Vietnam Effort................352

Chapter 23. Failure of Navy Advancement in Human Resources in the Post-Vietnam Era 361

Epilogue 375

Endnotes..381

REFERENCES AND SOURCES

An Index of Documents written earlier by Chester A. Wright from which information has been extracted and included in this manuscript.

Sources:

1. A WORKING PAPER; Historical Background of the Human Resources Management Problem Implicit in the Recent Amalgamation of the Stewards and Commissary Branches of the U.S. Navy by C.A. Wright. December 16, 1975; Naval Postgraduate School, Monterey, California.

2. ORIGINAL MANUSCRIPT; Black Men and Blue Water: An Oral History of the Stewards/Messmen Branch of the United States Navy by C.A. Wright. (date unknown)

    a. Authors Preface (30 Pages, P.1-30)

    b. Introduction (47 Pages, P. 31-78)

    c. Black Seamen: From the Dawn of History to the Conquest of the Americas (21 Pages, P. 79-100)

    d. Black Sailors in Early America: From the pre-Revolutionary Period to 1775. (60 Pages, P.101-161, includes Endnotes)

3. ORIGINAL MANUSCRIPT: Negro Seamen in the Pre-Revolutionary Period. (123 Pages, P. 6-129)

4.   ORIGINAL MANUSCRIPT: Messmen During World War II (29 Pages, P. 1-29)

5.   Negroes in the Navy: From the post-War of 1812 period to the Civil War Period.

6.   WORKING PAPER; The U.S. Navy's Human Resource Management Programs: In the Aftermath of the U.S.S Kittyhawk/ Constellation Racial Incidents

ACKNOWLEDGEMENTS

One of the first persons whom I wish to acknowledge for assisting me in this effort has to be Dr. Nathan E. Cohen the first president of the National Association of Social Workers, Dean of the School of Social Welfare at UCLA. While a master's degree candidate at UCLA, Dr. Cohen became my mentor. It is he, who on learning my background told me, "It would be both a tragedy and a shame to leave the story of the Navy's messboys untold. To do so would leave a little known segment of U.S. Naval History untold. He also doubted that an outsider who did not live and serve in that segment of Navy life could do justice to this part of the U.S. Navy's history.

I would like to acknowledge my late nephew, Eureal Bell, who worked so diligently and spent many days giving me direction for the presentation of this book.

I would like to thank the old black men who were holdovers from the area prior to the time when Negroes were reduced to servants (1898-WW1) and their subsequent denial of enlistment in the Navy (1919-1932). These old men especially those who were put ashore and assigned to the "lost battalion", at the U.S. Naval Academy at Annapolis, Maryland. This duty presented Black Chiefs and Petty Officers from exercising authority over white personnel. These old men, who bossed the black mess boys who served the midshipmen, answered my many questions. So, I wish to acknowledge the assistance of Chief Machinist Simmons, Chief Commissary Stewards Ray, Crocker, and McKinney.

There were 275 Black mess boys at the naval academy left in 1940. I must also acknowledge the sage advice of the black mess boys (some boys were 30 years old), especially section leaders, Clarence Wright, Milton Haskins, and "Head Boy" Scarface Davis, an honest but tough customer. He had to be because few arguments among mess boys were settled verbally. Most were settled with fists, ketchup bottles, china cups, etc.

I wish to thank my sister-in-law Frances Provost for her help in typing and correcting this manuscript. I thank her husband Chief Steward Paul Provost for their constant encouragement (Paul is a published author). This effort probably would have been abandoned and forgotten were it not for my wife, Billie Gale Jackson-Wright, who did all necessary things to keep me on the job. Billie has done all necessary, badgered, shamed or simply pushed. She has read, corrected and rearranged this manuscript.

Last, I wish to thank the White and Black scholars who dared to write and publish books in this basically unrewarding area. Acknowledgement is especially due to John Hope Franklin, Jack D. Foner, Carter G. Woodson, Lerone Bennett, Jr, and Arthur I. Maskow.

INTRODUCTION

In reading most histories of the U.S. Navy, one is left with the impression that only the White men served and earned honor and distinction in battle. The Stewards Branch of the U.S. Navy possesses a longer "historical reach" than is currently realized by even the more scholarly of navy historians. The scholar, who fails to grasp this in attempting to analyze the social, political and deeper cultural aspects of naval personnel affairs, will probably miss his mark by a wide margin. U.S. Naval History is about more than guns, ships, heroes, battles and dates. It is also a story of men, their behavior, and the greater society that shaped them and the major issues and events of their day. It is a story of governments that built ships and made personnel policy.

In this country, race has always been a consideration. When the Messmen Branch (re-designated the Stewards Branch on the eve of WWII) is looked at from a historical perspective, race becomes the context. The fact that this branch was made up of Black, Yellow and Brown men makes it impossible to address naval policy in the normal exclusively White men historical context. Consequently, such a discussion cannot avoid the adverse effects of race on Naval Policy.

The Messmen Branch did not simply occur along some magical or accidental continuum, but derived from social and political forces generated by White America. The creation of the Messmen Branch in 1893 occurred in response to how the broader society perceived the Negroes' "place" in that society after slavery had been abolished. That place was the bottom rung of the U.S. social, economic and political ladder. The U.S. Navy, being part of this former slave-based system, created the Messmen Branch to define an appropriate "place" in its organizational structure in line with the pervading social structure. Restricting Negroes to a servant's role was seen as the appropriate action. Historically, this was the Navy's first step backward, from 100 years of liberalism, into racist practices. From that point, merit, character and the capability of the Negro was not a factor in his service. Race and Color gradually became the determinants of his acceptability, placement and promotion in the U.S. Navy. The Messmen Branch stood as a stark symbol of bigotry, oppression and racism to all races of color in this country from 1893 until 1974, a period of 81 years! Its promulgation and length of perpetuation is truly remarkable.

The Messmen/Stewards Branch was arguably the most unique of all armed forces units. No other branch of any of the U.S. Armed forces, ever created, barred the service of White men! No other branch so rigidly restricted service to men of color, as was the case with the Navy Messmen/Stewards. No other branch created and sustained bigotry and the idea of racial inferiority, by personnel policy, as long as this branch of the U.S. Navy. No other branch hung onto such ideas as tenaciously as the U.S. Navy did. Regardless of the inefficiency, vulnerability to attack by black militants and the political liability, the U.S. Navy insisted on having a servant's branch long after it was politically correct or feasible to do so. A shining example here rests on the fact that only members of the Stewards' Branch were allowed to ride crack-fighting ships in World War II. They gave an account of themselves as Gunners. Yet, in spite of their being decorated for uncommon valor and their gallantry in action, they were not made eligible for the rate of Chief Petty Officer until 1949, four years after World War II. Their promotion was grudging and stingy. Only two Chief Petty Officers were granted Navy wide.

This is the story of the Stewards, Cooks and Messboys who manned that branch of naval service. This is the story of the men who fought and served under these trying circumstances. This is the story of men who served their country when to do so was to endure, or appear to accept the humiliating admission of one's own inferiority. In this story can be found the heretofore-unwritten chapters of one phase of the Negroes' march toward freedom in America, written by a man who participated in it.

It is finally the story of one of the most unique groups of men who served our country's Armed Forces. Regardless whether the member was a yellow man-Chinese, Japanese or Korean; a brown man-Philippino, Guamanian, Puerto Rican or Pacific Islander; or a Black man: all the men shared a commonly perceived perception that they were inferior. All members of the "Messmen's Branch"—its original name—or the "Steward's Branch"—its later designation—were neither perceived as nor were they called "Men". The perception of their skin color caused these people not to be perceived as "Men" but as "Boys", regardless of age, dignity or military bearing.

This perception of these men of color lasted so long until it became a "tradition", a tradition so strong that it outweighed "Law" or "Regulation". External to this branch, both tradition and usage of the term was "Officers and Men" or Officers and Enlisted Men". Since the days of the Navy's Apprenticeship Program, no Sailor has been addressed as "Boy". The only exception was the members of the Messmen/Stewards' Branch. One of the most unique features of the members of this branch has been their ability to deport themselves as "Men" while being perceived as "Boys" by their Officers, Enlisted Chiefs and Petty Officers. To do this required "mental trickery" of the first order, on the part of an individual, to pull this off, that is, to be a man and a person despite the constant negative perception of others.

It became a survival requirement. The Stewards, Cooks and Steward Mates of the U. S. Navy managed to do so, while looked down upon by their own people, the "so called" Negro, until that group became "Black"—that is, ceased to be ashamed of the color that God gave them, in spite of what racists and bigots said about them.

Among the unique features of these "so called" Messboys was that they were the only unit in the Armed Forces required to endure "total war". Messboys fought the Germans and the Japanese at sea as well as their racist Redneck shipmates on the docks. Negro leaders utilized them as a "key humiliation" in their fight for equality and failed at shielding them. Consequently, their own ill-educated fellow sufferers looked down on the Messboys. This author witnessed "punch-outs" and participated in them during World War II. Messboys usually gave a good account of themselves. Many a yokel was left nursing black eyes, broken noses and broken jaws, for payment, in telling local damsels that Messboys were "flunkies".

Although, until recently, having never been honored by White America, or indeed, Black America, their own people, Stewards, Cooks and Steward's Mates, by their behavior in battle, destroyed the myth beloved by bigots, that Negro men were "child-like, cowardly clowns". In doing so, they became the forbearers of our racially diverse Black, Yellow and Brown Admirals today. It is an irony of history that the only fighting ships named for Black Men in U. S. Naval history are named for members of the Messmen/Stewards' Branch of the service. The only medals awarded for gallantry in action, to Black Men during World War II, were earned by men in this service branch. In most cases, the ships were named for enlisted men and officers because they exhibited unusual bravery in action, at the risk of or loss of their lives.

To date three fighting ships have been named for Negroes. The first was named for Dorrie Miller who exhibited gallantry in action aboard the USS West Virginia, a battleship, during the bombing of Pearl Harbor. The second ship was named for Leonard Roy Harmon. Harmon lost his life in action aboard the USS San Francisco while saving the life of a White shipmate, in the Solomon Islands. A third fighting ship was recently commissioned, named for William Pinckney who showed gallantry in action aboard the USS Enterprise during the battle of the Santa Cruz Islands.

One thing not mentioned in general or in specialized histories is why there is an absence of Negro seamen from the list of World War II heroes. The reason is a simple one. Negro seamen were not allowed to go to sea, on fighting ships, as seamen until World War II was nearly over. Negro Messmen were always present at sea the entire time. Even the most liberal Naval Officer was not ready to make his own coffee, shine his shoes or make his bed.

Finally, I have specific points to make for your consideration:

1.) "So Called" Negroes were present at the birth of the Navy.

2.) We assisted in the freeing of this country and the freeing of ourselves.

3.) Our behavior during the War, possibly, foreshadowed the coming of the Negro revolt.

4.) We paved the way for the promotion of enlisted men to Officers and the promotion of Officers to Admirals of color, by our conduct in action.

This is their story. It is a story of the Stewards, Cooks and Messboys of the Navy. It is the story that American Historians have forgotten to tell. The story of a group of men who served this country in spite of itself.

Part I.

Black Sailors in Early America: From the Pre-Revolutionary Period to 1775

CHAPTER 1: AN INHERITED NAVAL TRADITION

1.) WHY THE HARSHNESS AND MALTREATMENT OF PERSONNEL IN THE BRITISH NAVY WAS MITIGATE IN THE COLONIAL NAVY

To fully understand the evolution of the role of Black Sailors in America, we must first examine the historical context in which they developed. America's Colonist inherited their naval traditions from stern and, brutal taskmasters, the officers of the British Navy. As mentioned previously, the sea was a cruel, harsh, and brutal profession for a man to follow. But Americans had no choice in developing a Navy and Merchant Marine. This became evident before the American Colonies secured their freedom from England. Colonial development depended upon the sea and some of the harshness inherited from the English was mitigated here; a fact often overlooked in most naval histories. As subjects of England, the British Colonies possessed no standing military units or military academies of their own.

The U.S. Navy derived from the colonial Merchant Marine in early America. Many trading, whaling, shipbuilding ventures, as in other countries, were corporate efforts. America was not yet a highly urbanized country with a large and impersonal population. So, merchantmen crews came from the same area and many knew each other. Captains knew many of their crewmembers families. Also, there were no generally available financial institutions such as we have today. Local families often bought investments in sea ventures. The U.S. Merchant Marine from whom the U.S. Navy emerged was not composed of the dregs (wretched debtors and scrapings of British jails or unfortunate men caught by "press gangs") of society as found on English ships. On our privateers and naval vessels during the Revolution and War of 1812, most men were volunteers. Brutality appeared later on the Merchant and naval vessels.

To ride a Privateer or Merchant ship where fellow community members and, even the Captain, were known to common seamen militated against the type of impersonal brutality found on British ships. So even when colonists, participating as privateers (actual reservist), under the British in England's War with Spain and France, American seamen fared better than those seamen of their masters, the British. This changed only after urbanization and competition on the sea came about. In the war against Spain, France, and Holland, American Seamen served with a different motivation. Where the "press-gang" was the principal recruiting instrument and, the Cat-O-Nine tails, the focal point of discipline for British seamen, all American privateers, were manned by volunteers. This in itself made the birth of American seamen, again, less brutal, harsh and traumatic than that of their British cousins.

Another significant difference was the service time commitment. American Sailors signed on for a voyage or a specific length of time. Sailors pressed into the British navy were required to serve for an indefinite period at the pleasure of the King. This could encompass most of a victim's useful life.

It should be pointed out here also that the Colonies, which later formed the United States, due to sheer need, had become a great maritime economic factor before the Revolution. We will return to this later. But slavery, the Sea and the Negro played paramount roles in the shaping of the western world long before the English Colonist of North America thought about Revolution. A mess boy drove this home to me one evening in 1943. We were stationed at Tulagi Island in the British Solomons. An Australian Colonial Officer told me that this was the former home of the Governor General of the British Solomons. We worked at the junior officers' mess on the top of a hill. From this high perch during the day, we could see Guadalcanal approximately 20 miles away and near its northern end, Savo Island. I had been telling this youngster, Harvey Wilkes, from Elizabeth City, North Carolina, about black sailors going ashore with Commodore Perry in Japan in1854; I said that one day, we would do so with Admirals William Halsey or perhaps Marc A. Mitscher of Task Force 58. Wilkes, who was quite bright, asked suddenly, "Have us Black folk always been dragged all over the world to fight in White men's wars that we don't know nothing about? I thought we were slaves when Perry went to Japan." I replied, "We were but the sea has been, traditionally, both the instrument of Negro enslavement and a conduit of the Negro escape to freedom". Hired Seamen were asked few questions. This was the only place in America where ones' ability, genetic endowments, fighting capacity and toughness outweighed his color, with the exception of the Officers' Corp level. Inclusion as equals had to wait a century and a half—until 1944, (from 1798 to 1944). Negroes were thought to be unsuitable as Officer material.

This man's comment about Black men being dragged over the World's oceans to fight in White men's wars that they knew nothing about, within a great degree of probability, is true. But, "being dragged" about to fight wars has not been the exclusive realm of Negroes. Many American Whites have found themselves, historically, and to this day, in the same plight, starting with the Treaty of Utrecht or before the

Revolution in this country. The English colonies never had a population large enough to provide significant manpower to augment British troops in Europe and her foreign Colonies at the same time. However, they did provide militia when the fighting was in America. Consequently, it was the colonial merchant sailor who was pressed into action on behalf of the crown, often as privateers.

2) COLONIALISM AND THE TECHNICAL INVENTIONS OF NON-WHITE EUROPEAN PEOPLE: THE TERRIBLE PRICE PAID BY NON-WHITES FOR FAILURE TO EXPLOIT THEIR DISCOVERIES

American history began with Colonial White men being dragged over the ocean to fight European and English wars, which they little understood. Spain, England, Holland, Portugal or France from the start, governed American Colonies. The Swedes played a minor roll here. It is a truism that all Kings possessed bottomless coffers, always in need of more gold and loot. These rulers helped themselves to their own people's money, property, persons or that of any neighbors' weak enough to allow them to do so. The last argument of Kings was swords, spears and pikes. Near and during the Colonial period the last arguments became guns. Europeans mastered this latter technology, built around gunpowder. The Chinese invented gunpowder but failed to turn it into a weapon because they had no iron. Both the Chinese and the Mongols tried to use their most available materials to harness and direct gunpowder explosions, but bamboo barrels with crude bronze or unhardened iron rings could not contain nor consequently control or direct the awesome power of gunpowder. Attempts to do so killed more of their own soldiers than those of the enemy did. So the Chinese restricted the use of its terrible power, which could have preserved their sovereignty, to fireworks at various celebrations. This awed, amused, and made their subjects happy but failed to preserve their freedom in confrontations with rapacious, power and profit hungry Europeans and later American expansionist. The end result of this mismatch in technology brought colonialism and slavery to the Western World.

Black Africans below the Sahara Desert, whom some Archeologists believe, were the first people to smelt iron, possessed the material needed to harness a direct Gunpowder but "had no powder". So Asia, Africa and the Western World fell to better armed European Armies and Navies, who had mastered the art of controlled and directed gunpowder explosions, by the use of hardened iron bore gun barrels. This deficiency aided and abetted slavery, and colonialism, which became a key factor in the economic world after the "Treaty of Utrecht signed April 11, 1713."[1]

Due to the demand for Seamen, American Colonists "were dragged" all over the Oceans to fight European wars. So as this writer explained to this bright mess attendant, Americans have a history of fighting in wars not of their making. Not just Black men but White men too. For example, Samuel W. Bryant says, "In 1689, the mortal enmity of Protestant England and Catholic France found expression in open Warfare, and in the American Colonies this contest of giants for trade and power brought about King Williams War."[2]

This was 70 years after the official accepted date of 1619 that Black Commercial Slavery began in North America. Bryant goes on to point out the affect of these two European Monarchs' squabble upon hapless American Colonist. French Canada instigated and, officered a series of raids by their Indian Allies on the Frontier hamlets of New England, while Canadian privateers busily raided the fishing fleets on the New Foundland banks. French Ships ranged American waters from Maine to the West Indies, seizing trading vessels and killing or imprisoning their crews in a frenzy of fanaticism."[3]

The British retaliated with a raid on Port Royal, Nova Scotia. This was known in the Colonies as King Williams' War. According to Bryant, "...in March 1702, Anne became ruler of England. In May, England and Holland declared War on France and Spain and the War of the Spanish Secession began. The Colonist know the War as "Queen Anne's War. Bryant says that this War became a War of privateers, and in the years between 1702 and 1707 England lost 846 Merchant ships but France lost a total of 1,346 ships and decimated their Merchant fleet."[4]

The British failed to take Quebec due, probably, to the incompetence of a haughty British Vice Admiral by the name of Sir Horeden Walker. This poltroon allowed light transports and two supply ships to run onto the rocks and lost 900 men. He sailed back to England after an aborted Quebec expedition, where his Flagship, the 70 gun *HMS Edgar*, blew up and killed another 400 men. He was so fortunate as to have all of his records burned in the blast. This prevented his just court-martial. But one must be careful about what one teaches daring subordinates. American Colonist were compelled to learn how to use guns not just to fight the English King's wars but to protect themselves against the rapacious demands made by that King and his greedy, arrogant cohorts. The King raised revenue by raising taxes on colonial commerce at will. This was done without any semblance of representation.

Reuben Elmore Stivers, in describing the emergent American character as "Rugged Individualism", says that "On the frontier in the New World there was at all times something or someone for the individual to contend with. This included cold, hunger, flood, fire, Indians, Spaniards, Frenchmen, Englishmen, and predatory American renegades."

Stivers said, "As a matter of course, a man voluntarily defended what was his own or voluntarily joined others to defend that which had common value. There usually was little alternative, for neither his society or his government was able consistently to defend anything for him. In America, most men had escaped European feudalism, so the individual always had to remind himself to mind his own interest. If that meant marching off, gun in hand, to help capture Louisberg in 1745, he did so, and the King's red-clad recruiters had little need to drag him from under his bed."[5] Stivers brilliantly pinpoints the basic forces that shaped the character of the oppressed (American Colonialists) and the oppressor (British Royalty and Common people) which were bound to clash in what we know as the American Revolution. This was a clash of ideas that was to change the World.

3) THE CLASH OF THE BRITISH AND THE DEVELOPING AMERICAN COLONIAL CHARACTER: THE FORCES THAT SHAPED THEM

Before trying to describe the Black experience as colonial life marched towards that fateful clash at Bunker Hill or, actually Breed's Hill, lets look at what shaped the British oppressor. According to Stivers, "This situation stood in stark contrast to the brutal conscription or impressment practiced in European Countries, and especially in Great Britain. There the Soldiers and Seamen were hired or commandeered as insensible machines of war, and duty frequently had to be learned by dancing to the melancholy tune of a Cat-O-Nine tails (a leather whip with 9 thongs with lead tips). As much blood might be spilt on the altar of discipline as in the engagement for which discipline was required.[6]

Here the term Volunteer, as perceived by Europeans and American Colonist stand in stark contrast to our use of the term today. Stivers says of European Volunteers if, indeed, they may be defined as such, "Theoretically, those who served in enlisted status in the British Army or Navy were Volunteers, but their enlistment was always for 'the duration', and the duration lasted most of a man's useful life. For every truly patriotic volunteer, 99 others might be oafs or adventurers garnered from jails, farms, gin mills, and poor houses or in exchange for the king's Schilling. As dismal servitude in the cheerless barracks of the Army or within the wooden hull of a man-of-war might be for the latter group."[7]

Stivers then points out that a new breed of man roamed free in the hills and valleys of the coastal colonies and its frontier... "He knew little of hindrance or restraint. He became accustomed to breathing an atmosphere of political liberty. When necessary, he willingly struggled with all comers, including if need be, the King's own men. By the end of the French and Indian War, great numbers of Americans had become proud men, a fact that caused some dichotomy, in that most were as proud of being Americans as they were of being Englishmen."[8] Having fought for England and himself in King Phillips's War, King William's War, King George's and Queen Anne's Wars, why not fight for his own commerce, person and liberty? This had to logically emerge as the central question in colonial existence.

While these events were shaping the character of early American White men, what was happening to the character of Black men? Consider the fact that King William's War occurred 70 years after 1619, the accepted commencement of commercial slavery in North America. And it was years afterward that, Americans participated in the raid of Louisberg, Canada in 1745. We must ask, "Did Blacks participate in these events as a people or were they like benign bacteria who did not make cheese or wine nor made anyone sick?" This was and is highly improbable and to understand this, today's thoughtful students of history must accept a premise and shed a myth. The premise is "men do not live contiguous to other men and fail to absorb certain parts of their cultural attributes. Since Black men, like White men possess rationality, memory storage, intellect, and intelligence in varying degrees, within the realm of probability, they participated in and learned that component of colonial culture that produced that era of U.S. History." In short, from the day of their arrival in North America their acculturation began. In addition to this, man created phenomena for all slaves, called a "breaking in", was introduced. Some writers refer to this method as the "seasoning" of slaves. Kenneth M. Stamp, who wrote the "Peculiar Institution", said of this "breaking in" process, "America gave these involuntary immigrants a vivid impression of the White man and his culture which they did not soon forget."[9]

4) CONDITIONS IN THE COLONIES THAT MADE AFRICANS IDEAL PROPERTY AS SLAVES

For the Negro, this seasoning or breaking in was a harsh, brutal "accelerated earning" period, which had two goals. The first was to rapidly teach the slave enough about American culture to exploit his/her labor; and, the second was to make this, as Stamp has labeled the slave, "troublesome property", stand in such fear that it could be controlled, directed and kept in abject subjugation, to the Master. To accomplish either of these goals required a degree of acculturation. Only the African's intelligence determined how rapidly he expanded this learning to include greater knowledge.

He often arrived with knowledge of agriculture, metalworking, cloth weaving, and other craftsmen skills. Hence, to think that Blacks stood around and ignorantly sucked their thumbs while White men made history as some racist-bigots would have us believe is both ignorant and improbable, as well as stupid.

First, the most needed resources in North America were laborers and fighting men. It was rapidly learned by White men that Black men were capable of both functions. From the first introduction into American society Blacks, though restricted to a circumscribed sphere, did play roles beyond that of picking cotton or singing "Swanee River" as Hollywood and many historians would have us believe. The necessities and needs of Southern society made Southern slave masters unable to totally limit the Negro participation, at all times. Crisis in form of Indian raids, wars, floods, drought and fever epidemics simply made such limitations impractical. House servants heard White men debate John Locke and Rousseau's ideas of governance long before 1776.

In striking for their own liberty, White men had to confront the dilemma of demanding freedom for themselves while holding Black men in Bondage. This bedeviled White Protestants and Catholics but failed to bedevil the Quakers, who fast became "the" Christians who knew and understood the difference in Christ's teachings about right and wrong. In spite of Slave status, Blacks were used where or when needed. One of the critical areas of need in early America was for men to assist with an expanding participation in sea borne commerce and to help on warships needed to protect that commerce. But long before sea borne commerce was developed, America had a great need for ships.

A plantation was a nearly "self contained", economic factory unit in its own right. Most plantations grew their own food, had their own spinning rooms and cloth weavers (many Africans were highly skilled weavers), carpenters, blacksmiths (another African skill), horse trainers, leather repair, vintners, etc. Larger, wealthier plantations built their own wharves. Rivers here meandered for miles from inland to the cities located on the bays and sounds. Hence flat boats, shallops, sloops and even good-sized schooners (a later addition) could be seen plying such rivers, as the James, Cape Fear, Potomac, Severn and the Peedee. There was another use for ships, especially schooners, which did not involve cargo for trade. These were often utilized as fishing boats. One can imagine the profit to be had by plantation owners by sending their own boats down the rivers to Albemarle Sound, Chesapeake Bay, etc., to catch enough fish to dry and lay by for the winter. Here one fed his slaves over the winter and eliminated the middleman in one operation, provided he had trained slaves as sailors. Africans, for centuries past, mastered the process of preserving fish by drying them. So plantation owners had their own people to process his fish as well as catch them.

The point here is that Africans arrived in the New World with certain skills readily applicable to the plantation economy into which they were unceremoniously thrown. They were not, in all instances, as most early White historians depicted them. They were not dumb brutes, who knew nothing but how to, perhaps, "Boola dance" for Jane and Tarzan as depicted in Hollywood movies. Hence, Black seamen were not unique to New England. Many Blacks came to the New World already possessed of skills in the areas of river navigation, surf launching and the retrieval of small craft. The need for these skills antedates the need for deep-water skills.

When one looks at the map of our eastern seaboard and checks its geographical features, two factors become self-evident: 1) Why there were no plantations in the northeastern colonies and 2) why a Black with some water borne skills was a real asset to southern planters. If one looks closely at the Atlantic Coast mountain ranges, he will note that from the north where the mountains veer towards the ocean, they tend to veer inland, away from the ocean, as one proceeds towards the Southern Colonies. This geographical feature made the south a land of wide, flat alluvial plains, as one travels inland there is a gradual change to fertile upland valleys and piedmonts conducive to the growing of agricultural products.

When the source of labor afforded by emptying jails and prisons, the kidnapping of the unwary poor Whites of England from city streets, the selling of debtors and the poverty ridden, landless European people into bondage ceased, Blacks became a harshly logical defenseless labor source. If such Africans were skilled river men or shore side sailors, they were a welcomed addition to any plantation located in the area below the line where rivers became navigable, for obvious reasons. Rivers were the principle mode of cargo transportation in early America. They meandered for miles from the ocean inland. Rivers were the main highways before the coming of the Conestoga wagon and automobiles.

Blacks got an earlier and better chance at becoming Blue Water Sailors in the New England area. In the South, Blacks who were enslaved at Charleston, Cape Hatteras, Norfolk and New Orleans areas also had blue water opportunities. There was a definite reason for Black men to be introduced to Blue Water in the Northeast or New England colonies. Here, where the Appalachian Mountains veer towards the sea there were no large plantations requiring the labor of slaves. Here most rivers are not navigable for any distance inland. Most are swift and boulder strewn. The land is poor and equally boulder strewn. Except for the Connecticut Valley, a man was hard put to wrest enough sustenance from that poor, rocky soil needed to feed his family, let alone a group of hungry slaves. So New England White men, of necessity, had to turn to the sea for a living, trade coastwise for grain and fish the Newfoundland banks for cod. Samuel W. Bryant said of early Americans and their perceptions of the sea, "The Sea had its demons too, but it was a less hostile element, and one that they had sailed over and to some extent mastered. It was their sole link with the civilization they had left behind in Europe, a civilization accessible only on its own harsh terms, but still a last resort as a refuge should their new homes prove to be untenable."[10] Here, Bryant refers to the unknown that terrorized Colonist, such as fierce Indians and trackless wilderness where men went to chop firewood and were never seen again, or wild beast found there. He goes on to describe the early Colonist's insecurity and self-perception; "...they were extremely conscious of being only a fringe of humanity clinging to the Coast, seldom out of sight or sound of the sea. If everything they had accomplished should suddenly be wiped out by marauding Indians or failing crops or epidemics, the sea could always be depended upon as a line of retreat."[11] Bryant goes on to point out that, there was some rich land pockets in New England and that some men became, by their standards, prosperous farmers. But these never reached the wealth of the southern Plantation System. "In varying degrees throughout the Colonies this sea-mindedness existed; it was a predominant trait among the English in New England."[12]

New Englanders were inclined to lead an amphibious life, farmer or not. Hence, a slave in New England was as likely to be a house servant as to be a hardy deckhand. Again, physical need and the desire to profit mandated that "New England Puritans never let God get in the way of profit."[13] So they emerged on the American scene as "the experts", on "the three S's: Sailing, Slaving, and Smuggling. Colonial shipwrights quickly became master ship builders. Samuel Bryant said, "...as the lines of their craft grew cleaner, another industry, slaving, had been developing with great rapidity."[14]

This was a fateful time for the historical development of this Country, and the Negro, in particular. To really understand how two foreign monarchs affected the course of American history in its embryonic stage one should read the Treaty that settled a war between Spain and England in 1713.

Two questions had puzzled me for most of my young life. The Treaty of Utrecht is the answer to the first question "what made the Negro a slave?" The answer to the second question of "why White men dislike Negroes?" rests in the darker side of the White Americans' unique psyches. Here the author can only speculate and offer premises. The answer to the first question was right under my nose thirty-six years ago as I sat on the beach reading at sunset at Seattle Harbor between Los Negroes and Manus Island, north of New Guinea. This first reading I remember with great clarity. I stood afterward until twilight gazing at the forest of masts of the myriad of fighting ships, Battleships, Cruisers, Flattops, Tin Cans and many, many amphibious ships, plus the vast array of transports, freighters, tenders and repair ships gathered for the assault upon the Philippine Archipelago. I asked myself, "What in the two-blocked-hell are you doing here? And, will you be lucky enough to ever reach home again"? Perhaps a bit of fear, added to my 10th grade education, caused me to miss the real significance of that treaty as it pertained to my social position as a Negro and an Officer's Cook.

For many needless years, I believed that, as my Grandfather believed, that "cotton made Negroes slaves."

This is a historical misnomer. Incidentally, many of my University educated students, even History majors, at the postgraduate school, believed this. For what it is worth, cotton did not make the Negro a slave. It, along with sugar cane, was simply the "accidental source of greatest economical application" of that diabolical institution as an ultra-cheap source of needed labor. Bryant said, "By Article 16 of the Treaty of Utrecht signed April 11, 1713, Spain agreed to take 4,800 Negro slaves each year for thirty years and this large order was to be filled exclusively by the ships of England and her Colonies. The Spanish and English Kings were each to be paid 25 percent of the profits from this business, and in England, the prospects of exploiting this monopoly were so highly regarded that Article 16 was hailed far and wide as one of the main rewards of the war. This is the possible locus of the greatest impetus to the creation of commercial slavery. "England and her colonies" is the key phrase here.

Here one may pause, if he is to really understand, and ask, "What did this mean to the seafaring community in the colonies?" Profit for hungry merchants, ship builders, canvas makers, cordage purveyors and makers of iron instruments. The introduction of Black men to revenue generating shore side applications was a major increase in profits as compared to their blue water sailing use.

That Community was not the only one affected. Where tobacco, sugar and naval stores (tar, pitch, masts, lumber and fish) had been principle exports, diversification had taken place bringing new crops such as indigo and rice, as well as the "experimentation with cotton". The mid-Atlantic and New England colonies had stopped merely drying cod and entered the sailing industry. Hence, able-bodied men were a dire need. Samuel Bryant points to the end of the quasi-slavery of White bondservants from Europe and England as approximately the end of the seventeenth century. Consequently, a new labor source for work on land and at sea had to be found. Africans uniquely filled the bill.

Bondsmen (poor women and children, or criminals) could be held to servitude for only a short, stipulated time. Furthermore, they were White and looked like any other Colonist. Thus, they could abscond, run away over the next hill or to the next village and blend in with other White Colonist making apprehension a real problem. Masters often found little sympathy in their attempts to catch White runaways as many of those charged with aiding and abetting by the law, were themselves former Bondsmen. However, Black Africans were another matter! They were not White and, therefore, could not hide among the general population. They did not have public sentiment on their side. They were the ideal slaves.

What really added to the enslavement of Africans was the fact that he was not a Christian and could be morally held in servitude, both he and his issue, in perpetuity! They were far more profitable than Bondservants as a labor source were. Bondservants had to be freed after a stipulated period of time. The massive profits reaped from the new industry made one of the Ten Commandments, do unto others as you would have them do unto you, irrelevant as Puritans, Anglicans, Catholics, and even some Quakers bowed to the god of profit.

Two additional questions regarding this period of Black Naval history bear some attention. In college settings such as the Naval Post Graduate School in Monterey, California and the School of Applied Sciences at Case Western Reserve University in Cleveland, Ohio, graduate students inevitably asked and argued: 1.) Since English, unlike the Greeks, Romans and Muslims had no codified history or tradition of actual human enslavement, how did they adapt so readily to such an institution in their colonies? 2.) Why did this happen in such a relatively short period of time? The questioners were graduate students, all of who had studied history at the college level and some of who were history majors. This perspective of the British was new to them.

To answer these questions, one must go back to the time of the Tudor Kings and examine the thinking and social constructs of the Elizabethan period in English history. Winthrop Jordan says, "Indeed, without some inquiry into Elizabethan thinking on the plantation societies while the Negroes became slaves."[15] I learned that most of the subject, it will remain impossible to comprehend why Englishmen became servants, students thought that English Common law was centuries older than it actually was.

Also, they did not take into account the meandering, stumbling path of common law development as it actually occurred. "For example," Jordan goes on to say, "thinking about freedom and bondage in Tudor England was confused and contradictory". "In this period of social dislocation, there was considerable disagreement among contemporary observers about what was actually going on and even as to what 'ought' to be going on! Statute and Common Law were sometimes considerably more than a century out of phase with actual and commonly held notions about servitude... Englishmen lacked accurate methods of ascertaining what was actually happening to their social institutions."[16] The establishment of British Common Law did not happen overnight, but over an extended period of time. Jordan also points out that by 1577 under the assault of developing Christianity, "villeinage" or "bondage" had all but disappeared in England. In the second half of the 16th Century, bondage had been replaced by the potent idea of personal freedom in England.

Personal Freedom had been accepted as the normal status of Englishmen. Understanding the foregoing factors makes it evident why English colonists lagged so far behind Portugal and Spain in grasping the economic and political importance of slavery. The question then comes up, if personal freedom was the accepted norm, why were White bondservants still being shipped to the colonies even on the eve of the Revolution? The answer to that question lies in the gradual evolution of change in social norms. Unlike today, social and technological changes occurred very slowly and over long periods of time. Jordan points out that there were always "overlaps" in practice as new ideas were gradually actualized. He pointed out that long after the invention and use of the tractor one could find oxen used to till adjacent fields.

A more current and germane example is the fact that Naval Personnel Policy in 1919 forbade the enlistment of Negroes even as servants. Yet in the period of 1919 to 1932 when Negroes were again allowed to enlist, records show that many seamen, firemen and machinists still remained in the Navy. There were some pre-WWI Machinist Mates and Chief Commissary Stewards as late as 1945, although the creation of the Messmen/Stewards branch in 1893 required that all Negroes be made servants.

So, White Bondservants being sent to the colonies in the sixteenth and early seventeenth centuries probably was the result of "overlap" in the slow process of social and political change. Further, being shipped out to the colonies, as a Bondservant was a potential step up the social ladder for an Englishman with no land and few prospects. Such people were often branded with a "V" on their chest for vagabond, and subjected to whippings and even hanged for petty crimes. As a bondservant, he did not have to contract his "person", but only his "labor", and that for a stipulated period of time. He could aspire to a prize almost impossible for him to gain in England; he could become a landowner instead of spending his life as a mere tiller of other men's land.

Probably the greatest boom in the colonial economy occurred in the maritime sphere. The demand for whale oil caused shipyards to proliferate along the coast. Slavery and the new commerce built around the selling of Black men, their women and children, produced profits that were mind-boggling. It created the concept of "triangular trade" and made it possible to sell virtually any ship that would float. Slaving was a dangerous profession that required a strong nose, ruthlessness, brutality, daring and cunning; it required a strong heart as well as a black one. But in spite of risk, the profits were unbelievable. Two good trips in a good Slaver to the African Coast could pay for a new ship and all subsequent trips were all profit. This enormous profit potential as previously stated, caused Presbyterians, Catholics and Anglicans to put Jesus "on hold" and bow to the god of profit.

5)   THE SEA AS A SOURCE OF THE SEEDS FOR REVOLUTION

American Colonists were a subject people, who often went to sea in peacetime, only to find themselves in the middle of some war started at the whim of an English or European Monarch. So Colonial sailors learned from bitter experience that once clear of the shoreline, a crew had better be armed and know how to fight. The alternative was to be impressed into some foreign man-o-war's crew or rot while languishing in some European power's prison. Being a subject people required other skills highly applicable to the slave trade. Like lower animals in a tight situation where flight or fight were the alternatives, colonial vessels too often found themselves in situations where they had to outrun or outgun a stranger or an enemy. All strangers, until identified, were perceived as enemies. Wars could have started after they left port; there was no "wireless" messaging system to warn them. Thus, colonial naval and merchant captains looked upon all vessels met at sea as potential enemies. Going to sea with guns was as much a tradition as avoiding the tentacles of the mercantile system or avoiding the port tax collector. Hence American Colonials had learned to survive in the "university of hard knocks" created by British quarrels with other powers. They now resented the English Kings propensity to perceive them as a mere source of profit instead of men, entitled to the same liberties as other English subjects. Colonist also resented a government beyond the seas, who without Colonial representation, saw fit to tax them whenever it capriciously occurred to them to do so.

For sake of clarity, lets recapitulate the march of events just before and after the 1713 Treaty of Utrecht. In the mid 15th century before this treaty, the English, French, and the Dutch had watched enviously as gold and silver poured into the Spanish Kings coffers. They watched large, slow, unwieldy Spanish galleons wallow in from Mexico, Peru, Chili, and the West Indies, laden with treasure. So the British developed the Caravel, a fast smaller ship but heavily gunned. It is said that this vessel could tack twice, unleashing two broadsides before the big unwieldy galleon could change its heading. They further found that the Spaniards had gobbled up too much land and had too many peoples under domination to effectively guard and control them. The English knew that they could be "had" and were ripe for the plucking. Black slavery and yellow gold caused Spain's days, as an empire, to be numbered.

Elizabethan Captains, if they can indeed be called such, were better pirates than naval officers. It is they who tested Spain's ability prior to 1588 by doing what some Historians call, "Singeing the King of Spain's beard". They would go into his harbors and burn his ships, raid Spanish Colonies in the West Indies and the Pacific Ocean. But it was England's great "freebooter", John Hawkins who found that gold did not necessarily have to be yellow. Spain and Portugal possessed "Black Gold", in the persons of African people.

Slaves were brought from Africa in Spanish, Portuguese and Dutch ships exclusively until John Hawkins of England raided the Guinea Coast in 1562, captured three hundred slaves from the Portuguese and sold them in Spanish West Indies. Spain, Portugal and Holland understood the enormous profit potential that could be derived from slavery long before the English.

Samuel W. Bryant in explaining critical events leading up to the Spanish/English naval battle of the Spanish Armada in 1588 said, "Besides their pillaging expeditions to the West Indies, the English had proved bothersome in the Pacific. Francis Drake in 1579 and Cavendish in 1585 had burned and looted Spanish ships and settlements. The galleons sailing back to Spain from the West Indies loaded with the wealth of the Incas and the Aztecs had been plucked like so many hairs from the King's beard."[17] Bryant goes on to explain that the Spanish Armada was a result of 20 years of insult and humiliation at the hands of English Freebooters; who led the British challenge to Spain's might and dominance of the New World, its Oceans, and Seas.

Philip II of Spain lost his gamble to eradicate his English challengers with the defeat of the Spanish Armada. He gambled all he had when he learned that Elizabeth of England had played him for a fool.

He miscalculated not so much the real condition of the political situation in England, but that wily female's ability to deal with her own problems."...King Philip seized what looked like a good opportunity to crush and annihilate England, a nation with a fast growing Navy, a Protestant religion, and a Queen who did not hesitate to use her womanly charms on the Spanish emissaries. Elizabeth bemused Philip with her wily diplomacy meantime by backing the practical activities of Drake, Hawkins, Cavendish and Frobisher on one hand, while protesting her good intentions on the other."[18] But this proud monarch could not forget the sacking of Santo Domingo, and the loss of many treasure-laden galleons, so he arrogantly played into Elizabeth of England's hands.

Her Captains lured him into "playing their game". The Spanish Armada of 1588 spelled the end. A North Sea storm and badly designed ships set in motion forces that were to, in time, cost Spain an empire and world power. The fast sailing English "Caravel" out-maneuvered and out-fought the big unwieldy Spanish Galleons; a viscous North Sea storm damaged or wrecked the remaining ships. Spain was never able to recover fully after this resounding defeat at sea.

In the pre-Revolutionary period in America, Black men had proven that they were men rather than "beast of burden", fit only to labor and kow-tow to White Masters. Blacks in many ways were better off, even as Slaves, in pre-Revolutionary America than they were in its aftermath; Slavery brought with it the propensity of White men to need the myth of Black inferiority to sustain it. For example, there were not enough men during that period to meet the almost constant pre-Revolutionary crises.

Both man and nature conspired against the early settlers of North America. There was a constant shortage of laborers and fighting men. As previously stated, the colonies consisted of a few souls a long ways from home facing a vast and hostile wilderness. In these vast reaches lurked a different Indian from the sedentary Peruvian and Mexican Indians, found and conquered by Cortez and Pizarro, or those found by the Spaniards in the West Indies Islands of the Caribbean. North American Indians were more like the Yaqui of northern Mexico who were renowned for their fierceness in battle rather than the Incas of Peru or the Aztecs, Olmecs and Mayas of Mexico. These had not been softened by centuries of sedentary living in cities. North American Indians still retained, when the White man arrived, the fierceness, resolution, bravery and stamina needed to survive in a harsher, less indolent, more demanding climate. Here the geography and climate ranged from trackless desert wastes to towering mountains and never ending forest, freezing cold and blinding heat. Here raged droughts, blizzards and hurricanes. Here roamed both wild animals and a wild, fierce and brave people. These met the White men on their own terms, fought the hell out of them, and in the main, refused to be their slaves. The few enslaved proved temperamentally unsuitable for slavery. They had a tendency to cease to function when deprived of their ceremonies, customs and traditional activities.

Hence, the most needed commodity in pre-Revolutionary America was manpower. As a consequence, Blacks were more needed and more valuable as workers and when the need arose, as fighting men, than they were after emancipation. From constant exposure to the White man's culture and mores, Blacks at the "prelude to", not the "beginning of", the revolt against England, had absorbed and inculcated the conceptual framework of what was at stake. They, consequently, looked upon this hassle between their masters and the "Master's Masters", as a possible opportunity to acquire their freedom. So it is not unusual that a Black man, Crispus Attucks, was one of the first men to die for the freedom and liberty of White men in America during the tax revolt in the Massachusetts Bay Colony.

So African Americans, "so-called" Negroes, or the more current term "Blacks", have always posed what the Swedish Sociologist, Gunnar Myrdal, has labeled an "American Dilemma"[19], and so titles his book. The dilemma in the historical relationship between Black and White Americans, in spite of Myrdal's optimism, has so far defied change. Rest assured it is not a one sided condition. The dilemma had adversely affected both Whites and Blacks. Bigoted White, Christian Americans have never been able to see Blacks as God's children too, though their Bible says so.

Blacks, since their arrival in North America, have been exploited, placed at the lowest rungs of the social, political and economic ladders and denied the simple status of being human in many instances. This frustrating and painful "conditional-relationship" existed long before the Revolutionary War. It was as if White America said to Black America at this Country's birth, "Nigger, I don't like you but I need you. I will use your labor, loyalty, fighting capacity and blood, but I will not allow you the fair and equal treatment bequeathed to other Americans at birth." This condition existed before the Revolution and it exists, although a bit less overt, to this day in many areas. Should Black men put their lives on the line in American wars?

Blacks who stood beside South Carolina White men in the Revolutionary war, and had fought Red men in the Yamassa Indian War in 1715, rode Privateers or were in the assault on Louisberg, in Canada, during the French and Indian War, had to grapple with this question. Unknown to most Americans, there was not one "French and Indian War", as taught in many U.S. Histories. There were actually <u>four</u> wars under this title. Each one of these touched the lives of Colonist. The first one of these Wars started in 1689, over who would be supreme in the commercial exploitation of the Colonial World, when Spain was proven incapable. The probable reason that the French and Indian War is dated as starting in 1754 is because this date ushered in the final phase of the fight for Colonial supremacy. It was known as the Seven Years' War in Europe. Where Colonial sailors were concerned, all of these Wars caused prudent Colonial Captains to arm their crews and teach them to fight. This was nothing new. Every time England's Kings and Queens got into a squabble with the rulers of Holland, France, Spain, or whomever, English Colonist had to fight or run at sea. But the reason that the last phase of this series of conflicts stands out in U.S. History as "The" French and Indian War is because its impact upon commerce and the daily life of colonists. The political relationship between England and her Colonies in its aftermath would never be the same.

This latter phase of the War lasted seven bitter years without let up. The conflict disrupted not just Colonial life and commerce; it disrupted world commerce and taxed both England's treasury, and armed forces, to the limits of endurance. England's rulers, in turn, made constant demands on her Colonies. This was intensified after the route of General Braddock's British Army in1755 near Fort Duquesne by an army of French and Indian allies. His army would have probably been destroyed were it not for George Washington, a young officer in the Virginia Colonial Militia, who taught its remnants guerrilla tactics.

The scarcity of manpower made it very improbable that Black men were excluded from combat. They have never been totally excluded from the casualty lists in U.S. Wars. Whether slave or freemen, necessity has always denied them such luxury.

The French and Indian War apprenticeship gave Colonist both the self-confidence and the enhanced know-how, which enabled them to confront their English Masters in subsequent revolt that we call the American Revolution. This was the prelude to the shots heard around the world. The shots exchanged at Lexington Green outside of Boston on April 19, 1775. Blacks were there with the minutemen in the persons of Lemuel Haynes, Peter Salem and Pomp Blackman. They were also present at Concord Bridge and the route of British troops. These Blacks who stood with White men at Lexington Green, and at Bunker Hill (actually Breed's Hill), did not arrive there as full blown, unthinking brutes, as many White historians would have us believe. They arrived at the flash points of the American Revolt with the ideas of freedom and equality germinating in their psyches just as other American Colonist did. As previously stated, most Anthropologist agree that if tribes, clans or so-called races live contiguous to each other, two phenomena are certain to occur, 1) genetic mixing of peoples and 2) an exchange of culture and ideas. Blacks in pre-Revolutionary America were no different, in spite of skin color, or the perceptions of White men. They endured the lowest status of the emerging society. Blacks are and were thinking, rational human beings. They swam in the same, "cultural sea", like other Colonist. They helped shape early American culture and were in turn shaped by that force and its contingencies.

Dr. W.E.B. Dubois spoke in the preface to Herbert Aptheker's" Documentary History of the Negro People in the United States", one of the few well-researched books on this subject. He had this to say: "Where attempts were made in the 19th century, historians were not prepared to believe that Africans even in America had any record of thought or deed worth attention"[20]. Dubois goes on to point out that, Historians have done little to preserve the historical records of ordinary people who, most certainly, contributed to history, as such. He said, "We have the record of Kings and gentlemen ad nauseam and in detail. With regard to Negroes in America, in addition to the common neglect of a society patterned on assumed aristocracy, came also the attempt, conscious or unconscious, to excuse the shame of slavery by stressing natural inferiority. That would render it impossible for Negroes to make, much less leave, any record of revolt or struggle, any human reaction to utter degradation"[21].

Hence, the myth that Negroes entered the Revolutionary War as ignorant, stupid, unthinking beings incapable of grasping the perceptions, and issues that created and perpetuated the "Spirit of 76" is more of the fabric of wishful thinking on the part of White men than historical truth. Social and political forces implicit in the Colonial march towards freedom on the eve of the Revolutionary War propelled Colonial Masters and Slaves alike towards that fateful moment of final confrontation at Lexington Green which created this Country.

In describing what became known as the Boston Massacre (March 5, 1770, just 150 Years after slavery started in the Colonies) few, if any White historians bother to mention the fact that of four Colonists killed at Boston, that one of the ring leaders was a Negro. Actually six men were killed, as two of the wounded died later.

6.) THE GAMBLE FOR NEGRO FREEDOM DURING THE REVOLUTIONARY WAR

Crispus Attucks who led the mob against British soldiers at what became known as the Boston Massacre and was one of the first men to give his life there was not a "fluke". Rather, in spite of his color, Attucks was a creature of his time with the same intentions as White men, freedom. Documentary proof abounds in factual documents depicting Negroes intelligently petitioning for freedom and leading rebellions long before the Revolutionary War. From what this writer has been able to determine regarding who and what this first Black martyr was is that Attucks was an itinerant seaman, dockworker, orator and rabble-rouser. He was employing his two latter skills when he fell, mortally wounded, in the snow.

John Adams, our second President of the United States and, at this time a lawyer at Boston, was charged with the defense of the British soldiers who had shot the Colonist down. Sam Adams, his brother, in whose behalf and organization for whom Attucks operated in the street, was one of the head "rabble-rousers" and agitators for freedom of American Colonies, quite a paradox. John Adam's argument before the Court on behalf of the accused British soldiers is very significant to both history and this writer's premise that Blacks played a part in the Revolution other than that of "good tobacco gatherers, servants and slaves".

John Hope Franklin's quote, taken from John Adam's actual argument before the Court is revealing. He describes the dissidents as... "A motley crew of saucy boys, Negroes, Mulattos, Irish and outlandish Jack Tars, led by Crispus Attucks, a runaway slave, and shouting, 'The Way to get rid of these soldiers is to attack the Main Guard.'"[22] Two historically significant facts emerge from this testimony: Blacks and Mulattos abounded in Boston. They were not segregated; rather they mixed freely and made common cause with White Colonist for American freedoms. Crispus Attucks, according to Franklin was not a boy. He was 43 years old, and had run away from Framingham, Massachusetts. He had made his own way and own living for twenty years.

In the ensuing revolt, Black men fought gallantly and died alongside White Colonist. Both John Hope Franklin and Herbert Aptheker tend to validate my premise that Blacks were not politically inert, ignorant bystanders, who stood by while White men fought for America's freedom. They were players and participants. If one reads Lerone Bennett, Jr.'s book, *Before the Mayflower,* or the writings of Carter G. Woodson, further validity is added. Aptheker, the writer, feels additional support is given to an earlier premise as to why myth, rather than fact, is still predominate in U.S. History and literature regarding Black people. Herbert Aptheker says, "A Jim Crow society breeds and needs a Jim Crow historiography. The dominant historiography in the United States either omits the Negro people or presents them as a people without a past, as a people who have been docile, passive, parasitic and imitative. This picture is a lie. The Negro people, the most oppressed of all people in the United States have been militant, active, creative and productive."[23]

All pre-Revolutionary Blacks were not slaves. This negative idea may have come inadvertently from the British experience (or lack there of) with the Romans. According to the Romans who attempted to enslave early Britons, they gave up on the effort and labeled Britons as stupid brutes, lacking in both industry and intelligence. These Conquerors subsequently threw up their hands in disgust, labeled Britons too stupid, in fact, so much so as to be unsuitable for slavery purposes. This Writer suspects that Britons did not deserve the stupidity-label, that they were merely stiff-necked, stubborn, and recalcitrant laborers who behaved in that manner on a mass scale as a tool of passive resistance and refusal to furnish free labor for the Romans.

Thus the British Colonist arrived in North America with no real solid perception of the practice of slavery as an institution. As a people who had participated in the import as a labor source. Further the social and political forces unleashed in England had pauperized small land holders and denied peasants the right to graze sheep or cattle on the Village greens found in most villages, thus denying this class the extra economic factor which allowed them to, at least avoid hunger. Consequently, landless, displaced small landowners and displaced peasants and debtors converged upon British cities creating unmanageable problems for City Governments. This population was tapped for badly needed labor in the Colonies as Bondservants.

Blacks, as slaves were not fully conceptualized in North America even by the mid-14th Century or by the end of the French and Indian War, which ended at the Treaty of Paris, February 10, 1763. This was not true of Spanish Colonist. For they had been exposed to <u>three slave systems</u> prior to coming to the New World. As examples: 1) Early Phoenicians, as traders, brought slaves to Spain. 2) Spain, as a province of Rome, was exposed to Roman slavery; 3) Moorish slavery arrived in April, 711 AD with the Moorish invasion. That exposure lasted nearly 10 centuries. So, at the birth of colonialism, the Portuguese and Spaniards were pre-disposed to Slave trading. This might help explain why the Portuguese started the slave trade at Jamestown in 1619 long before the British did.

Men tend to feel more comfortable with things of familiarity. So, indenture rather than slavery was tried first in British Colonies. The institution of slavery in the Portuguese and Spanish Colonies was a codified concept and its political, social and economic import was well understood long before the British realized its full implications. Hence, the first group of Negroes landed in Jamestown, Virginia in 1619. They were swapped for food by a Dutch Man-O-War, and were launched into Colonial society as <u>indentured servants</u>. Their status was downgraded to that of slave some years later.

Franklin in describing the time element in that change of status says, "So insensible were the Virginians to the unlimited possibilities of Negro labor that nothing resembling a spirited importation of Negroes began until the last quarter of the 17th Century"[24]. He goes on to point out that Negroes occupied approximately the same status as other bondservants for some years. For examples, they were listed in census enumeration of 1623 and 1624 as servants rather than slaves. He further points out the fact that recorded archives of "Early Virginia", as late as 1651 depict Negro Bondservants as having served out their period of indenture and were in process of receiving land and goods stipulated by law, as awarded to White Bondservants on expiration of their terms. This occurred, according to Franklin, for up to 40 years after Jamestown. There also exist records of Free-Negroes in the Colony during that period. The slave of the pre-Revolutionary and immediate post-Revolutionary War faced no such concerted degradation effort as occurred later. He did not have to contend with a sustained assault upon his mental faculties nor the whips, chains, lynching, maiming, and other brutal methods of total control of the Negro slave population of later years. These brutal and cruelly efficient control mechanisms attempted to ensure the "mental retardation" of slaves to the extent that their fawning subservience often made them appear either stupid or brutish and less than human. Behavior labeled often as stupid or clownish was action evolved as a last ditch effort simply to survive under, an often brutal system, by often brutal masters.

That this control system was efficient is attested to by the educational status of the slave population when finally released (not freed) after the Civil War in1865. It was found that 99.9% of the 4,000,000 slaves were illiterate. This brutal hammer had not fallen with its cruelly efficient behavior modifying evil by time of the American Revolution. This brutal method was perfected much later. Consequently, it was not unusual to find a Crispus Attucks, other Negroes and Mulattos making common cause with white men in the streets of pre-Revolutionary Boston, that fateful night in 1770, as a part of Sam Adams' mob of rabble-rousers.

Unlike those Blacks later locked away on rural plantations, these New England Negroes had heard the issues of the day debated in the street, at waterfront taverns and on the City green. Many knew the issues first hand as former prisoners of the British or French during the Revolution as a result of riding privateers and merchantmen, coastwise and on the high seas during the French and Indian War and other European Wars that Colonist were drawn into. Consequently when the Revolutionary War started there existed in the Colonies a small but seasoned cadre of Negro fighting men in an advanced stage of social and political development by Colonial standards. It may possibly increase the historical clarity of this era to point out that all White Colonists were not literate members of the "Gentry Class".

Most major cities in pre-Revolutionary War America, if these could be called so, contained an illiterate "under class" of White men. These were a by-product of a fast-fading Bondservant system, which had been providing cheap labor for the colonies incident to the decrees of English Kings, Queens, City Governments such as those of London and Liverpool. These actions were the solutions to social and political problems of that day and time.

These early forbears of today's "Social Service Engineers" solved their "people problems" by hanging, imprisonment, or deportation. Let's take, for instance, the problem of crime in 15th, 16th, and early 17th century England. Serious criminals such as marauders, rogues, highwaymen, etc., were disposed of by way of the hangman's noose and gallows, as was most rebel leadership. Petty criminals such as pickpockets, prostitutes, petty thieves and debtors were transported to the Colonies and sold as Bondservants. The mid-range of rebels and habitual criminals were deported half way across the world to the prison colony at Botany Bay, Australia or to James Oglethorp's experimental colony in Georgia. The rebellions in Ireland and Scotland furnished, as did the almshouse poor and street beggars, another lucrative source of White men sold into contractual, stipulated-time type servitude.

For the serious student to understand why Negroes, during the early slave period, were running around with White dissidents and rabble-rousers in the streets of cities such as Philadelphia and Boston, one must understand the progress of social conscientiousness and public sentiment in the geographical areas of early America. For examples: The march towards humane treatment of one's fellows in the Colonies, especially Bondservants and slaves, could depend upon many factors. Among them were 1) geographical accident; 2) the predominant religion of the Colonist in a given area; 3) and/or the degree of political or religious persecution of Colonist prior to arrival in America. For instance, the "Puritan Conscience" made the Colonist of Massachusetts uncomfortable with the dehumanization of Negroes. Neither the Amish nor the Quakers of Pennsylvania believed that other men should enslave their fellow man. All of these groups, as did the Huguenots of France who settled in South Carolina, were among the earliest anti-slavery advocates.

Neither the Catholics of Maryland, Polish Catholics, Irish Catholics, Presbyterians nor Anglicans, however, suffered pangs of conscience over human bondage or slavery. No political, social or scientific breakthrough affects all of a society's members simultaneously. This may be validated by the simple unobtrusive measure of mere human and institutional observation. We heard of Negroes in the Southern states being held in peonage and beaten or brutally murdered for protesting during the Civil Rights movement of the 1960's. This was not so in other areas of the country to the same intense extent. Political exception occurs in case of Revolution but even then the social change is a more gradual process. Thus, the White Bondsman System and the Slavery System were overlapping in time on the eve of the American Revolution. Bondsmen, as a cheap labor source was on the way out, with Slavery on the way, incoming.

Many newly released Bondsmen who failed to find a "social niche", where it was possible to survive, fled the small towns and rural villages flocking to the cities. There they found a complementary underclass of poor Whites, runaway slaves and free Negroes. Where the runaways are concerned, all oppressed peoples contain segments of the population haughty and daring enough to take a chance at freedom by either fighting for it or simply absconding. Negroes were not an exception. Hence, on the eve of the Revolutionary War we find a Black Crispus Attucks leading a mixed, motley mob of city dissidents against the British army of occupation. It is unlikely that recent Bondsmen or runaway slaves failed to understand the meaning of liberty or the concept of freedom. Against, England the small populations in Colonies needed all of the manpower ashore and afloat that they could get. So there was a definite role for Black men to play both in the prelude to revolt and during the actual commencement of hostilities.

There were major forces impinging upon the utilization of Negroes of British America on the eve of the Revolutionary War.

For example:

1) The march of England towards the mastery of the Sea after the Collapse of the Spanish Armada in 1588.

2) England's surge toward Imperialism.

3) The slow march, internally, in England towards the concept of The "Rights of Englishmen."

4) The near end of Bond Servitude in England and her American Colonies.

All of these forces converged as the American Revolution commenced and created a need for both Negro soldiers and seamen in the coming fight for American Independence. The Negroes did not disappoint their former masters when White America Needed them in the Revolutionary War—the war for White freedom. The Negroes, however, gambled on achieving possible freedom for themselves.

CHAPTER 2. NEGRO PARTICIPATION AND PERFORMANCE IN THE REVOLUTIONARY WAR

1) THE WHITE COLONIST DILEMMA: SHOULD THE NEGRO BE ALLOWED TO FIGHT IN A REVOLUTION TO FREE WHITE MEN AND REMAIN A SLAVE IN A FREE COUNTRY

On the eve of the Revolutionary war, a dilemma, in the form of a two-sided question faced Negro and White colonists. The question for Whites was "should Negroes, slave or free, be allowed to enlist in the colonial military". Although Negroes had participated in almost all prior crises and wars that required manpower. There was a dichotomy between this new fight for freedom, engendered by the Declaration of Independence and the institution of Slavery. It stated that all men were created equal. The question for Negroes was "if we are going to be kept in Bondage and subjected to extreme prejudice as free men, why should we risk our lives?" Prior service to these colonies had not brought equal treatment.

The solution to this dichotomy came from the pragmatism on both sides. David and Elaine Crane tell us that:

> "During the Revolution freedmen and slaves took up the cause
> of independence despite a ruling which excluded slaves on the
> somewhat incongruous grounds that their service would be
> "inconsistent with the principles that are to be supported". And

while Negro soldiers distinguished themselves in the early battles of the War for Independence, movement was afoot to rid the army of all black men. On November 12, 1775, General George Washington, motivated partially by prejudice and partially by fear of arming blacks, issued an order instructing recruiters not to enlist Negroes. Whatever his reasons, Washington nonetheless found himself in an awkward position when news arrived that the British army was eagerly welcoming free Blacks and runaway slaves. As Negroes, both slave and freedmen, began to flock toward the British lines, the American army was forced to modify its position. Owners were given bounties to provide slaves for the duration of the war. In some cases, slaves, turned soldiers were promised their freedom at the end of the war, and their masters were compensated at the going rate for human flesh."[25]

The following was taken from the Web Site "Africans in America/ Revolutionary Black Seamen:

"Unlike the Continental Army, the Navy recruited both free and enslaved Blacks from the very start of the Revolutionary War. This was done partly out of desperation for seamen of any color, and partly because many Blacks were already experienced sailors, having served in the British and state navies, as well as on merchant vessels in the North and South.

To both slave and free, privately owned vessels were more attractive than Continental or state navies. For runaway slaves, there was less chance of being detected by slave catchers, and for all crewmembers, there were greater financial rewards. Philadelphia's free Blacks, for instance, were more inclined to serve on privateers than in the Pennsylvania navy.

One of the most famous Black seamen was James Forten, who enlisted on the privateer *Royal Lewis* as a powder boy, was captured along with his ship's crew, and spent time on a British prison barge before being released in a prisoner exchange. Forten went on to become a successful businessman and a leader of Philadelphia's African American community.

Although Black seamen performed a range of duties, usually the most menial ones, they were particularly valued as pilots. Both Maryland and Virginia's navies made extensive use of Blacks, even purchasing slaves specifically for wartime service. Virginia's state commissioner noted that it was cheaper to hire Blacks than Whites, and that Whites could get an exemption from military service by substituting a slave."[26]

1) SO HOW DID NEGRO FIGHTING-MEN PERFORM? WHAT WERE THE RISKS FOR BLACKS IN PARTICULAR?

To answer these questions one must understand the manpower situation in both England and the Colonies. Reuben Elmore Stivers says that:

"During both the Revolutionary War and the War of 1812, unlike any conflict in which the United States has since participated, the number of men enrolled at one time in the continental and United States armies, including Militia, was always smaller than those facing the Maritime forces of the enemy. About 320,000 out of a population of 1,100,000 White males during six years of war but not more than 10 percent of these sometime participants were ever in the field at any one time."[27]

It is pertinent to point out here that Washington's boo-boo, rejecting Negroes for Army service, did not affect Negro sailors for reasons previously stated—hardheaded pragmatic, early Naval Officers who refused to reject Negroes before or after the Revolution. Hence the Navy was not a part of the dilemma. But what Stivers says next about this period is possibly more germane to answers to the questions posed. For example, in looking at England's manpower situation, he points out "that Great Britain increased the number of her sailors at sea from 16,000 in 1774 to nearly 70,000 in 1782; but, rather than assuring victory this manpower drain sowed the seeds of enormous discontent in the British Isles."[28]

He then points out that the Colonies moved from zero to just about as many men as England could allot to the sea services. Further, The colonists knew that a massive organized navy was not necessary to inflict damage on an enemy at sea. The French privateers in the past war had taught Great Britain and the Colonist that bitter lesson. Further, Britain knew the daring and courage of Colonial Reservist (Privateers men) as She had been compelled to press them into service in the French and Indian War and had taught the Colonist well. She had not found them lacking in bravery, aptitude, or ingenuity needed for privateering! Stivers says that this probably accounted for the English Navy's policy of refusing to exchange their imprisoned American privateers for British seamen in captivity in the Colonies until late in the war. At no time since has America had to deal with a situation whereby sailors outnumbered soldiers at any one time. The Sea during the Revolution was a scene of constant action.

2) THE NEGRO SOLUTION TO THE DILEMMA: MOST CHOSE TO FIGHT AGAINST ENGLAND THOUGH FREEDOM WAS NOT GUARANTEED

Negroes found themselves fighting on both the English and the Colonial side of the Revolutionary war. They were driven to the British side by the ineptitude of the Colonial leaders. George Washington and his backers, out of fear of Negro conspiracies or armed insurrections barred Negro enlistment. They failed to recognize that the Negro had already sided with the Colonists. They had fought at Lexington Green, Concord Bridge, and Bunker Hill just 18 days before George Washington arrived to take command. According to Peter Bergman, "Lemuel Haynes, Primas Black, and Epheran Blackmore, Negro members of the Green Mountain Boys of Vermont took part in the capture of Fort Ticonderoga."[29] None of this seems to have been considered before issuing what turned out to be a costly and stupid order to bar Negroes from military service. The situation was not helped by the harsh overreaction of the colonist. For example, Bergman points out that "Virginia law allowed the sale, banishment or execution of Negroes caught attempting to flee. It was enforced in 1776 when four runaways were hanged and twenty-five others were sold to the West Indies. So, Negroes had to do what they had always done, serve this country "in spite of itself" rather than with its blessing.

The number of Negroes serving in the Revolutionary War is most often quoted at 5,000. However, the more diligent historians point out that the number 5,000 represent the men in uniform. There were many others involved in building fortifications and roads, spying, and hauling supplies. Without this additional support, the war might have had a different outcome. Bergman says that, "In the period from 1774 to 1783, both before and after the ban on Negro service, between 8,000 and 10,000 Negroes served in the Revolutionary armies in various capacities; approximately 5,000 were uniformed regulars."[30]

General Washington became alarmed when Negroes began flocking to the British side in response to the promise of Lord Dunsmore to set them free. He reversed himself and approved the enlistment of men who had fought in the earlier battles. Congress approved this order, but, again, refused to countenance the enlistment of slaves. Circumstances, however, made this a moot point. For one thing, it was very difficult to coax White men into the Continental Army. Although there were over one million men of fighting age in the colonies, the Continental Army never exceeded 50,000 at one time. Bounties of land and money were offered to volunteers. Some states even offered bounties of slaves. Nothing, however, would attract significant numbers.

George Washington probably endured his lowest spirit at this lack of patriotism among colonial men. The number of desertions further hampered his efforts. "Washington went into the terrible ordeal at Valley Forge in December, 1777, with some 9,000 men. By March 1778, more than 3,000 had deserted. After Valley Forge, every able-bodied man, be he Black or White, slave or free, were welcomed into the continental Army."[31]

The navy, on the other hand, asserted its traditional independence. It ignored the order to bar Negroes from service issued by the Hancock &/Warren Committee and George Washington. Bergman says "the Negro soldiers generally fought in integrated units and were particularly effective as spies, guerilla fighters, and navy pilots. There were 20 Negroes on *the Royal Lewis* under Captain Stephen Decatur. Negroes saw action in major battles at White Plains, Saratoga, Stoney Point, Trenton, Monmouth, and Yorktown."[32]

Since Negroes were generally disrespected and considered not too bright, they were allowed to wander all over the countryside and even through enemy lines. This made them especially effective as spies. Lafayette says that his favorite spy was a Negro by the name of James Armistead. Armistead gave the British misinformation sent by Lafayette and returned with real and useful intelligence. He was able to tell Lafayette the number of troops, their distribution and supply situation, trails and possible routes in event of movement. Since they, the Negroes, were long time inhabitants of a particular area, they knew the geographical features, the depth and possible fording points for crossing rivers. On the mid-Atlantic coast, they were some of the best pilots. Pompey, a Negro spy, made possible the victory by "Mad Anthony Wayne at Stoney Point." John Hope Franklin's list of battles, in which the Negro fought, is more extensive than that of Peter Bergman. To Bergman's list, he adds Long Island, Eutaw Springs, Brandywine, Red Bank, Fort Griswold, Stillwater, Savannah and Bemis Heights. This would indicate that there were few battles in which the Negro did not fight! Bergman describes some of the Negroes who fought:

> "Peter Salem of Framingham and Samuel Craft of Newton, Massachusetts, both Negroes, were at Concord Bridge in April. Ceasar Ferrit and his son, John of Natic, Pomp Blackman and Lemuel Haynes of West Hartford, Connecticut were also present. Lemuel Haynes later became a theologian. Among the Negroes who fought at Bunker Hill in June were, besides Peter Salem, Titus Coburn, Seymour Burr, Grant Cooper, Cato Howe, Charlston Eads, Brazilla Lew, Sampson Talbert, Ceasar Brown (died in battle), Ceasar Basom, Alexander Eames, Ceasar Jahar, Cuff Blanchard, Ceasar Post and Salem Poor. Peter Salem killed the British Commander, Major Pitcairn. He later fought at Saratoga and Stoney Point. Prince Hall, later a pioneer abolitionist in Massachusetts, was also at Bunker Hill."[33]

When Prince Hall sought a charter for Negro Masons he was refused. Hall secured a charter from England. Negro Masons possess a longer, continuous history than Whites, as all of their charters were nullified after the Revolution.

In his memoirs, U.S. Navy Commodore James Barron, who served as captain in the Virginia navy during the war, recalled several Black men among the "courageous patriots who...in justice to their merits should not be forgotten." He mentions four slaves: Harry, Cupid, Aberdeen (who subsequently befriended Patrick Henry and was freed by the Virginia General Assembly) and the "noble African" pilot known as "Captain" Mark Starlins.

There is no question that Negroes participated in the fight that created this country. Further, how they performed leaves no room for shame. John Hope Franklin relates the following: "In the battle of Rhode Island, August 29, 1778, the Negro Regiment under Colonel Christopher Green distinguished itself by deeds of desperation and valor. On three occasions, the Hessian Soldiers who were charging down on them were stopped. 1,310 Hessians died while only 211 blacks were killed. In a later incident at Points Bridge, New York, Commander Green was surprised and killed. His Negro soldiers heroically defended him until they were cut to pieces. The enemy had to crawl over the dead bodies of his Negro troops to reach Green as he lay dying."[34]

The first question, as to how the Negro performed in the army, has been answered. Few, if any Histories include their performance at sea during the Revolution.

To answer the second question, "What was the risk for Blacks, to those willing to go to sea?" One has only to look at the intensity and scope of the War at sea. The risk to both White men and Black men was quite great. The British of this period mistreated and abused their own seamen. A Colonist of what they perceived as their own territory, was considered little more than a traitor and was treated harshly and disciplined severely at the least infraction. Whether he survived imprisonment or not was strictly a matter of genetic endowment or innate toughness. A seaman, unfortunate enough to become a captive could depend upon a starvation diet, baking in summer and freezing in Winter, while rotting (literally from filth induced scabies, diarrhea, scurvy, etc.) on some British hulks utilized for a prison. There was one way out; become a traitor and serve in the British Navy. This was offered incident to Britain having to stretch its naval arm of service to fight in all oceans. Her high handed policy of stopping and humbling other nations' vessels at sea, searching them and "impressing" any English appearing crewmen had angered non-belligerent nations who retaliated by harassing British merchantmen caught off guard. She desperately needed seamen. Stivers says that, "When American prisoners in the British prison ships Good Hope, Prince of Wales, and Jersey were regularly offered an opportunity to improve their miserable lot by enlisting in a British Man-O-War, very few did. Each morning guards shouted: Rebels turn out your dead! The corpses were passed up through the hatchway."[35] This did little to endear Colonist to their Motherland. According to Stivers, "...Many Americans were undoubtedly compelled to fight against their own Country and her allies. But for every American thus impressed, probably ten English sailors were persuaded to serve in American privateers."[36] To further answer the questions posed, a Revolutionary War seaman was almost certain to go to sea and most likely hear long guns talk. It was no place for the fainthearted as when in a fight or the misfortune of captivity he could expect no mercy, at worst he could end up hanging from a yard arm or in England's notorious Dartmoore prison, there to rot, starve or freeze. Unless one agreed to commit treason against his own people and serve England, a prisoner's untimely death certainly did not phase the Crown. Whether a person was Black or White made no difference. The harsh treatment was administered without impunity. In spite of the danger and harshness of sea service, Negroes saw action in all major actions in the Revolution.

Two of John Paul Jones' seamen were Black. Their names were Cato Carlisle and Scipio Africanus. According to Jones, these two men were two of his most loyal and dependable sailors. If you read any of Jones' biographies, you will find these two Black sailors who rode with him in his classic actions during the Revolutionary War.

But the power of the slave owners negated the service of Blacks in the Revolution.

It seems that the idea of picking his own cotton, doing his own sweating, and, his ingrained greed, denied the White man in Post Revolutionary America, the moral ability to pay Black men for helping him to obtain his freedom. Instead, Blacks were summary discharged from the U.S. Army. The U.S. Navy, what was left of it, refused to discharge Negroes. Also, they refused to discontinue the recruitment of Negroes. The Navy's policy toward Negroes paid off. The Army policy caused them to miss-out in the War of 1812 and to have, possibly, the best infantry in North America. Many Negroes had fought from Lexington Green to Yorktown, a period of eight years. Many of these Negro soldiers had no homes to return to. Most would have remained to form a nucleus of combat infantry, throughout the war of 1812.

To understand the military situation in the Post Revolutionary War period, one must understand that following the Revolutionary War, the United States virtually eliminated its Army and Navy. The U.S. Army that was left accepted no Blacks. The U.S. Navy created in 1798, continued to do so throughout the nineteenth century.

The smaller U.S. Marine Corps excluded all but a few Blacks since its inception in 1798 until 1942. Black soldiers had served in the War of 1812 but, in 1812, the Secretary of War, John C. Calhoun of South Carolina, responding to Southern slave owners, attempted to ban any further enlistment of Negroes and failed. As Negro veterans left the Army it became exclusively White until the American Civil War.

Understanding the power of Southern slave owners and their influence upon politics and legislative action, one can understand why the retardation to utilization of the Negro soldier was at great cost in the War of 1812. The only unfettered use occurred at the insistence of Andrew Jackson in 1815 after the Army had been thoroughly disgraced and humiliated in action. The Battle of New Orleans, in which Negroes were fully utilized, was the only Battle in which the Army really shone in the War of 1812.

CHAPTER 3.   THE AFTERMATH OF THE REVOLUTION AND THE WAR OF 1812

1)   THE 'PAYOFF' FOR NEGRO SAILORS FOR HELPING TO WIN 'WHITE FREEDOM' IN THE REVOLUTIONARY WAR

Though treated more harshly than Whites, the sea was a bit more democratic to blacks than a plantation. Leading towards the War of 1812, four phenomena converged, sealing the fate of Negroes. Ten years after White America acquired its freedom the first fugitive slave law was enacted by the new congress in 1793. The second blow fell a year later when a Yankee inventor named Eli Whitney patented the cotton Gin. The third was the rise of commercial whaling. The demand for whale oil fueled the growth in shipbuilding. From this activity, the fourth emerged. The growth in shipbuilding also brought technological advances and capacity, which helped facilitate the slave trade. From this point on, the rapid slide downward of the Negro to the status of "non—persons" commenced. This deterioration was more rapid on land than at sea. The ultimate barring of Negroes from enlistment in the sea services in 1919, Navy and Marines, and later, their reduction to servants and lackeys in 1932, was concomitantly set in motion here. The voice of slave owners, their greed and drive for profit, spoke as loud for the continued enslavement of the Negro as it did for the new freedom of White men.

This also marked the beginning of an enduring character trait that remains a part of White America's psyche, a more literally socially accepted part of their culture that remains a potent part of their behavior to this day. The trait spoken of has throughout U.S. History enabled White men to subvert their so-called Christian beliefs and/or consciences, sense of justice and to always exhibit a capacity to prostitute and compromise these at the expense of Black people.

Militarily, Negroes were paid in kind, for fighting for White freedom. According to Jack D. Foner, one of the first edicts coming from the newly freed American Government was to "restrict the armed forces to able bodied White males." The reason was harshly logical. How could America create contingents of armed Negro fighting men in their midst while, concomitantly continuing to hold the vast majority of these unhappy people in slavery? The latter decision had already been decided with the creation of the U.S. Constitution. The Negro emerged as 3/5ths of a man. Only whole men were to enjoy the new freedom, won in the Revolution.

Before the War of 1812 is dealt with as it pertains to Negroes, it is perhaps pertinent that we check our historical bearings. The first official U.S. Navy Department was established March 27, 1794. The U.S. Marine Corps was established the same year on July l, 1794. The prelude to the final establishment of the actual administrative unit that we know as the "Navy Department" occurred in October 1775. Its beginning was the appointment by the Second Continental Congress of a 13 member "Marine Committee." Some of those appointed were Robert Morris, Joseph Hewes, Henry Laurens, Richard Henry Lee, Stephen Hopkins, Samuel Adams, and John Hancock. These proved most prominent. The previous Naval Committee was composed of three people, later enlarged to seven who were superseded by the Marine Committee. So, it should be understood that the Navy Department only became a reality after two faltering starts and the impetus of necessity.

The first Secretary of the Navy was Benjamin Stoddert, who was a resident of Georgetown. He was a former successful merchant who succeeded in sending out a highly respectable force. Further, he laid down enduring foundations for Naval Organization and Administration. Europe was sure to test the new secretary's mettle. It did not take long for England, America's former master, and France, her recent ally to do so. During this period, the Tripoli, Morocco and the Algerian pirate kingdoms of North Africa exacted tribute and/or enslaved the crews of weak nations. America, newly freed, had no money in her treasury and no navy to protect them. This was primarily due to the attitude of Thomas Jefferson, who erroneously believed that the ocean barrier and neutrality would protect the United States. The United States rapidly became the victim of pirates in the Mediterranean Sea.

According to Dr. Frederick S. Harrod, Assistant Professor of History, U.S. Naval Academy at Annapolis, "Virtually from its creation, the Navy displayed a reluctance to accept Blacks. In August 1798, just four months after the passage of the Act authorizing the creation of the Navy Department, Secretary of the Navy Samuel Southard cautioned an Officer. He told this captain, who was about to enlist a crew for a schooner preparing for a cruise, that "no Negroes or Mulattos are to be admitted."[37] Since Naval tradition literally commenced with a deck stacked against Black men, the logical question is why did the U.S. Navy allow them to consistently enlist from 1776 until their final exclusion in 1919? They allowed enlistment for the first 133 (1776-1919) years of naval existence, in spite of a racist Congress, Senate and public. The most probable answer rests on the fact previously mentioned a chronic shortage of manpower in the early colonies. Pragmatic men don't go around, if I may use a time worn cliché "cutting off their noses in order to spite their faces". Thus Colonist probably harbored racist feelings but could not afford either the system or process that we call "Racism" as actual policy. Such a policy would have, in the 16th, 17th and 18th centuries, been not only impractical but self-defeating as well.

As previously mentioned one of the first lessons that the new nation had to learn was that the world is akin to a mean ghetto street where greedy bullies exist in abundance. The Revolutionary War officially ended on September 3, 1783 after eight bitter years of conflict. Less than two years later, the U.S. Navy ceased to exist. According to Jack Sweetman, on June 3, 1785, "Congress authorizes the sale of the one remaining American naval vessel, the frigate *Alliance*. For the next nine years, the nation had no Navy."[38] The newly freed United States did not lose its newfound freedom and does not rest upon any brilliance of post-revolution leaders. It rested upon the exhaustion and depleted treasuries of England, France and Spain, as there was no maritime defense. Much turmoil ensued as this fledgling country tried to gain its footing. For example, the Constitutional Convention occurred in 1787. It created authority, according to Jack Sweetman, "To provide and maintain a Navy. The process of ratification was completed in the summer of 1788 but years will pass before a Navy is actually established."[39] The Revolutionary Navy was never near such as would indicate the existence of an organized fleet of vessels specially designed as fighting ships. For example, it was not anything that remotely matched that of the British, Dutch, Spanish or French Navies. Then one must ask how did that rag-tag group of amateurs with their makeshift, converted, basically cargo type vessels inflict so much damage upon British commerce, and succeed in humiliating the greatest Naval power of its day?

To understand and so answer that question, we must "backtrack" and understand how American Colonial sea borne commerce survived during its existence as a colony subject to the whims of not just English kings and queens but those of other European monarchs as well.

American Colonists, as previously stated, often found out that they, as Colonist of England were involved in some stupid war, not of their choosing, after some European monarch had declared war. A war, too often resultant from some obscure disagreement between England and some other European King or Kings (Holland, Spain, France or a combination) which the Colonists often did not understand.

Further, kings and their advisors were always looking for money in order to fight wars or fill empty chests depleted by a previous war. This is the nature of kings. Since there was no telegraphs or radios, American seamen often found that a war existed, by being fired upon, without warning, boarded by some foreign crew, imprisoned in the hold of some hulk, their ships and cargoes confiscated and sold in foreign ports, while they rotted in that country's prison. Another jarring experience was that of going to sea under one set of regulations and returning to port only to find that the regulations (tariffs/taxes) had been drastically changed during their absence. This could result in part of a vessel's profits being, "ripped off," by a parliament or king 3,000 miles away. The sea was not a place for the faint hearted nor those lacking resilience or daring. Consequently, American Merchant Seamen learned to arm their vessels and the minute they cleared the harbor, to look sharply, be vigilant and be ready to run/or fight at all times. Hence New World seamen learned to be expert at laying guns, smuggling and to use to the fullest, the finer points of seamanship. Where on land the rigors of the Frontier shaped the American character, at sea the very circumstances in which they found themselves did so. Thus, in spite of not having the organization or ships, Colonists had astute seamanship, gunnery and daring. It is this that enabled them to give an account of themselves in the French and Indian, the Revolutionary War and War of 1812. In short, America was never dependent solely on its Navy.

The Merchant Marine, as forerunners of the Naval Reserve, and the privateers, were the backbone of sea fighting. Due to the culture that shaped it, the Merchant Marine formed a "Ready Reserve Force" capable of inflicting, until recently, more damage than the U.S. Navy. Most Colonial Merchant ships were "Privateers", in being, which enabled the Colonists to rapidly "show their teeth," when put upon. French, English, Spanish and Dutch history all attest to this, adding historical validity. Amidst all of this, what happened to Negro Navy Seamen in the aftermath of the Revolution and the scrapping of the Navy? The answer is probably the same thing that happened to White seamen. Probably, the vast majority did what they had always done. They drifted back to the Merchant Marine where they came from in the first place. This reserve force in being, a cadre of hard bitten men who knew how to fight and possessed the guts to do so, are possibly, the major reason that the United States was not remade into one of England's colonies again in 1812. Luckily for this country, this group of men knew how to both fight and sail. Their very occupation and its rigors imposed upon them the retention of the capacity to make split second decisions, to fight or outrun any strange sail that appeared on the horizon. This did not end because the War ended and the U.S. became a so-called Sovereign nation. Declaring that you were sovereign in that age (1700's) was an exercise in "bombastic futility" unless a nation had guns, men, ships, an army and the will to fight.

The questions are often raised, why didn't the adverse affects of European conflicts with the former colonist not cease at Yorktown? Why did the post Revolution policy based upon race fail? The reason was simple. It is one thing to sign a treaty, but another to possess the power to see that the other party does not violate it. The newly freed colonist one is reminded, had neither the money nor the power to compel England, Spain or France to abide by the Articles of the Treaty of Paris. Since the new nation had no Navy left, barring Negroes from service was a statement of intent and desire but without power or substance as Negro manpower was too badly needed. For sake of clarity, lets recapitulate the actions that set the stage for the War of 1812. According to Samuel W. Bryant, "on November 30th, 1782, articles between the United States and Great Britain had been signed, but they were not to go into effect until France and Britain made peace. And that did not finally come about until September 3, 1783, when the definitive articles were sealed by the treaty called the Peace of Paris."[40] The war lasted eight years and six months. The colonies were in a financial shambles, its commerce nearly non-existent, its coffers empty and its defenses likewise were gone. But this group of "country bumpkins" calling themselves the United States, had humiliated the mother country and in so doing, humiliated the mightiest Navy, and one of the best armies in the world. This victory revealed England's vulnerability to the other powers of Europe. Americans proved that England could not fight in all oceans at once nor engage all of her enemies simultaneously on the world's oceans. England had yet to learn what Spain learned after the defeat of her Armada in 1588. The English proved to be a proud, unforgiving, and arrogant nation. It is that arrogance that caused England to not listen to their colonial cousins after these so-called bumpkins, in the person of George Washington, tried to tell them that the old European military formations would not work in the new world. Here men engaged in guerilla formations, shooting from behind rocks and trees. Failure to listen had cost General Braddock his life at a place now known as Pittsburgh in 1755 in the French and Indian War. Even, after this error, which caused the Indians to become allies of the French, British arrogance so blinded them until years later Redcoats, "marching in formation," after the Battle of Lexington were routed by Colonists at Concord Bridge. But then thirty years later, another General Officer, Major General Sir Edward Pakenham, who could have attacked Andrew Jackson from the rear at New Orleans in 1815, arrogantly chose to let these country Americans see how English gentlemen faced "cold steel" in battle. They marched upright and in formation, to hell on the swampy flats of the Calumet Plains outside New Orleans. According to Samuel Eliot Morrison and Henry Steel Commager, "Instead, he chose, at 6 a.m. to direct a foolhardy frontal assault of some 5,300 men in close column formation against Jackson's 3,500 on the parapet, so well protected that the British, without ladders or fascines, could not get at them. "The result was more of a massacre than a battle. General Pakenham and over 2,000 men of all ranks were killed, wounded or missing. The second and third generals in line of command were fatally wounded. Exactly thirteen Americans were killed and 58 wounded."[41] You simply could not march in compact formations against men of the frontier equipped with the long rifle and survive. So if one wonders why Pakenham did not seize the advantage and attack Andrew Jackson's rear, military tacticians still do not know. His troops had routed the Kentucky contingent under Adair. Jackson called them cowards and these angry Kentucky citizens later made him pay politically. They would not vote for him for the next 41 years.

The truth was that the Kentucky group was hastily gotten together, poorly armed, clothed, trained, and with no logistics. This probably accounted for their poor performance. It's a fact that the Kentuckians had been in previous emergencies where they had acted with uncommon valor and were lauded for their "Long Rifle" marksmanship. They had given a good account of themselves in battle.

2) THE OUTSTANDING PERFORMANCE OF NEGROES IN THE WAR OF 1812

What is probably little known in most of today's history classes is that foreign Negroes fought on the side of American colonists in the Revolution, but against the United States in the War of 1812. There was a battalion of Haitian Negroes whom America scorns and mistreats today, with the French who supported the colonist at the siege of Savanna on October 9, 1779. West Indian Negroes were with the British troops who routed Adairs' Kentuckians and exposed Jackson's rear at the prelude to the Battle of New Orleans in 1815. Haitian Negroes fought again with Americans at New Orleans.

So whether Americans accept or understand it or not, Negroes did play major historical rolls both at its birth and at its quest for recognition as implicit in the War of 1812, when England sought to chastise it as a former colony. A native Negro/Freedmen regiment did fight with Andrew Jackson at the Battle of New Orleans and gave an account of themselves that earned his laudatory praise. Andrew Jackson did not keep his word with these Negroes after the War of 1812 and allowed the regiment to deteriorate and disband.

Their gallantry and participation did aid him in saving the seaport of New Orleans from capture and occupation by the British. This was one of the few instances in which a land force army shone in that War, at a time when virtually all of New England chose to divide the effort and look to their own selfish commercial interest. It is pertinent to point out here that Negroes served this country when it was barely able to serve itself. They were paid in shabby coin as usual and in the aftermath of 1812, their social and political status rapidly slid downward.

Incidents at sea prior to 1812 would finally trigger this second war with England. In this war, almost as if by fate, the caliber of

Negro fighting men would shine. The ignorant luxury of Racism simply could not be afforded. Once more America needed her sons, Black ones included. The country needed them fast and as many as she could get, Black ones, White ones, and Red ones if they could be induced. England, their American cousins soon found out, was a tenacious and all but implacable enemy. Masked behind the supposedly solemn peace agreement reached and signed at Paris twenty-nine years earlier, reclined "bad faith," on part of the former British masters. Britain still looked upon their American cousins at best as rustic simpletons and at worst, as an ungrateful bunch of bumpkins, if not quasi-traitors.

3) THE LACK OF UNITY IN THE NEW COUNTRY AND ITS COSTS

Even today, the position imposed on this newly formed Union of States by its logical birth pains is not very well understood. The states early proved to be united in form but woefully deficient in sentiment or substance. Unity based upon the sentiment of "national interest" had not been absorbed or even contemplated. This was the glue needed to bind this union of states into a "Federal Union," instead of a mere loosely knit confederation. Consequently, the "Self Interest" of each colony superseded any of the thoughtful, contemplative intelligence required to really understand that the strength of the United States rested upon the "mutual respect and caring. It required compromise or even sacrifice in the name of National interest. Samuel W. Bryant described the chaotic condition in which the colonies found themselves as they faced the second war with England. He said, "At first the coastal trade was active and prosperous, but soon various states, each functioning as an independent republic, began to compete with each other trying to lure trade away from neighboring states by levying port dues and taxes on ships and goods of their rivals."[42] James Madison was moved to point out that New Jersey, caught between Philadelphia and New York, was like a keg tapped at both ends, and that North Carolina between Virginia and South Carolina was like a patient bleeding at both arms. In short, each state said "to hell with their brother and looked at their own selfish interest." It is pretty hard to fight a common enemy while engaged in "a war of all against all" concomitantly. This was America as it faced English might in 1812. The West Indies trade had, as Bryant puts it, always had been a "projection of coastal trade." England struck at this lucrative aspect of U.S. commerce even as she hypocritically waved the olive branch of peace at the Treaty of Paris signed Sept. 3, 1783. She had, by order of Council in July 1783, first, closed trade with the British Islands of the West Indies to the former Colonist. Bryant says, " before the smugglers could evade the order in adequate numbers, thousands of slaves starved to death and with them hundreds of impoverished Whites; as a result of this sudden cut off of trade between colonial America and the West Indies."[43] The harsh conscience of the British King does not seem to have been touched by this catastrophe that befell Negro slaves nor indeed the deaths of his own people, resident in the West Indies. The American Colonist furnished much of the grain and meat that fed the large plantations in the West Indies.

The British closing of this trade to her former colony's ships was equivalent to a famine, intentionally induced. This action created a situation where slaves and powerless, impoverished Whites were the first to starve. There is one element of Naval History that the general run of U.S. Histories seem to not strongly stress; the principle reason for this is that the Colonist fought the English, in the Revolution, because of British interference with the maritime commerce of the Colonist. This same reason caused the United States to fight the Barbary pirates of North Africa and fight a three-year war with its former French Ally from 1798 to 1801, and finally the War of 1812 with its former British masters. The U.S. had a fifteen-year honeymoon after it won its freedom. This would not be called a honeymoon by today's standards where War ends all hostilities for specific intervals of time. So-called peace in the 17th and 18th centuries was always a comparative situation with the certain potential for rapid deterioration always present. It would be an error to misconstrue today's extended periods of peace with that of the 16th, 17th or later centuries. Another bit of U.S. History obviously overlooked or poorly taught, even at the University level is the fact that whereby France was a staunch ally during the latter part of the Revolution and up until the end in 1783. She was an implacable enemy ten years later in 1793. The time sequence here seems to be what is not emphasized. France, England, and Spain by 1793 were again in one of their seemingly endless wars. The newly freed United States had been doing exceptionally well, commercially but had no Navy to protect its lucrative commerce neither along the Coast nor beyond the seas. This time there was no French King to assist the U.S. Instead, France had been torn apart by the French Revolution. The Aristocracy was overthrown. Louis XVI and his Queen both lost their heads to mob demand, via the, "Guillotine" on January 21, 1793.

Thomas Jefferson, who was never a friend to the Navy, received a rude awakening in attempting to deal with these radical anti-aristocratic "Jacobins" and their "Directorate", or "Council". This was a far cry from dealing with the trained, suave diplomats of Louis the XVI. These were rude, harsh, angry men to whom force and opportunism appeared better tools of governance than that of the endless prattling and patience required for diplomacy. Finally Jefferson had to inform his Countrymen that there would be no peace with France unless the United States was willing to negotiate with her and any other power, for that matter, over the barrels of cannon or those of long guns. This nullified the slave owner faction and Secretary of the Navy Samuel Southard's racist and ungrateful attempt to bar Negroes and Mulattos from Naval service, who had fought gallantly and well, in the recent Revolution. The beginning of the Navy's construction in 1794 had "dragged on" with a parsimonious Congress producing nothing but hot air and talking endlessly. But when Colonial Commerce, which had nearly reached the pre-Revolution levels, started to plummet, incident to continued depredations by France, England, Spain, and the Barbary pirates, America stopped talking and started creating its first real Navy under its new Constitution.

The ingenuity of Yankee traders like Elias Haskett Derby had outfoxed England when she, two years after her defeat, closed the West Indies to U.S. trading vessels. Derby sent ships to Russia to trade. He, later, sent vessels around The Cape of Good Hope to China. According to Dudley W. Knox, this constituted approximately one third of this country's trade. Wily Yankee traders, seasoned and taught to fight in two Wars, the French and Indian and the Revolution, as Privateers went to sea armed to the teeth. Their daring tenacity and stubborn new found pride astounded European powers accustomed to the power to bully or over awe poorly armed, fainthearted overseas Colonials. This fact of survival in a harsh, ruthless, greedy and capricious world created a demand for brave, daring, tough seamen. This need has always determined whether White men in America allowed Black men to participate in the "manly profession of arms", and thus counter the slave owner's self-serving claim that the Negro peoples "innate inferiority", justified their enslavement. The sparsely populated Colonies and the infant United States always had a desperate need for manpower, even Negro men. In that historical instance that great societal leveler, necessity, again played a positive role in the continued acceptance of

Negroes in the Sea Services. The major character traits developed in early American Sea Captains worked in the Negroes favor as to their retention in what was left of the post Revolution Navy.

First we should understand the early Navy officers did not come from any elite Officer's Corps where they were taught to "go-by-the book", and to stand in awe of political leaders. Necessity imposed upon them a need to get the job done by "any means necessary", rather than worrying about "how they looked, politically, and/or socially". The by the book approach was left to the later Annapolis and West Point educated Army and Navy elite. This was a tough, pragmatic group of men who gave far more respect to what a man could do than how he looked, or the nonsense of the color of his skin. Most U.S. Naval Officers came from the colonial Merchant Marine. Years of survival in spite of British and/or other European powers, rather than anything that could have required their blessings, shaped them. Years of having to make the rapid decision on sighting a sail on the horizon, as to "friend or Foe" or whether to crack on sail run or turn and fight. In order to get a cargo home after running a gauntlet of greedy Europeans, Colonist often had to master the "fine art of smuggling", in order to keep the greedy fingers of English "mercantilism", from grabbing the profits on arrival back home. Consequently, the master of a vessel in the Colonial trade had to be a hard bitten, resourceful, wily man and above all, a practical sort. As such he was more likely to respect ability and dependability more than the color of one's hide. Checking the reality found in old ship logs and muster rolls may establish some validity to this assertion. On reading these it becomes evident that they did not obey the racist edicts of Benjamin Stoddert, first Secretary of the Navy or later, Samuel Southard, who attempted to restrict Naval service to White men. Nor did they obey the silly, impractical post Revolutionary edict that came from Philadelphia, restricting service to "able bodied White males".

Further validity may be added here when one reads the correspondence between then Captain Oliver Hazard Perry and his boss Commodore Isaac Chauncy before and after the battle of Lake Erie.

But on the eve of the War of 1812, Colonial America, though now a free Country, found itself in the same situation as that which preceded the Revolution, no ships and scarce manpower. The French rudely awakened her. The quasi-war with France may have been a blessing in disguise. It removed the last vestige of Colonial naiveté, even that of Thomas Jefferson, that Americans could live quietly as a nation of moderate "free holders", behind the Atlantic Ocean barrier; that if they were quiet and avoided entangling European alliances no one would bother them! Early leaders believed so deeply in this "isolationism", until they had to literally be dragged, beaten and kicked into the real world's harsh reality. Some insight may be added here if one reads Dudley W. Knox's depiction of the quasi-war with France. It had the odd blessing that caused Americans to really understand that coastline defenses with a "few harbor barges", would not keep out nor stay the depredations of its rapacious enemies beyond the seas. For this insight, lets start one year after the Treaty of Paris in 1784, and end with the birth of the "New Navy" in 1794, a decade later. Though six Frigates, the forerunner of today's Cruisers, had been ordered in 1794, four years later (1798), none of these ships had been completed and armed. Knox says:

> "Beginning in 1793, our sea commerce was also much annoyed by interference on the part of Spain, England and France. In the latter Country the great revolution led to French lawlessness on the Sea. Their privateers swarmed the Mediterranean and the Caribbean and even cruised the coast of the United States, freely capturing and plundering American ships regardless of our neutrality and our peaceful attitude towards France."[44]

> Like England, France took the attitude "Kick them again; they have no friends nor power"! According to Knox, instead of

responding to U.S. diplomatic protests or entreaties, the new Revolutionary rulers of France issued increasingly harsh decrees against its former ally. By the spring of 1798, conditions became intolerable and, President John Adams was compelled to act, ready or not.

Luckily for this Country, the post Constitution government removed naval affairs from the War Department where bumbling, corruption and little knowledge of maritime affairs seem to have been a major characteristic. The Navy was put on its own. They no longer had to put up with the slowness, extravagance and inefficiency in its administration of naval affairs. Even Secretary of War McHenry was glad to be rid of a job, that he seemed to know little about, and cared even less about. President John Adams warmly endorsed this change. Even if he was a racist like most of his contemporaries, Benjamin Stoddert turned out to be an able, energetic administrator.

Stoddert, the first Secretary of the Navy, arrived when war was imminent, but brought order to what had been chaos. He succeeded in creating a Navy, in spite of politicians, with six clerks, and one messenger. It took him only a month to get the first ship to sea. The nearest frigates to completion were the *Constitution 44*, *United States 44*, and *Constellation 36*. Stoddert rapidly purchased an East India man-o-war and armed it with 24 cannons. This became the U.S. Vessel, *Ganges*. Next he purchased the ex-merchant ship *Delaware 20*. Until these could get to sea, a few harbor barges and Revenue Cutters (now the U.S. Coast Guard) defended America.

4) THE U.S. NAVY AND ITS ACQUISITION OF A SENSE OF PLACE, SELF AND TRADITION IN THE UNDECLARED WAR WITH FRANCE: A FORCE IN ITS OWN RIGHT IN THE WAR OF 1812

By the end of 1798, Stoddert had bought up quite a few sound merchantmen, modified some, and armed most. Knox gives an excellent account of pre-1812 War chaos. Unlike the bumbling, politics laden War of the Revolution, the Navy that gave us two politically appointed bumblers, Esek Hopkins and Horsted Hacker, Stoddert could draw upon a group of battle tested officers who became such in spite of the Revolutionary Navy's poor showing. Consequently, by year's end 1798, there were available enough ships to form four reasonably well armed squadrons. This was never accomplished during the entire Revolutionary War. Stoddert seems to have picked his captains and Commodores well. He created a Navy from literally nothing and in spite of having to move his office from Philadelphia to Trenton; incident to an epidemic that hit the City. On the eve of this quasi-war, no war with France was even declared; America was blessed with a finer cadre of officers, as she would ever see again. Men such as Richard Dale, who had ridden with Paul Jones, "Irish Jack" Barry, Thomas Truxtun, Samuel Nicholson, Nicholas Biddle, Stephen Decatur, Sr., Joshua Barney, Isaac Hull, Joseph and William Bainbridge and the unlucky Captain Isaac Philips, C.O. of the *Baltimore*. When Lieutenant Bainbridge of the *Retaliation* was captured by two French Frigates, the *Insurgente 36*, and *Volontaire 44*, he was not held to account. To fight the two vessels would have simply ended in a massacre of his crew by the heavy-gunned units. So, even with the rise of nationalism, Bainbridge was forgiven. The rise of "Nationalism" however caused the unfortunate Philips, in similar circumstances to be judged harshly by the Navy and the government, and to be dismissed from service.

It is highly important that all Navy leaders and would-be leaders, whether they are Officers, Warrants or Enlisted men, thoroughly understand this incident in Naval History. The 20-gun ship *Baltimore* and her captain set the parameters of <u>negative</u> traditional combat-deportment, which remains a no, no, to this day. Captain Thomas Truxtun C.O. of 36-gun *Constellation* (later 38 guns) probably set the parameters of <u>positive</u> traditional combat-deportment that remains a traditional expectation to this day for all naval personnel. If one doubts that tradition outweighs law, all he has to do is to check what happened to Captain Lloyd N. Bucher of the *U.S.S. Pueblo* in the post Korean War period! When his intelligence gathering ship *U.S.S. Pueblo*, (AGER-2) on January 22, 1968, a hundred and seventy years after Thomas Truxtun established these parameters, was taken at sea by North Korean gunboats, Bucher was court-martialed. The Pueblo couldn't run or fight. The debate still rages as to whether Bucher or the Admiral who sent him to sea should have been court-martialed. This also established the code of Combat Conduct expected of future U.S. Naval officers to which Bucher fell victim. These established fighting traditions are taught at Annapolis and to all ROTC cadets today. The newly created United States demanded that naval officers, never, by their conduct and/or deportment allow their Country to be humiliated, that is in case of confrontation or combats. An officer is expected to stand up and be counted, to fight his ship to a finish. For his country's honor and his own reputation, it is expected that the commander will fight it out until all guns are silenced and her decks are awash.

While the new Navy was suffering its birth pains, what was happening to its personnel policy towards non-White peoples, Native Americans, Negroes, etc.? Negroes and Native Americans, in the period between the end of the Revolution and the War of 1812, were shielded from discrimination in the enlisted sector of the Navy. The "Shield" did not result from any action of liberal leaning White folk nor any protest on the part of the Negroes themselves. Negroes did not have to fight for acceptance. Chance, circumstances and history was on their side in the form of four "Whammies", blows administered by 1) England's closing the West Indies to Colonial trade, 2) an undeclared war with France, 3) extortion and piracy by Barbary coast rulers of North Africa, and finally, 4) the War of 1812. But these were not the only phenomena that shielded Negroes from being barred from military service on the Seas. The other factor that shielded Negroes in the Navy and Merchant Marine was again the hard headed, pragmatic, practical men who became America's first real Naval Officers. What turned Negroes against the Navy in the aftermath of the Great White Fleet's around the World Cruise in 1807 and 1808 should not be laid on early Naval Officers. To be sure, the early officers never thought that Negroes were Naval Officer material; given the social milieu of this era, this, socially, was probably beyond their imagination. This had to wait until WWII or 1944, after an inordinate number of White officers and men had lost their lives and, Negroes acquired the political sophistication needed to exploit the manpower needs of WWII. This resulted in the famed "Golden 13" who were the first Black commissioned officers. This first group of Negro Officers were picked from a cadre of outstanding Negro Enlisted men. They were not selected from college ROTC's, nor the Naval Academy.

So, when speaking of these early naval officers, who "thumbed their noses" at the racist and silly edicts pronouncements from federal government officials in the aftermath of "both" the Revolution and the War of 1812, it is historically relevant that we understand that only the "Enlisted Ratings" are involved. The Navy Officers' Corps remained "lily-white" until a year before the end of WWII. If it were up to the post Revolution government, which freed White men, no Negro would have been allowed to serve in either the U.S. Navy or Army. Orders were issued immediately restricting service in the Armed Forces "...to able-bodied White males". There was no problem here with the Officers' Corps, as there were no Negro Officers except for possibly Joseph Ranger, a slave who captained and piloted vessels for the Virginia Colonial Navy and remained on duty for 6 years after the Revolution. As for Enlisted men, Naval Officers paid no attention to politicians or their appointees where the enlistment of Negroes was concerned. There are historical notes that add much validity to this fact, if one researches the enlisted program and its development over the years. For example, according to Frederick S. Harrod, Associate Professor of History, U.S. Naval Academy, "Virtually from its creation the Navy displayed a reluctance to accept Blacks, but usually accepted them out of necessity."[45] In August 1798, just four months after passage of the Act that authorized the creation of the Navy Depart Secretary of the Navy, Samuel Southard cautioned an officer who was about to enlist a crew for a schooner preparing for a cruise. He told him that, "No Negroes of Mulattos are to be admitted. Remember, He said, "'The Navy', not its officers are charged with fighting its ships. Exclusion, however could not be rigorously enforced."[46]

What he says in relation to the Chesapeake Affair is very revealing, as to the Author's contention that Naval Officers did not obey the simplistic edicts barring Negroes from service. He goes on to say, "When the British boarded the American Frigate Chesapeake in 1807 to search for deserters from the Royal Navy, three of the four men seized were Black. Hence, there is historical proof that early naval officers continued to enlist Negroes whom they deemed skilled and fit for service."[47] Jack Sweetman says of the men taken by H.M.S. *Leopard* 56, from U.S.S.

Chesapeake 36. "The Chesapeake was completely unprepared for action; after 15 minutes of confusion, Lt. William Howard Allen saves the ship's honor by carrying a burning coal from the galley to fire a single gun in her defense. Barron then strikes his colors. Four of Chesapeake's company have been killed or mortally wounded and twenty, including the Commodore, wounded. A British boarding party seizes four crewmen."[48] According to Sweetman, one of the men turns out to be a British deserter whom the British took to Halifax, Nova Scotia and hanged. Sweetman does not say, but this unfortunate crewmember was probably a White person. It was possible but improbable that a Negro would look British enough for identification. Furthermore, most Negroes tend to look alike to most White men and the time lapse would have made identification more difficult.

The three remaining, who were Black crewmembers were impressed. It took four years of diplomatic wrangling before their freedom was secured. Only two of the three were returned home; the other died in England for the freedom and respect of this Country, a freedom that his people did not enjoy, a freedom reserved for White men only. However, unlike the harshness with which Captain Philips of the Baltimore was treated, Commodore Barron was not dismissed. He, instead, was Court Martialed, found guilty of negligence and suspended for five years.

The bitterness that ensued after Barron's court-martial simmered for years with some factions for Barron and others against him. No leadership on part of the newly formed Naval Officers Corps emerged to act as a mitigating factor in the dispute. There was fertile soil for the growth of a negotiated settlement of the dispute. Commodore Barron and the young national hero, Stephen Decatur were close friends prior to the Court Martial and could probably have been induced through sincere counsel by respected senior Naval Officers to forsake their grievances in order to protect the image of their service; forgive and forget. Instead, rancor and enmity were allowed to increase via real or implied insults, culminating in finally, a tragic, senseless duel between Barron and Decatur in which the latter lost his life. The duel occurred at Bladensburg, Maryland in 1820. Americans reacted with rage and long lasting chagrin. The American people seem to accept the assassination of its presidents with less sense of outrage than the killing of its national heroes. The killing of Alexander Hamilton by Aaron Burr on July 11, 1804 in a senseless duel had already caused distaste for dueling to enter the thinking of responsible leaders. Decatur's death set in motion forces that would cause dueling to be outlawed in most states. Louisiana was the last of the original states to do so.

It is ironic that Negroes were causal forces in both incidents. For example the bone of contention in the *Chesapeake/Leopard* affair, which humiliated the Country and caused Barron's downfall involved the impressment of four seamen, three of whom were Negroes. The lone White seaman turned out to be an English deserter. Hence, it turned out that the four-year diplomatic hassle with England needed to rectify the wrong, was a squabble over the freeing of three Negro seamen. The historical significance here would tend to validate the Author's contention that the U.S. Navy's Enlisted segment at the birth of the Navy was the most "liberal", of all branches of the Armed Forces. What is unsaid by Naval Historians, but implicit in that four-year squabble is that the Commander in Chief, the American people nor their Naval Officers gave a "tinkers damn" that the seamen were Negroes. What really matters was that they were members of this Country's armed forces. When any one humiliated or unlawfully imprisoned them, they concomitantly humiliated this Country. This lesson in reciprocal loyalty between Negro fighting men and their Country was lost on future generations of Armed Forces' officers and politicians. These later leaders, with the rise of racism and Jim Crow allowed aided and abetted the abuse of Negro servicemen at home and abroad. Later Armed forces, unlike their fore bearers, traditionally have made little or no effort to protect Negro servicemen.

Before we deal with Negro contributions, to the War of 1812, it is pertinent to point out that they played an unwitting, potent role, in both incidents, that probably equaled in potency for the War of 1812, what the Boston Massacre's affect was on the Colonial decision to revolt against England. The incident I speak of is, of course, the Leopard and Chesapeake affair. After that humiliation, America came to realize that war with England was inevitable. By the time that the arrogant British Parliament and King came to realize that, their former Colony, though weak and minus a treasury, still possessed the fierce pride and fighting capacity that forbade letting Britons continue to disregard their rights as a people, it was too late. When they realized this and killed in Council the harsh decrees leveled against their former Colonies, the United States had already declared war on England. Madison went to Congress and asked for a declaration of War on June 1, 1812. On June 17th, the British Cabinet revoked the humiliating "orders in Council", that so angered the United States. Had the wireless telegraph been available at the time war could probably have been avoided. Word of the Council's revocation arrived too late, for on June 18, 1812, Congress granted President Madison's declaration of War. At the start of the War of 1812 according to Sweetman:

> "...the U.S. Fleet (excluding gunboats consisted of 17 seaworthy ships: 9 frigates and 8 smaller vessels (sloops, schooners, etc.,). The Royal Navy numbers more than 1,048, including approximately 120 ships-of-the-line and 116 frigates."[49]

Again an angry American David took on an arrogant contemptuous British Goliath, as was the case in the Revolution. The cost to both would, in the end be great but would, in the end also let the British know once and for all time that these Untied States intended to remain free. Negroes were ready, seasoned personnel cadres as were Merchant Marine cadres. Gone was the naive idea that the U.S. Merchant ships could simply "pack-it-in" and go home after the surrender of Cornwallis at Yorktown. No government can exist without trade and commerce. However, post revolution politicians persisted in such contrary naiveté. So, when the Army went home after the Revolution, the Navy was allowed to die. The Merchant vessels armed themselves, as usual, and went to Sea and, as usual, manned by free Negroes, runaway Slaves, Native Americans and White men, one-step ahead of debtors' prison went to Sea with them. Sea Captains both military and merchant, always in need of personnel, winked at a man's past record. Those early pragmatists also continued to ignore racist edicts coming from civilian bosses and promulgated by the greedy, unprincipled slave owners, who during the Revolution, failed to allow their slaves to fight for fear of losing their "property". At a time when the Colonist so desperately needed fighting men, this caused many White men to be forced to face greater casualties and loss of life than if all races had been allowed to fight ashore. All were allowed as traditionally in the past, to fight at Sea. This tradition, of inclusion_rather than that of exclusion based upon race came from men, who had to deal with the real world of the Sea and its unforgiving harsh demands. The occupants of the drawing rooms and plantations and the Politicians wanting to make themselves look good were ignored again. As to the traditions of expected combat deportment, liberalism as to the enlisted branch emerged. The death of Stephen Decatur created the expectation that a naval officer would not be a ruffian but an officer and a gentleman. Louisiana was the last of the original states to outlaw dueling. The protection of the "Negro woman/White man" relationship traditional in Louisiana was a covert social reality, where some wealthy White men even had two families. He had one set of children by his White wife and another by his Quadroon or Octoroon mistress. Dueling was the method used to prevent overt discussion of the second family's existence. Negroes played a major role in the creation and maintenance of this darker side of Louisiana society and history. It is ironic that the expectation that a naval officer be a Gentleman coincided here.

England might have noted that though the States had no Navy to be compared with theirs as to tonnage, guns or numerical superiority, the newly freed Colonist did possess "Yankee ingenuity", guts, and tenacity. Its Merchant Marine had rapidly increased after the Revolution. All vessels were potentially warships or Privateers that had honed their sea-fighting skills in the quasi-war with France and the Barbary Pirates; this while playing dangerous at sea games, with the sore losers, British men of War. Perhaps the British forgot what Paul Jones had done to them in the late Revolution. For instance, how many ships one daring raider tied down seems to have been overlooked. Tories who had fled when the British Army was defeated possibly unintentionally misled the British. These, "British sympathizers", many of whom had fought against their own Country, never quite found, full social acceptance in England. This tendency to ever "look askance", if we may coin a phrase, at persons who have turned on their own people seems to be a human trait. What is left unsaid in such relationships is, "Can we really trust them?" Honor, even, among thieves and criminals is a human expectation. Probably the Tories in England, corresponding with those who had dared to come back home, were misleading to England in the 1812 circumstances. These people probably misread the attitudes of New Englanders who were bitter because of the retaliatory actions of the U.S. Government, which restricted trade with England and France. This hurt New England commerce badly. So, non-intercourse acts and acts of embargo had hurt New Englanders and was felt rapidly, sharper and with more impact than in the South. There, many plantations, which were virtually self-sufficient economic units as to food production, etc., contained better resiliency to abrupt economic changes. But, in New England where the leading economic factor involved sea borne commerce, the Embargo acts or non-Intercourse acts had a disastrous effect that was almost instantaneous. Fear of bankruptcies, loss of whole business ventures and debtors prison by ordinary people caused severe panic and bitterness towards the new National Government by former New England Colonies.

The newly freed Colonies had not developed the "group cohesion" needed to move with concerted National purpose. The British knew that patriotism was, as a result of the effects of embargo, at its lowest ebb since the Revolution in the New England States. They, therefore, sought to induce separation of New England from the Union and to possibly coax this region back into the British fold. Dudley W. Knox said:

> "The approach of war was further marked by an extraordinary incident in April, 1812...As a measure of war preparation, Congress met in secret session, passed a ninety day Act at Embargo which the President signed April 4, 1812. The object was to keep Merchant ships and Seamen at home as protection against capture immediately after the intended declaration of war and also to hamper the British Army in Spain which was being supplied almost exclusively by the United States."[50]

This sorry epic in U.S History reveals one of the great weaknesses of democratic government. The so-called "leaks", at high levels of our government, as played up in today's media is nothing new! Leaks, as such, are in fact as old as our governmental structure itself and thus, are an ongoing part of U.S. History. Knox goes on to point out that this secret session information was aimed at precluding costly mistakes of the past that had caused U.S. ships to be caught unaware at sea and in foreign ports at the start of a war. This often happened before causing immense cost to American Colonial shipping, including confiscation of ships and cargoes in foreign ports and the capture of unwary ships at sea. Knox says:

> "But several members of Congress deliberately defeated both objects, (secrecy) by sending advance word by express to the principal seaports as far as Boston. With advantage of this news and by working speedily night and day, American business men loaded and cleared several hundred ships before port officials could receive official instructions needed to enforce the embargo."[51]

Here greed overpowered even consideration for the safety of U.S. ships, seamen and indeed the Country, itself. The lack of "melding" needed for unification was all but nonexistent in that each state still thought as it did as a Colony and tended to look to itself, first.

One of the great miracles of the times is that the United States with such internal disabilities was able to defend itself at all as the War of 1812 began. . In spite of all, two developments that were to save this Country had occurred. Americans had learned to design and build ships to match any in the world. Joshua Humphrey's Frigates had no match on the Seas. The *Constellation* and *Constitution* had proven this in the War with France. The second development was that a hard cadre of officers and disciplined sailors had been nurtured and brought along. A small cadre, to be sure, but of a caliber to be reckoned with. An enduring foundation for the Navy was laid down between the Revolutionary War and the War of 1812. Thomas Truxtun had shown the French that the new Country could fight. When, in command of the *Constellation 36,* he soundly whipped the 40 gun French Frigates, *Insurgente* and *Vengeance.* In this war, according to Alden and Wescott, France lost eighty-four vessels, most of them privateers' ships. Being at war with England, she could send only a few Frigates to American waters. Hence, she took a whipping while attempting to take the same liberties taken by England in the abuse and impressing of American Seamen.

Further, newly freed Americans stopped the Barbary pirates from blackmailing the United States, seizing ships and enslaving their crews in the years between the Revolution and 1812. Under Commodore Edward Prebble, a strict, demanding but fair officer sent to the Mediterranean station in 1803, a new tough cadre of officers were taught and seasoned. These men under Prebble, "bearded", the Dey of Algiers in his own lair then proceeded to whip the Bashaw of Tripoli until that august potentate was compelled to sue for peace. In doing, this Americans did something that European powers had been unable to do for over a century. This small cadre of officers made up, in seamanship daring and gunnery, what the fledgling United States lacked in gross tonnage of War ships.

But what in this clash of U.S. and world events happened to Negro seamen who's lives were akin to the flotsam and jetsam cast adrift on a mighty river, drifting in any direction dictated by the capricious current flowing through the emergent life of the new Country? On one side were White men who respected the Negroes' loyalty and valor in the Revolution that freed the Colonist. On the other side were White slave owners who could only perceive Negroes as slaves, a source of profit, which worked and sweated while White men paraded like popinjays and sat on their butts, as gentlemen should, in accordance with the Plantation Society's dictates. So Negroes, existing at the whims and needs of White men, as the War of 1812 reached the flash point, were to fight their third war for the preservation of this Country's freedom.

According to Peter and Mort Bergman, "During the War of 1812, Negroes made up one sixth of the seamen of the U.S. Navy."[52] This is further proof that the officers of the early Navy paid little or no attention to orders issued by the Secretary of the Navy or secretary of War, aimed at barring Negroes from the Sea Services before the War of 1812.

For example, "On August 8, 1798, Secretary of the Navy Stoddert forbade enlistment of Negroes on Men-O-War ships. Before this, men had been recruited without reference to race or Color. This appears to have been the first attempted restriction against the enlistment of Negroes."[53] Before this, "On March 16th, the Secretary of War James McHenry, wrote to a Marine Lieutenant on the Frigate constellation; "No Negro, Mulatto or Indian to be enlisted."[54] Both the Secretaries of War and the Navy forbade Negro enlistment in the Marine Corps.

Though a few Blacks served, they were gradually eliminated and the Corps remained virtually lily-white until WWII. It is a tribute due early naval officers that they recognized the Negroes' fighting capacity and the genetic capacity to resist scurvy, to the extent that they did not allow the politics of race to cloud their thinking. They understood that in a sparsely populated Country, all manpower resources were needed to fight the War. Consequently, Naval Officers again literally ignored the racist prattling coming from government officials after the Revolution. Further validity may accrue that they did so when one reads the history of the period between the end of the Revolution and the War of 1812.

Bergman points out the fact that, despite orders to the contrary, Negroes were allowed to serve. For example, William Brown, a Negro, served as a "powder monkey", aboard U.S.S. *Constellation*. He was wounded in the engagement between Constellation and the French Frigate *L'Insugente*. Brown was rewarded for his gallantry by being granted 160 acres of land by the government. George Diggs another Negro served as quartermaster of the armed schooner, *Experiment* during that War. So they, the Negroes, never disappeared from the Sea Services. The Negro was always there regardless of the racist polices that government attempted to impose. Unlike the greedy slave holding class of dreamers, who let their greed lead them to think England could be beaten without Blacks, Naval officers dealt in the hard currency of reality. They again, as they did in all previous Conflicts, pragmatically ignored the color, race or National origin of recruits. This may account for some early American ship's rosters reading like that of today's United Nations, with the names of Negroes, Indians and any others available to serve.

While National policy was one of blatant racism, early Naval officers who were always in dire need of personnel, looked at a potential crewmember's ability to serve rather than his skin tint or his hair texture. This competition was waged by officers against: 1) An expanding frontier, which offered free land via "squatter's sovereignty"; 2) A Merchant Marine that offered better pay and a slightly less harsh discipline; and 3) Often lucrative privateer prize money. The foregoing were always formidable countervailing forces to personnel recruitment based upon race and color. Naval officers simply could not afford discrimination.

American people owe these early naval officers much, possibly even the freedom they enjoy today. Their Army on the eve of the War of 1812 left a lot to be desired and served a populace far from united for war. The vote to declare War was far from unanimous. In the House of Representatives, President Madison's administration could only muster a vote of 79 to 49 for War on June 4, 1812. The Senate, unaware that the British Prime Minister, Lord Castlereagh, had succeeded in getting the obnoxious "orders in council" affecting neutral shipping suspended, squeaked by with a vote of 19 to 13 on June 18, 1812. This type of division was sectional. The Northeastern Colonies never fully supported the War and had they known that the orders of Council had been suspended, Madison would have probably been denied his declaration creating the War of 1812.

This Writer considers this one of the most humiliating wars in U.S. History, if one is speaking of unity of purpose. Massachusetts Governor Caleb Strong, according to Arthur M. Schlesinger Jr., " declared a public state-wide fast" in order to protest the War. The State Legislature issued a statement proclaiming the War to be against public interest and stating that the State of Massachusetts will provide military forces only for defensive purposes. That is, only if Massachusetts, itself is invaded and to hell with the rest of the Country!

So the United States entered the War of 1812 ill prepared as usual. The Governor of Connecticut refused to levy Militia for any purpose other than the defense of his own State. The U.S. had neither a standing Army nor any money to pay Militia. We had no National Bank. Since Negroes were either in Slavery or quasi-free men (always suspect and extremely limited, as to liberty), they were a ready source of Military manpower. Their lot was solidifying as that of "permanent Slaves", in the newly freed American society, on the eve of the 1812 War.

Three things militated against the feverish post Revolutionary War Abolitionist movement. The first inhibitor was the birth of the concept of "Manifest Destiny", which resulted in acquisition of more and more land. This new land required more and more Slaves to clear and work it. Second came the invention of the cotton Gin, which made processing "short staple cotton" economically feasible, and third was the rapid emergence of the "Domestic Slave Trade", in the aftermath of the retardation of the African Slave Trade in 1808. Perhaps it is pertinent to point out that though the United States had entered into that solemn agreement between the so-called Civilized Nations at The Hague in the Netherlands in 1808, which barred further importation of African Slaves. America, though party to the agreement, did not actually participate in it until 1817. Ours, even then, was not a wholehearted effort. The United States winked at violations of that Treaty up to and during the Civil War. They probably only participated at all in order to pacify domestic Slave Traders, who viewed "imported Africans" as unfair competition. Consequently Negroes found themselves between a "rock and hard place", just as they were on the eve of the Revolution. As the War of 1812 approached, the condition of the Black Race was rapidly worsening in the Western World scheme of things. It is pertinent, also, to remember here that the War of 1812 occurred only four years after the non-importation agreement. The agreement did nothing to change the social, political nor economic status of the Negro people, as the need for Slaves to work vast new land acquisitions caused White America to exclude the Negroes as participants in the new freedom won in the Revolution.

The answer to the question, "Why did Negroes fight?" then is that they had nothing to lose but their chains or their lives, which were generally unrewarding anyway. And fight, they did, gallantly and well. The War of 1812 was one of the shinning hours in American History for Black men. This was so in spite of their situation. According to Jack D. Foner:

> "Between the Revolution and the outbreak of the civil War, the social, political and economic conditions of all Blacks steadily deteriorated. In the South, the post-Revolution liberalization movement came to a halt in the early 19th century, and subsequently controls on the slave population steadily tightened. In the North, Blacks lost the vote, faced increasing discrimination and segregation, and surrendered even their menial jobs to the Irish and German immigrants."[55]

Under these trying conditions the Maritime Service and the Navy were the only institutions in U.S. Society that welcomed the Negro, except the plantation. Foner goes on to point out that one of the principal indicators of a groups' status in society is their acceptance to serve in the Military. When a group is barred as Negroes were in

1820, the official end of the War of 1812, it was very indicative of their position in the society.

The social and political position of Negroes on the eve of 1812 is very pertinent to his position in U.S. Society today. Foner points out that discrimination against Negroes in the armed forces has always been unlawful and unconstitutional. For example, the constitution:

> "...Vests the power to regulate Military forces in both the National and State governments. Nowhere does it restrict membership in the regular Army or the Militia to individuals of any particular race. Nor did the Act of April 30, 1790, which simply defined recruits competent to enter service as 'able bodied men', deny Blacks a place in the Army."[56]

White Army officers restricted this, via interpretation, to mean able-bodied White men. Implicit here is a misnomer that lasted well past the 1954 Brown vs. the Board of Education decision, that all Northern Yankee White folks are good and fair to Negroes and all southern Whites and Rednecks, Ku Kluxers are unfair to Negroes. This caused a deflection in aim where by the Southern portion of the Country was labeled Racist, when in reality Racism was, is and always has been a "National phenomenon", rather than a sectional one. Racism was just a bit more visible and direct in the South. Foner points to further validity for this assertion in that the Militia Act of May 8, 1792, ordered only the enlistment of all able-bodied White men. Again the law said nothing about Black men but both North and South, with the possible exception of North Carolina, "interpreted" it to mean "White men".

Of consequence to Blacks and how they perceive their world, this Writer suggests that all had better understand that what White men write into the law and how the "gate-keepers" choose to interpret and enforce such laws was, in the main, during this period, never been meant to free Negroes. "You are a free Black boy, but you are really not free." Amidst this racist oriented stupidity, the Militia and the Army were denied the use of the tough, able bodies of seasoned Negro troops who had fought in the Revolution with distinction, at the beginning of the 1812 War. These seasoned Black men may have possibly steadied the bulk of untried soldiers and Militia who performed so disgracefully in 1812. The so-called War hawks turned out to be so much hot air, hawks without talons. In the early stages of the 1812 War the Army's performance shamed a Nation. A policy based upon Racism, in spite of the severity imposed by inexperience, poor equipment, and a rotten to non-existent logistics policy or supply system, persisted. This historically induced Army policy based upon racist assumptions lasted from 1812 to 1959, a period of 138 years, until the Korean War.

In the West, an Army led by General William Hull against Canada surrendered the port of Machilimackinac without firing a shot on July 17, 1812. This emboldened, the Indian Chief Tecumseh to ally himself with the British. This alliance so alarmed Hull, who had crossed the Detroit River with 2,200 men to occupy Sandwich, that instead of attacking, he retreated all the way back to Detroit on August 8, 1812. He retreated rather than face British General Brock's 2000 man Army. In the meantime, the garrison at Fort Dearborn near present day Chicago was massacred and the fort burned by Indians on Aug. 15, 1812. On the 16th of August, Hull, fearing another massacre surrenders Detroit to Brock, again without firing a shot. This was too much for the Warhawks. Hull was court martialed; charged with cowardice and gross neglect of duty. He was <u>sentenced to death</u> <u>on March 26, 1814</u>. His life was saved and the sentence commuted due to the intercession of powerful friends and his exemplary Revolutionary War record. The Americans finally won a battle by defeating the British at the small hamlet of Odensberg, New York on October 4, 1812. One of the sorriest inaction's of the 1812 War occurred on October 13, when, according to Arthur Schlesinger, Jr., et al.:

> "American General Stephen Van Rensselaer leads his 600 man force across the Niagara River to capture Queenstown Heights, Ontario. British General Isaac Brook was killed in the action, but the Americans were defeated by the 1,000-man British force when the New York State Militia refuses to come to Van Rensselaer's aid on grounds that their commission does not require them to proceed beyond the boundaries of the State."[57]

Van Rensselaer was a fighter and it was not his fault that victory was not his that day on Oct. 13, 1812. It is pretty hard to fight an enemy when the Governors of New York, Connecticut and Massachusetts are more interested in lining their "political pockets" and pacifying greedy merchants than protecting the honor and integrity of the Country. No dishonor should taint the name of Van Rensselaer, as he was given troops over whom he had no authority.

As if these humiliations were not enough, an Army led by General Henry Dearborn against Montreal had to turn back because his New York Militia refused to cross the Canadian border. This ended the assault from Plattsburg. Dearborn should be remembered as a fighting General. Again, one cannot fault him for ill-trained misdirected, cowardly Militia or perhaps "confused Militia" may be the better historical definition of these units. They were, after all, creatures of the governors of the several states and therefore subject to their political whims, commissions and orders.

The gallantry of the U.S. Navy saved U.S. freedom in The 1812 War, the only lights upholding American morale during these dismal times seems to have occurred at Sea on August 13th, when the 20 gun H.M.S. *Alert* was captured by Captain David Porter in *Essex 20*. Another boost to American morale came when in the fall, the fledgling Navy started to call the British to account at Sea. For example, on

October 9, 1812, Lieutenant Jesse Duncan Elliot caught two British men-of-war "sleeping at the tiller", and captured both H.M.S. *Detroit* and the *Caledonia* on Lake Erie.

This had followed the August 19th exploits of Isaac Hull who in the 44 gun Frigate *Constitution* fought the 38 gun H.M.S. *Gurriere* to a finish in one half hour. *Gurriere* was so badly mauled that she could not be made a prize of war and was blown up. Naval warfare intensified as fall came on. On October 17, 1812, Captain Jacob Jones over hauled the H.M.S. *Frolic* 18,600 miles off the coast of Virginia. The U.S.S. *Wasp* and the *Frolic* were evenly matched as the *Wasp* was carrying 18 guns, also. The *Wasp* decisively whipped *Frolic* suffering 10 casualties to 90 by the British. Eight days later off the Maderia Islands, Captain Stephen Decatur in U.S.S. *United States*, 44 guns, whipped H.M.S. *Macedonian*, 38 guns, boarded and captured her and towed her home to New London, Connecticut. British arrogance and contempt failed to deal with the fact that these, "Yankee Bumpkins", had designed a class of frigates capable of out sailing and out fighting anything in their class, afloat. This probably accounts for their continuing to send their lighter gunned Frigates against the constitution class ships. Hence Americans continued to wreak havoc upon them at Sea. The *Constitution* was probably the best ship of its class in the world.

Four days after Christmas, the 29th of December 1812, off the Coast of Brazil, captain William Bainbridge in U.S.S. *Constitution* 44 cut H.M.S. *Java* to pieces in an engagement. It's here that the Constitution earned the name "Old Iron Sides". As the New Year dawned in 1813, on February 24th, Captain James Lawrence in 18 gun U.S.S. *Hornet* sank the H.M.S. *Peacock* in a sharp engagement. The *Peacock* carried 20 *guns*. This was a badly needed victory as American morale had been shattered by yet another defeat suffered by the U.S. Army. A little less than a month earlier on the 22nd of January 1813, the Kentucky Militia under General James Winchester clashed with a combined force of British and Indians under British Colonel Henry A. Procter. Over 500 Americans were imprisoned. According to Arthur Schlesinger, Jr., "400 Americans were killed in battle or massacred by Indians."[58] This occurred at the western end of Lake Erie on the Raisin River near the Village of Frenchtown.

But, it seems that nothing good tended to last in this unwanted War. The next tragedy involved the Navy.

> "In a Naval battle 30 miles off Boston Harbor, the 38 gun *Chesapeake*, with an inexperienced and mutinous crew, commanded by Captain James Lawrence, is captured by the 52 gun Frigate *Shannon* commanded by Captain P.V. Broke. The mortally wounded Captain Lawrence exhorts his crew with the words, "Don't give up the ship."[59]

Though The *Chesapeake* was captured and towed to Halifax as a prize, but Lawrence's dying words became a rallying cry for American Seamen. Note that the British had tempered their arrogance. They had learned that Americans could and would fight. This is evidenced by the appearance of H.M.S. *Shannon* with 52 guns. The British had finally learned that second-rate ships nor second rate Englishmen would succeed in defeating their stubborn former Colonist, so in the latter part of that War they began to commit their best and heavier gunned ships to the fight.

Also note that Captain Lawrence had to deal with an untrained, mutinous crew when attempting to fight the Shannon. This is indicative of the constant hassle that the early naval officers always faced when they had to try to assemble a crew to commission a ship and get it to sea. As mentioned before, they had to compete with the frontier expansion, implicit in "Manifest Destiny", the Army and the armed American merchant corsairs given "letters of Marque", a license to engage in wartime commerce raiding. The latter had an advantage over federally commissioned vessels in that the pay was higher, the clothes cheaper and all crewmembers shared in the prize money obtained when richly laden Merchantmen were captured. Further, the discipline was not as harsh and a man could leave this service without the taint of desertion imposed by Commissioned Naval vessels. Thus it is very unlikely that any warship put to sea, did not have Negroes in their crews. One would probably also find Native Americans and new immigrants aboard an American Man O' War.

On March 27, 1813, one of early America's most able and unusual officers arrived on the Great Lakes. He was Oliver Hazard Perry, one of the Perry brothers from an illustrious Navy family. So as not to get these brothers mixed up, the other brother was Matthew Calbraith Perry, who would later become famous for opening up the hermit Kingdom of Japan to the Western World in 1854. Oliver Hazard Perry was unsparing of himself or his men. He not only had to fight a British fleet; he had to build a fleet to do so. This had to be done before the British could get their fleet ready. The prize was dominance of the Great Lakes and consequent domination of the budding Midwestern Territory. This was critical to winning the War of 1812 as he who controlled the lakes could concomitantly control communications between the newly formed New England and Midwestern Territory as well as all of the River arteries. They could disrupt communications and transportation between the rich, fertile, emergent Midwestern Territory and the Southern States. For example, the main transportation artery north and south connecting the hinterland to the great port at New Orleans was the Mississippi River and its tributaries. This was a massive staging area for armies and navies, which the Civil War was to prove. It afforded mass manipulation of the logistics needed to supply or rapidly transport these units. So Perry had neither an easy job nor light responsibility. How he discharged his duties could make or break the 1812 War effort.

The destiny of Negroes and their quest for respect and dignity had one of its most shinning moments when their paths crossed that of Captain Perry. If one reads Oliver Hazard Perry's papers, he would quickly assume that Perry was just another White racist. This Writer thought so when he read the component concerning this attitude towards Negro seamen, before the Battle of Lake Erie. When one reads his account after that battle it becomes rather clear that he spoke from frustration, illness and overwork to the point of exhaustion. After the victory, he was unstinting in his praise of the bravery, gallantry and fighting capacity of the Negro sailors who fought there. White racists do not readily share glory with Black men. The misconstruing of Perry as a racist was derived from his early communications with Commodore Isaac Chauncy, his boss. When Perry received a draft of men, he tersely wrote Commodore Chauncy, "That was a motley bunch you sent, Blacks, Soldiers and boys."[60] According to John Hope Franklin, Chauncy just as tersely answered in a message in which he "...cautioned Perry that he should be proud of whatever he received and added that the 50 Negroes on his ship were among the best he had."[61] According to the other sources such as Peter and Mort Bergman, and Lerone Bennett, Chauncy further told Perry that he had yet to learn that the color of the skin or the cut of the uniform could affect a man's qualification or usefulness.

This was quite a dressing down to receive from a senior by a junior officer. But in order to set the record straight, other factors bearing upon that incident should be known. Perry had served aboard ships, where there were very few Negro crewmembers. He had never had to depend upon them to the extent that he would before and during the Battle of Lake Erie. He had arrived at Presque Isle, Michigan on March 27,

1813, on the tail end of a bitter winter after a hazardous journey. He was not only to fight the British, but, had to build a fleet to fight them. On arrival he found literally nothing in way of skilled personnel or equipment. Every nail, bit of sawing, tools, hardware, cannons and food had to be dragged overland through snow, ice and mud via upstate New York or barged on inland waterways from Philadelphia or Pittsburgh. With Warhawks in Congress, who little understood the terrible effort or logistics, yapping at Perry and his Commodore's heels, he must have been a very overworked and harassed officer. Add to this the penuriousness of a Congress with an all but empty treasury and one may approximately understand the all but impossible commission of this young officer.

Further, the shipyard for constructing the heavier ships was behind a sand bar and a way had to be found to get them over this obstacle and out into the lake so that they could fight! His hours must have been measured not by a clock but by his stamina and degree of exhaustion. The British, who were about the same task as he, but possessing better organization and logistics had the majority of their ships prowling the lake. In an act of sheer indomitable will, Perry, on August 4, 1813, six months after his arrival, had not only built his fleet but also devised a way to get them floated over the bar and into deep water. He must have driven his Blacks, boys and soldiers as unmercifully as he drove himself and these new recruits do not appear to have disappointed him. Then Lady Luck smiled on him and indeed, his Country. Colonel Winfield Scott captured the 1,600-man garrison at Fort George forcing the withdrawal of ground troops from the shores of Lake Erie, once again causing the country's moral to plunge downward. The *Chesapeake* had been beaten and captured on June 1. Ten days after Perry's pontoons floated his ships out, Captain W. H. Allen in the 20-gun sloop *Argus*, which had humiliated England and raised American morale, was captured off the British coast by H.M.S. *Pelican*. (As a Privateer, *Argus* had captured 27 British Merchantmen.) So it was time that something good happened to this Country. The luck at Lake Erie was that when wind and water were right, the British were patrolling the other end of the lake. This allowed Perry and his ill, exhausted men to float his ships over the bar and into the deep water of Put-in Bay. Approximately a month later, Sept. 10, 1813, the moment of truth arrived for Perry, his "Jerry-built" ships, and untried crews. Opposing Perry was the seasoned, hard-bitten British Captain Robert H. Barclay. With typical British arrogance, he chose to fight when he should have run. He was out numbered 10 to 6 in number of vessels and felt that he could take Perry's measure in spite of the odds.

Perry and his crews, in spite of bad sailing errors on the part of some of his green Commanders, in a three-hour engagement, out-shot and out-fought these disrespectful representatives of the British King. His message to General William Henry Harrison remains a part of naval tradition to this day. It read simply, "We have met the enemy and they are ours". The Battle was decisive such that Lake Erie remained in American hands until the end of the War. His description of the account that his Blacks gave of themselves should be read to Negro youngsters once a week in order to stay their feelings of inadequacy and/or inferiority. Oliver Hazard Perry was no "glory hog". He eagerly shared the glory won at Lake Erie with his men, including the Blacks.

Franklin says:

> "...After the battle of Lake Erie, Perry gave unstinted praise to the Negro members of his crew and declared that, 'they seemed absolutely insensible to danger'. Other Naval officers spoke of the gallantry of Negro seamen. Nathaniel Shaler, the Commander of the Governor Tompkins said that the name of John Johnson a Negro seaman on his ship, should be registered in the book of fame."[62]

This is really a story of the heroism of two John's. John Johnson's lower body was shot away by a 24-pound shot. He lay dying on the deck. His last words were 'Fire away my boys. No haul a color down'. Another Negro Seaman John Davis begged Captain Shaler to throw him overboard, saying he was only in the way. He was mortally wounded at the time according to Franklin as he had suffered a similar wound as that of John Johnson.

The next shinning hour for Negro Arms occurred on the Chalmette plains that became known historically, as the Battle of New Orleans. Here Andrew Jackson was lucky where Negro-fighting material is concerned. Negroes here possessed a fighting tradition. To understand where this capacity came from, let's backtrack. Most people understand that France was an ally of the Colonist but few knew that Spain also assisted this Country's fight with England in the Revolution. It was as a result of this alliance that both French and Spanish Slaves and freed Negroes fought for this Country's freedom against England. So by way of backtrack lets go back to the year 1779 and the Revolutionary War Siege of Savanna. Here according to Jack D. Foner, "...545 free colored and slaves from the French West Indies fought in allied French forces with courage and skill during the unsuccessful siege of Savanna."[63]

Henri Christophe who later became ruler of Haiti fought here as a teenager. Most students of history get so hung up on France that they miss the fact that Spain held Louisiana as a Colony and later allied herself with France against England. Foner says,

> "In 1779, Governor Bernardo Galvez of Louisiana led 'a half-white and half-black Army in a successful campaign to drive the British from Louisiana and the Mississippi Valley. Later that year, "with more slaves and free coloreds added to his force", Galvez took possession of Mobile and Pensacola. Six black officers were cited for bravery in the campaign and were rewarded with medals of honor from the King of Spain."[64]

Of real historical relevance here is the fact that all White men did not, like Americans, perceive Black men as dumb brutes, too stupid and inferior in intellect to think and reason! Neither Spain, France, early Russian leaders nor Greek; Neither Roman nor Muslim civilizations perceive the African as an unthinking animal. The proof of this assertion may be found by studying how Africans were utilized by these societies. Among the Greeks, Romans and Mohammedans, gallantry, steadfastness, intrepidity or uncommon valor could elevate even a Slave in the society. Here we find a Spanish Governor of Louisiana, in 1779 freely giving Men of Color Officers Commissions and honors. The U.S. Navy did not do this until 1944, 165 years later! Under Napoleon Bonapart, France had six Generals of West Indian descent. One of which was the father of Alexander Dumas, the Author who wrote "The Three Musketeers". Peter the Great of Russia was given a small African Slave. On finding that this small slave was intelligent, Peter ordered him tutored along with his own children. This youngster was later educated as a Military Engineer and rose to be a Field Marshall in the Russian Army. This man, Abraham Hannibal, became the grandfather of Alexander Pushkin, a Negro and Russia's National Poet. In Ancient societies, the more competent and intelligent the slave, the more he was valued and utilized. This was not so in America. Intelligent slaves were often labeled troublemakers, instead of assessing their potential usefulness.

It is pertinent here to remind the reader that the U.S. Constitution never barred Negroes from serving in the Armed forces. It vested the power to regulate forces in both the National and State Governments. Nowhere does it restrict membership in the regular Army or Militia to individuals of any particular race. Nor did the Act of April 30, 1790, which simply defined recruits competent to enter the service, as "able bodied men" deny Blacks a place in the regular Army. But White officers interpreted it as such.

What have always hampered progress for Afro-Americans throughout American History are not the legislated laws. Afro-American progress, as a people, has been hampered by how White men have interpreted those laws when applied to Blacks and other non-White races. Whites have always acted as the "gate keepers". They have always found an interpretation that enabled the gate to be closed on non-whites. Just 29 years after the White Colonist received their freedom, the instruments aimed at preventing Negroes from acquiring their justly earned freedom was being put in place and solidified by law and economics. The Army, Militia and State Navies went to great pains to prevent Negroes from serving. The reasons were greed, avarice, fear and racism. The one way available to rise in the Society was possibly the Military. Americans have always honored heroes, sometimes regardless of color. If a people were not allowed to serve, Negroes could be kept in their places. If free, he was relegated to the lowest rungs of Society and always suspect. If one was a slave, "property", his place or low status was assured. Armed, a Black man might choose to fight for his freedom. All obstacles to retard Negro advancement were in place long before the War of 1812, as far as land forces were concerned. The weak impulse to free the Negro generated by their participation in the Revolution had already died by 1812. The rapidity of its demise is enlightening. Negroes in the Sea services fared much better than soldiers. Their hurts, if any, did not result from edicts issuing from the government because the Navy usually ignored these racist moves anyway. They, the Negroes, however were affected, just as Whites were by a scarcity of ships as President Thomas Jefferson dismantled the Navy and sold its ships. This militated against retention of seasoned manpower and ushered in years of demand for men from all races. Naturally Negroes were first to be cut, but not in all instances. Again at sea, a man's skills, competence, bravery and steadfastness could militate against a Negro being hired last and, fired first. Early Naval officers, as preciously noted, were pragmatic, hardheaded people and thus inclined towards respect for the caliber of the man. An incompetent dolt whether Black or White received short shrift by early Sea Captains. It is a tribute to early Naval officers that in spite *of* the Country turning rapidly racist, Naval officers hung on to their pragmatic approach until 1813 before being compelled, by the rise of Racism, to bar Negroes from service, "on the surface". They never did so in reality until WWI (1919). This can be appreciated when one realizes that the Virginia State Navy, one year before the Treaty of Paris ending the Revolution was finalized, sold all Slave seamen owned by the state. Many of these men had served and fought loyally for 10 or 11 years only to be sold again into Slavery to strange and often brutal Masters as payment for years of faithful service to that State.

Before leaving the position of Negroes at the end of the War of 1812, it is pertinent that we understand the forces that killed the post-Revolution liberal impulse. At its demise, there was an attempt to force the sea services to make a backward step into a policy based upon color and race. It failed but caused Negro slaves to be grossly restricted and maltreated by Slave owners. What caused legislation by States, North and South, to enact 'Black Codes'? These codes severely restricted so-called free Negroes and governed every move a former slave made and punished them, often brutally, minor infractions. These codes were an attempt, by Southern states after the Civil War, to maintain power and dominance over Negroes after they were emancipated.

Two things had always instilled unreasoning fear in the heart of these owners of this "uneasy property". First was that he would lose his property and thus have to earn his living by the sweat of his own brow instead of the blood, tears and sweat of another human being; his property. The second fear was that this property that he knew possessed a mind and a longing for freedom may come into possession of the means to kill his Master and take his freedom. This is probably a universal fear of all men who abuse, exploit and mistreat other men. This wariness was a necessity if one would subjugate and exploit his fellow human beings. This fear and need, on part of former slave masters did not disappear at the end of the Civil War, as evidenced by their attempted use of 'Black codes', to institute quasi-slavery.

The Haitian Rebellion of the 1790's scared the hell out of not just slave owners but those hypocrites who posed as respectable Christians. Both of these groups carried on commerce dependant upon the sale and transportation of men, women and children for purposes of reducing them to beasts of burden and one-step below real estate or chattel according to the U. S. Supreme Court. This latter part appears in the Court's Dred Scott decision of 1859 as handed down by Chief Justice Roger B. Taney. The eve of 1812 did not find the Negro naive as to why he should contemplate fighting besides White men again. He had been lied to and betrayed by both the English and the Colonist during the recent Revolution. Colonist promised freedom and re-enslaved most. England promised freedom but sold many to West Indian Slavers.

So contrary to fact, White Historians on emerging "twisted" Darwin's "theory of natural selection" to their purposes. These people, along with Slave owners, and industrialist applied the concept, "survival of the fittist", to human beings, particularly Black human beings. This is revealed in the U.S. social history and writings that appeared between the conclusion of the War of 1812 and the Civil War. In that period, as Europe completed the colonization of the non-white world, the justifications for doing so ranged from the "sublime to the ridiculous". Craniology, the belief that the size of the skull determined, via capacity, concomitantly, the intellectual capacity of races in relation to the size of the said race's skull appeared. Slavers said that Darwin's theory proved that "Negroes were meant to be slaves because they didn't have intellectual capacity like White folks". Hypocritical preachers forgot all about "we're all God's chillen" and joined the racist pack, with the exception of those few rare individuals who knew better and refused to keep their pulpits at the expense of defenseless Negroes.

Yet in the period between the Revolution and the War of 1812, as Americans waged a total war on Black people, they were not able to force early naval officers to close the door to Blacks wanting to enlist. So Naval officers stood pragmatically against a Government and a Country which went on binge of all-out downgrading of Blacks in order to justify Slavery and consequently the Northern hypocrites who hauled them to these shores to sell. In this terrible assault, the so-called Negro, found the Court/Judiciary, economic forces, political, educational, scientific, anthropological, medical, many theological and law enforcement institutions arrayed against him. The assault was total. No other people who came to these shores ever had to face such massive, negative forces as criteria for simply perceiving themselves as persons instead of beasts. It was not that God didn't create them, for he is alleged to have created beast, also. The aim of the assault was to define what God created the African for. The answer was simple; to toil, serve, fetch and carry for the White race, without pay. Did not Preachers, those great interpreters of "The Holy Writ", label the hapless African as Sons of Ham or his descendants? This took slave owners and slave sellers and buyers alike off the hook. But that "great leveler", that harbinger of common sense along with that pragmatism of the early Naval officer still caused Negroes to be enlisted. The great leveler was the behavior of the Barbary pirates towards American commerce and White people; they sold White folks into slavery! Then the former French ally, in the throes of revolution overthrew and guillotined its leaders. The new kids on the block, the Jacobins, formed a unit called the <u>Directorate</u>, which bore little allegiance to God, man or the Nobility, least of all former allies of the former Rulers. The newly freed Americans, with no Navy, no Army, and no money could not afford the silly acts of discrimination against the Negro demanded by the Slavocracys' representatives in the Congress. At least the Navy ignored such, during and after 1812. After 1812 the weight of negative mythology backed by "hacks" minus any semblance of scientific methodology, started to erode the "pragmatic stance" of Naval commanders. As the fight over Slavery intensified, so did the assault upon Black people as human beings. Even Navy officers could not "swim in this race-oriented cultural sea", without getting wet and absorbing the beliefs in the inferiority of the Negro. Real racism was probably born in this country during the period between the end of the War of 1812 and aftermath of the Civil War. The Negro slave had been quietly exploited for over two centuries minus much fuss. The debate over the Civil War had ended this quasi-silence. More debate occurred, over the Negro, between the end of the 1812 War and Fort Sumpter (1861), than had occurred over the two centuries. This debate as to belief was less one-sided as most Americans perceived the Negro as inferior and in his rightful place on the eve of the Civil War.

Part II.

From the War of 1812 to the Civil War and Post Reconstruction

CHAPTER 4. THE NEGROES' REWARDS FOR FIGHTING IN THE WAR OF 1812

1) THE RISE OF RACISM AND IT'S COST IN THE WAR OF 1812

The Army of 1812 had obeyed the edict that barred Negroes from service. In doing so, they missed out on the seasoned blacks that had fought in the Revolution. These were some of the best infantry cadres in the Western Hemisphere, many with 6 to 8 years of combat experience. Negroes were not "summer time" soldiers. They had no homes to run to. As a result, using raw untrained recruits, they were kicked all over the place. On the other hand, the Negro sailors, whose hardheaded Officers ignored the edict and kept their blacks probably saved the nation. They most certainly saved it from humiliation and many hardships. Negro sailors who participated in major naval engagements gave a strong account of themselves at both Lake Erie and Lake Champlain. They also measured up in the classic ocean engagements. Andrew Jackson, ignoring the edict, utilized Negroes at the Battle of New Orleans. It is a historic fact that they fought with distinction. In spite of it all, white America never rewarded them. Many were treated in the same manner as those, blacks, who ran away and joined the British when the war was over. Slavery was still a major economic force. Many of the 1812 War Blacks were re-enslaved at War's end.

John Hope Franklin says, "All during the war, Negroes, in search of freedom went over to the British. As in the war for Independence, the British promised freedom for all slaves. It is impossible to make an estimate of the number that escaped to British lines. However, some that did were sold back into slavery in the West Indies."[65] Franklin goes on to point out that some that fought for the Americans did get their freedom. Many more were returned to their masters at the end of hostilities; both sides betrayed the Negroes who fought. The degree of betrayal may be found by reading the Treaty of Ghent that ended the War of 1812. That treaty provided for the "restoration of property". Slaves were property. Consequently, hundreds were re-enslaved. A few remained in Canada.

2) THE SOCIAL, ECONOMIC AND POLITICAL FORCES THAT INSURED THE NEGROES' CONTINUED STATUS OF SLAVE AND SEMINOIC WAR

Slavery, as an economic factor, aided the concept of "Manifest Destiny". With the South's commitment to an agricultural economy, freeing slaves was out of the question. Cotton became "King" after 1812. Franklin says, "By 1834, the coastal states produced 160 million pounds, while Alabama, Mississippi, Louisiana, and other newly settled areas were dominating production with 297 million pounds; the demand for slaves increased and, naturally, the price for slaves went up.... Work was carried on primarily by Negro slaves."[66]

Franklin goes on to point out several forces that created and buttressed the Cotton Kingdom. He says, "1) The acquisition of Florida in 1819, 2) the settling of Missouri and its entrance into the Union as a slave state in 1821, and 3) the movement which culminated in the acquisition of Texas in 1845 were, to a large extent, a result of forces which emerged from the Cotton Kingdom."[67] These actions tended to create a balance, between slave and free states. Some historians think that this balance delayed the inevitable march toward a Civil War.

On the other hand, Negro sailors were still shielded from the march of these events. For example, the war with the Barbary Pirates, which began after the Revolution was still raging. Consequently, the demand for seamen was still high. Florida turned out to be a tougher area to subdue than expected. Slaves had been escaping to Florida for years. All attempts to recover them were thwarted under the Spanish and continued to be after Spain lost that territory. This became problematical with the Indians after the United States gained control. The Seminole Indians who had first hand experience with the earliest slaves, the Spanish and Portuguese, refused to cooperate in returning run-away slaves. A tenuous peace existed after the first Seminole War of 1817. However, this agreement did not include the forced return of runaway slaves living among them. The Payne Landing Treaty, signed by 15 Seminole Chiefs, an agreement to cede land and relocate west of the Mississippi failed because it was not a unanimous agreement among the Seminole Chiefs. When ordered to move by the October 28, 1834, edict, the dissident chiefs refused.

In November 1835, led by Osceola, the second Seminole War began. It was bitterly fought especially by the Black Seminoles and their descendants. These people had no intentions of peacefully submitting to re-enslavement. On December 28, 1835, General Wiley Thompson and his troops were wiped out near Fort King; Major Dade, with a company of 100 men, from Fort Brooke, was decimated near Fort Brooke. According to Foner, "Throughout the War, Black Seminoles liberated hundreds of slaves from plantations in Florida; at its conclusion, Officers sold hundreds of slaves from Florida back into slavery."[68] Most historians, after calling Thompson and Dade's defeats massacres instead of battles, end the discussion of the Seminole Wars here. However, Foner goes on to quote professor Charles Crowe who cites the post war experiences of several Black Seminoles as classic examples of "stubborn Black resistance" and refusal to surrender:

> "When peace came to Florida, some blacks made an incredible "long trek" to northern Mexico where they waged guerrilla warfare for many years against Texas planters. The planters were so skeptical about black courage that they invented fanciful stories about "marmeluke" soldiers from the Ottoman Empire to explain the troublesome dark skinned fighters."[69]

Texas White men had preached Negro inferiority, for so long until they came to believe their own mythology.

General Rufus Saxton, according to professor Crowe, said that "The Negroes would stand and fight with their bare hands".

This courage and fierceness on the part of Negro fighters was soon forgotten by white men due to their irrational need to feel superior or to soothe their conscience as they exploited Negroes and held them in slavery. Neither Negro sailors nor the U.S. Navy played a meaningful role in the Seminole Wars. The Mexican War of 1845 is possibly the only war fought by the United States where no <u>Negro Army contingents participated</u>. The U.S. Army allowed Negroes to be "body servants", thus, again, missing out on the available seasoned Negro Cadres who fought in 1812.

3) THE CONTINUED AND ENTRENCHMENT OF AND RISE OF RACISM: THE MYTH OF NEGRO INFERIORITY

But the U.S. Navy, in spite of the pressures of slaveholders, remained its hardheaded self and continued to recruit and train Negro seamen. There were Negro sailors in the force that landed and took Vera Cruz in the Mexican War. A Mexican Professor told the author about Negroes at Vera Cruz in 1970. Foner Says:

"Pre-Civil War America saw the Black as cowardly, childlike and with little fighting ability. By the 1850's, the deeds of Black soldiers had been effectively erased from both the pages of American history and the memory of most of Americans."[70]

He goes on to point out the fact that in 1858, a bill was passed by the Massachusetts legislature allowing Blacks to serve in the militia. Then Governor, Nathaniel Banks vetoed the bill. So that old myth that the Southerners were the "bad guys" and the "Northerners were the "good guys", so loved by the Yankees turns out to be so much mythology.

Southerners profited by enslaving Negroes and working for nothing. Northerners profited by going to Africa, acquiring cargoes of slaves to sell to a ready Southern market. So much for mythology. This author was surprised to find this mythology alive and a potent deeply held belief by bright Graduate students whom he taught at Case Western Reserve University (1968—1970), and officer graduate students at the Naval Post Graduate School at Monterey, California (1973—1980, during the waning stages of the Negro Revolution. It was a favorite defense used by Yankees in confrontations, often heated, between Northern and Southern students in his "Racism and the Military Command" class discussions.

4) THE RE-EMERGENCE OF THE ABOLITIONIST
    MOVEMENT: A HARD ROAD

The rise of racism and the consequent entrenchment of the concept of Negro inferiority was the most potent factor that slowed and delayed the U.S. march towards Civil War. This delayed and blunted the gradual emergence of the Abolitionist impulses so swiftly killed after the Civil War—the war of freedom. The post 1812 and the Pre-Civil War abolitionist faced a harder road than their Revolutionary War forbearers. The reasons are not hard to uncover when one studies the

Post Revolutionary War Period and the Post 1812 War Period. The economic policy of the emergent country, the United States, was literally dependent upon the acquisition, sale and the utilization of the Negro.

(Note: They mysteriously stopped being Africans and became Negroes en route to the United States.)

It does not matter whether one is speaking of Eastern banking and investment, the maritime industries, the building, buying and repair or the agricultural industry where cotton was "King". All depended upon slavery more than any other factor. This economic dependence became solidified between 1812 and the Civil War. In spite of the vast economic forces arrayed against them the Abolitionists re-entered the political arena and rose in power and became a major force. It is this group that kept the fires of disapproval of slavery burning such that a public awareness and shame emerged which eventually led to the Civil War. Although it was not the major issue leading to War, it was most certainly a constant that would not allow the war fever to die.

CHAPTER 5. THE CIVIL WAR AND THE POST-WAR RECONSTRUCTION PERIOD: THE FIRST ATTEMPT AT ESTABLISHMENT OF THE STEWARDS BRANCH FAILED

1) THE RESPONSE OF THE U.S. NAVY TO THE SEARCH FOR THE NEGROES' PLACE "BY THE BROADER SOCIETY"

The first attempt to relegate Negro men to the role of servants, in the U.S. Navy, occurred in 1842 when John C. Calhoun, the Senator from South Carolina, pushed a bill through the Senate stipulating the restriction of Navy Negroes to "cooks and stewards." It was hard enough to secure and maintain a crew in this harsh, exacting trade and it is quite possible that Naval officers and officials, pragmatists, as required by their age and position, assisted in defeating the bill. The House of Representatives "killed" the bill by refusing to vote on it, thus beating back the first attempt at political assault upon Negroes in the Navy. The Civil War gave impetus to the development of steam driven ships, but the sail to steam evolution was a gradual process. Coal driven ships required strong arms and shovels. This probably delayed the rapid downgrading of Negroes.

Since the fortunes of Negro service men have been always tied to the ups and downs in fortune suffered by Negroes in the broader community, one must conclude, in fairness to early naval officers, that they did resist racial bias. That they were able to retard its march for so long, is a tribute to, if not their altruistic instincts, most certainly their sense of mission and combat effectiveness. The historian, Jack D. Foner, further said of this era, "Despite the feelings of Calhoun, there was probably less prejudice and tension on naval craft than anywhere else in the society in the 1840's."[71] History does tend to repeat itself; for in the post Zumwalt/Holloway era, its present programs are rigorously pursued, the U.S. Navy may again become a refuge for oppressed minorities and women as well. Having been on the frontline of the integration effort by the military for seven years (1973-1980), as a teacher, consultant, lecturer and seminar participant, the Author can state unequivocally that the military Institutions are probably ahead of the U.S. Civil Institutions in their progress in Race-Relations. Need caused them to accelerate an effort in which they now lead.

According to the 1860 Census, one year before the Civil War started, 44% of the Negro population of the U.S lived in the Southern states. They constituted 37% of the Southern population. The national Negro population was 4,441,830, 14.1% of the total U.S. population. Of these, 488,070 Negroes were free while 3,953,760 were enslaved. Two million of the seven million white Southerners owned slaves. A mere 7% of the white Southerners owned nearly three million or nearly 75% of the slaves. 70% of the Citizens of Southern states owned no slaves at all! What was their "vested interest", other than "maintaining the southern way of life", in the upcoming war? The dream of slave ownership and the subsequent elevation in status resultant, seems to have been enough of a prize for poor Whites to shed their blood in the Civil War.

As a point of departure, one has to realize that every major compromise in early U.S. history revolved around the Negro.

First there was the debate about whether to make Negroes Bondservants or slaves before the War of Independence. Second there was the issue of whether to allow Negroes to bear arms in the Revolution itself. Third came the discussion of whether or not he should be set free after he fought in the Revolution. A compromise was reached at the Constitutional Convention where it was agreed that the Negro would not be a full citizen, but would be counted as 3/5th of a man! Fourth were two attempts to maintain a slave-free balance in territorial expansion. The Missouri Compromise of 1820 allowed Maine in as a free state and Missouri into the Union as a slave state; no slave states were to be established in the territory north of 36 degrees, 30 minutes north. Then the Kansas Nebraska act of 1854 allowed incoming states to observe "squatter sovereignty" which was later softened to "Popular Sovereignty" which allowed the citizens to decide for themselves whether to be a slave or free state. Underlying this action was an argument regarding whether railroad routes would favor the south or the north in the westward expansion. There were the questions of more land acquisition and whether that land would be worked free by Black men, or for pay, by White men. Failure to reach compromise here caused the Civil War.

Abolitionists rioted in Boston, and organized immigrants to move to the Kansas territory, which they would make it into a free state. Finally, the Compromise of 1850 allowed California to enter the Union as a free state, while no decision was made regarding New Mexico. Under this compromise, there was to be a strict fugitive slave law and a barring of slave trading; but no restriction on slavery itself by the Federal government. All of these compromises were made at the expense of the Negro.

What was happening to Negro sailors as the Civil War approached? As usual, after each war, the United States all but closed down its Navy. Both the Merchant Marine, and what was left of the Navy, still kept their Negro sailors, despite the constant pressure against doing so. One of the principal commercial seafaring ventures before the Civil War was the Whaling trade. According to Arthur M. Schlesinger, "Whaling provided a substantial portion of the nations economy before the Civil War...An average voyage was three years long...But the 1859 discovery of oil near Titusville, Pennsylvania, meant that Kerosene would replace Whale Oil in lamps and other uses. That meant that the great days of New Bedford and Nantucket were over."[72] It is important to note the date as this change made available a seasoned cadre of Negro sailors just in time, for the Civil War.

In this critical period, just as the Boston Massacre fed the fires of the Revolution, three critical incidents occurred that made further compromise impossible. The first was the Dred Scott VS. Sandford Supreme Court decision on March 6, 1857. Scott, a Negro, was taken from Missouri to the free state of Illinois; he also spent some time in Minnesota as manservant to his owner. Taking a slave north of the 36-degrees/30 minutes line was a violation of the Missouri compromise. Scott sued for freedom on those grounds. When the case moved to the U.S. Supreme court, the ruling, written by Chief Justice Roger B. Taney, was against him. Taney stated in that decision that the Negro had no rights that white men were bound to respect. He ruled on the grounds that "...no black person descending from a slave could be a citizen and that the Missouri Compromise was unconstitutional".

He further stated that any congressional prohibition of slavery violated the Constitution. The public outcry and the bitter debate that ensued split the Democratic Party thus ensuring a Lincoln victory in the approaching presidential election.

2) JOHN BROWN'S RAID AT HARPER'S FERRY INTENSIFIES THE MARCH TOWARDS CIVIL WAR

The second critical incident occurred when John Brown, an abolitionist who was largely responsible for Kansas being labeled "bleeding Kansas", in U.S. history, raided a Federal Arsenal at Harper's Ferry, West Virginia. Brown had moved to Kansas with his five sons in order to see that Kansas entered the Union as a free state. He was successful as signaled by the acceptance of the Wyandotte Anti-Slavery constitution on October 4, 1859. Brown perceived himself as an instrument of God. On October 16, 1859 "…John Brown, one of the most radical abolitionist led an armed group of five blacks and sixteen whites, including his five sons, that seized the Federal Arsenal. … first action in his vague plan to establish a "country for fugitive slaves."[73] This action gave most other abolitionist pause. They viewed the raid on a Federal Arsenal as going a little too far. Both the Federal and State governments sent military detachments to Harper's Ferry. Robert E. Lee led the Federal detachment of marines. Brown was defeated and taken prisoner within 24 hours. Only Brown and four others survived. Two of the survivors were Negroes, Shields Green and John Anthony Copland. They were hanged along with John Brown, Osborne Anderson having escaped. Amidst a lot of fanfare, John Brown was hanged on December 2, 1859. By most rules of logic this should have ended the affair. The culprits had been punished. But this did not end it. John Hope Franklin says that,

> "The effects of this raid on the South was electrifying. It made slaveholders think that the abolitionists would stop at nothing to wipe out slavery. No one felt secure because there were rumors of other insurrections to come and widespread complaints that slaves were insolent because they knew that their day of liberation was near. The whole south was put on a semi-war footing, with troops drilling regularly as far south as Georgia;

there was an increasing demand for arms and ammunition by the militia commanders of most states."[74]

The <u>killing of John Brown produced</u> the <u>abolitionists first true martyr</u>. For some reason, the death of another abolitionist, Elijah Lovejoy, earlier, had failed to do so. Lovejoy was a printer. He used his press to rail against Slavery. After his printing press had been thrown into the river twice, he still refused to be quiet. He was shot and killed by a mob on November 7, 1837, two decades before John Brown was hanged. Perhaps Lovejoy's death was too early in the anti-slavery campaign. Only two years had passed since John Brown's death when the fateful shots were fired at Fort Sumpter, which triggered the Civil War. John Brown's words would not die with him. According to Franklin, he had told a New York Herald reporter:

> " I pity the poor in bondage that have none to help them; that is why I am here; not to gratify any personal animosity, revenge, or vindictive spirit. It is my sympathy with the oppressed and wronged, that are as good as you and as precious in the sight of god... you may dispose of me easily, but this question is still not settled—the Negro question—the end of that is not yet. Upon hearing his sentence, he calmly said, "Now if it is deemed necessary that I should forfeit my life for the furtherance of justice, and mingle my blood with the blood of my children and with the blood of millions in this slave country whose rights are disregarded by wicked, cruel and unjust enactments, I say let it be done."[75]

It is this act of bravery that so impressed Americans that Union soldiers marched into battle years later singing, "John Brown's body lies a moldering in his grave, but his truth keeps marching on."

As for Negro sailors in the Civil War, as with the War of 1812, it temporarily slowed the erosion of their rights, which had accelerated in the 1840's and 50's. Frederick S. Harrod gives us some insight into the specifics of these changes. He says that this erosion steadily increased after the War of 1812. He says, further:

> "Although Blacks were permitted to enlist in the pre-Civil War period they did face some definite limitations on their opportunities once in the service. In the year 1855, most blacks signed on as "Landsmen" or unskilled men who performed a variety of menial tasks in all divisions on board ship. Throughout the 19ᵗʰ Century, Landsmen was also the service designation for domestics. It is likely that blacks in this classification performed the duties of Messmen, a category not created until 1893. During the Civil War, the pressure of increasing manpower needs forced the Union Navy to expand black enlistment. Rather than restrict black enlisted men to special units, the navy placed the races side by side in the same vessels as they had before the war."[76]

*There were five Negroes with John Brown in the attack on the Arsenal at Harper's Ferry (October 17, 1859), only one Negro survived, Osborne Anderson. He later fought in the Civil War as a union soldier.

Harrod also points out the contrast in the way the army treated blacks in comparison to the navy. The <u>Army segregated blacks by creating separate units for blacks</u> only. The Army's policy of separation implied inferiority. However, the Army did allow Negroes to go to West Point and to fill non-commissioned officer (sergeant) billets. The navy on the other hand had curtailed the positions a black could hold; but, by this policy, they avoided the time wasting debate over integration.

The Army was not allowed to officially recruit Negroes until January 1863. Lincoln could have actually recruited Negroes under the authority of the Militia Act of 1862. Lerone Bennett Jr. said of the Negroes in the Union navy, "<u>One out of four Union sailors was a Negro.</u> Of 118,044 in the Union Navy, 29,511 were Negroes. At least four won the Congressional Medal of Honor. Bennett said of the Negroes used by the Confederates, "The Confederates were first to recognize the Negro as a military asset and necessity of the war. As non-combatants,

Negroes were the muscle and backbone of the rebel war effort. The South impressed Negro slaves to work in mines, repair railroads, and to repair fortifications thereby releasing a disproportionately large percentage of whites for direct war service. The tragedy for the South is that their guilt and fear of arming Negroes caused them to wait until it was too late. Robert E. Lee was pleading for Negro enlistment up to his surrender at Appomattox."[77]

The precise number of Negroes who participated in the Union Army is really unknown and a source of dispute. Bennett says that 178,975 served; Bergman says 178,895, while Franklin says 186,000. Arthur Schlesinger gives a figure of 180,000, while 30,00 served in the navy.

The Negroes in the Union Army as soldiers still had to fight segregation, discrimination, and poor equipment. There was a tendency to use them for "fatigue" duty. According to the Military Fatigue Work Manual, fatigue work was defined as "menial and usually done as punishment". Many trained Negro combat units found themselves utilized as labor battalions. Many northern officers could only perceive the Negro soldiers as laborers. This caused even crack fighting units to be often mistreated by a command. The Negro units were often led by less capable white officers and suffered severe casualties as a result. The 54th Massachusetts is a case in point. However, poor leadership was not restricted to the Negro battalions. Whites, too, were needlessly slaughtered due to bad decisions made by poor leaders in this war. Arthur M. Schlesinger points out:

> "Black soldiers were in segregated units, usually under white officers. There were only about 100 black officers, Until 1864, blacks received only about half the pay of white servicemen. But, despite their treatment, blacks fought gallantly in several campaigns; about 68,000 black soldiers were killed or wounded. 21 Blacks won the Congressional Medal of Honor...president

Lincoln, referring still ambivalently to blacks as a physical force, would say "keep it and you can save the union. Throw it away and the Union goes with it."[78]

He goes on to point out the lack of ambivalence of the South. Given the fear that arming Negroes would be suicidal, there was little room for thoughts that Negro soldiers were stupid and cowardly as in the Union. However, in the last months of the war, desperation born of necessity found Jefferson Davis and Robert E. Lee agreeing that all was lost without Negro participation as more than a source of labor.

Lerone Bennett gives a precise and informative look at Negro participation in the Civil War army. He says:

"... Negro soldiers in the Union Army were organized into 166 all Negro regiments. There were 145 infantry units, 7 Cavalry, 12 Artillery, 1 Light-Artillery, and 1 Engineering battalion. The largest number of Negro soldiers, 24,052, came from Louisiana. Then came Kentucky with 23,703, followed by Tennessee with 20,133. Pennsylvania contributed 8,612, the largest number from a northern state. Negro soldiers fought in 449 battles, 39 of which were major engagements. Until 1864, Negro soldiers, from private to captain, received $7 a month whereas white soldiers received $13 to $100 per month. Negro units, with four exceptions, were officially designated United States Colored Troops. The exceptions were the 54th and 55th Massachusetts Volunteers, Fifth Massachusetts Cavalry, and the 29th Connecticut Volunteers. The highest-ranking Negro officer was Lt. Colonel Alexander T. Augustana, a surgeon. The Union Army employed some 200,000 Negro civilians as laborers, cooks, teamsters and servants."[79]

Bergman tells us that "Lt. Colonel Augustana, a Negro surgeon for the U.S.C.T., found it necessary to tell Senator Henry Wilson that the Army Paymaster at Baltimore had refused to pay him more than the $7 per month payment for Negro enlisted men. Augustana had rejected the payment. A letter from the Senator to the Secretary of War on April

12, 1864, resulted in an order two days later to the Paymaster General to compensate the surgeon according to his rank."[80]

Bergman goes on to tell us that Sergeant William Walker of the 3rd Carolina was <u>shot by order of Courts Martial</u> because he had led his men to stack arms and refuse to serve until the agreement under which they had enlisted, equal pay, was met. At least <u>three other Negroes died for similar protests</u> and over a score of the 14th Rhode Island Heavy Artillery unit was jailed. It was <u>not until 1864, four years after the war started that an army</u> <u>appropriation bill ordered equal pay for Negroes and whites.</u> Equal pay was made retroactive to January 1, 1864 for all persons who were free on the 19th of April 1861.

Reuben Elmo Stivers said that even the "Norsemen", who in European history, were the epitome of Sailor specimen, simply melted under the harsh southern sun. Other writers point to the fevers and insects for which northern-reared white men lacked immunity, as factors in the increasing need for Negro enlistment. The Army faced draft dodging and desertion on a mass scale. Add to this the fact that many new immigrants did not want to fight and some went home rather than do so. Stivers goes on to say that "The military recruiters had to fall back on an old disreputable, and previously, limited activity which swelled to big business as "runners", "crimps", and bounty brokers monopolized recruiting activities —seeking out "volunteers" and substitutes while making a profit on everybody delivered to a Service recruiting officer. These human parasites covered the nation with a well contrived and adroitly handled procurement network, and after April, 1863, few enlisted men entered either the Army or Navy voluntarily or involuntarily."[81]

Stivers describes recruitment, from the Navy's standpoint, as having been reduced to unofficial impressment. These parasites resorted to kidnapping, drugging, threats, torture, beating and false representation…anything to produce a body and collect a fee! This is a graphic illustration of the need that caused Negro enlistment to be expanded early in the war. Stivers does, however, offer the fact that the navy went to great lengths to ascertain whether a man was truly a volunteer. However, it can be said with a high degree of validity that without Negro contraband (runaway slaves), the riverine assault to secure the Mississippi valley and split the South would have failed or, at least, taken twice as long to complete.

While the Army and Congress debated endlessly on whether to allow Negroes to fight, the Secretary of the Navy, Gideon Wells moved at once to utilize Negroes and newly free slaves. Stivers tells us that:

> "As early as September, 1861, Gideon Wells adopted a policy of adding many of these Negroes to the National Naval Reserve force. Wells said, "The Department finds it necessary to adopt a regulation with respect to large and increasing numbers of persons of color, commonly known as contraband, now subsisted at the navy yards and on board ships of war. They can neither be expelled from the service to which they have resorted, nor can they be maintained unemployed; and it is not proper that they should be compelled to render necessary and regular services without stated compensation. You are therefore authorized, when their services can be made useful, to enlist them in the Naval Service, under the same forms and regulations as apply to other enlisted personnel. They will be allowed, however, no higher rating than boys at a compensation of $10 per month and one ration per day."[82]

It would have been totally irresponsible for Gideon Wells to give equal pay to the newly freed slaves at that time in U.S. History. First, his action would have been social and political dynamite. Congress was still debating whether to arm Negroes and let them fight in the army, a debate that was to last two years! Here, Wells had already recruited Negroes as fighting men and put them on the government payroll minus congressional approval. Wells was wise to deal with the cold currency of his worst need rather than to dabble in ideology. Dissension among his white sailors would have brought a political storm down on him and denied the Navy the critical manpower it so badly needed. His ships already practiced "integration". To include "equality", at that time in history, would have been to go too far. This would have raised a "no-no issue" that would have delayed or defeated his purpose.

By recruiting Negroes native to the areas, he got an intelligence bonanza. He got pilots and guides who knew the geography like the backs of their hands. He got spies and intelligence sources he so sorely needed. So, while the U.S. Army blundered blindly about the countryside and while the politicians debated, Wells filled critical needs. Stivers deftly points out that Wells had a sense of mission and common sense, when those were scarce commodities among military leadership. Seven months later, Wells expanded his policy and made it more specific by an official directive to all flag officers which stated:

> "The large number of persons known as contraband flocking to the protection of the United States flag affords an opportunity to provide in every department and ship, especially for boat crews, acclimated labor. The flag officers are required to obtain the services of these persons for the country by enlisting them freely in the Navy, with their consent, rating them boys at $8, $9, or $10 a month and one ration."[83]

The key word in Wells' quote is "acclimated". These Negroes bought time for the white sailors to become acclimated to the heat and fevers of the inland rivers of the southern states. That they served the navy well is proven by how they were perceived by senior officers. Flag officer Samuel Dupont said, "Some of these contrabands, who bring news…are very superior darkies. William, who went with the gunboats especially so. I intend to give him fifty dollars for his pilotage and enter him as a pilot; he knows every foot of the inland waters. These men risk their lives to serve us without the slightest hesitation...they seem to be insensible to fear, make no bargains about their remuneration, leave all that with entire confidence to us. Writing from the Arkansas River in January, 1863, Acting Rear Admiral Porter said the following: The Negroes are better than white people here, who I look upon as brutes and half savages. I have shipped more than 400 able bodied contrabands and owing to the shortness of my crews, have to work them at my guns."[84]

There is more than ample validation in the records that this group of Negroes more than measured up to the expectations of the navy and the officers they served under. The Navy started the Civil War as she began all other wars, in a depleted condition. But the Confederate Navy, luckily, was non-existent! According to Samuel W. Bryant, "Of the ten navy yards possessed by the U.S. Navy, only two were available to the south. Those two were at Norfolk, Virginia, and Pensacola, Florida. The U.S. Navy registers for 1861 listed 90 American warships. 42 Warships in commission were on their assigned stations. They were strung out over the oceans in the Far East, the Pacific and elsewhere. On the other hand, the Confederate navy was in pitiful shape, with 10 Warships mounting only 15 guns.

Gideon Wells moved very quickly and, by December, had assembled 264 vessels. With the rapid and sensible use of Negroes, the navy's manpower shortage was alleviated. The Army, even after it had begun to train Negro units and committed them to battle, continued to have unmet manpower needs."[85]

Jack D. Foner says, "Yet in July, 1863, at the very time when, in South Carolina, black soldiers were preparing to storm Fort Wagner, a bloody four day riot broke out in New York City to protest the Conscription Act of March 1, 1863. In this, the worst in American history, several hundred blacks were killed and thousands more fled the city. There were riots at the same time in other eastern cities. However, the black performance in battle did much to break down the resistance to troops. As one supporter put it, Copperheads would not be convinced that blacks made good soldiers even if they successfully stormed the gates of hell."[86]

The 54th Massachusetts Negro Regiment lost 247 killed out of a force of 600 in the assault on Fort Wagner. There were, according to Foner, "sixteen all black regiments making a total of 186,000 blacks in the Union Army...ultimately, blacks fought in 449 engagements, 39 of which were major battles. Sixteen soldiers earned the Congressional Medal of Honor."[87]

Five black sailors earned the Congressional Medal of Honor. In fact, one of the first heroes at sea was a black cook aboard the merchantman *S. J. Waring*. His name was William Tillman. When the *Waring* was taken at sea by the Confederate raider *Jefferson Davis*, she was turned over to a Confederate prize crew of five and ordered to Charleston Harbor. Tillman, it seems, had no intentions of being put back on the block and sold into slavery. When the *Waring* was about 60 miles from Charleston, Tillman took the hatchet used to chop wood and chopped up the prize crew as captain! He clobbered the Ship's Mate and took his pistol. With the pistol in hand, Tillman rounded up the four Rebel seamen and placed them in irons. After seizing control, he freed the other two black crewmen.

There was no one on board who could navigate. Tillman took command and, hugging the coast, took the *Waring* to New York harbor. This feat won wide acclaim.

According to James M. McPherson:

> "A Negro steward aboard the Schooner S. J. Waring was one of the first authentic northern war heroes. The "New York Tribune" said of this event--To this colored man was the nation indebted for the first vindication of its honor on the sea.." Another journal spoke of that achievement alone as an offset to the defeat of the

Federal Arms at Bull Run. The Federal government awarded to Tillman the sum of $6000 dollars as prize money for the capture of the schooner."[88]

A New York newspaper pointed to the fact that it fell to a Negro cook to give the north its first hero. According to Samuel W. Bryant, the *Jefferson Davis*, "In a lucky seven week cruise…Captured 10 merchantmen with a value of $225,000… The navy assigned eight war ships to track down and sink the elusive privateer.

James Lawson, a loader on the *U.S.S. Hartford* and James Mifflin, a loader aboard the *U.S.S. Brooklyn* were both given the Congressional Medal of Honor for their efforts at the Battle of Mobile Bay. Joachim Pease, Seaman aboard the *U.S.S. Kearsarge* was given the Medal of Honor for his gallantry in action in the engagement with the *Confederate Raider Alabama* at Cherbourg, France. Robert Blake, a Seaman aboard the U.S.S Marblehead earned the Navy Medal of Honor for gallantry in routing the enemy at Legarsville on the Stone River."[89]

Another Negro, Robert Smalls, who was a crewmember of the *Confederate Gunboat Planter* in Charleston harbor, seized it while its officers were ashore and carried it to sea. He surrendered it to the Union. The Union used Smalls piloting skills until the war was over.

He became a Congressman from South Carolina after the war and during the Reconstruction period. Reuben Elmo Stivers said in tribute after researching and writing his book, "Privateers and Volunteers", "It would be unfair to conclude this book without paying respects to two groups of people who have been more or less involved in it throughout. First, to the American Negro, who as a privateersman and volunteer, has been in our navy, as fine a sailor as has ever trod a deck anywhere. Nor do we forget the freed slave who was willing to contribute to the navy's victories in proportion to his gratitude for release from slavery."[90]

The Civil War ended, officially, on April 9, 1865, with the surrender of General Robert E. Lee at Appomattox Courthouse in Virginia. The period of time beginning in 1865 at the end of the Civil War and the year 1877 is commonly known, historically, as the Reconstruction Period. It was a time of huge changes, not only in the South, but all over the United States. The southern economy, disrupted and almost destroyed by the war, had to be rebuilt. With the freeing of 4,000,000 slaves, Southern society underwent massive changes. Cotton was still the backbone of the southern economy. But as one southerner said, how are we going to get our crops in without slaves? What had been formerly "property", was now, by law, persons entitled to equal rights, treatment, and protection under the law like all other citizens. In the north, the Industrial Revolution was well underway. Soldiers returned home to find massive changes, technologically and in the nature of work underway. Whaling and shipbuilding was out and railroading and Oil Drilling was in. The U.S government had to be reconstituted to deal with a whole set of new conditions. Southern state and local governments required restructuring and reestablishment under the new realities of non-slave populations and economics. Politics and social ideology were in a severe state of flux. The end of the war had brought new circumstances and tremendous change to all institutions. The concept of "one nation indivisibly" had to be reestablished.

The biggest questions centered on what to do with and about the newly freed Negroes? They were uneducated, lacked property and other resources. They were no longer the responsibility of their "masters", many of whom had been reduced to paupers, by the ravages of the war. Questions arose, such as "How are they to subsist and how and on what basis do we integrate Negroes into our new free and democratic society and economy?" Shouldn't our first order of business be healing the wounds of war and reuniting our country were the key questions.

How should we go about this? And, finally, how do we make functional a country suffering intense residual hatred; hatred between northern and southern white men and between former masters and their newly freed ex-slaves?

To say that Reconstruction was a massive and complex task is an understatement. Gaining consensus and commitment on how to best accomplish it proved impossible. The effort lasted only twelve years. Countervailing forces and other priorities proved to be its undoing. Reconstruction failed miserably and completely to obtain for the Negro even a semblance of social economic or political equality. The idea of such reduced even the southern intelligent gentry' class whites to quasi-maniacs where rational thought is viewed as a characteristic. What they really feared was political and social equality. They could not forgive the Negro at the time for his lawful freedom and claim to equality. Southern whites did not hate Negroes for merely being "black" during the slave period. To hate ones own property would have been stupid. To do so would have probably retarded the management of this "uneasy property" and hampered the acquirement of maximum productivity. It would have increased the tension in the relationship between master and slave. This, in turn, would have most likely increased the likelihood of abuse in the form of beatings, thus damaging, physically, a property whose value depended on its physical soundness and ability to perform meaningful labor. Hatred existed between poor landless whites and Negroes due to that class' need to feel superior to somebody. However, it was muted and could not be overtly actualized. All it took to prevent an assault on a Negro was for a thinking member of the group to remind his fellows "you all better leave that nigger alone; he belongs to Mr. "so and so".

Some writers contend that actions of the radical Republicans in the aftermath of the war caused the actual hatred between former slaves and their former masters to emerge with a vengeance. Led by Thaddeus Stevens, the radicals took back the presidential powers given to Lincoln to exercise in prosecution of the war and restored them to congress. The actions of the congress precipitated much of the hatred of Negroes by southern whites. Under the Radical Republicans, Lincoln's "with malice toward none" policy, which Andrew Johnson tried to continue to implement, was scrapped. It was replaced with "they are rebels and should be treated as such". Johnson, a poorly educated, crude bumbler, failed to hide his pro-Confederacy sympathies. He attempted to seat representatives from the Reconstruction states in congress, minus guarantees that they would observe and obey new laws pertaining to the Negro. These men had, in an attempt to maintain control over former slaves, written into state constitutions "black codes" which, in many instances were more onerous than slavery itself in their cruelty. For example, according to Peter M. Bergman:

> "The black codes were regulations written into State Constitutions that regulated Negro life. Generally, they made Negroes subject to virtual slavery if convicted of vagrancy. Children separated from their parents could be made slaves…The South Carolina Constitution of that year provided that: no Negro could enter the state unless, within 20 days after arrival, he had put up a bond of $1,000 to ensure his good behavior. A Negro had to have a special license for any job except as a farmer or servant. The license included an annual tax of from $10 to $100. Work licenses were granted by a judge and revocable upon complaint. In cases of revocation, the fine was an amount double the original amount paid for the license, half of which went to the informer. …Farm labor was required from sunup to sunset. …Visitors were not allowed without the Farm owner's consent. Any white man could arrest a Negro he saw committing a misdemeanor."[91]

The several laws and restrictions outdid slavery, where Negro oppression was concerned. The codes all but ignored the constitutional rights enjoyed by U.S. citizens of this country. The codes ignored any semblance of Emancipation.

So much for the white man's concept of freedom! Mississippi and Louisiana laws were, in many ways, much worse. Bergman, in shedding light on the fate of Negroes in other parts of the country outside of the south in the Reconstruction Period, points out that Wisconsin rejected a proposal to let Negroes vote. Minnesota and Connecticut also voted to deny Negro suffrage. So, not only former slave masters but, many northerners failed to perceive the Negro as free. The negative view of the Negro's new freedoms and his "place" in the social and political scheme of things was not limited to the south. Coming from poor circumstances in Tennessee, Andrew Johnson seemed to crave the acceptance and favor of the Southern gentry class of the former Confederacy. Instead of negotiating with the Radical Republicans in Congress, who were being pressured by the Abolitionist, he chose to attempt to seat the Reconstructed states in the Congress, black codes notwithstanding.

4)   THE FAILURE OF RECONSTRUCTION

Johnson took, what came to be known in history books, "a swing around the country", in an attempt to gain backing for his pro-Confederate policies. He overestimated the potential for support and underestimated the power of the Abolitionist impulse still present in the more densely populated North. Upon reading the harsh black codes, the Abolitionist realized that harsher treatment had to be meted out to the former Rebels to gain fair treatment for Negroes. They said, to hell, "with malice towards none". Congressmen were enraged and spurred into action by violence against Negro occupation troops in Memphis and New Orleans, followed by major riots in both cities. The local police, in both cases, stood by and urged the rioters on, instead of attempting to restrain them. John Hope Franklin says:

> "The rejection of the Fourteenth Amendment by Southern States, their enactment of Black Codes, the widespread disorder in the South, and President Johnson's obstinacy persuaded many people that the South had to be dealt with harshly. Consequently, the joint Committee presented to the Congress a measure... basis of the Reconstruction Act of 1867."[92]

Franklin goes on to describe the actions taken by this group of Congressmen, led by Thaddeus Stevens and Charles Sumner. The actions ordered, that before a States' delegation to Congress would be deemed bonafide:

1. The Reconstruction Act was directed at all former Confederate States <u>except Tennessee</u> (the only one in compliance).

2. Those charged with noncompliance are to be divided into 5 Military Districts, in which Martial Law will be instituted and a General Officer placed in charge of each district.

3. On the basis of universal suffrage, a convention was to be held in each state to draw up a <u>new constitution acceptable to congress.</u>

4. No State is to be admitted until it has ratified the Fourteenth Amendment.

5. All former rebels refusing to take an ironclad oath of allegiance are to be disenfranchised.

Johnson vetoed this bill on the grounds that it was both unconstitutional and unfair. He said that Negroes had not asked to vote. <u>He then inferred that Negroes were either too stupid and/or too ignorant to understand the meaning of enfranchisement! Congress overrode the veto, enfranchising all Negroes in the District of Columbia. They strengthened the Freedmen Bureau and began reconstructing the South</u>

<u>with Stern and, at times, severe measures</u>. After laying out additional plans, the Congress reacted to the insubordination of the President by unsuccessfully attempting to remove him from office. This, according to Franklin, pleased a "coalition of interests" which included crusaders, politicians and Industrialists. It also created bitterness and chaos that a century of time would not erase.

The race riots at Memphis and New Orleans ensured a Republican victory in the 1866 Election; by highlighting the real results of the Johnson Reconstruction policies. In the riot at New Orleans, city police played a major role in triggering the violence. The U.S. Army was slow to move in to protect Negro Convention Members. As a result, commented Herbert Shapiro, a reporter for the anti-convention New Orleans Times, "To see Negroes mutilated and literally beaten to death as they sought to escape, was one of the most horrifying pictures it has ever been our ill fortune to witness."[93] The U.S Army stationed in New Orleans failed to take any action to protect the convention.

"Before Martial Law was imposed…forty six blacks and two whites had been killed. Mobsters raped at least five black women. Racist had been driven beyond reason by the sight of Blacks in uniform. So intense was the emergent hatred that a white man shot to death another white man for having engaged in conversation with a black acquaintance in a saloon!"[94]

Herbert Shapiro believes that blacks in uniform was simply the straw that broke the camel's back; it was where southern hatred for Negroes was born and unleashed. The Government backed Negro in uniform meant not Negro equality but was assumed so by the former slave masters. His assessment of the cause and forces driving the hatred in the Memphis Riot is revealing. He takes umbrage at the widespread historical belief that lower class people, or "white trash", were the major perpetrators of hate and violence against the Negro during and after

Reconstruction. He points out that participation was not restricted to the lower class whites in the Memphis Riot. He says:

> "The Memphis violence was set in the circumstances of demographic change and was shaped by white Southerner resentment of Yankee conquerors. In 1865, a City Council census indicated that the city's black population had grown from 3, 882 to 10,995. In August 1865, the Freedman's Bureau census counted 16, 509 blacks out of a total population of 27,703 in the city. While blacks envisioned a new position for themselves in society, the fact of a black majority could be used to incite racial fears. Black assertiveness conflicted with renewed aims of white supremacy. Racist violence was a means of expressing defiance of a triumphant Union. One analyst... poses the question: was it not safer for southerners to focus their pent-up bitterness and frustration upon a symbol of defeat, the freed slaves in South Memphis, than upon the mighty Yankee? In the course of the riot, symbols of the Union, white and black, came under assault. White teachers (from the north and east), whites commanding black troops, missionaries and even local Freedman Bureau personnel were insulted and threatened."[95]

Shapiro goes on to describe why the Memphis violence could not be characterized in the conventional terms of lower class white resentment of black assertiveness:

> "...for a number of prominent Memphis whites led the mob, including the Tennessee Attorney General, William Wallace, and the Judge of the Recorders Court, John C. Creighton. The Federal inquiry into the riot reported that the city's mayor, John Park, took no action to suppress the riots. His influence tended to incite it still further. It was doubtless such support in high places that had encouraged the police in initiating... savage, almost merciless attacks on black Union troops. Police conduct seemed to be geared to inviting black retaliation."[96]

One is compelled to wonder why these black veterans, who knew how to fight, did not fight back. But, when one looks at U.S. Army history, the answer becomes evident. The Army has never backed black soldiers. They traditionally allowed civilian police forces and authorities to abuse them. The commanding officers at Memphis had allowed this abuse for months preceding the riots. These soldiers probably intelligently feared Army punishment more than they feared the mob. Before leaving the subject of upper class white participation in racial violence, it is interesting to note the origins of the name Ku-Klux Klan. It derives from the Greek word "Kuklos", meaning circle. Only the sons of wealthy southern planters were educated prior to Reconstruction. It is very doubtful that poor, uneducated white tenant farmers would possess the formal classical education required to be familiar with Greek or Latin. The organizers were probably men of letters.

Social equality was doomed from the start. The Negro became a symbol of southern defeat and a principle target of white hatred. The movement toward acquisition of political equality was real, but as fleeting as Reconstruction itself. Although there were three Constitutional Amendments passed in the attempt to grant political equality to the freedmen, this surge would end with Reconstruction and sleep until Brown versus Board of Education in the 1950's. The 13th Amendment was passed December 18, 1865 and outlawed slavery. The 14th was passed July 28, 1868, and validated the right to citizenship. The 15th was passed March 30, 1870, and secured voting rights for all male citizens. For a short period of time, a sustained effort was made to guarantee the civil rights and liberties of the now free Negroes.

For a short period of time, they sat as bonafide representatives in the state houses of the south and the U.S. Congress. "Two Negroes even went to the U.S. Senate. In 1868, South Carolina had a black majority in its legislature. There were 87 black and 40 white legislators. The white majority was not reestablished until 1874."[97] However, none of these efforts were to achieve lasting political equality. In fact, after this fleeting moment of political participation came the Compromise of 1877. Seventy-seven years (1954) were to pass before a significant assertion of political and social rights came again for Negroes.

As stated earlier, under leadership of the Radical Republicans in congress, a measure was passed that divided the south into five military districts under martial law. This required posting the largest peacetime army in the history of the United States in the South, ostensibly, to protect the persons and rights of the Negro. An exodus of war weary white men from army ranks caused Negroes to be retained in greater numbers and additional ones to be recruited. Consequently, this large peacetime occupation force contained probably more Negro soldiers in the ranks than ever before. As previously stated, this became the major source of post war hatred of the Negro. These Negro soldiers were a constant reminder of the South's defeat and impotence. This helped kill any chance of social and/or political acceptance by their former masters. This hate and anger fueled violence and intimidation via mobs, lynching, and Ku-Klux Klan actions unprecedented in U.S. history beginning around 1870.

Attempts to elevate the newly freed slaves economically represent one of the most dismal failures of the Reconstruction effort, north, south and across the country. Prior to the war, the principle product underpinning the economy was cotton. The South had been an agrarian economy dependent on free slave labor. In a prostrate south, all but destroyed by the war, the meaningful production of cotton had come to a halt. Most Cotton, Tobacco, Rice and Sugar Cane fields lay fallow and unattended. There was a gross absence of capital. Transportation facilities ranged from severely damaged to non-existent. There was severe deprivation and unemployment. Add to this situation, the fact that 4,000,000 slaves, 99% of whom were illiterate, had unceremoniously been dumped on the countryside and cities. Meaningful commercial contact between Southerners, who grew, baled and sold cotton, and the rest of the world had been halted by the war. The economic chaos was not limited to the south. Three changes, as previously noted, negatively impacted the North. 1) The discovery of oil at Titusville, Pennsylvania had sounded the death knell for the whaling industry and had repercussions all through the shipbuilding, supply and maintenance sectors of the merchant marine. 2) With the freeing of the slaves, slave trading and other slave-supported commerce engaged in by northerners came to a grinding halt. 3) Also, the mass production of materials needed to directly support the military and the war was no longer needed. The mid-west was largely spared due to its low level of industrialization and the demand for its foodstuffs in the north and the south both during and after the war. A full catastrophe was averted in the shipbuilding and associated industries by the strong demand for transportation of goods both at home and overseas. With the advent of the steam engine, there was an immense dire need for the construction of fighting and cargo ships, as well as crews to man them. This was the one bright light for the Negro in the darkness of industrial chaos, caused by the War's end.

The South faced starvation. The North faced the chaos of economic dislocation and a possibly severe post war depression. Complex is a mild word to use in describing the problems and forces unleashed by the end of the Civil War. The problems faced in guarding the civil rights and civil liberties of the newly freed Negro and finding an economic niche for this people was left hanging. It was placed on the back burner at the end of Reconstruction, signaled by the Compromise of 1877. The only positive and lasting prize left to Negroes after Reconstruction was probably the program developed to erase illiteracy and to provide education.

The Negro, a pawn in the post war game, was abandoned and forgotten as the Bankers and Industrial moguls of the Republican Party demanded reconciliation in the name of progress and the resumption of commerce between north and south. The effort to harness and use electricity and oil, to create the machines that would accelerate the industrial revolution took center stage and dominated national interest. Among the few positives of this period, in 1876, Edward Bouchet graduated from Yale University with a Ph.D. in physics, becoming the first Negro to obtain a doctorate degree. There were 571, 506 Negro children actively attending schools. And, finally Henry O. Flipper became the first Negro graduate of the U.S. Military Academy at West Point.

The Bergmans, in describing the Compromise of 1877, which ended Reconstruction, said:

> "In conference at the Wormly Hotel in Washington, D.C. on February 26 and 27, Rutherford B. Hayes promised southern delegates that he would remove Federal Troops from the South and leave the Southern states alone in return for the support of Democratic southern congressmen when the house voted for President. Upon Hayes's election, he removed the Federal troops from South Carolina and Louisiana. In the first five months of his administration, one third of his southern appointees were Democrats."[98]

This was the Compromise of 1877. John Hope Franklin points out that it was not the Negroes inability, nor their willingness to take advantage of opportunities offered. He says:

> "Indeed intimidation was most effective...after 1870, although the Ku-Klux Klan disclaimed responsibility for its increasing violence". The crops of Negroes were destroyed, their houses and barns burned, and they were whipped and lynched for voting Republican. The Federal Government was unable to rush to the defense of southern Republican Governments because it was

having difficulty in purging itself of corruption…Corruption discredited Radical Reconstruction. And, with its loss of conscientious but disillusioned supporters, complete home rule could be restored in the south."[99]

One has only to read the history of the U.S. Supreme Court between the end of the Civil War and the end of Reconstruction to know that this august body was not a friend of the Negro. The Court had, since the start of Reconstruction, been busy undoing gains implicit in the 13th, 14th and 15th Amendments. Finally, Franklin says:

> "The North had grown weary of the crusade for the Negro. Perhaps Stevens, Sumner, Butler and the Anti-Slavery leaders could have gone on with it, but younger people, with less zeal for the Negro took their places. Loyal party men, they were practical politicians who cared more about industrial interests in the North and South than Radical governments in the South. The assumption of Republican leadership by men like Hayes, Blain, Conklin and Logan was a signal for the party to turn to more profitable and practical pursuits."[100]

This was the beginning of the Separate but equal policies and practices which were to last for three-quarters of a century. Even the U.S. Navy, with its strong history of practical liberalism, could not withstand the forces at work in the U.S. society. I close this section with the following quote from Peter M. Bergman

(The Darkest Period):

> "After Reconstruction, practically all political rights given to the American Negro resulting from the conflict between South and North, were retracted. A gradual leveling took place. Before the Civil War the question was how to free the Negroes in the South from the violence of the Slaveholders. Following Reconstruction, the question became how to free the Negroes from the violence of all the whites, in the South and the North. Some of the worst conditions facing Negroes now prevailed

over the entire nation rather than just the Southern Region. In fact, this was the darkest period in the history of the Negro in America. Economically, the tremendous growing Industry used in this period the Negro as strikebreaker and as a supply for the army of unemployed reserve, and brought him in steady conflict with the masses of hard-working new immigrants."[101]

Amidst all this historical chaos, the U.S. Navy did what it had always done when politicians sought to tell the Service what to do. But after Reconstruction was killed by the Compromise of 1877 and the former slaveocracy gained power and asserted itself, the Navy faced a historical problem, the tendency of this country to rapidly disarm after each war. So it was imperative that the U.S. Navy put more energy into attempting to remain a viable service. This required friends in Congress who would see that it was stripped of Personnel and ships. So as racism and Jim Crow rapidly became entrenched into broader society the Navy too had to downgrade Negroes. This was so in order to remain accepted social members; such that their leaders would not offend new, increasingly powerful Southern Senators and Congressmen whom they depended upon for appropriations for ships and personnel. Along with the forces described here, other forces helped set in motion the downgrading of the Negro in the U.S. Navy:

1) Of 4,000,000 Negro slaves on Emancipation, 99.9% were illiterate.

2) The change from sail to steam technology required literate crews.

3) Naval officers serving in the Far East, e.g. Philippines, observed the abject subservience of colonized people, e.g. the kow-towing of the Chinese, and came to prefer that type of behavior to that of the Negro. Unchallenged by Congress, the U.S. Navy moved to rid itself of the Negroes by reducing all Negroes to a servant

role in 1893 and created the Messmen's Branch. In 1919 it barred Negroes from enlistment even as servants. This disbarment from service lasted thirteen years—from 1919 to 1932. Historically a projection of the slave system, the Stewards/Messmen's Branch was retarded in its march to a "lily white Navy" by the advent of World War II preparation. When allowed to enlist again on the eve of WW II (1932), it was stipulated that Negroes could be servants only. The Steward Branch, as a projection of the slave period lasted possibly longer as an institution, than any other unit in U.S. military history (1893 to 1974). This historical reach of the Stewards Branch as a negative retardant of Negro progress, has a longer existence than any military unit in U.S. History.

Part III.

The Post-Reconstruction Era Navy

CHAPTER 6.   THE END OF RECONSTRUCTION (1877)

The Reconstruction Period lasted from shortly after the Civil War (1865) until 1877, a period of twelve years. Peter M. Bergman says, "History knows restitution, and Societies have at times, moved by conscience or guilt, offered compensation to aggrieved peoples. The American Negro did not receive any restitution after emancipation. He profited for a time from the after effects mostly in regard to political rights. For a time, during Reconstruction, he was represented more widely in legislative bodies than at any other time up to the present."[102]

1)   THE REMNANTS OF OLD PRAGMATIC NAVAL OFFICERS STUBBORNLY HELD THE LINE: MAINTAINED A POLICY ALLOWING CONTINUED RETENTION AND RECRUITMENT OF NEGROES

It is relevant here to remind the reader that the Navy, whose first 100 years was the most liberal among the armed forces, neared its end during the post-Civil War Reconstruction. Concomitantly, the old hardheaded, pragmatic officers, who had refused to cease recruiting Negroes at the end of the Revolution and the War of 1812, were fading from the scene. They had also allowed Negroes to fight in the Mexican War in 1845. Just as the Negro got a momentary taste of <u>Civil Rights</u> as a result of the political hassles between southern and northern white men; they never received Civil Liberties. Forces were already at work to prevent this.

Socially, embittered southern white men were determined that although the Negro might be free, he would never be deemed equal. Politically, a compromise between white men over power at the Negroes expense brought Reconstruction to a rapid close. However, remnants of the old guard Naval Officers managed to slow the march of Jim Crow and segregation in the Navy. Frederick S. Harrod said, "During the late 19th Century, the Navy did not officially discriminate in the enlistment or assignment of Black sailors. In 1870, for example, the Bureau of Equipment and Recruiting informed one officer that colored Seamen and ordinary Seamen may be enlisted without limits other than those governing general recruitment. Blacks in this period constituted approximately a tenth of the enlisted force."[103] Harrod goes on to point out that even though Blacks were to be recruited in relatively large numbers, their status remained lower than that of whites. For example, more than three-quarters signed on as Landsmen, twice the number of whites in this rating. Yet, there still seemed to be a residue of the old pragmatic naval officer around. Harrod points out the fact that, once aboard ship, there were still naval officers who promoted Black men on merit instead of the color of their skin. This was done contrary to the march of Jim Crow and Segregation in the broader community. He says, "once on board ship, some Blacks served as Jacks-of-the-Dust (Storekeepers), Carpenters, Water Tenders, Oilers and other specialized billets. Nevertheless, as before the war, the majority continued to occupy Landsmen, Cook and Steward billets."[104]

In spite of extreme pressure exerted by the former slave masters, Harrod points out that with the coming of steam navigation and the Navy's organization of apprentice programs and the training facilities needed for this technological advancement, Blacks were still included.

Instead of foreign seamen or the scrapings of the docks as in the days of sail, steam navigation required a cadre of well-trained career men who were American born. "In the years 1880 and 1890, about 3% and 4% respectively, of Black sailors were naval apprentices, citing the great want of intelligent, literate native born seamen. In 1875, the navy began enlisting young men 16 to 18 years old to serve as naval apprentices until age 21. These boys were to receive an elementary English education and initiated into all the duties of sailors on a man-o-war."[105]

As late as 1874, when the cruiser USS Brooklyn was being crewed, sources of whites were still scarce. Blacks, many of whom were literate, were available who met the requirements for steam. For example, at emancipation, there were 4,000,000 Negroes of which 99% were illiterate. However, programs to educate the newly freed slaves were unbelievably successful. By 1900, the turn of the century, one in every two Negroes could read and write, according to Peter M. Bergman, "This, however, failed to stay the animosity of whites towards Blacks, which had been temporarily localized south by the Civil War and a flash of conscience in the north. Both Jim Crow and Segregation moved rapidly resulting in the legal codification of racism."[106]

2) THE DISAPPEARANCE OF OLD LINE OFFICERS AND ABOLITIONIST: THE SOLIDIFICATION OF RACISM, THE INTENSIFICATION OF DISCRIMINATION AND SEGREGATION

By 1893, the old guard naval officers were for all practical purposes gone; they were replaced by a new younger officer corps that bowed to the social and political will of a society which was creating a new form of quasi-slavery. New institutions such as the Sharecrop System were created and the accepted definition of "place" for the newly freed

Negroes at the bottom of the Socio-economic ladder were formulated. The U.S. Navy found a "place" for the Negroes in its ranks; it was the role of servant.

In 1893, the year the segregated Messmen Branch was created, Negroes were being lynched and the Ku Klux Klan ran rampant, the stage was set. The Federal Government acquiesced as the U.S. Navy created the "Messmen Branch" without opposition. It was an overtly backward step into a policy based on race and color that would last until the Post World War II era. This negative step nullified the positive utilization of Blacks that had served the U.S. Navy well since the Revolutionary War. It probably caused many white young men to lose their lives by being drafted earlier in the lottery than a non-racist approach that included Negroes.

3) THE END OF "LIBERALISM AS A COMPONENT OF NAVAL PERSONNEL POLICY

From the end of Reconstruction (1877) to the Spanish American War (1898, the plight of the Negro in the Navy spiraled downward. The Spanish American War afforded a brief respite. The first shot fired in the war at the Battle of Manila Bay was fired by a Negro, John Jordan, Chief Gunners Mate aboard Admiral Dewey's Flagship, the U.S.S. Olympic. Other Negroes were decorated for gallantry in action. In spite of outstanding performance in 1898, the temporary respite rapidly dissipated. The downward spiral of the Negro accelerated between 1898 and World War I (1914).

Although Negro soldiers who were some of the best trained soldiers in the war and displayed conspicuous gallantry in Cuba, the U.S. Navy failed to upgrade them.

Negro veterans homeward bound aboard trains after the war were mobbed and beaten when the trains stopped in Southern towns. These Negroes learned that they were still "niggers" and were not to forget their "place" in U.S. society.

The U.S. Army, its usual historical self, failed to intervene. In this racist atmosphere, the U.S. Navy continued to downgrade its Negro resource. Under the newly acquired colonialism, Negro cooks, stewards and mess attendants who had tasted Democracy were no longer considered subservient enough. So Naval officers who served in the new colonial outposts, who had seen the kowtowing of the Chinese and the Philipinos and the Guamanians decided to get rid of the stateside-bred "uppity Negroes" and recruit colonial peoples that knew their "place" and appeared to have no problem staying in it. Lest this author get ahead of himself, it was in the Post Reconstruction era that the stage was set for the U.S. Navy, after a century of bucking its own government decided to cease recruiting and preserving the right for Negroes to serve in this country.

CHAPTER 7. THE ABOLITIONIST DEMISE, BETRAYAL BY THE REPUBLICAN PARTY AND WHITE SUPREMACY: THE EMERGENCE OF NAVAL POLICY BASED UPON RACISM

The fact that an atmosphere was created that allowed the U.S. Navy to engage in legislating, unchallenged by the Congress or the Courts, points to the real potency and power of the post-Civil War march of racism. It does not seem to have mattered that reducing Negro men to servants, minus congressional action, violated the separation of powers embodied in the Constitution. Changes of this magnitude usually required an act of Congress. Violence against uneducated, defenseless, ex-slaves did not occur only in the southern states.

1) STARTING IN THE POST CIVIL WAR PERIOD WHEN THE NEGRO WAS SUPPOSEDLY "EMANCIPATED" RACISM AND BRUTALITY SURGED UPWARD. NEGRO WELFARE WAS TURNED OVER TO FORMER SLAVE MASTERS AND THE KU-KLUX-KLAN AFTER RECONSTRUCTION

The question comes up, Where were the abolitionists? They had worked so hard before the war to free the slaves. Men like John Brown, Elija Lovejoy and others had even given up their lives for the abolitionist cause. The Quakers of Pennsylvania organized the first Anti-slavery Society movement back in 1775. John Jay, Benjamin Franklin, Theodore Dwight, and William Lloyd Garrison were among the leaders, to name a few. They had caused many northern states to enact anti-slavery legislation and had fanned the flames of rebellion that culminated in the Civil War. They pushed hard for restitution as a part of Reconstruction. Then, when the new Reconstruction Laws came under siege, they disappeared. They vanished from politics and, it seems, off the stage of history.

They were probably the only forces that could have stopped the Compromise of 1877 that effectively ended Reconstruction. Again, all major compromises in U.S. history, including this one has involved white men compromising at the Negro's expense. The Compromise of 1774, the Missouri Compromise of 1820, the Compromise of 1850 and the Compromise of 1877 each involved giving away some form of Negro rights or preventing them from acquiring rights. The Abolitionist did not rise up or form any manner of protective barrier against the assault on Reconstruction. Most seemed to be more interested in finding ways to return the ex-slaves to Africa. When this proved unfeasible, they seemed to have lost all zeal and interest in the Negro. The greatest problem facing the Abolitionist in the post-Civil War period seems to have been their naivete. They failed to understand what the war had really accomplished and the stern resolve of the vanquished. I.H. Newby, said in reference to an article written by Senator John T. Morgan of Alabama, "In 1890, the South stood on the threshold of a revolution in race relations. Within two decades, Segregationist had radically altered the loyal and constitutional status of Negroes there; and the fortunes of the race plummeted. The advent of segregation and disenfranchisement meant the triumph of white supremacy and of the racial ideas it represented. Morgan summarizes the arguments just then crystallizing in defense of the new racial policies."[107] Seemingly unchallenged, Morgan goes on to present good insight, into the thinking of government figures, a decade prior to the turn of the century.

"...races are innately unequal, that race prejudice is natural and instinctive; that race mixture is biologically unwise and socially degrading; that America is a white mans' country in which white men will and should control race policy. Negroes are incapable of effective citizenship. The race has retrogressed since emancipation. History, science and religion support white supremacy and disenfranchisement does no violence to American Democracy. The future welfare of America depends upon the preservation of segregation and white racial purity. For all these reasons, extreme measures are justified in preserving white supremacy."[108]

To deal with the so-called Negro problem after he was allegedly free, white America had three possible choices: 1) they could be exiled back to Africa, 2) they could be forced to submit to disenfranchisement, segregation, and the quasi-slavery of the sharecrop system or 3) they could simply be exterminated. Banishment or exile was an early punishment for white men and Negroes who failed to adjust. This was a favorite punishment of Puritans as a method of dealing with sinners. It was used in dealing with both white and Negro malcontents in other colonies. John Hope Franklin said, "The problem of what to do with Negroes who would not adjust to American life was an old one... As the number of free Negroes increased, it came to be felt that they must be sent out of the country if property in slaves was to be secured. Certainly there could be no complete discipline of slaves as long as free Negroes were in their midst... Three thousand Negroes of Philadelphia, led by Richard Allen and James Forten met in 1817 to register their objection to colonization."[109] Paul Cuffy, a prominent free Negro ship owner, had proven the unfeasibility of sending Negroes back to Africa in 1875. The country had no money. Further, it did not grasp the magnitude or logistics involved. Martin Delaney, another prominent free Negro, criticized the Christian Church, labeling them hypocrites, for pandering to the slaveholders. After emancipation, that old problem showed up again. However, this time the question was not what should we do with free Negroes? The question was what could we do with 4,000,000 newly freed slaves? With no money in the treasury, mass colonization as a remedy, was unfeasible. The post Civil War Negro was saved from mass banishment to Africa or extermination by two factors. The first was an empty treasury, while the second was a new role, "sharecroppers", concocted by the former slave owners, as a profitable replacement for slavery. That system lasted for a period of 87 Years!

In light of this oppressive social and political atmosphere, as so eloquently described by Senator Morgan in 1890, the answer to the earlier question of how the navy was able to encroach upon the legislative powers of the congress to create the Messmen branch becomes obvious.

2) FORCES THAT INCREASED ACCELERATION OF THE NAVY'S NEW POLICY BASED UPON RACE AND COLOR: A) THE RAPID RETURN OF SOUTHERN OFFICERS B) THE CONCEPT OF MANIFEST DESTINY AND C) THE ACQUISITION OF NON-WHITE COLONIES

The final blows to naval liberalism came from two sources. A virtual flood of Southern officers returned to the U.S. navy after the Civil War. These men did not take kindly to the idea of black and white sailors berthing and messing together. Nor could they countenance black petty officers telling white seamen what to do in the boss/subordinate situations in everyday shipboard life. The second factor was the surge of manifest destiny and, later, the acquisition of colonies by America with subject non-white peoples to govern. After the Spanish-American war, The United States found herself responsible for Puerto Ricans, Panamanians, Cubans, Guamanians and Philipinos. Officers posted to colonial stations were exposed to a new "subservience", imposed on local populations by despotic rulers and they, themselves, as colonial masters and military peacekeepers. This foreign exposure had a decided effect upon the attitude of these men; especially those posted to the Far East and the China Station. They returned home expecting American Negroes to Kow-Tow and be deferential, as were the natives in these foreign lands. But the U.S. Negro had helped the country to free itself and in the process had been exposed to Democracy.

A crew composed of Chinese would make "Chop Suey" and cook a pot of rice for themselves on days when the white sailors ate steak. The Philipinos, who were excellent fishermen, would catch fish and make "Gidi-Gidi", a form of fish and rice stew, for their meals. American Negroes had the gall to expect to eat Steak like White sailors! Negroes had over two centuries of fighting for and observing the making of Democracy. White officers were often brought to anger when they discovered wily Negro Messboys engaging in "passive resistance" after being rudely shouted at or ordered about. Passive resistance might mean that the coffee was served lukewarm rather than piping hot. It might mean throwing good food in the garbage to drive up the officers' mess bill; or not serving the stipulated menu to them. The latter often occurred when naval officers took the Messmen's ration money, but ordered the steward to make stew for the crew on days when the menu called for steak.

Just as a "place" was ruthlessly ascribed for the newly freed slave in the broader society, naval officers engaged in a similar task. The navy task was more complex due to the diversity of crews of Messboys. But they had no political problems because words coming from Congress in this period indicated that no opposition would be forthcoming, regardless of what they did to or with the Negroes. Thus, the navy's march toward "lily whiteness" coincided with the thinking in the broader society.

3) THE U.S. NAVY'S POLICY ON RACISM: IGNORED BY CONGRESS AND THE COURTS, AND BACKED BY THE BEST MINDS IN THE SCIENTIFIC COMMUNITY AS TO THE INNATE INFERIORITY OF THE NEGRO

Attempts have been made over the centuries, to establish the intellectual inferiority of Africans or, so-called Negroes, "scientifically". The purpose has always been to buttress white superiority and to justify discriminatory social, economic, and political treatment of Negroes by Whites. Although efforts had been made for two and a half centuries, it intensified in the post-Reconstruction era. I. A. Newby, in critiquing an article by Robert Bennett Bean that appeared in the *Century* magazine in 1906 concerning the Negro brain said,

> "Prior to WWI, Physical and Social Scientist produced a flood of literature which purported to demonstrate racial inequality and Negro inferiority in particular. Inequality, they believed, was mental as well as physical, and mental inequalities have a physiological base. The most important organ in the human body is the brain. If Negroes are inferior to whites, it necessarily follows that the "fact" will be reflected in the brains of the two races. Negro brains, in other words, must be demonstrably inferior to Caucasian brains."[110]

Bean was a Professor of Anatomy at the University of Virginia. Bean's premise ascribes the alleged inferiority of the Negro to his brain and goes on to note the implication that that "fact" has for racial policy. Newby, in his critique, said, "It illustrates the scientific deficiencies characteristic of most literature on scientific racism, especially the author's willingness to use his "scientific" data as a basis of racist sociology. Despite the limitations of Beans study, the view expressed in it have been commonly held by segregationist throughout the 20th Century."[111]

Bean weighed and averaged white and Negro brains with great care and precision. His argument rested upon the size and shape of the Negro brain when compared with that of whites. His premise was that the larger and more perfectly rounded the shape was, the greater the weight of gray matter, the greater the intelligence and analytical capacity. Of course, his data supported superiority of the white man. White men went on a binge of theories, concerning the Negro's brain, during the historical period, after the Africans were enslaved and, later, when the darker people of the world were colonized for exploitation by Europeans.

They even invented a couple of pseudo-sciences, Phrenology and Craniometry, to support their efforts. Phrenology is the study of the conformation of the skull as indicative of mental faculties and character. This theory developed literally a cult among men of considerable intellectual standing. Craniometry is a science dealing with cranial measurements. Men so skilled were honored with the title "Craniometrician". Their skill was in calculating how many metrically measured ball bearings a skull could hold. Thus the exact weight of the brain could be deduced.

Lancelot Hogben, a contributor to Ashley Montague's The Concept of Race, said of this foolishness palmed off as science, "Indeed it will be difficult to believe that such hope could have sustained such stupendous persistence in fruitless and trivial exploits of repetitive measuration, if we do not fortify our credulity with the reflection that persons of intellectual standing enthusiastically subscribed to the cult of phrenology when Craniometry was still in the cradle. Even so, early measurements should have sufficed to dampen the ardor of the most credulous Craniometrician if rational considerations had any relevance to the issue."[112] Hogben then states what caused the two so-called sciences to lose, concomitantly, both credibility and popularity. He says, "The cranial capacity of Bismarck was 1965 cubic centimeters, and his brain weighed 1867 grams. The cranial capacity of Leibnitz, who advanced mathematics as few others of a very creative period, anticipated the study of Comparative Linguistics, and managed the financial affairs of the Elector who founded the Hanoverian Dynasty, was 1422 cubic centimeters. His estimated brain weight was 1257 grams."[113]

So much then for the physical and natural sciences of Biology, Zoology, Taxonomy, Anatomy, Physiology and Anthropology as they were all enlisted in the justification of slavery and colonialism. They were all enlisted at some juncture, to justify social and political policies.

4) PRESSURE FROM ENGLISH AND EUROPEAN ABOLITIONIST (1807-1865) FAIL TO HALT AFRICAN SLAVE TRADE AND FRUSTRATES U.S. NAVAL OFFICERS CHARGED WITH ITS SUPPRESSION

So, long after top European Scholars gave up on attempts to place the African somewhere between man and the apes, Americans embraced this task with gusto. The historical reason is understandable. The Abolitionist of England, led by Bishop Wilbeforce, as well as others on the continent, forced the Kings and statesmen to face the fact that slavery was a sinful abomination. So, the so-called "civilized nations" met at The Hague in the Netherlands in 1807. They agreed to cease removing Africans and selling them as slaves by 1808. Although the United States entered into the solemn agreement at The Hague in 1807, it did not send a ship to the African coast to aid in the suppression of the slave trade until 1817. Slavery was fast becoming a large economic factor for the Americans.

Though the United States entered into that agreement, this country with half dependent upon the free labor of slavery never supported the effort 100%. Instead it dragged its feet, delayed sending ships to help enforce the law and winked at slave smuggling up to and during the American Civil War. Thinking Naval Officers knew not to engage in rigorous enforcement lest they incur the wrath of Congressmen and Senators who represented the interests of the "cotton kingdom", New England shipbuilders, and slave cargo carriers. Even fair minded and conscientious Naval Officers found themselves frustrated. They were forced to often "play games" instead of preventing Africans from being enslaved and transported for sale.

This author feels it necessary to backtrack in order to set the historical stage for answering a question that inevitably arose in most of his classes at Case Western Reserve University. Most students did not know that not just the lot of Negro sailors but the lot of White sailors became harsher after the War of 1812. The question, "If Negroes were emancipated at the end of the Civil War and were free, how could they become worse-off during and after Reconstruction?" This question does pose an irony. There was rapid change in the maritime trades that affected ordinary sailors. Where once New England and Central Coast States utilized the maritime industries as dependable, economic rock it began to gradually wear away. Petroleum replaced whale oil. The primitive emergence of industrialization drew the interest of entrepreneurs away from shipping and those men controlled the capital for investment.

The above had to be explained and discussed before the calmer, more enlightened students could manage to be heard. At sea at mid-century, white sailors found their existence vastly different on shipboard in the 1850's than their predecessors did in 1812. Ships were larger but wages were lower. Segregation became a method for increasing production. For example, have one White on Watch and one Black on Watch and play them one against the other. The Navy had attempted to practice segregation during the Civil War but failed incident to personnel needs, which Negroes were able to alleviate.

CHAPTER 8. METHODS OF FORCED SUBMISSION AND EXPLOITATION: AFFECT UPON NAVY PERSONNEL POLICY

1) THE SOCIAL AND POLITICAL ATMOSPHERE SUPPORTING NAVY SEGREGATION AND DISCRIMINATION POLICY

The following appears on the back cover of Ralph Ginzburg's book entitled "100 Years of Lynching":

> "Mans inhumanity to his fellow man has rarely expressed itself more violently as it has in the lynching of Negroes by white Americans. Now for the first time, the whole-unvarnished story of this phenomenon as it appeared in the North and the South of the United States is told in this book. This book erases the myth that only Red Necked Southern Crackers engaged in lynching Negroes. Racism and lynching is a national phenomenon, not sectional. Included are true and thoroughly documented stories of Negroes lynched for white men's crimes, marrying white women, Negro mothers and wives raped and lynched when mobs were unable to locate sons and husbands, and Negroes lynched for no other reason except that they happened to be Negroes. Courthouses have been burned while intended lynch victims were on trial. Negroes have been lynched despite the best efforts of police and national guardsmen to save them; and Negroes have been lynched for offenses as petty as brushing against a white man's horse or refusing to dance when told to do

so by white men. Almost three hundred such cases are described and documented in this book."[114]

Even in a society of Christians, ostensibly governed by a new creed and constitution that opens with the words, "We hold these truths to be self evident, that all men are created equal,...inalienable rights, etc.", skin color makes null and void the biblical "all men are children of god". Inalienable rights and the American creed mean nothing for those whose skin is not the right color. Lynching, its lengthy practice and the violence done to society's creeds and religions, may possibly be the most accurate measure of the victims in that society's social order. The classic lynching of Negroes lasted for 87 years. By "classic" is meant the ritual-like taking of life by large mobs, unhindered by state, local or federal intervention. Blacks are still being lynched by small groups of white men in this country. Historically, to say no intervention is a valid statement. The proof rests in the number of lynching's and how long the phenomena lasted.

This discussion is included to assist the reader in understanding the atmosphere, environment and extent of the negative forces at work when the Messmen Branch was created in 1893. What the Navy did was mild compared to the behavior prevalent in the broader society. For example, a few of Ginzburg's news headlines are revealing:

New York Truth Seeker, April 17, 1880
First Negro at WestPoint knifed by fellow cadets...taken from his bed, bound, gagged, and severely beaten...then his ears were slit... cadet's claim he did it to himself.

Chicago Tribune, November 1895
Texans lynch wrong Negro, Madisonville, Texas...Lynching of Negro...on Tuesday night. On Wednesday it was discovered that the wrong Negro had been gotten hold of by the mob.[115]

Montgomery Advertiser, September 1919

Omaha, September 29, 1919. Mayor Edward Smith, who tried vainly last night to prevent a mob form lynching a Negro prisoner, died shortly after midnight from injuries inflicted by a mob, which began to lynch him too."[116]

Chattanooga Times, February 13, 1918

Blood curdling lynching witnessed by 2,000 persons.

Estill Springs, Tennessee, February 12. Jim McIlherron, the Negro who shot and killed...two white men and wounded Frank Tigert. The Negro was brought to Estill Springs on passenger train Number 5 arriving at 6:30. A crowd of about 1200 met the train...12 masked men stepped forward from the crowd and took possession of the Negro...as if by signal, others scattered among the crowd... Negro carried to ...spot where shootings occurred. (At 7:30 PM)...Negro being chained to a Hickory tree, funeral pyre being made ready. Little boys carry wood for pyre. (at 7:40 PM)...Red hot Crowbar is brought forward by masked man who jabs Negro's body...Negro grabs bar with bare hands...odor of burning flesh fills atmosphere...iron then applied to each side of Negro's neck, searing flesh...screams heard for half a mile rent air...Negro then implicated the son of a Negro preacher who was killed the day before by a mob. (At 7:50 PM) Coal Oil is poured on Negro's legs and feet. One of the executioners strikes a match...Negro begs for mercy."[117]

It was a lucky Negro who was simply hanged or shot! This was a pretty mild affair, ritual-wise. Castration, cutting off ears, noses and fingers, putting red pepper or holding red-hot irons to sensitive places was common practice. In many instances, Negroes were accused of insulting or raping a white woman. This seems to have triggered the ultimate fiendishness in white mobs as the most frequent reason for this lawless act was the alleged protection of "white womanhood". The news media, at the turn of the century, was as barbaric as the public it served. For example:

Bangor (Maine) Commercial, September 5, 1899

Veteran reporter…now visiting this city gives you an interesting account of his experiences. The news that there was going to be a lynching party spreads very rapidly in the south. I have attended, in my capacity, at least 12 lynching's. On two of these occasions, I have seen as many as three Negroes lynched. When arrested, they confessed their crimes and were placed on a pile of railroad ties…when the rope was ready, the crowd pulled the ties from under them. Before victims were dead, they were riddled with bullets… This lynching did not impress me half as much as one a short time afterward in which an innocent man named John Peterson was the victim. …Charged with the usual crime…near Denmark, South Carolina…he heard that he was suspected and surrendered himself to the penitentiary authorities…wanted their protection. The governor surrendered him…if he had been kept in the State Penitentiary until things cooled off, the outcome would have been different. Peterson…took back to Denmark by several officers. The crowd took the prisoner to the home of the man whose daughter was assaulted. She declined to identify him positively…not sure. (The) father of the girl started to blame her severely for not fixing the crime on the poor fellow…girl finally brought over to the point…Peterson was the guilty man. It so happened that two railroad lines crossed near that point…one of them, a train bound for Atlanta, Georgia, was due in a few minutes and a goodly number of the men wanted to board…to go to their homes. There was also a great demand on the part of *Reporters* to have the job done before the arrival of the train…the results was that one or two reporters took matters into their own hands and hurried (the crowd) along as a piece of newspaper enterprise. The crowd was too slow. The Reporters showed them how they ought to work. Execution took place in the usual way...and just as the train arrived, Peterson was dead and most of the crowd boarded the train...regarded as a well-arranged affair. It was afterward discovered that Peterson was entirely innocent."[118]

2) THE FAILURE OF THE COURTS, NEWS MEDIA AND GOVERNMENT TO ACT: ENHANCED THE DOMINO EFFECT OF RACISM

This section is included to give serious students of naval history an unadulterated view of the country's atmosphere when the Messmen Branch was organized as the first step towards a "lily white" navy. The total array of News Media, government, law enforcement and the courts, north and south, were involved in the post-Civil War hatred, discrimination and segregation of Negroes. What the U.S. Navy did was in keeping with what other institutions in American society were doing. These conditions seemed to worsen after Negroes fought in America's wars. The resentment of Negro men in uniform increased when the slaves were set free in 1865. This was odd in that the fear of Negroes trained to fight trying to free slaves no longer existed. Jack D. Foner says, "Although there is no evidence to indicate that black volunteers were any less disciplined than their white counterparts, the white press singled them out for special denunciation. Every incident involving blacks was made into a grave breach of discipline, while similar violations by whites were either overlooked or treated with tolerance and levity. It is evident that the "fourth estate" did not fail to unfairly indict Negroes, even in wartime."[119]

The effect upon military personnel policy was a decided change in the attitudes of Naval Officers and, a failure in government leadership.

Why the U.S. Navy acquired its "liberal stance" in its personnel policy on Negro enlistment caused heated arguments in my classes at the Naval Post Graduate School. As one well read White liberal student heatedly stated "Negroes helped free this country in the Revolutionary War. The U. S. Navy that defeated the British at the Battle of Lake Erie in the War of 1812 had 10% of its crew Negro. In the Civil War one fourth of the Navy was Black. We treated Negro enlisted men fairly and refused to discharge them when the Army did so."

It is hoped that via explanation of the forces at work in the broader community presented here will clarify why the Navy paid Negro loyalty with "shabby coin" after one hundred and eighteen years (1775-1893) of faithful service. The U.S. Navy is part of the U.S. social system and finally bowed to emergent racism. *

---

* For further clarification, the following three books are recommend:

1. "The Negroes Civil War", James M. McPherson
2. "The Negro Since the Emancipation", Harry Wish (Editor)
3. "The N.A.A.C.P.", C. P. Kellogg. (Pages 209-246)

CHAPTER 9. THE NEXT PUSH TOWARD A NAVAL POLICY BASED UPON RACE

1) THE U.S. GREAT WHITE FLEET ANNOUNCED TO THE WORLD THE U.S. AS A NEW IMPERIAL POWER: THE NEGRO EMERGED AS LOSERS

The Negro was not altogether without friends. According to Foner: "The New York Herald and The Cleveland Gazette said that the Navy had made a step backward and the Army and Navy Journal contended that the Navy was in violation of the Constitution."[120] This occurred on the return of the fleet and its triumphant parades and celebrations. Add to this the traditional tendency of Naval officers of this era to ignore "non-functional" directives from Washington and one may understand why little or no effort was made to implement this policy on any large scale until 14 years later. The first known application of this "new racism policy" was ruthlessly carried out on the eve of the "Great White Fleet's" world cruise (1907-1909). The fleet had assembled at Hampton Roads, Virginia. While lying in the Roads, word came from Washington informing the command that "tension between the United States and Japan had intensified."[121] There were many Chinese and Japanese stewards, cooks and Messmen embarked aboard ships of the Great White fleet. All Japanese in the Messmen category were summarily discharged, incident to friction between the U.S. and Japan.

This cruise required a maximum Messmen branch personnel effort. Shore-based units were probably already stripped to their bare bones. There was no time to recruit and give even basic training to new recruits. Nor did the departure time of the fleet allow recruiting, transporting and training Filipinos <u>or Guamanians, the most ready sources of needed servants</u>.

Personnel officers solved the problem by the ruthless abrogation of the rights of Negro seamen and ratings. As many Negroes as needed to fill the billets, left by departing Japanese personnel, were just as summarily ordered into the Messmen Branch. It is probably factual that this single act <u>ended the "old Navy policy of liberalism"</u> and set in motion the <u>actual</u> downgrading of the Negro people in the sea services. The U. S. Coast Guard seems to have rapidly followed by relegating Negroes to Messmen. According to Foner, "those Negroes who resisted this denigration and abrogation of Constitutional rights were coerced or beaten for their resentment and impudence. Many were put in the brig until time to sail. Charles F. Parnell, a Negro Petty officer, said bitterly after the world cruise in 1909. Everyone of us was transferred. We knew that the end of the colored man being anything in the Navy but a flunky had come."[122] This change, like all social change, however, did not occur as fast as Parnell perceived it. As previously mentioned, the final blow did not actually fall until WW I's <u>aftermath in 1919</u>.

2) THE BITTER RACIST CLIMATE IN THE POST WW I ERA CREATED A PERIOD SO DARK FOR THE NEGRO THAT THE "LILY-WHITE PROPONENTS" FELT FREE TO CARRY OUT THEIR FINAL ACTION OF NEGRO ELIMINATION

The climate in the United States in the post-WW I era was ripe for the final execution of the long ripening "policy of exclusion" of minorities from line branches of service. The summer of 1919, in the aftermath of WW I, was so bloody until it is known in U. S. history as the "Red Summer of 1919". Negroes did most of the bleeding. This brutal era seems to have been given impetus by the post-WW I perceptions of white men that "them 'uppity Niggers' that tasted equality in France have to be put back in their place." Whites proceeded as in a group-trance, characterized by behaviors that alternated between panic and paranoia, to ruthlessly and brutally re-establish the status quo. According to the NAACP, "This was a brutal era for Negroes in the civilian sector. Riots occurred at Longview, Texas, Knoxville, Tennessee. East St. Louis, Illinois, Chicago, Illinois, Omaha, Nebraska, Phillips County, Arkansas (City of Elain), Washington, D.C. and Charleston, South Carolina."[123]

Washington, D.C., the nation's capital experienced a race riot that lasted three days! The U.S. Army had to be called in to restore order. U.S. Marines and Navy sailors were the prime perpetrators. Navy sailors were also major participants in both the Chicago and Charleston, South Carolina riots.

Lynching escalated in the southwest, the south and Midwest, especially in Nebraska, Illinois, Indiana, Alabama, Texas, Louisiana and the Carolinas. In the normally "more civilized" southern state of Virginia the NAACP says, "There were 19 verified lynching's and 12 probable in one year, 1918."[124] Nor did the cheapness with which black lives were held end in the next two decades. All during this writer's early life (1922-1940) he heard and saw ignorant, poorly educated, poor whites swagger about the streets of Hope, Arkansas, bragging that "if you kill a good mule, ya hafta buy one. If you kill a nigger you can hire one." There were four lynching's in Hope. Two of these occurred in this WW I period. One victim was my father's friend. It is no wonder, in light of the virulent racist character of this era, that the services moved to downgrade Negroes. Where the Navy is concerned downgrading did not suffice. Naval policy caused the near eradication of Negroes from its roles. Negroes, as previously stated, were even barred from enlistment in the Stewards Branch in 1919 after World War I. The Navy, unlawfully, refused to reenlist Negroes who had served honorably. This rejection of Negroes and recruitment of Colonial persons of color account for the author's bosses on entering the Navy in 1940, being Philipinos and Guamanians.

The U. S. Navy and other branches of the Armed Forces are, after all, mere institutional components of the U. S. social system. It is, of course, the nature of systems that what happens to one part (civilian sector), affects, in varying degrees, all other components. The stage for eventual eradication of Negroes from Navy rolls had been carefully set in the prelude to WW I. As an example, when the Great White Fleet returned in triumph from its round-the-world cruise in 1909, no Negroes were allowed on parade. The Navy also barred Negroes from the national military review at New York in 1912. When Negro leaders and the press questioned this second attempt by the Navy to make Negroes invisible, Foner says, "On April 12, 1913, a number of New York leaders wrote to Secretary of the Navy Josephus Daniels. The Secretary responded that careful consideration would be given to 'the alleged discrimination against colored men in the naval service.' The communication was turned over to Rear Admiral Charles J. Badger, in Command of the Atlantic Fleet. On May 26, the New York Times reported, "Secretary of the Navy Daniels and Rear Admiral Charles J. Badger have completed an investigation of the charge of discrimination against colored enlisted men and find that the charge is unwarranted as there is no evidence of discrimination."[125] * Both Badger and Daniels conceded that <u>the only Blacks in the Navy were in the Messmen Branch. There were whites in that branch also but they were not all allowed to parade</u>. Then Badger claimed that only deck and gun crews were to parade. Both statements were poorly conceived lies as many Negroes served in the Fireman and Seaman ratings until, during and after WW I. Negro non-steward ratings were in charge of the USS Cumberland, barracks ship for all mess attendants at the Naval Academy, Annapolis, Maryland in 1940. This was this writer's first duty station as previously mentioned. As a matter of authority, a commanding officer could order any man he chose to parade, on pain of courts-martial if he refused. Until very recently, there was no power more absolute than that possessed by sea services captains. In fairness to them, there is no more awesome a responsibility. A bill was introduced in Congress in July 1914, which prohibited Blacks from serving as Commissioned Officers or Non-Commissioned Officers in the Army or Navy. This bill was killed in committee and never came to vote. In June 1916, while Black troops were engaged (10th cavalry) in the Mexican Expedition against Pancho Villa. Southern Congressmen sponsored a bill to eliminate Black soldiers and sailors from the Armed Forces by preventing the enlistment or re-enlistment of "any person of the Negro or colored race in the military services of the United States."[126]

3) NEGRO EXCLUSION IN THE AFTERMATH OF WW I (1919)

Negroes had a rare white friend in Newton D. Baker, Secretary of War. Baker fought this bill tooth and nail on grounds that Negro soldiers had proven that they were brave, intrepid and brought honor to the uniform in the fight at Carrizal, Mexico, as recently as June 21, 1916 (10th Cavalry, Company C., 10 killed).

In the bitter aftermath of WW I the military responding to the climate of the times, and an unsympathetic President Woodrow Wilson coldly, illegally and with ruthless precision paid Negro veterans with the "shabby coin" of denigration and discrimination based upon race. Jack D. Foner said of the services reactions to the civilian climate of this era:

> "The Air Corps totally rejected Blacks. There were no new line officers; the total number remained at two. The exclusion of Blacks from the Marine Corps remained complete. Not only were they unacceptable in uniform, but the Marine Corps headquarters in Washington refused to hire Blacks even as Messengers. Black Americans were enlisted in the Coast Guard only as menials, and from 1919 to 1932 the Navy virtually closed its doors to Black enlistment."[127]

It is pertinent to repeat here that in 1919 even Black stewards were barred. "Every one was doing it" was the rationale. But racist stigma has clung with greater tenacity to the Navy, than to any of the other services. This book does not allow for discussion all of the reasons why. Though not the complete reason, it is most certain that the Steward's/Messmen Branch played a major part in "setting the glue". To be sure, the Army has suffered more "racial incidents" and far more bloody ones than the Navy, yet the public seems to have a short memory where their Army is concerned. Negroes tend to have just as short a memory of past wrongs done to them by the Army. This is not so where the Navy is concerned. The probable reason seems to rest in the fact that the Army's incidents have tended to be sporadic. Consequently, they have been perceived in the collective mind, minorities included, as fleeting variables along the continuum of history. Unlike the Navy the Army had no definite branch, such as the Stewards, to act as a constant symbol of racist policy toward minority peoples. The total exclusion of Negroes in 1919, even the recruitment of Negro Messmen, proved unfeasible. As the "two-ocean Navy" concept moved from the drawing boards to reality, it became readily evident that enough menials to serve this vast organization could probably not be gotten from Guam or the Philippines. So a trickle of Negro Messmen were allowed to enter in 1932 in preparation for the manning of two ocean naval vessels, which were being built. <u>Further, Guam and The Philippines might be lost in a Pacific War.</u>

Like all naval history and tradition, which derived from the civilian merchant fleet, the Steward's or Messmen's branch has its roots there also. Even though the Steward's Branch (Messmen) was 'informally' established in April 1893 the policy <u>of strict</u> <u>restriction to that Branch was not actually fully enforced until many years later. Social change and political change is never instantaneous. This tendency to "overlap" probably accounts for Negro ratings still being on duty as late as World War II.</u>

As previously mentioned, it took from 1898 to 1907 and 1908 for the downgrading of Negroes to a servants role to lose its "gentlemen's agreement" existence. The discharge of all Japanese stewards, cooks and mess attendants, just before the sailing of the Great White Fleet in its around the world cruise, caused the "cat to let out of the bag". Here Naval Officers ruthlessly and unlawfully forced Negro Deck ratings into the Stewards Branch in order to replace the Japanese. The outcry of the Negroes made it impossible for the downgrading to be hidden because Southern Senators and Congressmen served longer terms in Washington than those of other regions, furthermore, as a result of seniority, they assumed Chairmanships of most of the Armed Force committees. They held the purse strings. This, combined with the disappearance of the old hard line Naval Officers who had bucked the Washington politicians at the end of four major wars, left the door open for the U.S. Navy to segregate and downgrade Negroes without cause. This enhanced the march toward Negro exclusion from enlistment and a possible lily-white Navy. This last attempt at "lily-whiteness" failed, incident to personnel needs of World War II.

CHAPTER 10. THE FORMATION OF THE MESSMEN/STEWARDS BRANCH (1893)

The Steward's branch, formerly the Messmen branch, historically has been a thorn in the side of the U. S. Navy. No branch of service in the U. S. Armed Forces has caused more bitterness, political strife and hatred. The reason for the problem in this particular branch rests with the end of traditional 'liberalism' in Navy policy towards minorities around 1907. This total retreat from liberalism occurred between the Spanish American War and WW I. The rise of Racism and bigotry is implicit in its birth. This, in the broader U.S. society, meant the rapid emergence of segregation, Black codes and brutal lynching of Negroes.

The United States Navy, in early American history, was formerly the most "liberal" branch of the U. S. Armed Forces and remained so, except for its officers corps, from the Revolutionary War to the Spanish American War. For example, the Navy did not obey Congress, in the post revolutionary period, which ordered service in the Armed Forces restricted to "able-bodied white males" by Act of Congress in 1792. For example, according to John P. Davis, "Joseph Ranger, an ex-slave who had won his freedom by service aboard five ships of the Virginia Navy during the war, remained in service for six years after its close. Some of the best pilots on the Atlantic Seaboard were Negroes born in the Albemarle Sound and Cape Hatteras areas. Further, ten percent of the sailors who fought under Oliver Hazard Perry at the battle of Lake

Erie in the War of 1812 were Black."[128] Again Congress, on February 18, 1820, the year of the Missouri Compromise at the end of the War of 1812, allowed to be issued from the Office of the Adjutant and Inspector General the following message: "No Negro or Mulatto will be received as a recruit of the Army."[129] Again the Navy stubbornly paid Washington no attention. The Navy traditionally had been a haven for freed Negroes, runaway slaves, Indians who broke tribal law and white men "on the lam." In 1845, the first surge of "Manifest Destiny", under President James K. Polk, which saw U. S. soldiers invade Mexico, for the first time in U.S. History, no black contingents were present. This is probably the only time in American history that a war was fought without the presence of sizable black units in the Army. This was due to the Army's obedience of the post-1812 order from Washington. There was, however, as proof of naval disobedience of this policy, Negro sailors, who were with the naval forces that took Vera Cruz. At the start of the Civil War, while the sages at Washington "hemmed and hawed" over whether to enlist Negroes, while its Army got shipped, Gideon Wells, Secretary of the Navy, ordered Negroes enlisted. Over 800 firemen in Farragut's river campaign were Negroes as early as the spring of 1862.

It is probably no accident that Americans produced the pragmatist school of philosophy; early naval officers were, perhaps unwittingly, most certainly members of this school. The core of the character of early American Naval commanders centered on this no-nonsense school--a school that respected only that which was practical. If a man could endure the harsh existence, brutality (cat-o'-nine-tails was used into the middle 19th century), bad food and not succumb to scurvy, he was unique in his own right. Early Naval officers, recognizing this, tended to judge men by their skills and their toughness--,"color be damned." These hardheaded, pragmatic men did not waste their time nor clutter their ship's rosters with such mundane factors as ethnicity or color. Rosters were written as to a man' s function. Men were listed as Gunners, Coopers, Carpenters, Landsmen, Seamen or Able Seamen, etc. Furthermore, Negroes and American Indians, via possibly genetic endowment, exhibited greater resistance to the scourge of "scurvy" than Whites. So, old Navy captains perceived them as men, dependable crewmembers.

This poses a problem to the scholar attempting to trace the history of Negroes in the Navy. Attempts to do original research in this area requires knowledge of what was in vogue as to the names applied to male "slave property" in the social period under study. In early America and the antebellum period of the south, one finds names for slaves taken from ancient Greece and Rome, such as Aristotle, Socrates, Cato and Caesar. This was later replaced by a given and a surname, usually that of the master to whom a slave or freed man belonged, or once belonged. Color bias does not tend to appear in the Navy's written records until the 19th century. The U. S. Navy's step "backward"[130] into racism-based personnel policy, which generated today's human resources management/race-relations problems, is historically of recent import and does not reflect early Navy policy. It is a gross injustice to early naval officers in identifying this group with the 20th century racist image acquired by their descendants. Those tough, practical men dared to place fighting capacity, skilled craftsmanship, combat effectiveness, toughness (a requirement) and mission above the color of their men's skin. There are no lofty journals, backed by an academic association, that could be said to assure academic rigor on this subject. Rather, a probe of materials possibly existent on the forgotten shelves of the Navy's own archives, studies that, until recently, were feasibly done quietly and held in strict censorship, as back copies of Negro newspapers and journals constitute the only real source. There is a reason for this that rests on the peculiar history of the Steward's branch and the politically volatile nature of its approximately 82 years of existence (1893-1975).

The Steward's branch, by its very birth, humiliated the Black race in the United States by relegating all persons of color, including, later the yellow and the brown, to be servants, regardless of intelligence, education, skin or craftsmanship, as an only mode of serving their country in the "sea service." Indians and Mexicans were exceptions, for the reasons that the Author has been unable to uncover. The birth of this branch also marks, historically, the first backward step by the Navy, from the most practical and liberal of all branches of the Armed Forces to possibly its most bigoted and most racist, with the exception of the Marine Corps. The Steward's branch has caused, politically, more harm to the public image of the Navy, and more pain to minority peoples, than all of the other branches combined, including the Naval officer's corps, which was not opened to minorities until WW II.

The fact that Negroes in the Army came home from France in WW I "covered in glory" brought the humiliating policy, pursued by the Navy, into sharp, antagonistic focus in the Negro community. The 8th Illinois was an all-Negro infantry regiment out of Chicago (re-designated the 370th Regiment). The 15th New York (369th) was another Negro infantry regiment out of New York City as part of the 93rd Division.* They returned from Europe, possibly, the most decorated units in the American expeditionary forces that served in Europe in WW I. Jack D. Foner, a contemporary author, says of these troopers, obviously unwanted by their own U. S. Army officers, except as laborers:

> "The four regiments of the 93rd Division were integrated into the French Army. Equipped as French units, carrying French rifles and eating French rations, they knew equality denied

---

* The 92nd was also an all Negro Division.

them by their own military. They operated in the area of the Meuse Argonne near Saint-Mihes Champagne, and in the Oise-Aisne offensive from the early summer of 1918 to the end of the war. The total casualties for the 93rd Division amounted to more than 3,000, with 584 killed-—a casualty rate of about 35 percent. The 369th alone lost 851 men in five days, and according to its commander that unit spent 191 days at the front, longer than any other regiment in the AEF. In that period the regiment reportedly never surrendered a foot of ground or had a prisoner taken. By the war's end, about 540 officers and men of the 93rd had been decorated by either the French or American government. Casualties for the 92nd Division amounted to more than 2,100, with 176 killed."[131]

These U. S. Negroes were the first allied soldiers to cross the Rhine River. The 369th Infantry received the Croix de Guerre en masse.[132] They were given a ticker tape parade up Broadway in New York on their return." According to the Negro Reference Book, the 371st and 372nd Regiments received this decoration also, France's second highest award. All that once proud Negro sailors could claim was, 'We Served good soup, kept the coffee hot and shoveled a lot of coal (many coal-burning ships were operated in WW I)'. Many of these older holdovers, who were not servants, were "beached" in the post-WW I era and placed in positions where they did not supervise white seamen.

When this writer entered the Navy in 1940, his first station of duty was the *USS Rheina Mercedes*. Negroes (over 300 mess boys) actually slept on the USS *Cumberland* at an adjacent berth. This was in order to comply with the criteria of "total-segregation". Our Petty Officers were all Negro relics of the bygone era of "Naval Liberalism" which died between 1898 (The Spanish American War) and 1919 (World War I). Among these were Chief Motor Machinist Mate Simmons and T. L. Crocker, Chief Commissary Steward, who later trained the Naval Academy Boxing Team. There were several others, Chief Commissary

Stewards Ray and McKinney, and First Class Machinist Joe Carter. These old men were "walking history books" on events leading up to the formation of the Steward's branch. They witnessed the reduction of Negroes, Orientals and Filipinos to Messmen in W W I, and the "force out and discharge" of non-White general service personnel in 1919, and suffered the frustration and humiliation of not being able to work in their rates because of their color. These were arrogant and proud men and their behavior toward us Messmen was ever ambivalent. They did not seem to know whether to scorn us, as symbols of their degradation, or feel sorry for themselves and us mess attendants, as Negro victims of circumstances. It is from these old men that this writer received much of his oral history. The Steward's Branch, after its birth, became a pawn in the power-game played by Negro leaders, who sought dignity and freedom, and status-quo racists. Both became so caught up in the game that they failed to understand, or care, what their actions did to the psyches and moral of the Stewards themselves. Secondly, they didn't grasp the effect upon the perceptions of the whites who observed the stigma attached to serving officers, and, finally, they did not see the actual importance of the branch as a factor in the Navy's mission. It has taken from 1893 to 1975 for this branch to become, truly, a part of the Navy. It to their demise as part of the Navy for knowledge of their role in Naval history to become known. They did not have eagles on their rating badges reinstated until mid W W II. The "Eagle" is the symbol of a Petty Officer's authority. Stewards and Cooks wielded authority minus this symbol. And, finally, for its real importance to be recognized by even the Naval officers, whom the Stewards served for 82 needlessly bitter years, most of the time served was under heart-rending conditions.

J. H. (Dick) Turpin related much of this to this writer. He was 79 years of age at that time and had been decorated twice. He was decorated in 1898 when the USS Main blew up at Havana and again when the USS Bennington blew up off San Diego in 1911. Dick retired as a Master Gunner, served 30 years in the Navy and for many years was Master Diver at the Bremerton Navy Yard. He co-invented the underwater cutting torch and was recalled in WW II as a Lieutenant Commander. It is to him that I owe much of my oral naval history.

I could understand clearly what Chief Turpin related to me about that era (1919-1932) as my first three years in the Navy was without the supervision of "White Chief Petty Officers". As I previously stated, there were three Negro Chief Commissary Stewards and the one Chief Machinist. There were also two First Class Ships Cooks and one First Class Machinist mate. These men had direct supervision of the more than two hundred Negro Mess Boys that served the Midshipmen at the Naval Academy, Annapolis. They wore Eagles on their rating badges, something that Chief Stewards were not allowed to wear until World War II. We Mess Boys only had dealings with White authority when we had screwed-up and had to go before the Mast for punishment. Then one had to face the White Chief and Captain. These men, my bosses, had not been allowed to work in their Rates since Negroes were barred from enlistment in 1919, as to do so was a no-no. They would have had to tell the White men what to do. Stewards and cooks were not allowed to boss White men in any way.

After over a century of bucking slave master, Congressmen and Senators, virtually their own government, to understand why the Navy, for pragmatic and practical reasons, decided to bow to the march of domestic racism, and to reduce Black men to mere servants requires a look backward. Reconstruction ended in 1877. The Messmen Branch of the Navy was created sixteen years after that brief experiment (1893). In that period the U.S. Navy reaped a harvest. The Civil War caused a vast leap forward in food service. How it was caused and what was needed to prevent "scurvy" from decimating ships' crews and infantrymen seemed to have been solved. In the past it had been seen as a crucial problem during the Civil War and its aftermath. The genetic endowment that caused Negroes and American Indians to be able to resist this disease, which could decimate whole Crews and Armies of Whites, seems to have been better nutrition. This fact weakened the arguments for continued "inclusion" of Indians and Negroes. While one door was closing, another was closing concomitantly, that of the rise of Racism and a definition of "place" for the 4,000,000 newly freed Black slaves. It was decided that they would never enjoy the equality with White men. Instead, they were to be discriminated against, segregated and lynched, if they failed to stay in their "place". It is this era in U.S. History that allowed the birth of the Messmen/Stewards Branch of the U.S. Navy and the assignment of the Negro to a servant's role.

Part IV.

Negroes in the U.S. Navy During the Spanish-American War (1898)

CHAPTER 11. THE INTENSIFICATION AND THE CONTINUED RISE OF RACISM: IT'S AFFECT UPON NAVAL PERSONNEL POLICY

The downgrading of the Negro intensified in the aftermath of the Spanish American War in 1898. The early pragmatic officers in the U.S. Navy, which had shielded Negroes in its enlisted ranks since its birth, finally bowed to the march of racism and Jim Crow. The U.S. Navy began to turn its back on the Negro in 1893, as previously stated, with the creation of the Messmen Branch. This effectively brought the navy in line with other institutions in the U.S. social system, most of which had already instituted segregation, discrimination, and Jim Crow policies, lynching and other laws, aimed at exploiting Negroes. The Civil War had checked that trend in the navy; and now, the need for men in the Spanish American War provided a momentary pause in the march to policies based on race.

1) THE POST SPANISH-AMERICAN WAR EXCELLERATION OF JIM CROW AND THE ACCOMPANYING MARCH OF SEGREGATION AND DISCRIMINATION IN THE NAVY

It is ironic that a Negro, Chief Gunner's Mate John Jordan, fired the first shot fired in the Battle of Manila Bay from Admiral Dewey's flagship, the U.S.S. Olympia. Racist senior military commanders, at this point in history, have failed miserably in getting past their own racist perceptions of the Negro and have preferred criticism of Negroes to truth and fairness.

For example, Theodore Roosevelt,* a former Under Secretary of the navy, the organizer of the "Rough Riders", and, later President of the United States, could not, with any consistency, tell the truth when it came to the Negroes behavior under fire in the Spanish American War. He told one story, and then when some political gain was at stake, he would describe the facts differently.

When assessing the Negro performance in the Spanish American War, one must understand that, probably the most disciplined and well-trained cadre of veterans in that war was black! Most of Theodore Roosevelt's Rough Riders were, indeed, "rough" in that they were untrained volunteers and former cowboys who knew little about battle tactics, cavalry or infantry. Roosevelt, who was more of a politician than he was a general, led them. These Negroes were regular U.S. Army veterans (9th and 10th Calvery, 24th and 25th Infantry), who had been on the western frontier fighting Indians for the past two decades. One of the worst blemishes on Roosevelt's record occurred when he disparaged the fighting capacity of Negro soldiers.

2) THE OVERT POLITICAL UTILIZATION OF RACE AND COLOR AT THE TOP OF THE U.S. POLITICAL LADDER AFTER THE SPANISH-AMERICAN WAR

• Roosevelt often lied in the name of political expediency, or engaged in distortion concerning the positive behavior of Negro soldiers who served in Cuba, as he sought the Presidency. This should not be a surprise, as the post-Civil War, United States, North and South, were on a binge-like search and demanded that the Negroes' "place" would be below that of White men

"For example, Theodore Roosevelt, who had earlier extolled the bravery of black troops in a widely publicized magazine article, now declared that they were 'peculiarly dependent upon their white officers', and that black noncommissioned officers generally lacked the ability to command and handle men, like the best class of whites."[133]

It would appear that Roosevelt, in order to secure victory in an upcoming election, stooped to the low level of telling other racist in this country "I am a racist too". Foner says of Roosevelt's disparagement of Negroes:

"He described an incident during the critical period of fighting at San Juan Hill, when the Spaniards were laying down an intense barrage of fire. Under the strain, 'none of the white regulars or Rough riders showed the slightest sign of weakening'. But he had to draw his revolver to stop a group of black infantrymen from fleeing to the rear. Faced with the threat of being shot if they did not return to the front, the black soldiers 'flashed their white teeth at one another, as they broke into grins and I had no more trouble with them."[134]

This would have been humorous had it not been for the pain that it caused Negro soldiers and civilians. For here is revealed the reality that Roosevelt often depicted in political posters. He sits astride his charger, standing in the stirrups, saber in hand, leading the charge up San Juan Hill. This was a farce. He led the charge from a safe position in the rear! The story further reveals that the Rough Rider leader did not know what was going on. It turns out that the so-called scared, cowardly Negroes fleeing to the rear consisted of an orderly detachment of Negro soldiers who had been ordered to the rear by a white officer. They came down to pick up more ammunition and trenching tools. This story almost caused the Republicans to lose the Negro vote, as it angered blacks all over the country. Booker T. Washington and other Negro leaders had to spend full time going about the country in an attempt to 'patch the pants' on account of Roosevelt's boo-boo. Prior to this, Roosevelt and Major General Nelson A. Miles had given unstinting praise to Negro soldiers for their service and gallantry in Cuba.

According to John Hope Franklin, "Sergeant Preston Holliday of the 10th Cavalry", writing in <u>The New York Age</u> on May 11, 1899, said that "The Negroes who were going to the rear had been ordered to do so by Lieutenant Fleming. They were to bring up rations and trenching tools and to carry wounded men to a safer place. Lieutenant Fleming, at the time, made explanation to Colonel Roosevelt."[135] Less than a year after the War, Roosevelt found it expedient to make these untrue remarks about Negro soldiers.

3) THE FAILURE OF THE PUBLIC OR THE NEWS MEDIA TO FAIRLY ASSESS THE PERFORMANCE OF NEGROES IN THE FIELD

Regardless of how the Negro performed beyond the seas, whether in Cuba or later in the Philippines, the preferred perception at home was always one of cowardice and stupidity. This was one of the most shameful periods in U.S. history as pertains to the treatment of the Negro soldier. Whether it was a northern newspaper or the Atlanta Journal, the newspapers and politicians grabbed anything that could be said to put the Negro fighting men down. Negroes must have appeared truly stupid for fighting for a country that allowed them to be abused and mistreated, in this manner.

The answer lies in the intelligence and strong desire of the Negro to not give white racist absolution in their need to perceive Negroes as inferior. Consequently, Negro leaders, throughout this country's history, confounded racist by encouraging Negroes to fight in its wars. It was a way of making liars out of those whites who said that Negroes were not men. Franklin also says "It has been claimed by many that the 9th

and 10th Cavalry saved the Rough Riders from complete annihilation at Las Guasimas. One southern white officer said, "If it had not been for the Negro Cavalry, the Rough Riders would have been exterminated. I am not a Negro lover. My father fought with Mosebys Rangers and I was born in the south. But the Negroes saved the fight and the day will come when General Shafter will give them credit for their bravery."[136] As far as we can tell, the General never did so.

This clearly validates the contention that regardless of the Negro's gallantry, bravery or willingness to shed his blood for the United States, this country has never found a majority of white Americans willing to grant them laudatory praise. Instead, Negro fighting men have, historically had to fight two wars. The <u>first</u> is against America's enemies. The <u>second</u> one is against the deeply embedded racism, ever present in this society.

John Hope Franklin is almost dismissive of the Negroes naval service in the Spanish American War. He says, " The service that Negroes rendered in the navy was relatively inconsequential because they were employed primarily in menial capacities. He does mention Elijah B. Tunnell, who was killed aboard the *U.S.S. Winslow*, which was under fire from shore batteries at Cardenas."[137] Charles Blatcher tells us, "Six black soldiers were awarded the Medal of Honor for valor in the Spanish American War.

The White public greeted the black veterans with mixed emotions. Some were greeted with speeches and parades; and a few were assaulted and lynched. Charles Young, the third black graduate from West Point, was the highest-ranking black officer to serve in the Spanish American War. Prior to World War I, Colonel Young was forced into retirement". Young was given a medical discharge. He rode his horse from Chillicothe, Ohio, to Washington, D.C. in order to prove his fitness for duty. The Army grudgingly assigned him to the Ohio National Guard. The government later sent him to Liberia to help train that county's army. He contacted one of the numerous fevers there and died."[138]

THE MALTREATMENT OF RETURNING NEGRO SOLDIERS AND THE DEATH NELL OF RECONSTRUCTION

Jack D. Foner tells us that beginning in 1899, troops were mustered out of the volunteer service:

> "...Black volunteers, after being officially discharged, returned to their homes by troop train. As discharged soldiers, they were subjected to local police rather then the Provost General. When the train carrying the 3rd North Carolina from Macon reached Atlanta, members of the police force climbed on board and engaged in "much clubbing". As a result, the train that pulled out of Atlanta for Raleigh contained "many bloody heads". Another assault upon black troops occurred in Tennessee. When a train carrying the 8th Tennessee (or U.S. VI) reached Nashville, black soldiers were asleep in their coaches. About 75 policemen and 200 civilians entered the cars with pistols and clubs and proceeded to beat the men "over their heads and bodies". A sheriff who participated in this affair stated gleefully "it was the best piece of work I ever witnessed...inspiring...And if a darkie even looked mad, it was enough for some policeman to bend his club...over his head."[139]

Three years after the Spanish American War, Hiram R. Revels died at Holly Springs, Mississippi. George H. White then became the last Negro holdover from the Reconstruction period. He had been elected from North Carolina in 1896 and, again, in 1898. He was aware that he would not be elected again. Politically, he was the last vestige of the effort of Reconstruction. Congressman White's farewell address to the Congress gives an insightful look at the political atmosphere of Washington and its effects.

"When White rose in Congress on that day in 1901, men shifted in their seats to get a better look at him. For better or for worse, they would not be seeing the likes of him again soon... He reviewed the whole dreary story... the rise of Negro political power, the undermining of Reconstruction, the gutting of the fourth amendment, and the birth of Jim Crow. "Now, he said the circle had come full cycle". And, so it was time for goodbye. White went on to say, "This, Mr. Chairman, is perhaps the Negro's temporary farewell to the American Congress; but let me say, phoenix-like, he will rise up someday and come again. These parting words are in behalf of an outraged, heart broken, bruised and bleeding, but god-fearing people. (They are) faithful, industrious, loyal, rising people—full of potential force."[140]

It would be over half a century before this prophecy would be fulfilled. What Congressman White failed to say was that the Negro's road would be long and hard. That the brutality and discrimination he faced would seriously challenge his survival as a people.

But survive as a people they did. They mastered the art of survival both physically and psychologically as a people, in spite of the constant assault of racism. They survived physically in a country that allowed "lynching's"—another term for "murder to go unpunished". The historical period between the Spanish American War of 1898 and World War I (1918) was possibly the darkest period in the history of the United States if we exclude the post-War period which was so brutal it became known as "The Red Summer of 1919". Not just lynching but Serious Race Riots reached literally across country.

CHAPTER 12. THE PROUD HISTORY OF THE STEWARD'S BRANCH

The Steward's Branch of the U. S. Navy was established on April 1, 1893, as the last residue of the Reconstruction period came to a close As Negroes were disenfranchised in U. S. society, moves to downgrade them in the service also emerged. The establishment of the Steward's Branch did not bear the official sanction of Congress. Instead, its implementation was done in clandestine secrecy. The Author has found no "written orders" that accompanied its inclusion in the Navy personnel structure. Tradition was already in place, so "verbal instructions" were passed that ordered all new recruits to be restricted to the Steward, Messboy and Cook categories. All others were to be mustered out until no Negroes existed in the line-ratings. This effort at "regulation via gentlemen's agreement" seems to have fallen flat on its face, probably due to, again, the hardheaded, practical characteristics required for command at sea. It would appear that those naval officers who possessed "crack Negro ratings" simply ignored the order. Proof of this may be found in the fact that Negroes fought in line branches of service, five years later, in the Spanish American War of 1898.

However, the history of the Steward's Branch did not really begin in 1893. It had years of historical precedence that lie buried in tradition and necessity. Life at sea, at best, during the 17th, 18th and 19th centuries was harsh. One of the greatest sources of irritation and bad morale at sea was the lousy quality of the food. Early New Englanders, like their English forebears, were probably the world's worst cooks. Unlike the

French, they possessed little tradition of the gracious living aspects of good cuisine. New Orleans and Charleston were two of the few centers in early America where a decently prepared meal could be found. It was a lucky sea captain, indeed, who possessed a runaway slave or freedman who had been trained or exposed to this French culinary tradition in one or the other ports. Or one who had been a "house Negro" in one of the upper-class homes, and whose owner happened to be well traveled and knew European culinary arts.

If a cook could take the hardtack, salt pork, beef and sometimes salt-horse and potatoes and other coarse fare and make it palatable he was, in spite of color, a valuable and cherished member of any crew. Since many merchant ships captains, during the sailing ship era, often carried their wives to sea with them. A well-trained cook and steward was a prized and welcome addition. It was one of these stewards and cooks who gave the Union forces in the Civil War their first hero and a badly needed boost to their morale.

After the humiliating surrender of Union forces at Fort Sumpter in Charleston Harbor, the South moved rapidly in getting ships to sea. Their Privateers were soon raiding Union shipping. Although we told this story earlier, it bears repeating in this context. In June, 1861, the Schooner S. J. Waring, bound out of New York for South America, was captured at sea by the rebel privateer Jeff Davis, who put a prize crew aboard consisting of a Captain, a Mate and four seamen.

The Negro who acted as Steward and Cook on the *Waring*, William Tillman, was tersely told that he was the property of the Confederate States and was to be sold when the vessel reached Charleston. The Negro had other plans. His plans did not include submitting to being sold back into slavery on the Charleston "auction block." That night Tillman took the hatchet used to cut firewood, killed the prize-crew captain, clobbered the mate and took his pistol. With pistol in hand

Tillman rounded up the four rebel seamen and placed them in irons. After seizing control of S. J. Waring, Tillman freed the other two black Waring crewmen, reversed course and pointed the *Waring's* nose toward New York where he arrived five days later.

The Stewards and Messmen branch has derived its roots from the civilian merchant fleet as did most U.S. Naval history and tradition. Approximately a year later, in the wee hours of the morning of May 13, 1862, Robert Smalls, a slave, stole the confederate gunboat Planter. He piloted it out of Charleston Harbor and surrendered it and its valuable cargo to the Union Navy. Smalls and his crew received one-half the Planter's prize money. He served as pilot of the Planter and other vessels of the blockading forces throughout the Civil War. Probably Smalls would have failed miserably without the intelligence furnished by stewards who served the commanding officer and his staff on the Planter. Only these men knew the movement of the Planter's officers.

My first station of duty was the U. S. Naval Academy's "lost battalion", the Messmen. Administratively, we came under the CO of the Severn River Naval Command. He and his staff were berthed aboard the *USS Rhenia Mercedes*, a Spanish cruiser and trophy, sunk and re-floated at Santiago, Cuba in 1898. This served as berthing for all whites. All Negroes (200 plus and later 300) were berthed across the pier on the *USS Cumberland*, a relic of the days of steam vs. sail, but we went to mast aboard the Rhenia. My first trip to mast was enlightening. The Captain asked black Joe Carter (1st Class Machinist and Master-at-Arms), a holdover from the earlier Negro line group, "Joe, what has this Nigger done?' Joe went into his Uncle Tom act (he saluted the Captain three times) and I received five days "cake and wine" (bread and water). This was the fall of 1940 and correctly indicates the position of Negro Messmen on the eve of WW II. My crime was "silent contempt," a phrase that I had to look up in a dictionary. In rapid succession, the

Navy underwent massive changes, mind-boggling in their rapidity, with negative conceptual effects upon the minds of Negro Messmen.

WW II occurred December 7, 1941. Suddenly, Negro leaders brought the Messmen Branch under intense fire. As pawns in the game of Negro equality vs. White status quo and tradition. We, in our ignorance and with little understanding as to why, caught unmitigated hell. We already were prime targets for "red necks". Now we became targets of scorn and ridicule by our own people, fellow Negroes.

Due to racist reaction to Negro equality in France during the war, white hatred in the aftermath of WWI, a Congress that turned its back, three uncompassionate Presidents (Coolidge, Wilson and Hoover), and the general social climate, the stage was set. We were frozen in the nebulous vice of tradition. Yet Negroes represented a red-flag-like constant, a target at which militant Negro groups could aim in their efforts to secure equal treatment for minority servicemen (NAACP effort is not limited to Blacks).

Further, Negro leaders found the new Secretary of the Navy, Frank Knox from Tennessee, just as intractable on the issue of racial equality as his predecessor, Josephus Daniels. Here it is relevant that the reader understand the time sequence between the advent of WWII and the rapidity with which the new, astute Negro leaders launched their attack on the services and their discriminatory policies. The devastating raid at Pearl Harbor, which caused U.S. entry into WWII, occurred on December 7, 1941. According to Lerone Bennett:

> 'In January 1941, A. Phillip Randolph, the President of the Brotherhood of Sleeping Car Porters, advanced the idea of 100,000 Negroes marching on Washington. By June, Negroes all over the United States were making preparations to entrain for Washington."[141]

Randolph exemplified the new political sophistication of the Negro leadership forged in the bitter aftermath of WWI. Walter White of the NAACP, Channing H. Tobias, T. Arnold Hill of the Urban League and men such as A. Phillip Randolph led the Negro community. With a more enlightened constituency, they let Washington know that Negroes would no longer willingly serve in its armed forces, while being treated as second-class citizens by their country. We were really confused. For example, we knew of no other way of Negro service, than that of segregation and discrimination.

It is said that Franklin D. Roosevelt sat in shocked silence when he heard of this plan. After all, he had a good "track record" in the Negro struggle and, in fact, was the only President since 1919 to even address himself to the deplorable condition of America's Negroes. The spectacle of 100,000 Negroes marching in the Capital, in wartime, could not be tolerated. President Roosevelt got in touch with Fiorello LaGuardia, Mayor of New York, and Eleanor Roosevelt, his wife, and asked them to try to dissuade A. Philip Randolph, in his march on Washington. They failed. Randolph had been jailed in WWI for advocating Negro refusal to serve in the Armed Forces. He had taken on the railroad's powerful Pullman Company and in a ten-year fight won the right to a Union.

Invited to Washington by the President (June 18, 1941) he proved just as intractable. Randolph said, "Something has to be done now!" Roosevelt, being both an astute and practical politician, asked Walter White if Randolph was "bluffing." White said no. He next asked, "What do you want?" Randolph stubbornly replied, "Equal work opportunities in war industry and equal treatment of Negroes in the Armed Forces." The end result was that the President issued Executive Order #8802, which forbade racial and religious discrimination in war industries, government-training programs and government industries, on June 25th.

Randolph called off the scheduled march on Washington the same day. Bennett has said of Randolph: "Asa Philip Randolph is one of the most remarkable Negro leaders in American history. His march on Washington gambit was certainly one of the most brilliant "power plays" ever executed by a Negro leader."[142]

Before departing from this area of colorfulness, service, and style of stewards, as individuals, I would like to address a few words to those White and Black commissarymen who will have to interact more closely with Filipino and Guamanian contingents in the rating, in the event Commissary and Steward ratings are merged.

The Filipino's are not the docile "houseboys" that Hollywood movies would have you believe them to be. Neither their history nor their heredity supports such an ignorant mythology. The same applies to the Guamanians. This writer can speak with some authority to this issue having worked and lived with the two groups for over a 21-year period and through two wars. Nor did I learn of the fighting capacity of Filipinos recently.

I learned of it as a child in my native home, Hope, Arkansas, from old Negro men, Veterans of the 9th and 10th cavalry. These old men, instead of going to New York with Theodore Roosevelt and his "Rough Riders", for a ticker-tape parade after San Juan Hill in 1898, were sent from Cuba to the Philippines to put down the *Aguinaldo Rebellion*. It is they who told me why the 45 automatic pistol was invented. To you who do not know, it was invented because neither the 44 nor 38 caliber pistols could stop the tenacious Moro fighting men. These men were known to continue to charge and kill after being hit six times by ordinary pistols of that era (1898).

The 45 caliber was designed to knock these forebears of the Filipino down. In the veins of the Filipino flows some of the fiercest fighting blood on this planet. These so-called "little Brown men" are descendants of fierce Malay tribesmen from Southeast Asia and Indonesia, Negritos, Chinese merchants, pirates, Spaniards and Americans, none of whom are known for their docility or willing subservience.

Historically, the man who discovered the Philippines, Ferdinand Magellan (1521), lost his life as a direct result of underestimating the fighting capacity of Filipinos. Magellan took advantage of a quarrel between two rival chieftains in order to strike awe in the minds of the Filipinos. In a joint assault on Macatan Island, Magellan told the Filipino contingent to stand aside. He wanted them to see how Spaniards fought. He set fire to the Filipino village. Angry Filipinos led by Chief Datu Sayu defeated the Spaniards, armor and all. Magellan, known to history as the first White man to "circumnavigate the globe," did not do so. He was slain by Filipinos at Macatan Island. Juan de Saicedo returned to Spain with Magellan's last surviving ship. When Spain conquered the Mariannas Islands they had to nearly carry out an act of genocide in the attempt to subjugate the Chammors—the fierce fighting natives of Guam.

In World War II, the Japanese learned that Guam was one of the worse islands to conquer and/or govern. The Chinese members of this branch were not docile, none-war-like peoples. Most of them had witnessed the European colonization of parts of China and many had participated in the resistance. However, even the Chinese had to eat. So, many ended up signing onto U.S. ships on the China Station in the post-colonial period. This was the source of Senior Cooks and Stewards when the author entered the Navy.

As for the Black Messboys, Cooks and Stewards, the story is one of a constant fight for survival. When one really researches the history of Black men and the United States Navy, he or she is in for a surprise. For example, White students, even those with Degrees in history, had bought into the recent naval history that the U.S. Navy had "always" been a racist organization. My students at the Naval Post Graduate School were surprised to learn that for its first 100 years, the Navy, except for its officers corps, was one of the most liberal institutions in American life. The "sailing" Navy, unlike the "steam" Navy, allowed no mistakes. The sea, in the days of sail, was a harsh place, where one mistake could prove disastrous and possible lost of a ship. Recognizing this, only hardheaded, practical men rose to command. They looked at a man's skill, competence, ability and whether he could be depended upon in a fight, rather than the ridiculousness of what color he happened to be. This luxury came about with the coming of steam navigation and its comparative increase in safety. The unforgiving harshness of the sea, in the day of the sail ship, did not allow for the luxury of placing men via their color rather then their character and ability to perform. Racism in this milieu was simply impractical, a liability.

CHAPTER 13. WORLD WAR I AND THE FINAL PUSH FOR A "LILY WHITE" NAVY

World War I, more than any other war, validated the contention that the United States advanced technologically, economically, and politically, but defied all logic in moving backward socially and legally. The judiciary had sunk to a new low. It had allowed the bulwark of new Negro freedom, the 14th Amendment, to be trampled. It outlawed the "grandfather" clause, but allowed states to use this instrument in ways that used it as a loophole, which prevented Negroes from voting in 1915, but failed to put any teeth in the law. Southern States simply moved on to literacy tests, lynching's and riots as tools for Negro disenfranchisement. The United States entered the war on April 6, 1917. To understand the social and political conditions created, let's look at the violence level. Martial law had to be declared in the East St. Louis race riot, which raged from July 1st to the 3rd. An accurate count of the number of Negroes killed is not available. Lerone Bennett estimates the number as between 20 and 200. "On July 28th of that same year, 10,000 Negroes marched down Fifth Avenue in New York City in silent protest against lynching and other racial indignities."[143]

On the military side, things came to a head on August 23, 1917 when long suffering Negro soldiers of the 24th Infantry Regiment rioted at Houston, Texas. The 24th Infantry Regiment, veterans of the Indian wars, Spanish American War and the Philippine Insurrection, led by Aguinaldo, had been relegated to "guard duty" at Camp Logan, a National Guard training camp. The riot was a result of the white citizens, along with the police, being allowed to abuse and mistreat black soldiers when they were off duty. Two Negroes and 17 whites were killed. Jack Foner details how the army reacted. He tells us:

> "Between October and late <u>November 1917, sixty four black soldiers</u> were Court Martialed at Fort Sam Houston for murder and mutiny. After the most "perfunctory trial", <u>thirteen of them were sentenced to death, forty-two received life sentences, four were given long prison terms</u> and five were acquitted. Details of the Court Martial, as well as the verdict, were not made public until after dawn on the morning of December 11, <u>when thirteen men sentenced to death, had been summarily and secretly hanged without a review of the sentences by either the President or the War Department since military law specified that the area commander had final authority in time of war.</u> However, the attorney for the NAACP insisted that this provision applied only to troops in action. <u>The northern press joibla ned southern newspapers in justifying the execution of the thirteen blacks.</u>"[144]

This would tend to validate the Author's contention that "Racism was and is a national phenomena."

This action was carried out by the Army mostly on the words of the abusers...the police and civilian mob members! The U.S. Army, true to historical tradition, did not come to seek justice. They, as usual, came to blame and persecute their own soldiers, Negro soldiers. No record has been found where the state of either Texas or the Federal Government charged any of the white mob members with breaking the peace or any other crime. One of the black soldiers, knowing that he would not receive any justice, committed suicide prior to the trial. Foner goes on to say:

> "In a speech at Brooklyn's St. Augustine Church, the Reverend Dr. George F. Miller condemned the speedy executions as a military lynching to placate the South. In two additional trials,

sixteen more men were condemned to death and twelve received "life terms". Black organizations, especially the NAACP, worked to mitigate the harsh sentences imposed by the military. In February1918, the NAACP presented a petition with 12,000 names, to President Wilson, asking clemency for the condemned men. In response, the President agreed to review. As a result, 10 of the death sentences were commuted to life imprisonment. The other six were hanged. All told, the War Department indicted 118 men and convicted all but 8 who testified against the others in return for a promise of immunity. <u>Nineteen were hanged and sixty-three received life sentences</u>."[145]

According to Foner, Woodrow Wilson was no friend of the Negro. "In 1921, President Harding, after receiving a petition containing 50,000 signatures, reduced the sentences of those still imprisoned. A majority of the men had been released from prison by 1924. But it was not until 1938 that the last soldier was freed."[146]

As Negro soldiers fought to free white men in Europe, American racist fought just as hard to make sure that the Negro did not forget his "place". In Chester, Pennsylvania, on July 25 through 28, 1917, a race riot cost the lives of five people; and in Philadelphia, the "city of brotherly love", four were killed and 60 injured on July 26 through 29. Even a war failed to allow the whites in the United States to momentarily forget their need to persecute the Negro. Despite all of the negatives arrayed against him, the Negro soldier performed admirably beyond the seas.

Before we begin this assessment, we must understand that the U.S. Army, the President or Congress did very much in the way of securing, training and equipment to ensure the battlefield success of the Negro soldier. In fact, the Army Generals did just the opposite! That the Negroes fought at all in the war was not due to any change in attitude of the Generals who ran the Army. If they had their way, Negroes would have been confined to hard labor in various activities such as stevedores, ditch digging and hauling supplies. The Army also held the mistaken belief that southern white men should be assigned to command Negro troops because they were more capable of handling them. Underlying this was the unspoken belief that they were hard drivers of Negroes capable of exacting maximum production, being descendants of slave owners. These gentlemen, ostensibly, knew the Negroes place and could keep him in it.

In the aftermath of the brutal, unfair treatment of the 24th Infantry at Houston, the Negro community still simmered in anger. Many Negro leaders, among who was A. Philip Randolph, a young activist and labor leader, and Chandler Owen, a law student at Columbia University, preached against Negroes joining the Army. These two men were socialist, and co-editors of a magazine called "The Messenger". Through it, they issued fiery diatribes against Negro participation. The situation was not helped by ignorant racist in the ranks of the Generals. Foner says:

> "The war would see an intensification of the armed forces racist orientation and further deterioration in the status of the black soldier and sailor. Military leaders now came to believe that the ability to serve in combat was largely a matter of race and that blacks were not suited to such a role. If used at all, their service should be limited to that of labor troops in the army and menial tasks in the navy."[147]

He gets down to the heart of the matter when speaking of actual Army policy. He says, "The general white policy was to make use of blacks to help fight the war, but to do so in ways that reinforced rather than denied the conception of them as inferior, and not fit to serve as equal men."[148] Newton D. Baker, Secretary of War, faced a dilemma; he had to placate both backward, racist Generals and Admirals, and an angry divided Negro community whom he needed for total mobilization. The rivalry between the Booker T. Washington and W.E.B. Dubois camps seemed to have cooled after Washington's death in 1915. Dubois went along with the NAACP in support of the war, but Baker had to make a positive move in order to get the majority of Negroes to support the war. Negroes would not just be needed as troops, but also as workers in agriculture to feed an army of this size, and as financial contributors in the war bond effort to finance the war. So Baker consulted with Negro leaders. According to John Hope Franklin:

> "Because of the mounting race friction which attended the Negro migration to the north, the continued lynching of men and women, and the German propaganda which was circulated in the United States, (Baker) deemed it wise to bring into government a Negro...who enjoyed the confidence of his people. Consequently, the Secretary of War announced on October 5, 1917, the appointment of Emmet J. Scott, who for eighteen years had been the secretary to Booker T. Washington. He was to be Special Assistant to the Secretary of War and would serve as confidential advisor in matters affecting the interests of the ten million Negroes in the United States and the part they were to play in connection with the present war."[149]

Franklin goes on to point out that this appointment caused Newton D. Baker to be widely commended. This seemed to counter the negative assertion made earlier by him that the Army had no intention to solve the so-called race problem. As if Baker was not experiencing enough problems with racist Generals, Admirals, a Southern born President,

Woodrow Wilson, and an unsympathetic Congress, the Senate and the Draft Boards posed yet another problem. They played racist "games" in the middle of his efforts to supply the needed manpower through a massive mobilization. The draft legislation contained no specific racial provisions. Foner points out that the same Board registered both black and white draftees. Also, "Baker assured the NAACP that the army would be free of racial discrimination and that black soldiers would be justly treated."[150] Newton D. Baker thought he could assure this. He was badly mistaken. Where, through his role as Secretary, he could apply a modicum of pressure on the military, here, he was dealing with racist civilians and local governments who were under the assumed protection of States Rights. They, historically, did what they pleased with the Negro, law be-damned! Jack D. Foner says:

> "The local Draft Boards registered and classified both blacks and whites...In spite of Bakers assurances, blacks confronted gross prejudice and discrimination at every stage. The local Draft Boards exercised wide discretion in deciding who would be drafted and who would be deferred. Deferrals were composed almost exclusively of whites. Across the nation, local boards required registrants of "African Descent" to tear off one corner of their registration questionnaires so that they could be more easily identified. The boards eventually accepted a greater proportion of black registrants than whites for military service...because of their advantaged economic positions, more whites qualified for occupational deferment. Many single whites with practically no dependents were granted exemptions, while black men with large families dependent on them for support were drafted."[151]

34.1% of the blacks were accepted for drafting while only 24% of the whites were. Blacks constituted 9% of the registrants, but 13% of the draftees! Foner goes on to say that a larger percentage of blacks were also found <u>physically qualified</u> for general military service, 74.6% of blacks against 69.7 % of whites. Draft Boards regularly inducted blacks that were physically unfit while excluding whites with similar disabilities. Foner further says:

> "No wonder Randolph complained. The Negro is tubercular, syphilitic, and physically inferior for purposes of degrading him, but physically fit and superior when it comes to sending him to the front to save white men's hides."[152]

So, as usual, black men had to fight on three fronts; 1) against racist draft boards, 2) then against the army charged with training, berthing and equipping him and 3) to prevent the army from placing him in labor battalions rather than in fighting units. The Negroes did most of the sweating while whites sat on their butts or did the strutting when not in the field. In spite of Emmet J. Scott's best efforts, his answering of hundreds of complaints, his proper liaison with the NAACP, Urban League, and black churches; he was often stymied by the realities. While Negroes were barred from the Marine Corps and served in the navy in the most menial capacities, they served in almost every branch of the army except the Air Corps. John Hope Franklin dismisses Negro participation in the navy and marines with one sentence: "nothing to report!"

Negroes were given lousy, castoff equipment. They were sent for training to the most run-down camps. Many froze to death or succumbed to disease. The army went along when southern whites objected to the presence of Negro troops in their areas. The extremely racist press aided, abetted and helped influence the areas that Negroes were sent to in the south for training. "Blacks entitled to deferments were railroaded into the army, while whites with no legitimate excuse for exemption were allowed to escape the requirements of the draft system. In parts of the south, black sharecroppers were not drafted if the planters they worked for filed requests for their exemption, while independent black farmers, with large families were arbitrarily drafted. Out of 815 white registrants in Fulton County, Georgia, the local draft board exempted 526. Only *six* out of two hundred and twelve registered blacks were exempted from service. In that case, Secretary Baker suspended the board for violations and appointed new members.

The lot of Negro soldiers was one of harassment by white civilians with the U.S. Army usually on the side of the civilians. Foner, quoting

W.E.B. Dubois as saying, "Major General Charles C. Ballou, in command of the 92nd Division, had served in the ill-fated 24th Infantry Regiment that suffered the disaster at Houston. He was one of those officers previously mentioned "who knew how to handle Negroes". Whenever any occasion arose where trouble occurred between white and colored soldiers, the burden of proof always rested on the colored man."[153] For example, Ballou issued a command directing officers and men to refrain from going "where they were not wanted, regardless of legal rights". This Directive, known as Bulletin No. 35, resulted from an incident in Manhattan, Kansas. The manager barred a black sergeant stationed at nearby Camp Funston from entering a local theatre, even though his exclusion violated a Kansas Law prohibiting discrimination. Admitting that the theatre manager was legally wrong in denying the sergeant admission, the bulletin claimed that, nevertheless, the sergeant was "guilty of a greater wrong in doing anything, no matter how legally correct, that would provoke racial animosity". It concluded with the warning: "White men made the Division, and they can break it just as easily if it becomes a troublemaker".

Further validation of the fact that the army's senior officers had neither faith nor respect for Negro men, as soldiers or simply as men, can be found in their behavior towards even proven veterans. Further, they held deeply, the racist myth that the Negro was unfit, due to a lack of intelligence, for leadership as officers. Because they believed this myth, they conned themselves into believing that fellow Negroes also believed this, and, consequently, a "Negro would not obey another Negro"; only white men could command Negro units! Due to the ingrained white attitudes and belief in the innate inferiority of the Negro, quite a lot of confusion as to how to best use the Negro existed. The record from history was that if given a chance to fight, he would probably fight on a level that required recognition. The U.S. Army solved this dilemma by making sure that combat ready blacks not be allowed to go overseas.

Foner tells us that "None of the four black regular army regiments saw combat, as a unit, in France during World WWI. Instead, regiments were kept at stations in the United States and its island territories, while a large percentage of soldiers were used to provide non-commissioned personnel for the two all Negro (92nd and 93rd) Divisions."[154] This, it was probably assumed, would deny the Negro a chance at earned battlefield glory and ensure his failure as a soldier. Franklin points out a shining example of the Army's chicanery. He says: "The problem of training Negro soldiers while in the United States was one that plagued the War Department from the beginning of the struggle. While the Army was committed to the activation of an all Negro Division, the (92nd), no arrangements were made to train the men at the same camp. Thus, the men of the all-Negro division were trained at <u>seven widely separated camps</u>; all the way from Camp Grant in Rockford, Illinois, to Camp Upton in New York."[155] I have not been able to find, in researching U.S. Army history, a situation where any other divisions were sent to the front without its units ever maneuvering or practicing together as a whole. Another Negro Division, the 93rd, was never brought up to full strength; and after training in different locations, units were organized and sent overseas at different times to join various fighting units of the French Army."

This design for failure backfired. How does a military entity, Regiment or Division, develop identity, image or esprit de Corps under these conditions? The Negro in World War I did so, however, which is a tribute to the resilience and common sense of the Negro people. They did not participate in their attempted contrived failure, by the Government.

One of the foremost and exasperating problems for the Secretary of War, the country and the Negro was the behavior of racist elements in U.S. society. Negro historians, including Lerone Bennett, Carter G. Woodson, John Hope Franklin, Jack D. Foner, and Richard J. Stillman all agree on this.

They devoted extensive space to the racist behavior of whites in their writings. This behavior retarded the war effort and attempted to destroy Negro morale prior to and during World War I. Even while Negroes were being trained to fight for this country, racist southern communities demanded the luxury of "NIMBY", or "not in my back yard". At the start of the mobilization, when a southern community raised a ruckus because Negro troops were to be stationed for training near them, politicians complained and the Army responded by moving them somewhere else.

This was costly, stupid, and it severely retarded the war effort. A big conference was held in Washington, D.C., to deal with the problem in August of 1917. At first, the War Department presented the feeble and ridiculous argument that Selectmen (or draftees) must have the privilege of being trained in their own areas of muster. But as mobilization needs rapidly escalated, the inefficiency of this became apparent to the Secretary of War, and even racist Congressmen and Generals. In the end, troops, regardless of their color, were sent north and south to wherever an open facility and billet existed. The friction between Negro soldiers and white civilians became a first order of magnitude problem. Racism permeated every facet of American existence. Space does not permit examination of all U.S. institutions, so we will concentrate on one, the Christian church.

The Bible, a canon that claims the moral high ground in guiding human conduct, ostensibly governs the Christian church. Negroes organized the Federal Council of Churches to investigate and report on the treatment of soldiers. According to Franklin, "Complaints flooded the War Department that Negroes were being continuously mistreated and insulted by white officers. They referred to Negroes as "coons, Niggers, and darkies", and frequently forced them to work under unhealthy, laborious conditions…(they) made it extremely difficult for them to advance…(they) indiscriminately assigned them to labor Battalions. The friction between Negro soldiers and military police, and between white and Negro soldiers continued until the end of the war." Franklin tells us:

> "At Camp Green near Charlotte, North Carolina, they found that there were five Y.M.C.A buildings but none for the 10,000 Negroes. A sign over one of the buildings read, "This building is for whites only". At Camp Lee near Petersburg, Virginia, white soldiers patrolled the ground around a prayer meeting to see that no Negroes attempted to enter. According to these Rednecks, Jesus was for white folks. When the 15th New York, later named the 369th, was sent to Spartanburg, South Carolina, white citizens decided that these uppity New York Negroes needed to be reminded of their "Place" In October, 1917, when Noble Sissle, the talented drum major of the infantry band, went into a hotel to purchase a newspaper, the proprietor cursed him and asked him why he did not remove his hat. Before Sissle could answer, the white man knocked his hat from his head. As the young soldier stooped to pick up his hat, he was struck several times and kicked out of the place."[156]

When soldiers of that regiment heard about the abuse of Sissle, they gathered and were ready to Rush the hotel. The timely intervention by the bandmaster, Lieutenant James R. Europe, prevented what could have resulted in another incident like the one at Houston.

Europe got the group under control. But the next evening, it took the intervention of Colonel Hayward, the commanding officer, to prevent the 369th from marching on Spartanburg and shooting up the town. Emmet J. Scott rushed to South Carolina and pleaded with the soldiers to not cause another Houston incident, which, he said, would bring dishonor on the regiment and the race. Scott lost a lot of prestige by this action, among Negro soldiers and civilians.

The army's racist top echelon finally understood their three choices. 1) They could leave the Regiment at Camp Wordsworth and risk a blowup. 2) They could move them to another camp and give the Redneck element the impression that all they had to do was "show resentment of niggers" to make the Army jump to their tune. Or, 3) they could send the 369th overseas. They chose option Three, throwing a monkey wrench into the group in the top echelon's plan to keep the Negro away from the battlefront as long as possible. This caused the 369th to be the first Negro Combat Unit to reach the front. The Army policy was to put the Negroes arriving in France to work in any unglamorous occupation that was needed.

Where their own countrymen did not want Negroes, even if segregated, in their Divisions, the French, due to their heavy needs, readily accepted them. So these Negroes in World War I ended up in the French Army. It is said that Ferdinand Foch saw the strong Negroes of the 369th digging ditches and asked, "are they fighting men?" Can they shoot? Upon getting an affirmative answer, he asked that they be given to the French Army. This was readily agreed to, as the American Generals did not want them.

The negro had gone so willingly to war for the United States, he of course, had faith that a new attitude of justice toward him might result. The Negro fighting in Europe was not simply fighting Germans; he was fighting indirectly for his privileges at home. However, his experience during the war had spawned a new spirit of determination "not to accept passively the assaults and indignities that had been their lot in the past," but to fight for their rights. In the words of DuBois: "We return, We return from fighting. We return fighting."[157]

In what has become known as "The Red Summer of 1919", it is interesting to note how the Negro soldiers were "welcomed home". Upon their return from Europe in 1919, there were 25 race riots and 76 Negroes were lynched. 70 were lynched in the first year of the post war period. John Hope Franklin says, "Ten Negro soldiers, several still in uniform, were lynched. Mississippi and Georgia mobs murdered three returning soldiers each; two were lynched in Arkansas. Florida and Alabama took the lives of Negro soldiers by mob violence. Fourteen Negroes were burned publicly, eleven of whom were burned alive. White soldiers, sailors and marines participated in the killings of Negroes in Washington, D.C., Chicago, and Charleston, South Carolina."[158]

White soldiers, sailors and marines, whom the Negroes went to fight beside in the American Expeditionary Force, never enjoyed the privilege of comradeship, due to racist policies of segregation and discrimination. So white servicemen came home from France just as racist, and probably more so due to the fact that they had heard of Negroes dating French women, a major taboo in America. Consequently, instead of standing up for their comrades in arms, they played a major role in the riots, lynching's and murders of Negroes. In the Chicago race riot, Sailors helped beat and kill hapless Negroes trapped in the downtown loop area. In Washington, D.C., sailors and marines were the main perpetrators of the rioting and violence against Negroes. Josephus Daniels, Secretary of the Navy, refused a request to restrict them to their bases. Sailors and marines triggered the riot at Charleston. The only military official to act responsibly was the commanding officer of the Charleston Naval Yard. This rare gentleman ordered his marines to form a line just inside the Negro neighborhood and turn around a mob led by marines and sailors bent upon burning the houses and beating their occupants. These marines met the mob, led by their fellows, with fixed bayonets.

They arrested the leaders and commandeered cabs and other vehicles to return them to the bases.

This awful knowledge rested in the memories of older Negroes, mothers and grandmothers, on the eve of World War II.

With all of this negative history behind them, Negroes, at the end of World War II, found themselves in their usual condition—the expectation that they would fight and willingly die for the liberty and freedom of White men in Europe, something the U.S. Negroes had never enjoyed. But this time, led by better-educated and more astute leaders, Negroes demanded that the racist policies, formerly accepted, be changed. This time would not be "business as usual", a "Negro, White man thing." This new Negro leadership did not arrive with "hat in hand" and pleading for just treatment. They arrived demanding just change, in the demeaning racist policies. In other words, there would be certain costs for their participation in this war.

Part V.

Negroes in the U.S. Navy During World War II

CHAPTER 14. U.S. MOBILIZATION FOR WWII: THE STATUS OF NEGROES

On the eve of World War II, there was a significantly lower number and percentage of Negroes in the military than any of the prior periods of our history. The Navy, in a last futile attempt at "Lily Whiteness", which began with creation of the Messmen branch in 1893, barred all Negro enlistment in 1919, including as servants. They were not again allowed to enlist until 1932, when the two-ocean Navy concept's personnel requirements dramatically increased the need for manpower. Even then, Negroes were allowed to be cooks, stewards and Mess attendants only. The army maintained the basic theme, blacks must be kept in segregated units with only limited numbers permitted into combat arms. The army banned blacks from the Air Corps, the Artillery, Engineers, Signal and Tank Corps. The Navy excluded them from all units except Messmen units. An Army War College report entitled "Use of Negro Manpower", dated November 12, 1936 reflected the strong racist sentiment, prevalent in military thinking in World War I and beyond. It said:

> "As an individual, the Negro is docile, tractable, light-hearted, carefree and good natured. If unjustly treated, he is likely to become surly and stubborn, though this is a temporary phase. He is careless, shiftless, irresponsible, and secretive. He resents censure and is best handled with praise and ridicule."[159]

Navy Admirals, Marine and Army Generals socialized together on the Washington circuit. They interacted and exchanged ideas both on and off the job. It is most likely that this military thinking affected all branches of the military. It was certainly a factor on the eve of World War II. As in all prior Wars, the U.S. Military found itself in dire need of manpower. A massive mobilization would be required to prosecute such a venture. There were only about 5,000 Negroes in the Army out of a force of 230,00 and less in the Navy (4,000). There were none in the Marine Corps.

As with past wars, the age-old question regarding Negro participation reared its head. Given the treatment that Negroes had received in the past and were continuing to receive from society in the United States, why should he risk his life for this country yet again in a war? Why was he willing to go in harms way, to forget past wrongs, to work and shed blood for a country that had never granted him the civil rights and liberties given to other Americans? Maybe a review of the author's personal circumstances might be enlightening, in this regard. It was certainly not patriotism that pointed the Negro towards the armed forces. Other forces were at work, such as poverty, unemployment and discrimination, and/or, injustice and segregation.

I was a refugee fleeing from the poverty and insecurity that the state of Arkansas provided for its Negro citizens. In Arkansas in the 1930's, if a Negro man made $1.00 a day, he was lucky. Some white men were intelligent enough to know that one could not put out maximum labor on an empty stomach, so there were a few who offered 75 cents a day and one hot meal. Or, one could pick cotton for 35 cents per hundred pounds. I had learned from World War I veterans, that Negro soldiers were not backed by the Army and had been lynched for daring to wear their uniforms after their discharge. This is why I chose the navy. I had not heard of many sailors being lynched. Perhaps whites knew that most sailors had been servants, were not uppity and knew their "place". Additionally, the armed forces offered a prize unheard of for Negro civilians in Arkansas. One could earn a check each month for the rest of their life! An old WWI veteran had explained to me that if I was lucky enough to not get my head blown off in a war, and stayed alive for twenty years, this would be my prize. Incidentally, an 8-hour workday was unheard of at that time. Organized labor was dangerous even for white men to discuss. A workday was "from can see to can't see" or from sun up to sun down. So, it was the ever-present unemployment and poverty that made Negroes overcome their unwillingness to participate in the WWII mobilization.

However, mobilization did not proceed as smoothly as in past wars. Anger over discrimination, segregation and unfair employment practices retarded the growth in numbers of Negroes willing to enlist. The armed forces found the Negro willing to bear arms, but not at any price this time, as in prior wars. Negro leaders assailed the Roosevelt Administration with demands for fair employment in the war industries and an end to segregation and discrimination in the armed forces. Yes, there would be a price for Negro participation in this war!

Mobilization, this time, faced a new Negro and a new people, who had learned to fight back if attacked, how to use marches and picket lines, mass boycotts and organized political action. They had been smart enough to not let the "Communist" use them, which would have increased the distrust and alienation from their fellow citizens in this country. The Negro would not engage in Mobilization unless his social and economic condition was changed…no more business as usual.

Lerone Bennett describes it this way:

> "At the beginning, Negro Americans expressed deep skepticism about a second world war to make the world safe for democracy. In a letter to the editor of the Raleigh News and Observer, a Negro observed: The Negro races of the world are very suspicious of the white man's intentions;…another Negro, according to Gunnar Myrdal, said, "just carve on my tombstone, here lies a black man who died fighting a yellow man for the protection

of a white man". This mood of dissatisfaction and bitterness even erupted before Pearl Harbor. In an unprecedented show of unity, the NAACP, the National Urban League, Negro churches sororities and newspapers asked America to put up or shut up. American Negroes had not forgotten their treatment after helping Woodrow Wilson "make the world safe for democracy in WWI or their payment in the "Red Summer of 1919". They had not forgotten that it was Negro blood that made it red."[160]

Peter Bergman says that, in 1940, "There were fewer than 5,000 Negroes of the 230,000 men in the army. There were 2 Negro combat officers 500 out of the 100,000 Reserve officers."[161] This paucity of Negroes in the army had to be remedied. The Selective Service Act was passed on September 16, 1940. In 1940 Bergman says, "The NAACP began a coordinated drive to desegregate the armed forces. Walter White of the NAACP, T. Arnold Hill of the Urban League, A. Philip Randolph and other Negro leaders submitted a 7-point program to President Roosevelt. The NAACP also petitioned the Senators for Selective reforms so that Negroes would be freely inducted."[162] This action retarded the rapid mobilization of Negroes, which the army desperately needed. The President attempted to deal with this problem in October 1940. Bergman says, "…President Roosevelt announced that Negro strength in the army would be proportional to the Negro percentage in the total population. Those Negro groups would be organized in every branch of service, combat as well as non-combatant. That Negroes would have the opportunity to become officers and to attend officers' training schools; that Negroes would be trained as pilots, mechanics and technical aviation specialists. However, Negroes and whites would not be mingled in the same regiments because that would produce situations destructive to morale, and detrimental to preparation, for national defense."[163]

This last statement, failure to end segregation, dogged the war effort from 1940 until 1945, from beginning to end. It adversely affected not just the army, but all other branches of the armed forces.

However, poverty, unemployment and memories of what Roosevelt had done to relieve the suffering of Negroes caused by the depression brought increased Negro support for the war effort. The humane treatment of Negroes by Roosevelt and his wife, Eleanor, also helped overcome this problem. Roosevelt showed daring in meeting some of the demands of the Negro leaders. A. Philip Randolph, who had been jailed during World War I for fighting the governments' treatment of Negroes, proposed a 100,000-man march on Washington. As a labor organizer, he had waged a 12 year fight with the powerful Pullman Company to get a Union of Pullman Porters recognized and had won. According to Lerone Bennett, Jr., Randolph fused the coalition effort with his proposed march. This alienated many white liberals, who saw it as bad politics. President Roosevelt was against the march. Fiorello LaGuardia and Eleanor Roosevelt, both very popular and well liked in the Negro community, nation wide, got Randolph to come down to New York City Hall, where they attempted to dissuade him. Randolph stubbornly refused to call off the march, and next he was invited to Washington. Bennett says:

> "President Roosevelt sat behind his desk flanked by the Secretary of the Navy and the Assistant Secretary of War. He was cordial but cautious. He challenged the right of the group to put pressure on the White House. He was doing the best he could and intended to do more. The march must be called off. Randolph was adamant. Unless something was done quickly, he said 100,000 would march on the White House. The President (said), "we cannot have a march on Washington. We must approach this problem in an analytical way. Randolph (said) something must be done at once. The President (said) something

will be done, but there must be no public pressure. Randolph (said) something must be done now.

The argument grew heated. FDR switched suddenly. "Phil, he asked in obvious allusion to Randolph's beautiful diction, what year did you finish Harvard? Randolph, who was not a graduate of any college, smiled. The tension relaxed. Bennett goes on to describe how, after calming the argument, he then went on to just as skillfully put this problem on hold in a manner that ensured Negro participation in the mobilization effort. He turned in the interval in which Randolph was "cooling out" and asked Walter White of the NAACP, "Walter, how many people will really march"? White replied, "no less than 100,000". The President knew that White and his NAACP were members of the coalition pushing for an end to discrimination and segregation. Roosevelt next fixed his gaze, face to face, with an intensity that Walter White later described as penetrating and lengthy, to ascertain whether he was bluffing."[164]

White was a friend to Franklin and Eleanor Roosevelt. This friendship had been built upon integrity, trust and a deeply held respect. Bennett says:

> "The President shrugged. "What do you want me to do? A. Philip Randolph said he wanted the President to issue an executive order barring discrimination in the war industries and armed services. Seven days later, Randolph had his order. Executive Order 8802 banned discrimination in war industries and apprenticeship programs. On the day the order was issued, June 25, 1941, Randolph called off the march on Washington."[165]

Roosevelt went a step further. He appointed a Fair Employment Practices Committee to push his policies. War Industries did a better job of compliance than the armed forces that dragged their feet during the entire war. But Negroes, out of respect and trust for Franklin and Eleanor Roosevelt, rapidly joined the Mobilization. The Fair Employment Practices Committee had not been equipped, for political reasons, with the teeth to punish Federal Contractors who discriminated against Negroes! But they quickly learned that it was uncomfortable and newsworthy to appear before the committee. It damaged the image of their company to have to do so. Thus there emerged an unusual degree of compliance.

On the military side, there was a far harder nut to crack. Here, Roosevelt and his proponents of change in discriminatory practices ran into an all but impregnable wall. This wall was composed of racist civilian War Department employees and their bosses. Included were Henry L. Stimson, Secretary of War, John J. McCloy, Assistant Secretary of War, Frank Knox, Secretary of the Navy and many old Generals and Admirals. A number of them had been present in 1919 when all Negroes were barred from naval service. They put up massive resistance to any change in race relations that would remove discrimination and segregation. Stimson said that they had tried this before and that Negro officers ended up making fools of themselves. Knox, according to the Negro Reference Book, said: "The policy of not enlisting men of the colored race for any branch of service but the Messmen Branch was adopted to meet the best interests of general efficiency". John McCloy said, "I do not think the basic issues of the war are involved in the question of whether colored serve in segregated units or mixed units."[166] Negroes did what they had to do, to serve this country.

McCloy's statement would be humorous if it was not so stupidly hypocritical. At that time, the world, and even most Negro teenagers knew that one of the major issues and selling points for going to war with Germany was Hitler's "master race" theory. Thank God that the Negroes were wise enough to look past these old-line racists to their own self-interest and the interest of the nation.

Even so, this racist foot-dragging caused a momentary lag in Negro recruiting. Franklin says:

> "...in the first year of operation of the act, only 2,069 Negroes were drafted into the armed forces. In the following year, more than 100,000 Negroes entered the services, while in 1942, approximately 370,000 Negroes joined the armed forces of the United States. In September 1944, when the draft was at its peak, there were 701,678 Negroes in the army alone. Approximately 165,000 served in the navy, 5,000 in the Coast Guard, and 17,000 in the Marine Corps. A rough estimate of the total number of Negroes in the armed forces in World War II places the figure in the neighborhood of one million men and women...approximating the ratio of Negroes in the general population."[167]

But this generation of Negroes was backed by a legacy from WWI. Unlike in the riots of Chicago and Washington, D.C. in the Red Summer of 1919, when confronted by white supremacists, they fought back and killed some white men. This had never been done before! Down through the history of this country, white racist had simply lynched or murdered the terror-ridden unarmed Negroes at will. In the 1940's, white men were made to pay with their lives for abusing Negroes. Further, this more militant generation had fearless, highly intelligent, politically astute leaders.

They had adroitly learned to use the concentration of Negro voters in the urban areas of large cities to affect local and national elections. Franklin Roosevelt's election ended the one party voting by Negroes. Up until that time, those that could vote, voted Republican, the party of Lincoln. My father was a life long Republican. He talked about how Woodrow Wilson, a Democrat, had lied to the Negroes. Then, as President, he had ordered the re-segregation of Negroes in Civil Service jobs in Washington, D.C. Wilson did nothing while Negroes in the city were being killed until the Negroes armed themselves and fought back! My father would then say acidly, "then that cracker-democrat called out the army to stop it". I will never forget my fathers' anger each Sunday when, after church, he would break out his Negro newspapers and bury himself in them. He subscribed to the Chicago Defender, the Pittsburgh Courier, and the Kansas City Call Bulletin. He brooked no disturbance. Later in the evening, Negro men in the neighborhood who could not read would gather and ask, "what them white folks doing to niggers"? He would hold forth for an hour or more. He would read to them about Negroes up north who were forced to be strikebreakers to keep their families from starving; about them being attacked by white union members who wouldn't let them join the union. He would read about what was happening to Negroes in the Democrat-ruled south which most of these men came to learn about. Most had relatives in Louisiana, Texas or Tennessee. There was seldom a week that the Negro newspapers didn't have a headline, "Negro lynched, or burned, whipped or beaten". Every now and then, after dad had read of some lynching, one of the men would jump up and scream, "I know that boy and his whole family! He ain't raped no white woman. Dat whole bunch be church folks. Dey done made a mistake!"

My older brother was the family jokester. We, in childish ignorance, used to laugh when he said, "Here they come" (talking about the men who came to hear the news), "They coming to see how many niggers were fast enough to survive last week." Ignorance shielded us children from the insecurity with which our parents had to live every day.

I will never forget an incident that happened in 1932. I heard my father advise some men in the neighborhood to save some money to pay poll taxes so that they could vote for Franklin Roosevelt. When they left, I said, "daddy I thought you said cracker-Democrats was no good and that they hated Negro people, just like Pitchfork Ben Tillman and the rest of that sack-suit wearing lynch mob. How could you tell black folks to vote for him?" I said, "He's probably kin to ole Theodore Roosevelt, who you said was a two-faced, no good lying cracker." I will never forget his reply.

He fixed me with a long quizzical look, not believing, as he told me later, that I had been listening that carefully while he was reading to his friends and neighbors. He told me that this Roosevelt and his wife Eleanor were different white folks. He said that Franklin Roosevelt was not like that lying, loud talking cousin of his, ole Theodore. I was still shocked that he would vote for a Democrat, so, I asked him, " but how can you trust him when you said that Negroes were fools to trust that other Democrat, Woodrow Wilson?" "He's a different white man and he and his wife, Eleanor, don't seem to hate Negroes for being black. He won't allow black folks to starve like that cracker, Hoover. I've been reading about him and I know he's different from them others. He is a lot smarter upstairs than those fools and he knows what to do."

My father probably characterized this kind of thinking among Negroes. These well-informed post WWI fathers were being asked to offer up their sons in this second gambit to "make the world safe for democracy". This is possibly the key reason why Franklin Roosevelt was able to, in spite of retardation by racist southerners in the house and senate, the tradition bound Generals and Admirals and their civilian bosses, get massive Negro support for his mobilization program.

Roosevelt was a man of action with rare intelligence. He was a doer not a talker. He immediately moved to relieve the suffering of both ignorant, illiterate Negroes and whites. Both had been victims of the "share Cropping System", which had replaced slavery. He launched the Agricultural Adjustment Administration (AAA). Farmers were given cash benefits for plowing under their unneeded cotton, wheat and tobacco crops or slaughtering their hogs, rather than putting them on an almost non-existent market. While farmers' cash benefits rose to billions of dollars under AAA, many of the grants intended for Negro farmers were dissipated or misappropriated. Many landlords took advantage of illiterate sharecroppers and tenant white farmers by keeping the checks for themselves. Franklin explains that, "The Negro illiterate was not the only victim of this dishonesty. Uneducated white sharecroppers and tenant farmers were cheated as well. These people learned the white southern elite, when it came to money, thought as little of them as they did of the Negro. The landowners often simply forced the white tenants off the land and continued to pocket the checks from AAA. This compelled white victims, who had been told all of their lives that they were "better than Negroes", to realize that they shared a common problem with the Negro. They too were being cheated and lied to. Thus, blacks and whites were compelled to engage in a common cause to achieve common benefits. This was the first time since the brief birth and death of the Populist Movement led by Tom Watson of Georgia in 1892, that a split occurred in the Democratic Party."[168]

Other scholars have written about this era and its unfair treatment of Negroes and poor Whites. For example, according to Bergman:

> "...both attempting to gain the Negro vote, at first by friendship, and finally by bribery, intimidation, and fraud...As Tom Watson, the Gubernatorial Candidate, explained, "now the people's party says to these two men, you are kept apart that you may be separately fleeced of your earnings". You are made to fight each other because upon that hatred is rested the keystone of arch financial despotism that enslaves you both. You are deceived and blinded that you may not see how this race antagonism perpetuates a system that beggars you both."[169]

Unfortunately, in 1892, the Rednecks showed their true colors and alienated the Negroes as did Tom Watson and the Democrats. Now, nearly half a century later, under the New Deal, poor white sharecroppers and tenants found themselves faced with making common cause with Negroes for the first time since the post-Reconstruction era.

When the Roosevelt Administration found out about the mass cheating and misappropriation of funds, they moved very quickly. They created a program whereby these unfortunates would be paid directly. Landowners then moved the tenants off the land and kept the checks for themselves. So, white and black victims jointly organized the <u>Southern Tenant Farmers Union</u>. This organization, in the years leading up to WWII, was fought tenaciously by southern farmers, using race prejudice and anti-union sentiment as the principle weapons. In spite of this assault, Negro and White victims learned from this organizational effort that they could vote and cooperate in the effort to influence the economic factors that served them both. Nevertheless, the <u>disenfranchisement effort moved</u> <u>forward in most southern states.</u>

Franklin Roosevelt had another card to play. He created the Farm Security Administration or FSA. John Hope Franklin points out that, although the Agency was woefully under funded, Negroes learned better farming and marketing techniques. Loans were funded and many were able to buy land and own their own farms for the first time.

CHAPTER 15. MESSBOYS AT THE NAVAL ACADEMY: THE LOST BATTALION AND BANCROFT HALL

The following discussion is included to give the reader some insight into the social environment and interaction of sailors in the Stewards/ Messmen Branch. The use of the vernacular is designed to maintain reality. It is hoped that these personal experiences of the author will better inform the reader regarding the actual conditions that were experienced.

Most Negro Messboys arrived in the Navy with certain advantages as to Military life. We were already possessed of a sense of discipline. In the Southern States in the 1930's and 40's, a Negroe's welfare and often his survival depended upon doing what he was told by White men whether at work or not. Further, one's father or mother was not charged with "child abuse" for whipping a sassy young'uns butt. Parental authority was absolute in most Southern Negro families. As one of my friends laughingly said to another messboy, "Boy you 'talks back' too much. Who raised you anyhow! My ole man would seize a little Nigga like you, grab him a limb an light into thrashing your ass like he was killing a snake." Most of the group laughed and probably remembered when that disaster befell them. Harsh language? Yes, but very real and absolutely necessary behavior for Negro family heads in the South, prior to WWII, if their children were to survive.

The use of corporal punishment was a very serious business for Southern Negro parents. It was not only administered by mom and dad but also by aunts, uncles or any grown up friends of the parents. The Black youngsters had to be taught early and well lest he or she should mouth off to some White man or woman and get beaten, or worse, lynched or "put in jail", (usually beaten if arrested). To prevent this, a community's adults watched each other's children, looked out for them. If a neighbor or friend popped you on your butt, you hoped that they would forget to tell your parents because you would probably get whacked again. So the better part of valor was to shut your mouth and hope that the neighbor did not report you to the ole man. There was nothing more hair raising than to have a Negro family head fix a youngster with a steely eye and say, "Boy, you giving folk the impression I ain't raisin' you?" This was as serious as a heart attack because one could take bets that he would be given the unpleasant job of choosing his own switch! Hence the Navy, even Annapolis was a piece of cake compared to where many Messboys grew up.

To be sure, the naval academy was harsh duty for a messboy. If one appeared in formation dirty or in a scroungy, wrinkled uniform he was made to wash his whole "Seabag". This included all blue and white uniforms, underwear, socks, hats, towels, etc., about a three-hour job, scrubbing by hand or three days in the brig on bread and water. If caught wearing another man's clothes, the cost was five days bread and water. If you loaned a friend clothes and he was caught, he had to lie or you were punished for loaning the clothes in the first place. If one was 5 minutes late he got three days bread and water for a first offense. A second time got the culprit 5 days. Insolence and/or insubordination earned one a deck court-martial with 10 days on "cake and wine". More serious offenses earned one a "summary", courts-martial whereby he got 15 to 30 days on bread and water or was sent to prison at Portsmouth, New Hampshire (desertion, serious assault, etc.).

We hit the deck at a quarter to (0500) 5:00 am washed up and dressed by 0530 and had breakfast. We were in formation and on the march to Bancroft Hall by 0600, all four platoons (40 to 50 men each). "Reveille", pronounced *revalee* aboard the U.S.S. Cumberland, was a true nightmare for the uninitiated. At 4:45 am bedlam reigned in the form of the Reveille Crew composed of the duty chief, the bugler and the duty section leaders. All hell broke loose each morning when a galvanized wash bucket was hurled against a steel "bulkhead", (ships don't have walls), followed by loud screams, with language such as, "Hit the deck me lads! Time done run out on you! This is the navy Mr. Jones. Drop yo cock and grab yo socks! Reveille, Reveille wake up and see you might want to pee, Reveille, Reveille." Behind this bedlam came the most hated man on the ship, a tall, black dude named "Scales the Snake", due to his long neck, prominent "gooz up pipe" (large Adams apple) blowing, "I can't get'em up" on his bugle. He did not have a long neck for no reason. He could blow a bugle loud enough for it to be heard all over Severn River basin. His name, "the Snake", came from his other duty which was to check for extra-sound sleepers or "laggards", who failed to "hop to" or answer the first call to Reveille promptly. On finding such, ole Scales would sneak back and inform the culprits section leader whose job it was to see that all-hands and every mother's son hit the deck promptly on demand.

The mornings after payday, when many of these dudes had been up all night drinking, "come on momma les fight," (cheap store bought booze) or "alligator piss," (bootleg concoctions), was a morning of fights and near riots. Now, we all who were tough enough, slept in hammocks, which when properly lashed to their "Jack staves" or hooks, hung six feet off the deck. There were nearly 200 Messboys at Annapolis most of my tour of duty. The catch was that there was only about 90 places to hang hammocks! So if a dude hung his hammock in the same place each evening, it was wise to "walk around him" because he could take care of himself. Someone was sure to challenge ones right to that spot with, "Say man that's my spot." This was usually followed by "I've decided that I'm tired of sleeping on the deck an what do you aim to do about it?" This was an "all stop situation" and somebody was gonna get whipped. The Author witnessed many of these "all stop situations". These two dudes would run together like two trains, with teeth bared, fists flying and on occasion the use of a brass fire nozzle or switchblade brought into play, as an equalizer. The one who was able to walk away got the spot. So the act of telling a drunk or laggard to hit the deck was serious business when told by him, "I ain't coming. I feels that them damned midshipmen don ate they vittles already!" The only out left, a section leader with any self-respect, was to dump the Culprit out of his hammock or suffer a complete loss of respect and/or prestige. Now, if the dude slept in a hammock, as previously mentioned, he probably had a reputation already as a "touch hog". So he usually came off the deck lashing, kicking and punching. Most of the time he got beaten and locked up. If you hit a section leader at "nap town," (Annapolis) you had to be "put on report", that is "formally written up", which required the intervention of the "White Folks", face the man, "Hard hearted Joe Benson, the Captain."

The code for fights between ordinary Messboys was simple, "Effen yo fist ain't hard don't let yo mouf be big". This was unwritten but known to all and was handled just as informally. All fights were "finish fights". It was over when one combatant failed to get up. No one was going to stop a fight until this happened except in an instance when an opponent challenged some one woefully over-matched. In such cases some "hommie" (from the same state) would intervene with, "Say man, whyn't you pick on somebody yo size?" This involved taking his place and dealing with the cowardly bully who specialized in picking on small, weaker members. These scuffles were not reported to "The Man", for very practical reasons. There would have been as many Messboys in the brig as those out and ready to serve midshipmen.

This was so, so long as no one got banged up enough to require hospitalization or time off from duty. In such instances the offending culprit, the winner of the fight, was dully charged with the unforgivable act of "damaging Navy property". One day when the Author was standing by to go before the "mast" he heard Captain Benson break his iron decorum for the only time during his 3 years at Annapolis. This ramrod straight Martinet was chastising a messboy who got mad in a crap game and busted another fellow's head with a brass fire nozzle. When he asked Gunner Davis about the condition of the injured party he was told, "They had to put six stitches in his head but that's alright. The problem is he gits dizzy when he stands up an he ain't talking right, yet. The Doctor said something bout a concussion." The Captain asked how long before he could return to duty. The Gunner said about two weeks. Benson turned red and literally screamed at the guilty culprit, "You, you rapscallion have damaged 'Navy property'". The messboy mumbled, "Suh, I ain't broke no dishes." (We were punished for breaking dishes). Allow me to explain, "When a messboy tended to be clumsy and broke over a certain amount of the midshipmen's dishes he was logged each time. If the amount exceeded the quota allowed during a certain period of time, he was punished by 5 days bread and water in the brig." Captain Benson mimicked the culprit and then said, "I am not talking about no dishes you idiot. Don't you know that you Messboys are Navy property? When you held up your hand and said," I do", you dunderhead, you belong to the Navy and I want you court-martialed. About 10 days in the brig on bread and water might just teach you to control yourself."

At this point Gunner Davis, a redneck, but with a "soft spot" for us Messboys, diplomatically intervened with: "Cap'n, I want to see him punished too but we are short of Messboys in the Bancroft Hall. Lot of 'em is sick with "Cat Fever (mild flu)". Benson looked scornfully at the culprit who stood dumbly with his ridiculous white hat changing hands and said, "Alright, you got 5 days bread and water, you also got 2 weeks restriction on board ship, starting the first pay day when you get out. And I want you mustered with the "prisoners-at-large" on this ship 3 times a day so I can see you for the 2 weeks. You understand that boy? And don't you show up here again!" Yassuh sur, he answered.

This "Navy property" dig dawned on me, the Author, after I got through basking in the laudatory praise of the Arkansas boys, for fighting ole Willie. My broken hand had swollen and began to throb. If I couldn't answer Reveille, march to Bancroft Hall and serve my 22 midshipmen in the morning, I would have to face the man. There were often bets made as to whether a dude would answer the bugle the next morning. If one proved soft and couldn't, he was sneered at, looked down upon because he got another messboy in trouble. If I showed up in front of the man he would probably throw the book at me. He was proud of our boxing team. So, I probably would be castigated for allowing Willie to break his hand on my hard head again and jailed.

I had earned the right to sling my hammock in a corner of the marine deck by force-of-arms (fists) and had sustained that right two times. One time a dude took my hammock, a no-no, and laid it on deck to sleep on. Nothing engendered more ire than to return from liberty after consuming a half-pint of Jack Daniels, walking from town in the snow at 0100 and finding ones hammock gone. When such occurred, standard procedure dictated that the culprit be reported to the duty watch stander. In this way the victim avoided 3 days in the brig for having a dirty hammock. This person accompanied the injured party, with a flashlight, in a search of the ship. When the offending party was found the watch stander rousted him out and the owner of the hammock whipped him to the glee of every one awakened by this ruckus. The culprit usually came up with some lame excuse like, "Man, this was jes a mistake. I thot that it wuz mine." He usually got, "Nigga, can't you read?" from the watch stander and another two or three shots upside his head in order to get his undivided attention. Such culprits could expect no mercy, sympathy or warm understanding. This was "serious shit" because a dirty hammock found at formal inspection earned the owner 5 days bread and water. The tragedy here was that many Messboys couldn't read! Literacy was no great requirement for the early recruitment of Messboys. An assumed capacity for subservience was demanded; the right attitude as to one's "place" was the central focus of acceptance in the Navy. If such unfortunates sat at a "strong table" of homies from his home state, these might teach him rudimentary reading. During his 21 years as a "Division Whip" (leading assistant), Chief Steward or Division Leading Chief (master chief), the Author taught 6 White boys (total illiteracy – x-mark types) to read and write letters home. He made a near regiment of Negro Messboys learn this art, and, has always been mystified by High School Graduates from, say, New York, Chicago or California schools who, after 12 years of schooling, were functional illiterates. The Author never found a High School graduate, from the Northeast, Midwest or South who was illiterate during his watch (1940-1961). He does not know why the Northeast is so successful but he does know why the South and Midwest were so. As late as 1968 when the Author was Faculty Field Instructor, to graduate students at Case Western Reserve in Cleveland, Ohio, teachers were allowed to "paddle" Junior High students' bottoms. At H.C. Yerger High School, Hope, Arkansas, and in most Southern states, Whites left discipline up to Negro teachers and parents. Those old Black

Southern teachers of reading probably never had a course in psychology but they were masters of motivation. The author was motivated by Mrs. Ella Yerger in the second grade, so well that being pretty industrious, and reasonably sharp, he did not have to have the process repeated until the 8th grade by Professor Hamilton, who whipped the entire class (girls and boys)! As Nathaniel Garett, a homey from Arkansas, told the author, "Man, I wuz busy checking out them pretty country girls. One day I wuz called on to read and stumbled and mumbled over a whole page. Dat teacher called me down front and seized a limb, then lit into lashing and whipping my butt like she wuz whipping a mule. She seized me by my jaws and said, 'you ain't stupid, you're lazy!', and thumped me on top of my head an said, 'you better get your lessons, boy!'" Garret told the author, "Chester, that was one of the worst days of my life. My sister got home before me and had blabbed to my daddy bout me being whipped. I had been laughed at during recess, before the girls. I trudged six miles home with my back and butt stinging off and on, called a 'numb skull' and totally humiliated, only to find my ole man waiting in the yard with that 'look' on his face. It was the one he assumed when he was totally pissed off. This look was reserved for those too slow and lazy to pick and chop their share of cotton or forgot to slop the hogs or feed the mules. The ole man said, 'Come ere boy!' He seized me by the collar, lifted me up to eye level and slapped me a couple of times and said, 'Boy what you doing up there at that school shaming me an yo momma before dat teacher like I ain't raisin you?'" Boy, the next day I could hardly sit down at school. Man, that made me, 'wake up smarts' that I ain't knowed I had. Garret laughingly said, "I became the neighborhood scholar." Other children came over to my house to be tutored in the three R's. The teachers later told my dad, "That boy got a head on his shoulders", as I strutted at church wid all that learning. Well, so much for the motivation and education of

Southern Messboys. I never knew one who finished high school and couldn't read. Nobody was 'trucked', feeble minded or not, one's best was demanded.

Back to the U.S.S. Cumberland and my broken hand. My homies, Quinten Berryman, Leon Campbell and R.L. Snell slung my hammock and helped me to get in. I lay awake with the hand throbbing all night. The next morning my homies lashed up my hammock and stored it in the hammock netting topside. My hand had swollen and hurt like hell. Someone said, "That pharmacy mate likes juice." I got a half-pint of Schenly's Black Label (store bought booze). "I'll go and get you some of them 'dope pills' from him." This was done. When the bugler blew the call to muster on the dock, I looked out and saw ole tough Willie, cast and all heading for formation.

Hell, the traditions, mores of Annapolis Messboys were just as non-forgiving as those imposed on the midshipmen we served. I had to march to Bancroft Hall or be considered a 'poot butt' (a punk, blowhard, a phony of no consequence). Now here one had to enjoy the respect and real comradeship of his shipmates. If he didn't he couldn't make it in Bancroft Hall because this required carrying trays with six large heavy porcelain bowls of food, carrying dish racks full of dishes and placing 22 heavy metal chairs on the mess table quick and on demand, an impossible task with one hand. Me an ole Willie made out, the boys from the Louisiana table helped Willie and my Arkansas homies helped me, such that we did not have to face the man. It was two and one half weeks before I could, "Swing 22" (serve 22 midshipmen) by myself. Life at the Naval Academy was a harsh proposition for the timid or lazy messboy. If one did not, "hack it", or just couldn't master the work or endure the stress, just learn to live with it, he was summarily dealt with. If he was merely inadequate, he was given an inaptitude discharge; if he was a bad actor, he was court martialed and punished or given a bad conduct discharge (BCD). Serious crimes such as aggravated assault, gross in subordination, disrespect of an officer (peace-time, wartime, more serious) causing serious injury to a sailor, murder or desertion (30 days over the hill with no intent to return) required prison time usually at hard-labor at Portsmouth, New Hampshire or Terminal Island, California. In most instances, on termination of sentence, the culprit received a BCD or worse, a dishonorable discharge (DD).

Weaker members had to have the support of his homeboys in order to hack it. His table had to have a reputation for taking care of their "own people" and be willing to "go to general quarters" (fight) when a homey was mistreated or (threatened) braced, by bullies. Woe to the person who did not enjoy the support of homeboys.

The author, 10th grade intellectual and, "touch hog", of the Arkansas Table aboard U.S.S. Cumberland, enjoyed immense prestige and respect among his peers at Annapolis. This was not minus certain costs. For example, when new youngsters had navy "forms" to fill out, they were often just short of terrified. Many had never, in their lives, done so. They all knew, from their fathers signing a share crop or land rental agreement between a Negro and a White man, who was going to be the "bottom part of the hot dog, " who was going to be screwed. This was the locus of the unreasonable fear of paper forms to be signed. Forms usually were for checking on insurance status or trying to get an allotment sent home to an ill father or dependent mother. As the "Resident Intellectual" for Arkansas it was my duty to alleviate the fear, coach the victim in filling out these "mysterious, White man's forms" and seeing that such was given to the proper yeoman in the personnel or disbursing office. Now the duty "hawg" (shack bully with the long teeth) was another matter. After punching it out with ole "bad Willie", and breaking his paw, the author was referred to as that "bad Arkansas mother." He had enhanced this reputation by engaging in a "chunk-out" against a Texas touch hog, in Bancroft Hall. A chunk out occurred when two antagonist settled a difference by throwing as much of the midshipmen's china, (plates, cups, bowls, etc.), as one could get his hand on, as rapidly as it could be thrown upside the head of ones opponent. The author considers this one of his luckiest shots. This was serious, destroying the government's property. It was a foregone conclusion that the culprits were going to "face-the-man" and do some hard time (eat bread and water and work). This was illegal. When on bread and water, one was not supposed to work but to discourage such "breakage". In Bancroft Hall, this was waived. But, Gunner Davis, Master-at-arms (M.A.A.), knew and disliked this bully, who was 6'-3" and weighing 200 lbs., always picked some plantation, half-starved messboy weighing 130 or 140 lbs., to jump on. So Davis interceded with Captain Benson. The upshot was that the antagonist drew, "time" and the author drew "restriction" and again additional prestige and respect.

The duty of the touch-hog was to intercede and prevent smaller or weaker Messboys on the Arkansas table, whom some big bad dude had braced, from being beaten up. The ineligible-cowards were always on the prowl for some easy mark to beat up and thus enhance their reputations. My job was to see that this was not accomplished at the expense of some inoffensive Arkansas crewmember. These situations usually began and ended like this: when I, as touch-hog, approached some bully with, "Say Man, my cousin (cousin or not you made him so in order to add gravity) told me that you said that you were going to beat him up. You are a bit big for that "ain'tcha?"" "Aw man, the little nigger got a big mouf so I intend to shut it when I ketch him." At this point I fix him in intense, pointed eye contact and inform him in my coldest voice. "Effen you hit my cousin, you gonna have to hit me. I promised his momma I'd look out for him. And if you hit me I ain't gonna like it. Do you git it?" Now, if the dude hesitated you hit him with this, "if you got a problem man, we don't have to wait, you go git yo big ass out heah and let's let the "shit go down" right now! If the dude lacked heart it usually ended with, "Aw man, I didn't know that, that little fart wuz you cousin but you tell him to keep his big mouf shut", and mumbled under the breath, "I ain't scared of you." This was said minus to getting to his feet. Then you knew you had braced him, successfully and thus, maintained your respect and prestige as, "duty touch hog."

One time, the author got away by accident. The dude he braced probably could have kicked his butt. But, the Author ended the confrontation with, "Listen, Nigga, I'm a busy man. My people got a lot of them damn form papers and need me to show them how to fill them out. Shit, effen you want to "go down," let's git it on!" The dude backed down, surprisingly. The mystery was cleared up later on that evening when this dude showed up in the Arkansas corner. Did the dude change his mind? No, he had a form to be filled out to get his widowed mother an allotment. Now, even illiterate Messboys were proud. So you don't "front him off" in front of folks. I discreetly took him behind the dynamo, located on the Marine Deck and one of the few places of privacy aboard. Here, by flashlight, his form was quickly filled out. I told him to wait till morning to sign. I got up early and taught him by "sound" how to write his name. I made a lasting friend. Illiteracy should never be equated with intelligence. This guy was very bright. He never forgot and went on with a little help to learn to write a letter home. Some of the shrewdest people that I met in the Navy were illiterate. They were remarkable at hiding their illiteracy and "reading" people. Their perceptions and social skills were highly developed, probably as tools needed to avoid letting people learn of their inability to read and thus suffer humiliation. The author can grin today at his own part and ignorance while at Annapolis, but there is since acquiring maturity, education and a bit of wisdom, a bit of shame too. Yet, one cannot judge us too harshly. We, after all, were handpicked by the Navy for ignorance and a capacity for subservience, and not for our intelligence. Many were intelligent but had to play the role of buffoon in order to serve.

For a Southern Negro small town or farm boy, Bancroft Hall was a terrifying place during his first months at the Naval Academy. Here he had to become a tough dependable, functional cog in the fine-tuned machine that fed 2,500 midshipmen and cleaned up in just short of forty-five minutes. Not half-clean but absolutely so such that not one water spot remained on a piece of china or silverware. White table clothes were to be spotless and the deck clean enough to sit on in a white uniform without it acquiring a stain or spot. This is how Section Leaders explained requirements to new comers. Personally one had to maintain a clean body, fingernails, hair, etc. and no spots or dirt on his white uniform. To enter formations in violation was 3 days bread and water and possible inaptitude discharge for chronic offenders. White uniforms were worn year round regardless to how cold it got in winter, except while aboard ship or on liberty.

One other thing that the author forgot to mention was that the hopeless messboy assigned to the Naval Academy had to function in two harsh spheres of existence, one on the Cumberland, described earlier and the other in his workplace, the Naval Academy's Bancroft Hall.

The preparation for formation, inspection and entry to the other world, the world of the Academy was something that had to be mastered by every messboy or else. If one slept in a hammock, this had to be "triced", up quickly at reveille and carried two decks up to the "main deck" to be properly stored. An explanation is due here.

"The U.S.S. Cumberland was a bastard-relic between the "age of sail" and the "age of steam." As such she had both an engine room and boilers but also a capacity for sail power in the form of 3 masts. Like a sail ship her main deck and poop deck aft were "open" (uncovered). Around the main deck was built-in compartments called, "Hammock Netting." It is here that all hammocks were stored neatly, prior to morning formation. One was punished for not taking down his hammock, tricing it up, and seeing that is was properly stored prior to morning formation. Cumberland was a lousy sail ship. She was top-heavy and when she was made a barracks ship for Messboys, her main deck was covered.

The pre-formation inspection was carried out by Section Leaders, who in their rigor, a marine drill instructor would be hard pressed to match. Often, a surprise inspection by the Duty Officer of the day would be called. This dude in sparkling white arrived unannounced. This clipboard yeoman was a terror. These eagle eyed, no nonsense, handpicked men possessed a capacity for sight and smell that was remarkable. It was their duty to see that the Navy's midshipmen were served by "Clean Messboys", not approximately or half but ultra-clean. Formations were often subjected to unannounced physical (hands, nails, hair, etc.), inspections. Since Messboys were marched in formation to Bancroft Hall 3 times a day, one time for each meal, it was all but impossible to be a "scroungy" person and go undetected. For example, the pre-noon formation was the usual inspection. Here all men were inspected for both neatness and cleanliness. Here shoes must be shined, neckerchiefs unfrayed, white uniforms spotless and on command all hands were held forth and fingernails were inspected for telltale dirt under the nails.

Ever so often a surprise morning inspection was held in order to trap the unwary laggard. This type usually came from ashore, too drunk or lazy to shower and wash off "last nights tryst", and simply crawled in his "sack", overslept and had to fall out for formation half clean. Now old timers at Annapolis would sagely advise a homey to simply hide, miss formation and accept 5 days bread and water rather than be caught and marked down as "scroungy" and dirty. To be so marked brought down the wrath of the Head boy and your Section Leader whom you had shamed by giving the impression that they were not doing their jobs in "shaping" you up. These could really put the "righteous-heat" on a dude, which, if unchecked, could earn the culprit an inaptitude discharge, if scrounginess was adjudged to be a chronic habit.

When this was suspected the heat was intensified and the pressure was constant such as inspecting the suspect's locker and making him scrub his entire sea bag, every stitch! Then such suspects were "hard-assed" by unannounced "hard-inspection" whereby the culprit got both an outside and inside inspection. The outside inspection is self-explanatory. The inside was the ultimate in humiliation of having to drop your pants, have your drawers and T-shirt inspected and your socks checked for odor. I looked out for suspected members of the Arkansas table. As the touch hog and resident intellectual you looked out for your homies as a matter of expectation. The Author possessed prestige and even respect of the Section Leaders. I understood, better than most, the whole dynamic of the scrounginess label, since I came from a family of 12 children, lived in a house minus a bathroom (these were for white folks), with an "out house" for a toilet. Each Saturday evening, three no. 3 washtubs were filled with water, heated in the big black wood-fired pot where his mother made soap, hominy and boiled both the family and white folks clothes. We did have running water but what about my small farm and plantation reared fellows? Many of these had never seen an indoor bathroom or ever had running water or a simple hydrant for baths? We Wrights stepped into the first tub for removal of surface dirt, into the second for scrubbing and soaping down and into the third to be rinsed.

My oldest sister, Mildred, and my mother carried out this mass production effort. Mid-way in this evolution the water became so dirt laden until it had to be dumped and fresh water brought in. Only three families in my neighborhood had a bathroom.

But, what about the share crop/plantation raised brothers? These very often entered the navy with the following knowledge of water: it oozed out the ground at the "sump" (spring). A good, "water well" was a luxury. Many had to walk a block or two to the sump, chase off the water-moccasin snakes, crawdads and frogs to get a bucket of water for cooking, drinking or bathing.

James McClendon, a retired Chief Steward and a successful real estate agent in San Francisco told the Author that when he came to the navy, his family had to walk several blocks up to the Big house from their shack to get a bucket of water. The man whom his father sharecropped for was too cheap to dig them a well and only allowed them to go to town when he took them in his wagon. He even made out their grocery list and did the buying.

The Author often interceded with Section Leaders to get the heat lifted off some poor devil that had been targeted as a person with dirty-habits. Utilizing his primitive diplomatic and negotiating skills, the Author often interceded in hassles on these peoples' behalf. He was usually met with "What damned business is it of yours?" I would shrewdly say, "I ain't meddling. You a boss and knows a lot more than me. But I was told that you wuz tough but fair, that you wasn't no "Uncle Tom' who jess mistreated yo folks so as to please the White folks." The Section Leader on seeing that I didn't pose a threat would say "OK, boot, let's heah why that little scroungy Nigga, that's makin all of us colored people look bad with his dirty ass, should git the heat often his behind." The Author, "I kin tell by the way you talk and ack that you momma and daddy was probably 'quality-folks' an smart. That po fella's momma and daddy can't read. He had never seen a bathroom or head (navy for toilet area) until he come in the Navy, ain't neva been in a bathtub or shower. He ain't bad, he's jess country and thanks you don't bath till Saturday." I knew to not appear too smart myself and if the part about bathing once a week drew laughter, I knew that I had gotten to the Section Leader (often he already knew but had forgot where he came from). Usually the Section Leader would say, "But Scarface Davis said to put fire on that Nigga. An when Scar says do something he mean it and no shit or excuses about it". The Author, "Why don't you explain to him and tell him that I will teach that farmer how to wash his butt and keep his clothes clean. An I'll stay on his case till he do."

Scar Davis was tough and a "most-military mother" (messboy definition of a martinet) but he was very bright and luckily, for such farm boys, he had not forgotten his "Roots" either. So as a negotiator , the Author, prevented quite a few country boys from ending up "kicked out" with an inaptitude discharge. This was damned serious. You did not get caught going over to the Naval Academy's Bancroft Hall neither dirty nor unkempt. Everything at the Academy was spit and polish including Messboys and seamen. Many were sent home, that did not know what the word inaptitude meant. Before going ashore you were inspected. If not up to par, you stayed aboard.

The Author's first day in Bancroft Hall was just short of terrifying. The size of the place to new men looked like an oversized football field with tables and chairs. There were large clocks at each end with large numerals. One could stand in its center and have difficulty ascertaining the time of day. It was so large until the Head boy had to direct the crew by loudspeaker.

In preparation for Bancroft Hall we lined up in two long lines facing each other single file that nearly reached the length of the dock. On the command, "Count-off," we did so, by singing out loudly one, two, three, and four. Having completed this, again on command the order came to execute a "squads left." At this order, the no. 1 man pivoted sharply left, no. 2 executed a half-pivot, no. 3 and no. 4 would swing around forming a shoulder-to-shoulder squad of four. In this way squads were formed into four neat platoons. This execution was beautiful to watch. Often tourist visiting the Academy would line up to see the Messboy's' "lost battalion," on the march. One elderly White lady wrote a letter to the Commandant, Rear Admiral "Rusty" Wilson, commending him on the smartness, cleanliness and military demeanor of his Negro midshipmen. She, further, suggested that he get as many Negro boys there as possible where they could be disciplined and taught to keep their Bodies clean, so that the country wouldn't have so much trouble with them. The Admiral's cook shared that one with us, which caused howls of laughter and "doo say, nigga midshipmen!"

This lady probably misconstrued us for midshipmen because all "plebes," (first year men) at Annapolis wear white hats with a blue band around the top and a white sailor uniform during their first year and had to double time (run) every where they went unless in formation. What she failed to observe was that a plebe's white hat had a ½-inch blue band of color around the top, which the common sailor did not. We had expert mimics among the Messboys. We had one who could mimic Captain Benson's voice, posture and demeanor who, when addressing Messboys, always commenced with, "you people." He could also mimic the martinet – Commander of midshipmen whose accent was almost British. For example he did not address midshipmen Jones as such, he would say, "midshipman Joons." It did take humor to survive at Annapolis. So on learning of our new status via the Admirals cook, the mimics spent a week addressing each other and their homies as Midshipmen Washington, Jones, etc. with great ostentation, pomp and circumstance. Once I was ordered to "front and center" and to recite the first stanza of Kipling's poem, "If," just as first class midshipmen ordered plebes to do on command. A good time was had by all. We had expert mimics among the Messboys. It did take humor to survive at Annapolis.

But if a messboy "hacked it" at Naptown, Annapolis, he could hack it anywhere the Navy sent him after his tour of duty there. When World War II commenced, it was from this station that the Navy acquired ready disciplined cadres of messboys, needed to man the new ships, sliding rapidly down the Ways and awaiting commissioning. Many of us were placed in Rated men's positions (Stewards and Cooks), while still not rated. A good example is that of my own history. Where it formerly took years to become a Rated man, the War reduced this to weeks. As a mere Third Class Cook, just out of the Naval Academy's cooks and stewards school, I was sent to Motor Torpedo Base #15. This outfit was packed and ready to sail. It was to repair P. T. Boats. Although I was a mere Third Class, I was put in charge of the Officers' Mess and all personnel; a position usually held by a First Class Steward. This outfit sailed for Guadalcanal and we ended up being put ashore on Tulagi Island, about twenty miles away, across Sea Lark Channel. I was a Watch Captain in Officers' Mess on Tulagi. After the Admiralty Islands invasion, we were sent to Los Negros Island and billeted with the 58th SeaBees. In what would have taken years in the peacetime Navy, I had in months been promoted to First Class. I came home after the invasion of Leyte in the Philippines. As a First Class, we were not allowed to be ("Petty Officers"), I was in charge of four hundred men, (eight platoons of fifty men each). My Officers wondered where I, at my age, got the discipline and leadership skills. I used to tell them, with a grin, that I was trained at the U.S. Naval Academy.

CHAPTER 16. THE MESSBOY'S REQUIRED ADAPTATION FOR NAVAL SERVICE

There probably never was in Naval History a more colorful group than the "highly select" group of Negroes who served the Navy's Officers Corps between WWI (1919) and the end of that service: In 1974. At that time it was stricken from the personnel structure. It is possible but not very probable there ever will be another group of Blacks like this group. They possessed a toughness balanced by a certain shrewdness; a native intelligence that enabled them to survive, thrive and even prosper in a climate of unabashed racism that would have broken and/ or crushed lesser men. The stewards, cooks, and Messboys of the Navy mastered one of the most exacting "survival arts", ever imposed upon an oppressed group of minority peoples; that of perceiving one's self as somebody when a near totality of a powerful society stated and believed that "you were nobody". The brown Filipino or yellow Guamanian, Chinese and Japanese fellow sufferers came from stable, basically homogenous cultures where they were allowed to belong as members. The Black members of the Stewards Branch had no such society where they could claim universal social acceptance. They existed in a psychosocial and political no mans land, where one's very identity was an ongoing challenge.

However the Negroes suffered, besides the disability of "color", being forced to try to become social members of a culture which, from its earliest history, misused and rejected them, shamelessly exploited, abused and brutally lynched those that tried to be men. This was a society where it was blatantly stated that Blacks were not wanted. The often-stated phrase was, "They should send all of you niggers back to Africa", is a presumption of racist bigotry even today. Most members of the Stewards' Branch managed to "hack it", that is, to remain persons with a picture of themselves that they could live with, in spite of the sustained harsh psychosocial and political forces arrayed against them. Most of this group arrived in the Navy already skilled and toughened by the cruel slings and arrows of rejection and racial discrimination. Most had endured harsh apprenticeships in their native southern states, where poor white-redneck failures made it a game to goad and/or belittle them. In the Navy, one did not have to deal with the "terrible reality" of possibly being lynched, burned alive or beaten half to death, for simply failing to observe the black/white protocol, talking back or mouthing off justifiably to a white man, or losing one's temper and smacking someone. This hardening process made most of the Navy's Officers and men's occasional redneck antics seem tame. Thus, we officers' servants could let "racist trash" fall off our backs like water off a duck's back and inwardly dismiss it with the aplomb of a duck getting a shower bath! Of course quite a few Messboys failed in the capacity to withstand the "psycho-social heat" implicit in their contrived social milieu and fell by the wayside. These never really developed that art of being "two-selves", one for dealing externally with white men and one for dealing internally with one's inner-self or psyche.

The author knew many friends and shipmates who failed the "exacting-adaptation" test required of Blacks. This had nothing to do with the "military-adaptation" required of all new Navy men, regardless of color. Blacks had to learn to appear to stay in their place, "physically" (never showing anger or defiance, etc.), but escape from the concept of "place" on the inner "mental-plane" of day-to-day existence. The failure to do so was usually manifested by:

1). * Mouthing off to some officers more than once. The first offense usually earned the culprit a stint in the "brig" on cake and wine (bread and water). A second offense of this nature was looked upon as ingrained-insolence, a character flaw that directly challenged the sense of place perceived by white men. There was attitude involved here, not knowing his place. This was a "no-no" and was not forgiven. Such hapless fellows were discharged with a "bad conduct discharge" (BCD) or worse an "inaptitude discharge" or (ID). This later made future finding of employment nearly impossible, as people did not know whether the person was stupid, crazy or some kind of sexual deviate.

2). Get kicked out by getting into a "funk" failing cleanliness requirements, refusing duty or becoming alcoholic, being constantly over leave, tardy or going "over the hill" (running away). This usually elicited a BCD or ID.

3). Defiance (unacceptable attitude), usually manifested by beating upon some nasty white person or Uncle Tom. This was a sure way to a "kick-out" as one violated both the "concept of place" but worse showed no intent to perceive ones self as having such. Many of these failures were sent to prison.

4). Intentional violation of sanitary rules. Now White people of this era had sold themselves on such facts, as Black people were not only inherently stupid but that they were also dirty. So all a Negro messboy had to do to get kicked out was to become

---

* Commanding officer could order an enlisted man jailed for five days on bread and water minus any really formal court process.

scroungy (dirty clothes and dirty body and stink real good), catch the "claps" (gonococcus infection) two or three times, or pretend that he lost control of his bladder. We were food handlers and were inspected, underwear, fingernails, etc. each day. The author knows one messboy from Kentucky who peed "his way out" of the Navy! He simply said, "I don't have to take this shit" and urinated in his hammock every night. The Navy gave him a medical discharge. The concept of the "dirty nigger" was always a source of amusement to the author who knew families who could barely eat each day though they worked like horses. Their children usually possessed one or two sets of clothes. The lucky ones had a Sunday-go-to meeting set of clothes. Most Black women washed and kept white folks and their houses clean. We knew and observed poor whites that were called "poor white trash", that couldn't afford a Black washerwoman. Blacks were clean compared to these unfortunate, mean and usually ignorant people. So a standing joke among Messboys was what will happen to "Miss Ann" and her young'uns if "Ole Saffire" went on strike?

5). Finally, the most pitiful failure of adaptation was the "Uncle Tom", the Steward who lost the respect of both white officers and Black Messboys; no one respected informants. This person projected behavior that made us ashamed of being Black. He was the boot licking, fawning, grinning at "ole Massa's" non-funny jokes, while bucking his eyes like Mantan Moreland or Step'n Fetchit. Worst of all, this type "finked" on his own people, humiliated and got men punished, unfairly, in order to please "his white folks". This type earned the unmitigated contempt of his fellows and usually had to seek company elsewhere and became a pariah. In the language of Messboys "the dude became a phony, a piss poor imitation of a white man".

For the sake of clarity, let's depart from the mundane scholar bit that I might acquaint you with the climate, behavior and expectations of this era through my personal experiences. The entry gates were not fully opened to Negroes until 1939-40. This writer entered the Navy in July 1940 with the first large-scale flood of Negro mess attendants recruited since 1919 and after their total exclusion in 1919. He was inducted at Little Rock, Arkansas, and sent to Unit B-East, a cluster of wooden WWI buildings at Norfolk Naval Training Station for "boot training." We were rigidly segregated. Whites lived in modern, warm, red brick barracks, some of which had bunks to sleep in and recreation rooms. Our quarters consisted of a long house-type empty room with a "poop-deck" (elevated platform) for "hammock" storage and starboard and port "jackstaves" (steel pipes running the length of the building). There was not one chair or bench for "boots" to sit on in the whole complex. We broiled under the July sun and froze chilled by the wet, late, September winds off Hampton Roads.

To give the reader real insight into the interactive behavior, based upon Black/White expectations, let's review my early service. The Navy was highly selective in those days of the 'great depression' of the 1930's. In order to gain entrance as a mess attendant 3/C (third class) at $21 a month, one had to acquire character references that would do honor to today's Naval Academy candidates. Further, it was common knowledge and a source of wry humor to us that you had to be: (a) a southern Negro, and (b) not too smart. The Navy discouraged recruitment of "uppity northern Niggers." The sincere, first class yeoman, who recruited me, said, in hindsight, he really wanted to help me. My first papers were turned down because the well-meaning white members of the "southern aristocracy" in my hometown of Hope, Arkansas, Mrs. K. G. McRae, the daughter of a former Governor of Arkansas, and Judge Leonard K. Lemly, "political boss" of Hempstead County, slipped up.

They said that I was <u>intelligent,</u> in order to get around the fact that I was a tenth grader. According to the Yeoman, this made me suspect in the eyes of the recruitment chief! The Yeoman told me, "I like you boy." His coaching session with me went like this. I remember it with the clarity of an automobile accident: 'I'm gonna be straight wid ya. You talk too good and you look white men in the eye. This could cause you trouble. You simply don't ack lak a nigger enough." He did not have to draw a mural for me to comprehend him; I had been coached in this art form as a survival tool. He further told me, "Them big shots hurtcha wid all they big shit words". Now if ya really want to git in, you go back and git some solid ordinary white folks to recommend ya." This I did and made sure that they stressed that I was <u>"obedient"</u> rather than <u>"intelligent"</u>, and that I "knew my place." This, however, was not enough. The Chief was still suspicious and wanted to see me in person. I said to myself "Oh hell, that cracker ain't gonna let me in." The Yeoman sent all other prospective recruits to lunch. We ate in the kitchen of a white restaurant, standing up with the plates lined along a vegetable preparation table. My face obviously fell at the thought of missing free vittles. I had fifty cents and was 112 miles from home. I had hoboed up from Hope, Arkansas, on a freight train.

The Yeoman seeing this said, "You wanta git in dontcha?" "Yes sir," I said, to which he replied, "Then stop thankin bout ya gut and listen", he told me while rehearsing it for me (he was a great mimic of Negroes). "Stop saying 'Sir' like a white man and say 'yassuh,' an when ya talks tu tha chief, don't look em in the eye. Kinda look down atcha feet and cock ya head to one side and scratch it whuther it itches or not, you understand? Now let me see ya do it." As I was going through my act he stopped me with, "Aw hell boy, not lack that for Christ sake. What in the 'two blocked hell are ya doin? Aintcha never saw Stepin Fetchit or ole Mantan Moreland at tha pitcha show?" "Yassuh," I replied. He then said, "You'll never git by the Chief, an dammit, I needs you for my quota."

I wondered in bewilderment what expressions such as 'quota' and 'two-blocked-hell meant. I smiled inwardly because his next statement put me on familiar ground. He said, "Kinda shuffle and don't smile like a cracker; Kinda giggle." As he demonstrated, I cracked up laughing. He became very stern and said "You gotta put down some John, understand?" I was well schooled in the southern darkie art of shucking and jiving. I damned well had better have learned this well in order to survive in Arkansas. After further explanation (the Navy wants "good southern boys"), I passed with flying colors.

It is surprising how many of the Navy's stewards, cooks, and Messboys managed to survive with a modicum of dignity and self-respect in tact, remain men and prosper under these circumstances. But many of these wily, shrewd, mentally nimble, tough fellows did so. They even raised families on Messboys pay by "moonlighting" as janitors, waiters, etc. while ashore. They rose to heights of human-survival and managed to be "somebody" when most of U.S. society said they were "nobody"; an unusual feat in itself. In spite of intentionally distorted U.S. History, the Battle Record of the Navy's Messboys speaks for itself. They were men who performed and gave a good account of themselves. They did so in the best traditions of the U.S. Navy.

It is said that the true measure of the quality of any pudding is the tasting. If one wishes to check out the quality of the "fighting capacity" of the Navy's cooks, stewards, and Messboys, the author suggests that they simply sift the action reports of the Navy's crack fighting ships. Here in the dusty archives read the casualty lists of those killed in action, missing in action, and those grievously wounded. These unemotional, dry, dusty ship's logs speak with greater eloquence, authority, and truth than any written Naval history; most of which is marred by the negative concept of race and contain more omissions of the true story of Black men than commissions.

CHAPTER 17. NEGRO PERFORMANCE IN WWII: STOLEN HONOR

This part of the story is about the honor historically due Blacks, who, down the continuum of time in this country, have displayed gallantry, courage and intrepidity on America's battlefields here and beyond its' seas. Honor was omitted, or insidiously and unfairly stripped from them by Hollywood, amoral historians, educators, politicians and behavioral scientist over a period of years.

Freedom has never come cheap for Black people in this country. Most of the time it has been paid for in blood. It is both fitting and proper that we honor Alonzo Swann as well as other surviving Navy Cross recipients. Above all, we must honor those Black youngsters who lost their lives a long ways from home, who were buried in alien seas, and whose families never had the privilege of looking upon their faces a last time. All paid dearly for something desperately needed by Afro-American citizens --, heroes. Lack of these, as a part of our Black children's knowledge base, stunts and impairs their self-image negatively. This is the locus of self-hatred that has made many Black inner city youngsters, today, a clear and present danger to not just themselves, but to other citizens as well. It is damned hard to "act like somebody" when one is made to feel like "nobody". Finally, as to the surviving crewmembers of *U.S.S. Intrepid*, the US Navy owes them a lasting debt. A diving aircraft is always a serious danger to an Aircraft carrier such as the Intrepid. This is easily validated by the loss of:

1. USS Lexington lost May 28, 1942 - Battle of the Coral Sea

2. USS Yorktown lost June 7. 1942 - Battle of Midway

3. USS Wasp lost September 15, 1942 - Battle of the Eastern Solomons

4. USS Hornet lost October 26, 1942 - Battle of Santa Cruz Islands

5. USS Princeton lost October 25, 1944 - Battle of Leyte

Just to name a few? This is just some of the carriers lost. Many more were flown into by Kamikaze planes and were lost or suffered severe losses in men killed by the hundreds. For instance, the *USS Ben Franklin*, which was turned into a funeral Pyre for 600 men incident to air attack but managed to limp 13,000 miles home. The aim here is to really pin point the importance of what these Messboys in Gun Tub 10 did so that a layman can understand. Any old carrier steward knows that there are no non-combatants aboard a carrier. The chance of death is shared equally by all hands incident to the fragility of a fast carrier. It can inflict more damage probably, than any other ship with the exception of ballistic missile carrying atomic submarines. It cannot take as much punishment as it can deliver. The reason is to be found in her cargo consisting of hundreds of gallons of aviation gasoline or jet fuel, torpedoes, bombs, shells and the planes, themselves. When fueled and loaded with bombs, a hit on any of these by a diving plane could cause the loss of a ship and hundreds of lives.

So on October 29, 1944 when all that stood between the *USS Intrepid* and her possible destruction and severe loss of lives, were 16 Messboys, stewards and cooks, who were gallant and courageous enough to stand fast and stay the course with a resultant terrible, and tragic cost. These were men, whom America thought were only fit to shine shoes, peel potatoes, cook, make beds and serve coffee! They were there because two white men, Naval Officers, Captain W. D. Sample, who allowed their training, respected and believed in them, and Captain

Joseph F. Bolger, later Vice Admiral Bolger, allowed them to fight rather than restricting them to washing pots and pans.

One of the most tenacious men that this writer has ever met was former Stewards Mate Alonzo Alexander Swann. Swann fought the U.S. Navy for 47 years over the perceived wrong done to him and his shipmates for service aboard the U.S.S Intrepid. For corroboration, let's begin with the unbiased perceptions of a white reporter, Jerry Shnay, who worked for the Chicago Tribune. The story was also published on December 26, 1992 in the Patriot News of Harrisburg, Pennsylvania. It Said:

> "All that stood in the way of a Japanese suicide plane and the flight deck of the U.S.S. Intrepid that day in 1944 was Gun Tub 10. While other gunnery crews had abandoned their posts, Swann's battery blazed away with 20-millimeter cannons across the aircraft carrier's deck toward the oncoming Kamikaze. The firing was accurate, shooting away the plane's left wing and most of its tail. But at the last moment, instead of crashing into Leyte Gulf, the plane veered and slammed into the battery, turning it into a blazing funeral pyre. Nine men were burned to death and six others, including the 19-year-old Swann suffered serious injuries. The Navy says that each of the six were awarded the Bronze Star medal; but for 48 years, Swann has insisted that they all had been promised the Navy Cross, the highest award for gallantry the Navy has to offer.

Since this reporter was writing about an event that occurred 48 years before, this writer sought out a report closer to the actual event. He found it in a report by Ray Coll, Jr., written for the Honolulu paper,(The Honolulu Call Bulletin), and published Wednesday morning, December 13, 1944. Coll was a war correspondent who was actually aboard the U.S.S. Intrepid that fateful day (October 29, 1944) as an eyewitness. He said:

"When this correspondent was on a big carrier with Admiral Halsey's Third Fleet not long ago, there was one day that will be long remembered. We had been launching strikes against airstrips on Luzon. The first strike was back and circling the ship for landing when general quarters sounded. Some of the Japs were evidently following the planes home...Suddenly ships near us opened up frantically and then our ship started firing. I looked up and suddenly saw a plume of smoke. And, it was falling directly toward us. The other ships kept firing as it passed over them and then were silent. Only our ship was firing. But the plane kept falling and as it came closer, I could see pieces of the wing and tail flying off as our bullets seared into it. Smoke continued to billow forth like a long black streamer. The Jap came in just abaft the smokestack. I thought he would hit the flight deck but it did not. I got up and dashed to the other side of the ship and there was a blinding sheet of flame as the Jap plane scraped the edge of a Gun Tub and went into the water.

But that blinding sheet of flame had covered the crew in the Gun Tub. When it cleared, I couldn't see any of the crew. Some of the guns they had been manning were twisted up at a bizarre angle and others looked okay. A crew of medical corpsmen and others were running to the spot. I wondered about those men who had been manning the guns an instant before. They were Colored boys, a picked crew from among the Mess Attendants. They already had a record of shooting down one plane out of three downed by gun crews on the ship in a previous action. They were mighty proud of that achievement. There were 16 of them".

Then Coll vividly describes what price the Negroes paid for standing to and shooting down the plane. He said:

"Then I saw the corpsmen climb down into the Gun Tub and soon they were tenderly lifting out bodies up to the stretcher-bearers. They were naked bodies and they were white. I couldn't understand. Then it dawned on me. They had been badly burned by that sheet of flame; their clothes had been burned off and so had their skin. They looked puffed and distorted. I wondered if Saunders (I'll call him that) was among them? Saunders was our room boy and he had been telling me about his crew knocking down a Jap. He was a good boy and couldn't do enough for us. We used to chat once in a while, while he was making up our room. After all clear was sounded, I learned that nine of that crew had been killed and seven wounded, one of who died later".

There is a bit of history here that is often overlooked. Although Saunders had just done a man's job, even a kindly, astute white man showing genuine concern, still was obviously comfortable in calling him a "boy". William H. Davis provides further insight and history of Gun Tub 10 in an article written for the navy human resources magazine, "Our Navy". He was assigned to start a training program for the new, all Negro Gun crew. Davis admits facing a real communications problem with this crew. Davis says:

"These men, mostly boys, had wanted a "topside" battle station, a few guns to fire ever since the ship went into commission. Stewards and Steward Mates spend most of their time in the galley, the wardroom or at their cleaning stations. They are the colored boys aboard ship... A gunners mate 3/C helped me with the boys that first day and from then on took over the guns. He was a Mexican boy, but also an American from San Juan Capistrano, California. Everyone called him "Papoose" because he looked like a Red Indian. Davis admits he had become frustrated and hoarse while trying to teach this crew the technical language of gunnery; such terms as target angle, gun elevation and relative bearing, etc. So after a while, Papoose took over. His patience and the determination of the colored boys produced a combination that produced quick results. In 30 minutes, he was giving them loading and tracking drills, and the six guns were waving in unison. Under Papoose's leadership, the Stewards and Steward Mates quickly gained the respect of everyone in the gunnery department. They treated their jobs with the utmost seriousness. They practiced with the spirit of competition and fought with the spirit of loyalty and courage."

Davis, in describing the attack and its aftermath says, "when the plane struck, there was complete silence. The Altoona, Georgia boy spoke to me before I could find the right thing to say to my men. "Oh God Sir, he spluttered". The Jap Plane and Tub 10 went up in flames together. Some of the gunners, strapped to their shoulder bars were burned to their guns. Nine died in all and many were seriously wounded. One of them was Papoose (real name A. Chavarrias), who lost his leg and died a few hours later." Not one man had left his station. The next day the ships' plan of the day carried an expression of condolences by the Executive Officer. In part, it said:

> "We are saddened by the suffering and death among our shipmates. But we saw an example of sheer nerve hard to equal and impossible to exceed. Our gunners kept up their fire until the Jap crashed among them. In this instance, we saw unadvertised courage of our men serve their guns in the face of certain death. It wasn't necessary to whip up their courage, it was there…"

All of the men were buried at sea. The memory of Gun Tub 10 will live forever with the ship. Before closing this discussion of Gun Tub 10, there is, in fairness to the gunners who abandoned their stations and ran, an explanation for their behavior. To the unaware, this would appear to be an act of cowardice. That is not so. As a flattop crewmember, this author heard the gunnery officer tell his officers to instruct the men that when an enemy plane is struck such that its pilot is no longer in control, do not remain at the guns. Get the hell out of the way, when one understands that further hits will not enable gunners to change a suicide planes direction. To stand and shoot, in that instance, would constitute a waste and needless loss of life.

Obviously, the men of Gun Tub 10 stood and shot at this plane until it, literally, flew down their gun barrels because they thought they could still make it change direction or blow up and miss the ship. They, at great cost, partially succeeded in preventing death and serious injury to possibly hundreds of their shipmates.

What happened in the aftermath of this gallant act is what angered Alonzo Swann and triggered his 48-year fight with the Navy. Swann, a 19-year-old Stewards Mate got out of the Navy in 1945, an angry and very disappointed young black man. The source of Swann's anger was that his shipmates had given their lives for their country, but had been cheated and disrespected in payment. They were not cheated or disrespected by their Officers or shipmates. They were cheated and disrespected by some *desk-huggers* at the U.S Department of the Navy! On February 15, 1945, a Meritorious Mast was held at which nine members of the U.S.S Intrepid crew were awarded citations and the Navy Cross for gallantry in action on October 29, 1944. Receiving the awards were three officers and six enlisted men. Among them were Captain J. F. Bolger, USN, Commander W. E. Ellis, USN, and Commander T. S. Wallace, USNR. The Enlisted men included Eli Benjamin, STM 2/c, USNR, Harold Clark, STM 1/C, USNR, Johnell Copeland, STM 1/c, USNR, James Dockery, STM 1/c, USNR, Que Grant, STM 1/c, USNR, and Alonzo Swann, STM 1/c, USNR

When the results of this Mast reached the Navy Department in Washington, someone decided to downgrade the Black enlisted men's awards from the Navy Cross to the Bronze Star! All of the men were ordered, on the grounds that a mistake had been made, to return their commendations and medals. This was done after the war had ended. One of the enlisted men, Que Grant, refused to turn his in. This proved to be critical later in Swann's case. Swann was rebuffed at every turn, over the years, as he sought records of proof, for possible action by the

Navy Review Board. Finally, in 1984, he sought the assistance of Larry Dickey, an aide to Congresswoman Katie Hall, (D-Indiana). Dickey began looking for proof. According to the Chicago Tribune, Dickey later became aide to Peter McCloskey, Hall's successor; so he was able to continue the search.

Finally, pertinent documents were found. A copy of the Meritorious Mast was obtained along with a copy of the press release in which someone in the Navy ordered that the word "Navy Cross" be deleted and replaced by "Bronze Star". Swann then learned that Grant had kept his award. With this solid proof, Swann hired an attorney and took the Navy to court in 1990. Two years later, 1992, Swann, now 67 years old, got his date in court.

U.S. District Judge Rudy Lozano ordered the U.S. Navy to award Swann the Navy Cross. The judge said that Swann had been denied his medal either through error or by racial injustice. Alonzo Swann told the author that he considered the event to be a Pyrrhic victory in that only he was ordered to receive his medal in this ruling. Further, the Navy still had the right to appeal. Swann was obviously unaware of the vast racial and social climate changes the U.S. Navy had undergone by this time. As it turned out, the Navy Department awarded the Navy Cross to all of the Gun Tub 10 survivors and chose not to contest the court ruling.

Leaving the subject of Gun Tub 10, it is pertinent to remind any present or future commander that it is weak and a dereliction of duty to tolerate racist or bigots and now "male chauvinist pigs", the new time bomb in a command. Such tolerance neglects to consider the potential damages such people are capable of inflicting upon a command or a Service. Such damage is immeasurable and may come in form of race-riots or highly new-worthy sexual type incidents embarrassment, severe damage to a service's image, its fighting units and consequent prestige;

not to mention political hurts that tend to take on a life of their own. Bigots and Racist, or sexist, it is repeated here, can always be depended upon to act stupid and embarrass their commands as they tend to not posses the capacity to put the welfare of their service first. As an example, they would let their personal feelings tell them that Captain Bolger, who was there and who recommended that Tub 10 survivors should be decorated, and his task force Commander Vice Admiral John S. McCain, "made a mistake!" No, these two extremely capable officers made no mistake. Some unthinking bigots at Washington, in the Navy Department's bureaucracy made the mistake, hoping that amidst the exigencies of War no one would ever find out.

Long after this unthinking, amoral bigot was allowed to downgrade the gallant Cooks, Stewards and Steward Mates, the hurt that he did to the U.S. Navy's image remained a potent negative force that acted as a retardant to Navy recruiting years later. This type of highly publicized media incident tends to take on a life of its own. For example, this matter still finds ordinary people, especially minority communities, that are unaware of the giant strides made by the U.S. Navy, in the Human Resources Management and the Race Relations areas during and after the Viet Nam War era. Uniformed, these people still perceive the Navy in its old negative, racist and sexist role.

To the informed, the post Elmo Zumwalt Navy is a vastly different organization. The author, on leaving the Post Graduate School, observed a Navy that was way ahead of the civilian institutions in the broader society, when it comes to actually dealing with the problems of racism and sexism in its ranks. By comparison, the U.S. Air force Academy recently had its superintendent fired over the mistreatment of female cadets. West Point has also suffered from Human Relations problems. Annapolis seems to have handled, positively, its sexism, racism and gay/lesbian problems. The Author feels that Admiral Zumwalt supervised the creation and promulgation of one of the best Human Resources Management efforts in U.S. History, an effort for which he has never received proper recognition, and /or honors, from his fellow Admirals or his government. Having met and talked with the Admiral, on two occasions, I know that Elmo Zumwalt knew that he would pay a price for doing something about racism. Nevertheless, he ordered all Officers, getting a graduate degree at the Post Graduate School, to take courses in Human Resources (course Numbers mn3811 and mn3822).

The U.S. Marine Corps has also avoided being dragged through the mire of press, so far. This Author was invited to the U.S. Marine Headquarters, by Lieutenant General Leslie Brown, while teaching at the Naval Post Graduate School. General Brown turned out to be a very understanding senior officer. He pushed for, and succeeded in getting the Marine Corps to upgrade its Human Resources Management effort. He is probably responsible for Marine students being sent to the Post Graduate School program. So far, his effort seems to have had positive results. The Marine Corps has, so far, escaped the humiliation that has dogged West Point and the Air Force Academy. When the author retired from the U.S. Navy in 1961, he had 21 years of Service. During the 21 years he was selected for one of two promotions "Navy wide", on two occasions. He was one of two promoted to Chief Petty Officer in 1949. It is important, here, to note that Chief Stewards were not granted the authority of Chief Petty Officers until 1949, four years after WW II. Possibly, of equal importance, is that when the Navy created two grades above E-7, in 1959 (Grades E-8, Senior Chief and E-9, Master Chief), the author again took one of two promotions, Navy wide. He was allowed to jump E-8 and take the E-9 exam, by the officer in charge of Submarine Administration, Mare Island, California, Captain Lowel Stone. What is relevant here is that he, as a Mess Boy, Steward 1/c, Chief Steward and Master Chief Steward at Annapolis, in the Pacific Fleet, and later an Assistant Professor of Human Resources Management at the Naval Post Graduate School, Monterey from 1973 to 1980, saw and knew many Admirals and Generals. To this day the author remembers those Senior officers who possessed the character and sense of fairness needed, to overcome the Racism, which permeates this society such that their leadership could be brought to bear, when their country and their service was in dire need. When the Negro Revolt threatened to demoralize this country's Armed Forces, some moral Officers came to the forefront and did what was required, in order to prevent this demoralization. This Country and their Services owe these remarkable Officers a debt that will, one day be realized.

CHAPTER 18. GOALS OF NAVAL PERSONNEL POLICY: THE SELECTION OF MESSBOYS 1932-1974

As mentioned before, at the end of the US Navy's "disbarment period" (1919-1932) during which Negroes had been wrongfully and illegally denied the opportunity and privilege of serving their country in the Sea Services, necessity intervened from an unplanned quarter. This has always forced limited acceptance of Negroes in the U.S. Armed Forces. The Philippines, an American Colony since the defeat of Spain in the Spanish American War (1898), had the temerity to demand their freedom from their American masters in the 1930s! Herein lies a story unknown or ignored by most Naval historians. In the Naval histories consulted by the author not one index contained a heading for Negro Messboys, Messmen or stewards. Nathan Miller does deal briefly with this subject in his depiction of the Zumwalt era (see page 402). But the only mentioning of Negroes in Simon and Schuster's massive 700 thousand-word encyclopedia of World War II refers to the Island of Negroes in the Philippines. As in most other sources, unless one is interested in the humiliation of slavery, Blacks simply do not exist; nor do Stewards, Cooks, or Messboys. So reiterating the Negro/Philippine section may be forgiven.

To do this lets pose a question. Since the Negro was brought to America to slave and work in the white man's fields and wait on his table and historically has filled this role in U.S. society, why were Filipino, Guamanian servants, Chinese and Japanese acquired by the Navy in the first place? This answer is important if one is to understand the source of the massive resentment of most naval officers of the Negroes' reentry into the Navy in 1932, after being barred from enlistment in 1919. It further clarifies why the Negro messboy of the 1930's Navy had to master rapidly certain survival skills if he was to become a career Navy man. Otherwise he was "kicked out". The United States did participate as a Colonial power prior to and after the Spanish American War. When China was coerced into often unfair trade agreements and being forced to address Christianity as a religion, the United States was there to help enforce and to get its share. The U.S. Navy and Marines were the guardians of this country's so-called rights in the Far East. They were there also to let European powers, (England, France, Germany and Russia) know that the United States was no longer a mere participant but a "player" in world affairs, that we had an Imperial Power.

In the Administration of the Philippine, Samoan, Puerto Rican, Cuban and Panamanian colonies, while protecting these U.S. interest, and, while dealing with the emergent powers of Japan and others, exposed older naval officers to the "fruits of Colonialism." These old "China hands", for example, knew what it was to observe and experience "complete subservience", including the act of "kow-towing", by Chinese, (placing ones forehead on the ground or floor while prostrate), before ones "betters". Now the American Negro, from the Southern States, may have learned to fool the white man by grinning at non-funny jokes, casting down his eyes or appearing dumb but "kow-towing", really? No way! The brush with U.S. Democracy eliminates this ultimate act of subservience.

The problem here was how Negroes were socialized. For example, no nations in the Western World could match those in the East in the Creation of despotism, as a tool and mode of social and political control. Chopping the subjects' head off or ordering other suitable torture befell any underling who dared to question the authority of his superiors. Whether you are referring to Mongols, East Indians, Tartars, Tibetans, Chinese, Japanese, Malayasians or ancient Siamese Societies, no European Nation ever equaled the Far Eastern or those of Southeast Asians' rulers in the art of "Despotic-control" of a populace. The upper class Filipinos is no piker here either. These old China hand-type Naval Officers knew that Orientals were conditioned to despotic rule, and its offshoot, expected subservient behavior; the oriental servant's culturally induced subservience, was perceived by them as genuine. Again, no people living contiguous to each other fail to learn from each other. Herein rested the white officers' problem with Negro Messboys. Probably little or no effort is required in such learning as man is, by nature, an "imitator". Negroes were never placed on "reservations" like war-like native Americans. They were always allowed to live contiguously to White Americans. How else could "Ole Marse Charlie" get his cotton picked, his sugar cane cut, his indigo, rice and tobacco harvested and his woman waited upon, except by exploitation of black labor? Negroes were, like it or not, by exposure to "Democratic/Republican" government concepts and principles and understood their meaning. They may not have enjoyed its full fruits but they certainly understood its concepts and its possibilities of eventual freedom. White officers knew of this longing. So we Navy Blacks were more carefully watched and more readily and more severely punished than Orientals.

Consequently White officers had to spend an inordinate amount of time contemplating whether "Ole Shine" was playing games with him or was being truly subservient and knew his place. Doubt on part of Naval officers was unlike what us Black Messboys were used to: as in, "Nigger, are you getting' uppity with me?" Officers and gentlemen used the more proper "Boy, are you getting smart with me?", when they doubted a Black Messboy's sense of "place".

Before leaving this subject, it is pertinent to point out that what is written here is not with any intent to disparage either the Pacific Island People (Filipino, Guamanians) or those of the Orient (China, Japan), as they were, as much victims of their situations as the Negroes were. We shared communality as underlings. They were all looked down upon as inferior beings. Most Southern Negroes, from landlocked states, probably had never seen a Filipino, Chinese, Guamanian or Japanese prior to entering the Navy. The author had only seen one oriental in his life. One Chinese man somehow ended up in Hope, Arkansas, married a black woman and had one son.

One time he asked his father, "why his eyes were hurt", having never observed Mongoloid eyes. His dad, after he quit laughing, told him about people, not just Chinese who also suffered that affliction, genetically. He then told him, "His eyes aren't hurt and he can probably see a damned sight better than you." Many years later in the British Solomons, the author had to disabuse a lot of White Marines and sailors of this ignorance. "They can't see too good, especially at night!" Where American serviceman got this from, the author was never able to ascertain; but it was wide spread among the troops. The author while at Tulagi Island, had to tell many young "90-day wonders", (reserve officers) bound for the invasions of the Northern Solomons, that these shiny 2nd Lieutenant and Ensign's bars on their shoulders or that shiny watch on his wrists could cost them their lives. Japanese snipers high in the palm trees would make the Martins and McCoy marksman of Tennessee feuding fame look like a piker. A flash from a shoulder bar or a shiny watch reflected by the sun's rays could get one a bullet between the eyes from marksmen in the dense jungles of the Southwest Pacific. I knew nothing about Orientals prior to my arrival at Norfolk.

But Negro hayseeds fresh from plantations in Alabama, Georgia and other states of the Confederacy had to learn to work with Orientals. Contrived relations were established between Oriental Messboys and newly recruited Negroes. During the author's early naval career he thought that Orientals simply did not like Negroes or thought they were white. They disliked us just as any ole honky did, so he thought. He thought also, being ignorant of their culture, that they were simply "Uncle Toms" who happened to not be Black! Further, older Negro stewards and cooks warned us new Southern yokels, "Boy you betta watch them "Chinks and Flips" (Chinese and Filipinos); they will tell them white folks on you and mess you up." Notice that these older Negroes ignorantly utilized the same derogatory terms for Orientals as white sailors and officers used.

It was much later that the author came to understand, that the social distance maintained between these servants and us was a result of social engineering, on part of officers. The aim of these trained military strategists, whom we served coffee, was nothing so lofty as "divide and conquer" as we were already victims of this. The aim was to "divide and control" as an end.

It was much later that he understood why these Oriental servants who shinned the same shoes, served the same coffee and made the same beds as us Negroes appeared to perceive themselves as "better" than their Negro fellow servants. He, by sheer accident obtained this revelation in this manner, on several occasions. He would often hide in an empty room to write letters or study. The Messboys compartment was a place that existed somewhere between chaos and bedlam where, simultaneously, there may be crap games, arguments, tussles, the "dirty dozens", etc., forming a loud symphony. He was capable of sitting quietly in a corner and reading amidst all of this. He could simply lock on to his subject and "tune out". But occasionally the longing for "quiet contemplation" took over. Privacy did not enter into his needs. Being reared in a small house with 12 sisters and brothers had disabused him of the idea that such was possible indoors. But, quiet, he could obtain by simply going into the surrounding forest, even in Arkansas. While hiding with a book in a storeroom one day he overheard an officer, whom he really liked, indoctrinating the newly arrived head steward who was a Filipino.

This gentleman told the Filipino that under no circumstances was he to put a Negro in charge of the wardroom, galley (kitchen), pantry (salads/baking) or the staterooms. His reasons were that Negroes were dirty, stupid, undependable and sloppy and would mess him (the head steward) up and get him in trouble. He said, "Keep them in the wardroom or staterooms so you can watch them." He ended this session by sternly telling the steward "You keep those people in line (their place) because if there is a screw-up, I am going to blame you. Do you understand?" The author laughed, since white officers had a problem here, how in the hell did he think some foreigner could do so when he had a problem with us. "Now, you are a good boy, and I know that we can depend on you." This "boy" was 42 years old. The author stayed in hiding and was not about to let them know of his presence. He did wonder why the Navy wanted them at all if they were that lousy, as a people.

From this, the author learned the reason for negative Oriental behavior towards them, mistrusted them and retarded the promotion (some Negro Messboys remained 2nd class for 4 years) of Negroes, were a result of fear, that they would get them in trouble. There were never too many Japanese in the Navy during my watch (1940-1961). Mistrust of Japanese nationals had occurred in the prelude to the sailing of the "Great White Fleet", (1907); most were discharged. One officer told him that the Japanese were quick, tricky and could copy anything. They were wily, sneaky scoundrels.

Later, an old warrant officer told the author, "Them damned Japs probably drew every turret and gun on them ships before they put them out. They probably sent all them plans to Japan." The Japanese do not appear to have been sought in any great numbers between the Great White Fleet era (1907-1912) and World War One. As previously stated, instead Chinese, Filipinos and Guamanians were recruited. It is these that filled the void when Negroes were barred from naval service in 1919, in the aftermath of WWI. As the old Asiatic type officer disappeared via attrition, the re-admittance of Negroes probably became more acceptable. Further, the "two ocean navy", as a concept, combined with the Philippines demand for freedom, made the recruitment of the Negro a necessity as it had been throughout American History. There was a grudging need to be met.

The first wave of Filipinos, Chinese and Guamanians were inundated by the flood of Negroes needed to man the vast armadas of fighting ships for WWII. According to Jack D. Foner, in July 1940, the navy issued a call for 4,700 volunteers, including 200 blacks needed to work as mess attendants, cooks and stewards. When several blacks sought to enter naval service in other capacities, Rear Admiral Chester W. Nimitz, acting for the Secretary of the Navy, succinctly stated the official position. "After many years of experience, the policy of not enlisting men of the colored race for any branch of the naval service except the Messmen branch was adopted to meet the best interest of general ship efficiency."[170]

The author entered the navy on July 2, 1940 amidst all of this discriminatory rhetoric which dominated the Negro press. He got in by a "hair's breath", as his father stubbornly refused to sign his papers. He was told "Boy, I didn't raise you to be no damned flunky or servant!"

He was a follower of Marcus Garvey and was adamantly against him settling for a life as a mess boy. His mother's pleas finally won out with, "What is there for him here in Arkansas?" He was too poor to go to college so that settled it. It was a tradition among Southern Negroes to first educate the girls to keep them out of white folk's kitchens. Two other items, germane to the social and political situation that impinged upon the Navy's recruiting policy, based upon race and color are pertinent here.

There were actually three waves of Filipino recruits. The <u>first</u> along with a few Guamanians was used to replace the Negroes denied enlistment in the aftermath of WWI (1919). The <u>second wave</u> was brought in after WWII to replace discharged (1946) Negroes (most were reserves). The <u>third wave</u> was brought in to replace Negro recruits, in the aftermath of the Korean War, and advent of the Negro revolution. This was caused by the Brown decision of 1954, which triggered the "Negro Revolt", which in turn made the retention of large cadres of Negroes on the Navy's roles as servants politically untenable. Poverty, at home in the Philippines made this source of servants always available. Many of these later waves of Philipinos were better educated than were most American recruits.

The Chinese, a resourceful and entrepreneurial type people, finally released from the intense racism formerly leveled against them in the Western States, all but disappeared from the Stewards Branch as a meaningful bloc after WWII. Most of them left to open their own businesses (restaurants, markets, laundries, etc.).

The author is waiting for the U.S. Navy's reaction to the rise of Philippine Nationalism which caused the navy to be "kicked out" of the Philippines with especially the closure of the Massive Naval Facility at Olongapo (Subic Bay) and the Airforce Facility at Clark Field. Will the source of Filipino recruits dry up? If so, by which mechanism will it dry up? Will it be A) Philippine pride, or B) American Chagrin? Philippine Pride will probably not play a part, as poverty is a constant pressure for Philippine immigration. Further, the Filipino/American Community in the U.S. is a critically needed source of dollars, "hard currency", enjoyed by its government.

American chagrin could be a factor in that the U.S. incident to the rise of anti-immigration sentiment and its political ramifications could cause the navy to shut that recruit source down. They could do so minus political fear in today's political climate. We shall see. Further, the Philippines had, with State Department pressure after WWII, forced the Navy to cease and desist from recruiting Filipinos as servants only. Will the Navy nullify this by ceasing to recruit Filipinos? Again, we shall see.

The post WWII Filipinos were better educated than their predecessors but, "cultural comfort", still inclined them as a group to be "Clannish" and to exclude Negroes from their cliques aboard ship. For example, while teaching at the Naval Post Graduate School, the author was approached by a Black disbursing clerk and a storekeeper, two West Coast reared sailors, and asked if he could help them. They had been referred to him by one of his former white officer students whom they had complained to. They had families in California but were frozen in the Atlantic Fleet because, as they explained to him, Filipinos dominated "placement power" at the Navy Personnel Department and gave preference to Filipinos for West Coast assignments in that this was the locus of most Filipinos in the U.S. They told him to not go to Treasure Island; that Filipinos dominated supply and disbursing there. They were angry and threatening to "go public" or write their congressman. He advised against this as such incidents often damage the service in a manner that hurt innocent and guilty alike, further, the navy would be forced to defend itself, probably to exclusion of reasonable solution to their problem. Further, too often, in such incidents the senior officer present (SOPA) is the last to know!

He knew from experience that the navy's new leadership had better understand that, "It is always the better part of valor to settle the navy's problems in-house, in the family." When such minor problems are allowed to jump the boundaries of command, they can become subjects for a hungry media (newspapers, television, magazines, etc.) and anything can happen. Here a problem of the magnitude of a traffic ticket can, by media-manipulation, be made into a federal case. Because the navy is a Government Agency, such problems are automatically political with a tendency to take on a life and identity of their own. Out there in the so-called "real world" amidst the clash of media and the political response to such, the distortion causes an issue's end to bear little resemblance to its beginning. So, the author made a few discreet calls to the Navy Personnel Office at Washington. The two youngsters got their transfers. So the news media was denied a Negro/Filipino "thing", to be served up at the navy's expense, by nipping it in the bud. News, after all, is "what the dudes at the scene decided to make it", often with very little relationship to the original facts. It may be an old cliché, but an ounce of prevention here is indeed worth a pound of cures. To cure infers already letting the patients get hurt. If one does not believe this, for validation, ask the poor devils who got caught up in the "Tail hook" incident, where even many non-participants got egg on their faces, as did the service in general, innocent and guilty. It is not necessary that we attempt to assess the damage to the Navy's image, as it will take years for this corrosive force, "tail hook/sexism", to spend itself.

As a Division Whip or Chief and Division leading Chief, the author, did not waste his time criticizing, hating or speaking disparagingly of Islanders, Orientals or the few Black Puerto Ricans and Panamanians after he learned that the schisms between them and the Negroes were, basically, cultural. The author learned everything he could about Filipinos, Chinese, etc., their history, culture, especially their social/ cultural mores.

He carefully studied the mores of the various members of the yellow, brown and black peoples whom the Navy and the American people had chosen to mark down as inferior or "lesser human beings". He became quite adroit at a skill that he was too poorly educated to name or define. He speaks, of course, of what we know today as "<u>Inter-Cultural Communication</u>". He was very successful in leading, educating, teaching and correcting multi-racial divisions ashore and afloat. One of the best places to learn and master the art of "Functional Inter-Cultural Communication" was the U.S. Navy. The term "functional" means to not just perceive Inter-Cultural Communications as "Knowledge in being", but as a very potent and useful leadership and problem-solving tool. In mastering the functional component, he served his commands, his men and his service positively over a period of years. The author has been very fortunate in having good mentors in the form of older Chiefs (1932-1936 boys). Many of these were very bright and were probably more efficient at "applied Inter-Cultural Communications" than most University Professors. This is not a "way out assertion" when one looks at the juxtaposition of a Chief Steward and a University trained behavioral scientist. Where an Ivy League Professor could hide behind words and errors for years, while teaching students totally dependent upon him for their grades, a Chief Steward had to deal in the "hard currency of reality", or else. The "else", could prove disastrous by resulting in 1) a collapse of division morale, 2) A full-blown brawl or riot, 3) occasional killings.

Few naval officers understood the dynamics inferred by the clash of values and culture at work in a large division of Messboys composed of

Filipinos, Guamanians, Chinese, Virgin Islanders, Black Panamanians, an occasional Japanese or Black Puerto Rican combined with Southern reared Negroes. The blame here does not fall on the backs of Naval officers. The fault lies in an act of omission in American education. A fault that has not been corrected to this day, is that it is quite possible, in this country (in 1995) to go from the first grade in elementary school to a Ph.D., and never have to take one course in Inter-Cultural Communications, as a requirement!

So, the story of this chapter, a story of many "Messboys", does not deal merely with a few who were outstanding. It is complex in that it must include the main components making up the "Social Milieu", wrought by the inter-action of often uneducated or illiterate Southern Reared Negroes and upper class, Sophisticated University, and Annapolis educated officers, along with the inter-action between cultures totally alien to Negro Messboys (oceanic/oriental). How to maintain harmony in this maelstrom required first-rate leadership. The first Inter-Cultural Communications failure that the author encountered was at Annapolis, Maryland, at the U.S. Naval Academy where the hard-core of Naval Leadership is indoctrinated, trained and educated. When Civilians were removed, according to the old timers there, in the 1930's Navy Messboys as waiters in Bancroft Hall replaced them. Here they served the Brigade of Midshipmen.

That old relic, the *U.S.S. Cumberland*, from the eras when the navy was moving from Sail to Steamship-driven vessels, was brought in and utilized as a barracks-ship. At first there were both Filipino and Negro Messboys occupying the main deck and mess decks and White marines (there were no black marines yet) on the third deck. This was designated the Marine deck. As the concept took hold and Negro recruits were again allowed to enlist and started to pour in, friction between Negroes and Filipinos intensified. Disharmony and fights became common. If a Negro hit a Filipino and broke his jaw, he couldn't work for a month. If a smaller Filipino equalized the fight by sticking a knife in a Negro, a good hand could be lost. So, all Filipinos were transferred. As the "two ocean" Navy ships started to come off the blocks, Negro recruiting was stepped up. Where the Navy had formerly allowed only "good Southern boys" to enlist, it had to, because of necessity and the Draft Act, take Negro men from the Northern and Midwestern states. The arrival of tough ghetto type Messboys from Philadelphia, New York, Chicago, etc. caused a different standard of conduct to be demanded of the Marine detachment.

Where some Southern reared Negroes took a certain amount of Marine hazing and kidding as good natured hassling, this "New Negro" did not laugh at the non-funny jokes of white men, and resented such names as "shine, jigs," etc. They would punch it out with any Marine that used the "N-word" (nigger) in reference to them. So the Marines were transferred and U.S.S Cumberland became "all black". White sailors lived aboard the *U.S.S. Rheina Mercedes*, an aging Spanish cruiser taken as a trophy of war at Santiago, Cuba in the Spanish American War in 1898. This had been brought to Annapolis as a trophy of war and was utilized as a barracks ship for white sailors and home to the Chief of Staff of the Severn River Naval Command and his family, Captain H.H.J., Benson, called by Messboys "Hard Hearted Joe". Here was bred many of the Stewards who rose to chief and fought in the classic battles of Guadalcanal, Midway, the Mariannas islands, etc.

The Messboys at Annapolis had been hand picked because when the author arrived there in the fall of 1940 it was like going home. Northern Negroes had not arrived in mass. There was only a trickle, but the entire South was a microcosm here. On the mess deck, Messboys from the same state occupied most tables. There was the North Carolina, South Carolina, Georgia, Alabama, Arkansas, Texas, Kentucky, Louisiana and

Tennessee tables. Messboys from the former Confederacy dominated. If some "odd ball" (Northern or Western Negro) happened to slip into the Navy and ended up at Annapolis, he had a problem. For example, the Tennessee table was a particularly mean table. The author heard the following one morning, "Say man, where you from?" A timid new recruit who came aboard the day before replied, "He from Delaware. We ain't hear bout no damned Delaware. You get yo butt up from heah and go eat wid yo Delaware folks." This poor dude sat too long after being told, so three big dudes picked him up and threw him out into the walkway. Amid laughter and hoots, someone said, "Where in hell is this Delaware? Hell, I don't know. Let's eat."

The author never met but two Negroes from Wyoming during his 21 years of service. One name Dilahunt from Casper and another named Chuck Settles, from Cheyenne. Ole Dilahunt sat down at a table one morning and one of the "loud and wrong" toughs asked, "Boy, where you from?" Dilahunt replied, "I hails from Casper, Wyoming." "What you doing sitting heah?" To which Dilahunt replied, "Would you like to move me?" Now this was big medicine; all other tables were silently watching and waiting. This group-surveyed ole Dilahunt's six foot, three inch frame, all 225 lbs. of it. They observed the rust cups on the two-ham-like fists, and became highly interested in where Casper was and whether they raised cotton and sorghum in Wyoming, to the guffaws and hoots of the other tables. It's a damned good thing that these toughs "ate crow" because as it later turned out, probably only "Barnacle Bill", the sailor could wreak as much havoc as Dilahunt in a brawl. We had many of these in the streets of Annapolis with civilians over the hands of the local damsels. Annapolis, Maryland had some of the most beautiful black women in the United States and we did not disappoint them, to the chagrin of the local males. Marines and cops quite often had to restrict us Messboys to one side of the street and civilians to the other during an after-brawl, and an uneasy truce. Many Messboys got married at Annapolis.

Another dude who would sit where he damned well pleased was C.R.A. Wright (Clarence), a coalminer from West Virginia and a rough man in a fight. Clarence's mother encouraged him to join the navy after two of his uncles were killed in mine explosions. Here it is pertinent to point out that all Messboys were not uneducated, backward people as the navy thought and sought via recruitment. Many were exceptionally bright and entered the navy as a last resort, incident to the poverty inflicted by the "share crop system" and great depression. Wright, a lifetime friend, had to quit college (Bluefield State College), due to the depression, after 2 years of attendance.

The Louisiana table was basically a nice group. You could not be quite sure whether they were black or white. They were ultra class conscious but otherwise all right, except for one tough cookie named Willie Morris. Most were of Creole extraction with light brown skin, straight hair, keen features and spoke a "French-patois". Willie was an oddball among these Grefonhs and mulattos. He was black, built like a short version of a Mac truck. He had a torpedo head, was good with his fists and tough as nails. He grew up in the tough ghetto of New Orleans known as "Gert Town". The author knows first hand about his hardhead, because he broke his right hand on it, and it aches as He sit's here writing after all of these years. When Morris and the Author came to blows, he was runner up for the Maryland State welterweight Boxing Championship. The way this fight started is that he and another fellow were playing a game called "Whose Smartest?" Many Messboys played this, and the aim being to show the opponent up, "cap" on him, as stupid or dumb to righteously make an ass of the unlucky opponent. The two got into an argument as to when and where the battle of New Orleans was fought. Willie insisted, "Any fool knows that the battle was fought in 1812 and that is was fought at New Orleans like its name said." The other messboy betted $2.00 that he was wrong. He, as the, "resident-intellectual" in all of his 10th grade education splendor, was asked to hold the bet and rule on who was right and who was wrong. A crowd gathered to see Morris make an ass of this young "boot" (new recruit).

When the answer that the author gave was in favor of the young recruit, Morris disagreed and demanded his money back. He said that it would be unfair and he refused. He handed the bet to the recruit and said "Wait until I get my history book from my locker and I will show you where you're wrong." To which Morris replied, "'Nigga', you ain't gonna get nothing. You gonna give me my damned money or I'm gonna knock you on yo ass. You think you smart anyhow. I thinks you mo yellow than smart." He said, "You've got to bring ass to get ass and I don't know whether you be man enough to knock me on my ass."

This was an "all-stop" situation whereby all conversation ceased. A chant started in the crowd," fight, fight", as the crowd gathered. Now, ole Willie didn't believe in observing the marquis of Queens-berry's rules outside the boxing ring. He often failed to observe these in the ring. For example, the author had observed him to butt an opponent with his torpedo head and open up cuts over his eyes. One of his well-meaning friends said, "Chester don't fight him, he's a boxer." At this point, he replied, "I don't give a damn if he's a sword fighter." Then the "signifiers" (signifying as in, signifying monkey = to razz, incite to fight, etc.), took over with "I know Willie ain't gonna let no boot, (I was new aboard ship also), take his money" coming from the Louisiana boys. Then oh lawdy, "I heard that he badmouthed Willie's mom. They yelled, "Get him Willie", while the author's supporters from Arkansas, came on with, "I know Chester don't take no shit." "Chester ain't afraid of that dude." "Lash on to his ass Chester, you a Arkansas boy!" While he was reveling in the choice language of his Arkansas cohorts ole Willie sneak punched him. He found myself sitting just where he had said he would knock him, on his butt, with blood slowly dripping from his nose. Marcellus Whiteside, a Texas boy out of Waco, a member of my boot-training class (Class #15, 1940) said, "Oh lawdy, that Nigger done spilt Wright's blood. I know Wright's gonna put on his spurs and ride that dudes ass now." He got up and lit into ole Willie. He rocked his head back and drew blood from his eye. The ferocity of his attack stunned and surprised old Willie. Now, he had seen lesser lights stay down when they weren't knocked out, as a better part of valor, after one taste of Willie's right hand. He suppose that he expected him to do so. With a look of surprise, Willie lowered his head to butt, but he wasn't there. They were standing toe-to-toe trading broadsides when ole Willie laid a particularly vicious shot upside his head. His hand cracked like a stick, "pow"! About two seconds later he paid him in kind and broke his right hand on Willie's head. The fight raged over three decks for nearly 15 minutes before Chief Simmons, six feet four inches tall and weighing 245 lbs., caught up with them. Simmons was the master-at-arms of the ship. He was a former Fleet Wrestling Champion, a machinist and a post WWI "hold over". This giant of a man picked Willie and him up by their necks like two chickens and ordered them to cease and desist. But the minute he turned them loose, they tore into each other again. At this point Simmons, probably to avoid a brawl between the Arkansas and Louisiana contingents called in "Gunner Davis", a first class Gunners mate, a white man and master-at-arms (MAA) on the Rheina Mercedes, anchored across the dock from the Cumberland. Now, this was serious, as the Messboys said, "bringing in the white folks", Gunner Davis, in the words of the Cumberland Messboys, was a "righteous-Redneck", a white man who liked Negroes and was not contemptuous of them.

Davis tried to prevent them from having to go before Captain Benson by having Willie and him march across the Academy to the Midshipmen's Hospital, on the other side of College Creek. While sitting side by side getting their broken hands set and wrapped with Wet Cast, Ole Willie, still smarting because he had lost a bit of reputation, tried to intimidate him with, "You know I'm gonna git-Chu, dontcha boy?". He jumped up and hit him over the head with his half-finished cast, sending white plaster up the wall, and they went at it again, turning over the medicine table and wallowing in it. For some reason, the hospital did not call the Marines, which they usually did out of fear of possible knife play when Negroes fought; so they were not locked up that day. All of this was caused by ignorance. The Navy had intentionally, as a matter of personnel policy, hand picked us Negro Messboys for this, "sterling-quality". Any messboy, who proved too well educated or intelligent for his role of servant, in the Southern sense, funny, backward and/or subservient, was probably rejected at the recruiting station. He would have flunked the all-encompassing test of knowing his, "place".

When the author returned aboard, with a cast on his broken hand, nothing was said. But, when Ole Willie returned with his hand in a cast (they were sent back separately, to cool off), there was trouble. He caught hell from Chief Commissary Steward, T. L. Crocker. Chief Crocker was a remnant of the era before Negroes were restricted to a, "servant's role", only in the Navy. He castigated him for having a head hard enough for Willie, one of his most promising boxing team members, to break his hand on. Crocker said "Damn it Willie, you should have known better than to hit that burr-headed farmer with yo fist. Why didn't you hit him with a fire hose nozzle or a damned chair or something? Now you won't be able to do nothing in the ring for two months, damn your soul to hell." As I stood chastened and Willie stood dumbly staring at the

Chief's retreating back, Crocker complained loudly of the pedigree of, "Dumb assed Southern Niggers with cockle-burrs in their hair," that those fools in Washington were recruiting for sailors.

On the mess deck as the author passed the Louisiana table, He was greeted with sneers and jeers. He was still mad as hell, in that Crocker assumed that he would peaceably hold his head at the proper angle for Willie Morris to knock his brains out. He was in no mood to listen to this drivel from a company of ignorant equals talking "smack", so he stopped and walked back to the table and told the one with the fattest mouth, "I have another hand. You want me to break it on your stupid head?" As if on command the two-table contingent from Arkansas stood and Ireland, a section leader said, "You dudes pipe-down"; an "all-stop" situation" ensued, the calm before the storm. Before GI cups, plates, fist or brass fire hose nozzles could be brought into play, the icy voice of "Scar face" (Alphonso) Davis cut through the bubble. The all-stop situation became at once very real. Scar Davis was, "Head Boy", at the Naval Academy. When Davis spoke, every mess-boy in the Severn River Naval Command listened and he had damned well better do so. Scar said, "I think you men heard Section Leader Ireland tell you to pipe-down. You are to assume here, after that a Section Leader represents me. Do all of you boots understand that? I don't want to hear one peep out of you chickens until I finish my dinner." The Louisiana/Arkansas groups ate the quietest meal that the author witnessed during his 2½ years aboard the U.S.S. Cumberland. He had never seen a Negro man wield such absolute power over a group of Negroes. It usually took a White man to do this. Scar could, even Command Complete Silence! This was a feat in itself. But lest we go too far afield the Narrative Continues.

The scene, the "Marine", or lower deck, the place of the Arkansas boy's area amidships, the author is surrounded by the contingent who had heard about the continuation of the fight at the hospital. There were his, "homies", little Albert Daniels, R. L. Snell, Quentin Berryman, F. Ireland all wanting to know why he ruled against that Louisiana braggart, "tough Willie," and could he prove it? Here, the author, after all of these 54 years (1941-1995) finds himself laughing uncontrollably at the shear ridiculousness of this scene. It went like this:

I, Chester A. Wright mess attendant 2nd Class, 10th grade, H. C. Yerger High School, Hope, Arkansas, resident intellectual, U.S.S. Cumberland, drew myself up pompously, as a scholar should, and prepared to dispense information. I am surrounded by my Arkansas homies and a few of the Louisiana boys who had sneaked within hearing distance to see if I knew what I was talking about or had cheated Willie out of his two dollars. I, with great drama, opened my locker and pulled out a battered high school history book that I had purchased for 75¢ at the second hand store. I read solemnly, "The Battle of New Orleans was fought on the Chalmette plains outside of New Orleans on January 8, 1815." I then explained that this was outside New Orleans, not "in" it. Further, the war of 1812 lasted three years and the battle did not occur until its end in 1815. At which one Arkansas boy turned and told the Louisiana bunch, "Y'all knows better'n to think you as smart as Arkansas Niggers or that you can whip folks from Arkansas. You not only got asses made of yourselves, but ole bad Willie got his butt kicked too." Loud guffaws and hoots followed this.

As the author stood warmed by the adulation and cheers of his fellows, he warmed to his subject and told them that Black men helped Ole Andrew Jackson to whip them "Limeys" (British) at "Nawlins". That a battalion of 250 "Free Men of Color" from New Orleans under Daquin and one composed of Negroes from Santo Domingo (Haiti) fought at New Orleans. Then he explained that the Battle of Bunker Hill was a mistake, it was fought at Breeds Hill and that this often happens in history, and here, Bill Clinton's advisors need a history lesson or two. The President, when recently braced about the U.S. intervention in Haiti, by the newly victorious Republicans in 1995, was almost apologetic! He need not have been because this is the one group of Blacks in the world that "all" Americans owe a historical debt that was never paid. Oh, we owe the Africans too for buying or stealing, some say 12,000,000 of their people and working them for nothing for three centuries. This is usually dismissed by Euro-centrist Historians with that, "Everybody was doing it", that lame, shuck and jive bit. But Haiti cannot be dismissed so easily, that is by Historians who possess a shred of integrity. For it was the Haitian Negroes who helped make what became the United States possible. It is shameful that most of the author's graduate students at the postgraduate school at Monterey did not know this. This was followed by, "Sho nuff, you mean Niggers helped free White folk again them Limeys?" He continued, "Were it not for the sound whipping administered to the Napoleon Bonapart Army by the Black slaves of Haiti (1791-1794), the United States would probably be facing the same threat of disintegration, as that faced by Canada over the Quebec question between the French and English speaking Canadians. So much for the 10th grade intellectuals, and such. But before we leave this area, lets deal with a few facts that Bill Clinton's staffs needed to be aware of to save their boss from having to engage in quasi apologies over the Haitian Intervention. If the 20,000 picked French troops sent by Napoleon had succeeded in putting down the Negro Slave Rebellion on Haiti he (Bonapart) would have had no need to sell the United States the Louisiana Territory. Out of 20,000 Frenchmen only 5,000 of the original left marching in formation. This was not a simple defeat of French Arms by a group of Black yokels. Their leaders were Toussaint L'ouvetuer, an ex-corporal, Jean Jaques Dessalaines, a field hand and Henri Cristophe, an ex-boot black. There was severe "emotional cost and loss" usually omitted by all but a few, even Black Historians. As previously mentioned, Field Marshall Victor LeClerc, Pauline Bonapart's husband commanded the French Army sent to Haiti. LeClerc lost his life there and was sent back to France in a casket. Napoleon, Master of Europe, was compelled to practically give Louisiana and the present day Midwestern U.S.A., which was part of that territory, to a newly freed, weak nation, the United States.

This is what the United States owe the Black, and now, pitifully poor, malnutrition-ridden people of Haiti. These people fought and died by the side of White Americans at the Siege of Savanna (3 Sept. – 28 October 1779) and at New Orleans (8 January 1815), in order that this country might acquire and keep its freedom from England. The author was justifiably proud, that evening at being able to prove that he was right. A second source of pride was that he possessed this knowledge, "before" he entered the Navy. The Arkansas Boys went wild, strutted and bragged, saying, "Don't 'f' with us, boy. You might get yo ass whipped and get an ass made and a foot o' yo-self to boot!" So ole Chester Wright, mess attendant 2nd Class, got not only a reputation as a "smart mother" but a "tough mother" as well and reigning "touch-hog" (boar with the long tusks) on the Arkansas table at Annapolis. He had gotten this knowledge about Louisiana and Haiti out of books, purloined by Mrs. Thelma Rector, in the White neighborhood, she was Thelma, but in the Negro neighborhood she was Mrs. Rector. She was the "intermediate librarian" who made the excellent library of Judge L. K. Lemly, political boss of Hempstead County, available to the author. She ran the judge's household with authority, denied most Negroes in Hope, Arkansas. The judge knew that she raided his library for him. He once told him, "Boy, you be careful with them books. Don't you get them dirty or tear them up." Pointing to his copy of Kipling's Ballads and Poems, which he was reading. He told him that the book cost more money than you make in a month! Needless to say, he was very careful with the judge's books.

As he lay there in his hammock, with the wind howling down Severn River and broken paw just starting to throb, he thanked the judge and Mrs. Rector. Most of his fellow Messboys were not so lucky. Most of his friend's came from sharecrop farms and shantytowns of the mean rural, southern communities of the South. These men had been allowed to attend school between planting and harvesting time. Very few Negroes or Filipinos had ever had all new clothes and three regular meals a day, before entering the Navy. Most had been, intentionally, kept ignorant and poverty ridden.

CHAPTER 19. THE EFFECTS OF EXECUTIVE ORDER #8802 UPON THE MESSMEN'S BRANCH

"Old Nameless" refers to the nickname of the *USS South Dakota*, 35,000-ton battleship, and the secrecy surrounding her entry into the Pacific war. The Navy did not want Japanese intelligence to know the true strength of its forces in the Southwest Pacific. They knew that the new battleships, the *USS Washington* and *the USS North Carolina*, had arrived because they had felt their sting. What the Japanese did not know was that accelerated building of the next new class of battleship had started to bear fruit. While the old ships damaged at Pearl Harbor were being repaired and modernized the four new ships, the *USS South Dakota, Alabama, Indiana* and *Massachusetts* began to slide down the ways.

The *South Dakota* was the first of this group to reach the beleaguered, out numbered and outgunned US forces which hung on tenaciously at Guadalcanal in the British Solomon Islands. US forces had to, prior to their arrival, fight Japanese 14 inch gunned battleships with 8 inch gunned heavy cruisers, PT boats and old "tin cans", (destroyers), many of whom dated from World War I. This lasted until the battleships *USS North Carolina* and *Washington* joined this hard-pressed group in the Solomons.

So, when the *USS South Dakota* arrived amidst a cloak of secrecy in fall 1942 she was code named "Battleship-X". Her name was not to be mentioned in any radio or written message transmission. The

South Dakota was referred to, by common sailors as "Old Nameless" at first, and later, as simply the "SODAK"; this must have run Japanese intelligence crazy, in trying to translate her name. The mess boys of Gun Tub 10 aboard the *USS Intrepid* may have been the first gun crew in the fast carrier fleet but they were not the first in the Navy.

For example, the C.O. of the USS *South Dakota,* Captain Thomas L. Gatch, had stewards, cooks, and Messboys trained as gunners aboard the *USS South Dakota.* When Gun Tub 10 saw action October 29, 1944, the mess boys of Old Nameless had faced their "moment of truth" two years earlier at the Battle of Santa Cruz Islands, October 26-27, 1942: the fight for Guadalcanal. They saw action again on November 14-15, at the Battle of Savo Island, north of Guadalcanal. According to Jack Sweetman, in speaking of the Japanese effort:

"Admiral sends combined fleet - four carriers, four battleships, fourteen cruisers and 44 destroyers south again in another attempt to destroy the US Naval forces supporting the struggle for Guadalcanal. The U.S. forces, commanded by Vice Admiral William F. Halsey consisted of two carriers, the Hornet (CV-8) and the Enterprise (CV-6), the battleship South Dakota (BB57), Six cruisers and 14 destroyers."[171]

As usual Americans were out numbered and outgunned. But there is another factor usually not mentioned by history, the guts, confidence, courage and intrepidity of American youngsters. This caused the Japanese, who did not know the American character, or probably not the history that shaped it, to underestimate American fighting men. What the quote fails to mention is that in the Battle of Santa Cruz Islands, though planes sank the Hornet, she gave as good as she got. According to Carrol Storrs Alden and Allan Westcott, much more was involved besides the ratio of ships, for example: culture, character and courage just may have had something to do with the out come at Santa Cruz. The Hornet had just raided Tokyo! The Japanese wanted to sink her more than any ship afloat. "This action resulted in the loss of the United States Aircraft Carrier Hornet and damage to the Enterprise and South Dakota. The Destroyer Porter was also lost.... In this engagement the new battleship, the South Dakota, commanded by Captain Gatch, successfully fought off sustained aircraft attacks and gave protection to a second carrier... The Hornet came through two bomber and torpedo plane attacks, shooting down fifty out of fifty-four planes.... The defense by the South Dakota indicated the increasing possibilities of heavy well-managed anti-aircraft fire. In the first onset of twenty bombers from 11:12 a.m. to 11:30 a.m., 'all were shot down', and the second flight of forty torpedo planes and bombers was met, according to press descriptions, met by a curving wall of glowing steel from the great ship... In the third assault the battleship was hit by only one 500 pound bomb."[172]

The Negro Messboys were there that day and gave an account of themselves, that gained for them the admiration and respect of the SODAK's crew. Many years ago while in transit at Treasure Island Receiving Station, while in the shower room the author met a stewards mate (designation was changed from mess attendant in WW II), whom he only remember as "Fred". What drew his attention was Fred's back, which he asked him to help him scrub. He was covered with scars and small eruptions. The conversation went like this and is remembered after all of these years (1947-1994) though he can't recall Fred's last name. "Say man, did 'boss Charlie' take his whip and put you in your place for being an 'uppity nigger' when you went down to "bam" to visit your folks?" This was said in jest. Fred replied, "No, man, them Japs dropped a bomb on us on the SODAK." He went on to tell him that the ack-ack (anti-air) battery in the forward bow of the South Dakota was manned by Messboys and that he was hurt when the Japs dropped a bomb on the second turret. He said that about every six months, small pieces of shrapnel from that bomb worked its way to the surface of his back. He usually had to go to the hospital and get it picked out when his back got inflamed.

For years after this the author wondered if ole Fred's "lying and shucking n' jiving, blowing smoke", was his way of saving face. This was something that all stewards, cooks, and Messboys did in competition for the dates with the local damsels of Frisco and Oakland. "Old timers", laughingly labeled, "instant, self inflicted, heroism", as in "yeah man you be a hero, jes like them white folks", followed by a good razzing among ourselves. In later years the author came to realize that this had a serious side effect, "Self defense" for instance, when attempts by our own Negro people were made to make one feel cheap. These Negroes had read the Negro newspapers (Chicago Defender and Pittsburgh Courier) during the NAACP's fight with the Navy over discrimination that said that Messboys were nothing but "flunkies"! For example, when a Negro seaman or fireman told a girl that us Messboys wasn't nothing but "flunkies", for the white man-"bootblacks n' tater peelers", this often ended up causing heads to be busted, teeth to be knocked out and, in extreme cases, switch blades, to be put into play. We knew from hearing Naval officers talk that these new Negroes, "Seamen", were never going to be allowed to go to sea and ride a crack fighting ship. This was because if a Negro became a leading seaman or a petty officer he would have to tell a white man, "what to do". The US Navy literally fought attempts at integration up to the end of WW II and most Negroes who were not Messboys were formed into "labor battalions" and kept ashore. Bad morale, incident to this, probably caused the costly Port Chicago blow-up, which brought to light before the public, the Navy's policy of not allowing Negro Seamen and Petty Officers to go to sea.

So us Messboys, on being called flunkies, fought back with "you uppity Niggers think salt water is some kind o' salad dressing! You ain't never rode nothing but the (Frisco or Coronado) ferry. You ain't never rode the "Big Blue", nor heard a "long gun" talk (the roar of cannons)." There were also some stewards and Messboys scornfully called by deep-water sailors, who had seen action, "Market Street Commandos". This type "Uncle Tommed", cosied up to and snizzeled around staff officers, worked at their houses and polished their cars in order to stay ashore and not ride the Big Blue, where they would get their butts shot at or off. Knowing our scorn and wanting to be accepted, the usual response to these old vets was, "Boy if you heard one of them Jap 14s roaring you'd wet yo pants", followed by guffaws and much gagging. So to share beer and booze with veterans, this type told outrageous lies about the sea battles they never fought. They were self-made heroes, whose ocean was Market and Fillmore Streets, in old Frisco town.

For years the author wondered if Fred was one of these dudes. But years later ole Fred showed up aboard the USS Princeton (CVA-34), with a fighter squadron during the Korean War. He was Division Leading Chief and had to let Fred off to go to the doctor to get shrapnel removed. While teaching at the Naval Post Graduate School, he sheepishly found that Fred was not lying and that he had to have been aboard SODAK, at the Battle of Santa Cruz Islands, to know the details he described. He was not the type to read a detailed written report. He had been broke when he met him at Treasure Island years before, so he put $5.00 in his pocket, took him ashore and they talked for a couple of hours. According to a book that the author found in the Post Grad School Library written by Gilbert Cant, "*The US Navy in the Pacific*", Fred had told him accurately what happened. Gilbert Cant was a war correspondent and was on the South Dakota that day at Santa Cruz. He told how "Old Nameless" danced and pirouetted like a ballet dancer in motion, while hanging off USS Hornet's quarter during twists and turns at high speed as she attempted to evade Jap planes.

One of the most vivid pictures to emerge from WWII shows the anti-aircraft burst and falling planes at Santa Cruz, as the Enterprise and South Dakota maneuvered in a dance of death. Cant says: "A Jap plane penetrated the screen and dropped a bomb on the second turret of the South Dakota. The bomb bounced and exploded in front of the bridge killing or injuring many up there. Captain Gatch had his throat cut by shrapnel and only quick thinking and skill saved his life. Colored Messboys manned the anti-aircraft battery in the extreme forward bow. When the bomb exploded it showered these youngsters with shrapnel. The force of the explosion knocked these Messboys down on deck. As the battle raged and the sky was blackened by shell bursts, these youngsters got calmly up and put their guns back into action, and continued to fire."[173]

This later event is where Fred got his back sprayed with shrapnel, all of which had not been removed five years later. Many Messboys paid in blood for reclaiming the honor of Black men insidiously stolen by opportunistic, dishonest, money-grubbing hacks posing as historians. Only a few reporters, the "new breed" of white historians, who emerged after the Brown decision of 1954, have dared to touch "the black thing", with any degree of scholarship or honesty. The tragedy here is that Black children are denied this bit of history, which could possibly enhance their sense of male pride and womanhood.

According to Nathan Miller, between the South Dakota, Hornet, Enterprise, and their destroyer screen, "The Japanese lost about 100 planes, along with their experienced aircrews. This would seriously cripple the Japanese war effort later as it helped in the deterioration in the quality of Japanese pilots."[174] This messboy, Fred, told the author that the South Dakota knocked down 32 of 34 planes that flew against her at the Battle of Santa Cruz Islands. Since Negroes were not usually decorated, he did not ask him if they were commended. He regrets the not asking, he did, however, know of a rare few that were so honored later and usually given letters of commendation along with Dorie Miller, and Leonard Roy Harmon, whom we will meet later. The scholarly history of the Negro by John Hope Franklin lists only one member of Gun Tub 10 for the Navy Cross, STM 2/C Eli Benjamin.

The author is sure that Franklin did not know that the Navy later took the cross from Benjamin! Franklin was a very careful researcher, yet it can be understood why he missed this fact. It can be understood why it took Alonzo Swann many years, even with the assistance of congressional representatives and the force of the Freedom of Information Act, to obtain the papers which revealed the other six men who earned Navy Crosses, and had been unfairly downgraded.

He does mention Harmon and Officer's Cook 3/C, William Pinckney. Harmon earned the Navy Cross for meeting the unwritten criteria "No greater sense of valor exists than that of a man who gives his life to save the life or lives of his shipmates". This he did aboard the heavy cruiser *U.S.S. San Francisco*, November 13, 1942, according to Admiral King,

"One of the most furious battles ever fought."[175] It was a fight to prevent U.S. marines on Guadalcanal from being bombarded unopposed. This action in the wee hours of the morning on October 11, 1942 saw an American task force led by Rear Admiral Daniel J. Callaghan, and Rear Admiral Norman Scott, composed of cruisers and destroyers against a Japanese force that contained two battleships! Here we are talking about six and eight inch gun cruisers going up against two battleships with fourteen-inch guns. The carnage was terrible. The action at point blank range was confused to the extent that three Japanese units ended up firing on each other. American commanders gave an account of themselves. They paid dearly in lives, casualties and ships sunk. On "the Canal" the sick, exhausted marines were not shelled. The American price was two Admirals, Norman Scott, with his flag on the *U.S.S. Atlanta* (a light anti-aircraft cruiser), died on the bridge with his ship in the melee, and Daniel J. Callaghan, carrying his flag in the eight inch gunned heavy cruiser, *U.S.S. San Francisco*, took on the HMIJS (His Majesty's Imperial Japan Ship) *Hiei*, which carried eight fourteen inch rifles. This battle was a true David and Goliath action.

In trading salvos, the San Francisco took part of a salvo that carried away most of her super structure. It is said that she looked like a barge when she limped home. A fourteen-inch shell, which is as tall as a man and weighs in excess of 1,200 pounds, landed on the San Francisco's bridge killing Rear Admiral Callaghan and Captain Cassin Young. The senior officer left alive on the San Francisco's bridge was Lieutenant Commander Bruce McCandless. The San Francisco was badly damaged such that her admiral and commanding officer died, but she had punished the Hiei so badly that she was found the next morning sailing in circles. This would indicate that the San Francisco had shot away or severely damaged "Hiei's" rudder to the extent that she lost steerage and maneuverability. This enabled planes from Henderson Field on Guadalcanal to catch and sink her the next morning. When the San Francisco was put out of action, the heavy cruiser *U.S.S. Portland* took on Hiei. The *U.S.S. Laffey*, a small destroyer took up the fight along with another "tin can", the *U.S.S. Cushing*.

According to Alden and Wescott, "Laffey fired all port torpedoes at a battleship at close range, crossed her bow and demolished her bridge with her five inch guns."[176] Nathan Miller said when these two ships were knocked out, the Destroyers "O'Bannon", "Sterett" and "Monssen" continued the fight. Seven of eight destroyers were sunk, only the "O'Bannon" survived. Here one wonders how amidst all of this valor and uncommon gallantry a messboy could earn a Navy Cross. According to the "Frisco's" crew, Leonard Roy Harmon STM 1/c, lost his life in order to save that of a friend. Seeing a glowing shell coming in on the San Francisco, he, instead of diving through the hatch, shoved his friend through first. That selfless decision cost him his life and placed his name in the history books for uncommon valor. Harmon died a second later as the shell struck the ship. Harmon received a Navy Cross for heroism. The USS Harmon was named and launched in his honor.[177] One of the first ships named for a Negro was later named for him. William Pinckney Cook 3/c, " when a bomb exploded aboard his ship, the U.S.S. Enterprise, he saved his comrade's life at great risk of his own. Awarded the 'Navy Cross.'" The real story was that the bomb explosion turned the compartment into a "hot box" and knocked most unconscious.

Another navy Cross was earned by Elbert H. Oliver, Steward's Mate 1/C, whose citation reads, "Although wounded himself and bleeding profusely, took over the station of a wounded gunner and maintained accurate fire against enemy torpedo planes. He was awarded the Silver Star (not mentioned in 1976 Black Reference Book)."[178] Neither the Black American Reference Book, no other Negro Histories mentioned the gallantry of the Messboys in Gun Tub 10 or those on the U.S.S. South Dakota. The author found only authentic naval history that really gave the Messboys, Cooks, and Stewards credit for gallantry in action. In light of this, these publications cannot be blamed for such omissions. Also, they do not mention Charles Jackson French, Mess Attendant 2/c. When his ship had been abandoned (U.S.S. Gregory) during the battle of the Coral Sea, he tied a rope around his body, attached it to a raft carrying fifteen wounded men and swam for nearly two hours to prevent the raft from drifting ashore until beyond enemy fire. What is not said here by French's citation is that there is more to this story, oral history.

The author, while Chief Steward aboard the *USS Princeton* (CV-37), met French on a visit to the home of Chief Steward Stacey Benton, a "homeboy", from Hope Arkansas, who lived in San Diego. Stacey was a dear childhood friend of his older brother, Eugene, and the first Black sailor that the author ever saw. It is he who put the Navy career bug in his (the author's) head. When the Princeton entered San Diego and tied up at North Island, "his first stop" was at Chief Benton and his gracious wife Genivieve's home. Charles Jackson French's wife turned out to be Jettie Mae, Stacey's sister. He and French spent an evening over a bottle of Jack Daniel's charcoal filtered booze.

He told him the following, "Man that fight at Guadalcanal was a bitch, and them Japs damned nigh whupped us. I never thought that I would ever see home again. Them Japs sank four of our cruisers in thirty minutes. They got the *Quincy, Vincinnes, Astoria*, and the Australian cruiser *Canberra*. I knowed a lot o' them fellas that got hurt and burned up bad. Then we heard that the aircraft carrier WASP had been torpedoed in the Eastern Solomons. I thought that them Japs must be jest better than us. Then I heard that they lost some ships too. That made me feel good. But us "Tin Cans" caught hell all the time by them Jap airplanes. From the landing in August (August 7, 1942) until December them Japs put fire on us "Cans", and we caught hell. We lost the Blue, Jarvis and O'Brien and them was new "Cans". Us older ships didn't have a chance cause we didn't have enough ack-ack, so we lost the U.S.S. *Little*, the *Calhoun* and my ship, the *Gregory*." French said, "When Gregory was hit by them planes a lot of us got off before she sunk and many of my friends wuz hurt. I was on a raft with some of them and we started drifting towards land. I knowed that if we got close enough them Japs would kill us. They, we had been told, would soon as kill a man already wounded as any body else. So, I being lucky enough to not get hurt jes put a line around my middle and started a paddling away from the beach. Then I got the hell scared outta me. I noticed they wuz sharks a circling around that raft a waitin for they dinner. So I thought what's wurse them sharks or them Japs; at least them sharks will be quick. I don't know bout them Japs. They be some mean "mothers". So, I jest keep paddling. I nearly peed on myself when one of them sharks teched my feet. I jes froze and tried to surface and float, git my feet outta the water. There wuz a whole lot of other folks in the water, some of um hurt purty bad." Then French laughed uproariously and said "I guess them sharks decided to not have "scairt-nigger" for lunch!"

Then he changed from laughter to what the author had trouble discerning. It was anger, frustration, then tears. On questioning him, after waiting two minutes or so, he said, in a more subdued, angry voice: "When we wuz picked up and the hurt ones wuz taken to be worked on, we wuz taken to the rest camp with the others. I heard they came up wid some of that "race-shit", that "you a culud boy" mess. I wuz told "you can go over there where the culud boys stay." Then some of them white boys, what wuz on the raft, and other sailors from the Gregory's crew said "He ain't going no where!" He is a member of the Gregory's crew and he damned well will stay right here with the rest of us. Anybody who tries to take him any where had betta be ready to go to "general quarters" (ready to fight) with all of us."

The boy who did the talking was from either Alabama or Georgia, according to French. "So for near on to five minutes there be a standoff, us covered with oil and grime in our hair and all over our clothes, in our eyes, and them clean master at arms folks. We musta looked like wild men." Anyway one of the master at arms said, "Them fools mean it. Just leave them alone. We got other folk who need help. Them "crackers" retreated, tucked they tails and left!"

This conversation with Charles Jackson French occurred shortly after the Korean War. The author attempted to probe for the cause of such intense emotion concerning an incident that happened years before. French's shoulders shook; tears coursed down his cheeks. All the author could get from him was, "Them white boys stood up for me."

French, according to friends residing in San Diego, was claimed by alcoholism, in later years. From close questioning of friends, it would appear that he returned from the Pacific Wars, "stressed out", from seeing too much death and destruction. He was probably discharged with mental problems and left to fend for himself. Here the Navy must not be blamed as what we call, "post traumatic stress", today, was probably not a gleam in the theoretical eye of that inexact science that we call psychoanalysis at this early date. So this gallant Messboy died alone with his own terrors, anonymously. The author was told that French's death did not rate two paragraphs in the San Diego press, in passing into history. No, Dorie Miller was not a freak! Plenty other Black Messboys, Stewards and Cooks stood to their guns and gave their lives or suffered grievous injuries to prove this.

As the author prepared to close this chapter out, he received from an older White member of the crew, of the USS Essex (CV-9), the ship that bears the name for this class of carrier, copies of that ships Action Reports for 25 November, 1944, Luzon, Philippine Islands. This gentleman and I have shared tidbits of research after meeting at the K-West and B-West National Conference in Oakland this year (1994). His name is Richard W. Streb and he now resides at Roanoke, Virginia. He is one of the first White authors I have ever met who has shown a real interest in stewards, cooks and Messboys as people, human beings.

It is his sincerity that possibly drew me to this man. Admittedly I had been made suspicious of older White men, as they came from a period in US history that took for granted, and as fact, that Black men were a bit less than human and cowardly. This was an era in which we were lynched, beaten and imprisoned, often for nothing except our color. So on first meeting Mr. Streb, I went into my "defensive, cautious mode", as only a Southern reared Negro instinctively does, on being approached by an unknown White, as in "what does this cracker want"? But it's a funny thing about "sincerity"; its beam shines across racial lines and even suspicions! So this author had to pause and, sheepishly so, listen. I shall always be thankful that I did. Streb was it turned out, in search of truth concerning not just about White crewmembers of the USS Essex, but Negro members as well!

Now a White man cannot just tell a 1920's Arkansas bred Negro, such as I, whose "racial radar" was honed razor sharp as a survival-tool before entering the Navy, and who dealt successfully with 1940s Naval officers as a messboy, any ole cock'n bull story. So probably unknown to Mr. Streb, he underwent the most intense scrutiny, possibly ever received by him, in the first few minutes that he talked with the author, at the Parc Oakland Hotel. Yet his sincerity still rang true. On going to his room, observing his research and really talking with him, I was surprised, pleasantly so, to find that Mr. Streb was not a "user nor a phony". He was a person, a very humane man, genuinely interested in the stewards, cooks and Messboys, who suffered grievous injury and death, as they gave their lives, gallantly, aboard the USS Essex. To this day he believes remain unrecognized. This White man actually sought to tell their story. A few Black Messboys, Cooks and Stewards who gave their "all", a long ways from home. Further it developed that he sought to do so in a way that bestows honor upon the Black fighting men of this country and the command in which he served during his youth, many years before, in WWII.

The moral of this story is "don't bitch about White men who judge you by your accident of 'color', while you hypocritically do the same yourself." We Blacks and Whites do swim in the same 'cultural sea', and if not very careful absorb the same fruit, that of racism and other stupid and harmful products.

What follows is taken from the research that Streb has been gracious enough to share. Note that the Action Report from the *USS Essex* (CV-9) is dated November 25, 1944 and like most such war reports are marked "secret". Thus, minus the "Freedom of Information Act", would have been impossible to obtain. Also note that the entire Action Report is not entered here, as it was quite lengthy (five pages). Hence, only the Stewards, Cooks, and Messboys (STM's) are included in this abbreviated version, they include those:

1) killed in the initial attack;
2) reported missing (presumed lost);
3) those who died of wounds later aboard ships and;
4) those who were wounded.

The stars and arrows were not a part of the original report. They were placed there so that those unfamiliar with the rating designations of the stewards' branch of the Navy may become so. This branch no longer exists. It was stricken from Navy structure in 1974. Many of today's officers and men would not know either what or whom they designate in the naval personnel rating structure for this era of Naval history.

CK= Officer's Cook

ST = Officer's Steward (changed to SD in WWII)

STM = Steward's mate, or non-rated member of the Steward's Branch

These were designated Matt or Mess Attendants prior to WWII. CK and SD indicated petty officer "duty" and STM indicated non-petty officer duty. In order to see that no person of color would ever wield power over a white person, these men were not granted the same power enjoyed by white petty officers until 1949, four years after WWII!

The members of the Stewards' Branch were "mock-petty officers", until President Truman intervened in 1948. Regardless to how they were treated, these unusual fellows who were told that they were inferior and treated as such, stayed the course fought and died for this country. They were a truly remarkable group and, as previously noted, probably the most historically unique of all contingents that fought in the WWII Navy. The USS Essex Messboys, Cooks and Stewards did not, it seems, have any one to demand recognition for them and the terrible sacrifice they made. So, let's allow the Essex's own Action Report speak for them. There were many more besides these men, killed, wounded or reported "missing in action", (blown to bits, blown overboard and unrecovered or burned beyond recognition).

The following is an excerpt from Action Report#2, cited by Richard Streb:

> "November 25, 1944. Operating in TG 38.3 about one hundred miles east of Luzon, launching strikes against shipping in Manila area. At 12:56 *Essex* hit on the port-edge elevator at frames #69 and #70 by Japanese suicide, torpedo aircraft (Judy). At 13:26 flight operations resumed. 16-17N; 123-30E. End.

Earl Leopold:

> On 25 November 1944 I was in the main (gun) battery plot when the guns started to fire. I was connected by phones to the gunnery officers and the guns. I heard someone shout, "he's going to hit us." The guns fired; then there was a big bang...I herd a report that a Kamikaze had struck the 20-mm platform,

which was above the tire repair shop. I knew it was bad... I experienced great fear. I was on the circuit. There was a lot going on, lots of gun firing going on. <u>There were twelve guns on the platform, with two white guys and twelve blacks on it.</u>

I had to report on the Mark 14 and the other gun damage. Twelve guns were mangled, useless or off the platform. When I got there, the fire was already out. One of the guys killed, a black guy-I used to exercise with him on the flight deck. The guy always gave me a steak sandwich- never took any money. He was a real nice guy. I wish I knew his name!"[179]

Leopold is talking about Edward Emanuel Brown from Pittsburgh, PA. Streb put him in touch with the family. Leopold maintains contact. Eight black and eight white sailors were killed in the above action. These otherwise officers' servants wanted to fight and most were volunteers. They had to fight in order for Blacks to get their own Gun Batteries. They had something to prove and did so at a terrible cost.

In closing this chapter I would be remiss not to mention our own Norman H. Bell, AKA "Bigfoot", second National President of Units K-West and B-East, Inc., a Georgia boy who served his country, his service and his shipmates, with honor, for thirty years in service and many years after he retired. Chief Bell was at Pearl Harbor December 7, 1941 during the devastating attack there. He served aboard USS Langly (CV-1), the Navy's first aircraft carrier. ADMIRAL W. F. (Bull) Halsey later cited Bell for bravery and intrepidity in action aboard U.S.S. Zane (DMS-14), during the Guadalcanal campaign.

The citation reads: "for skillful and effective performance of duty, under adverse conditions while acting as first loader of gun number one of an escort ship during an engagement with enemy destroyers in the Solomon Islands area on October 25, 1942.While Bell's gun was in action he was rendered unconscious by an enemy near miss. He was revived by the medical officer and immediately asked to return to his station. He resumed his position and continued to load the gun rapidly and efficiently throughout the remainder of the action. His conduct throughout was in keeping with the highest traditions of the naval service."

Wallace Baptiste, who rode the U.S.S. Zane's sister ship, the U.S.S. Trevor, had his nerves all but shattered in that fight. Baptiste later became a "well off" businessman in Oakland, California and is a member of K-West and B-East.

The two men who gave birth to K-West and B-East, the Navy Stewards Veterans Association, are Chief Stewards Clyde Oden and Jackson Seaberry. Both men were in the six months of bitter fighting around Guadalcanal. Carriers, Cruisers, "Tin Cans" and Transports all contained contingents of Messboys, Stewards and Cooks. There were three carrier battles fought there, the Coral Sea, Eastern Solomons and Santa Cruz Islands. Clyde Oden had the USS Hornet shot out from under him and abandoned her by swinging across on a line to a destroyer, at the Battle of Santa Cruz Islands. Jackson Seaberry, a member of the "Gator Navy" (amphibious units), rode the "USS Jackson", a fast attack transport that landed marines in many invasions in the march across the Pacific. The author personally saw the USS Hayes, Adams, and Jackson at Tulagi, Bougainville and Los Negroes Islands. These Messboys heard a lot of long guns talk.

It is not possible to name all of the men of K-West and B-East here who fought in WWII, Korea and Vietnam. But, if there is a hell for the Navy Officers' Stewards, Cooks, and Messboys, it probably won't bother them too much. Many Naval Officers' servants rode steel ships to hell and back, starting at Pearl Harbor and ending in the Sea of Japan. Most served a bitter apprenticeship. So if there is a hell for them, in the words of Rudyard Kipling, "They'll be squatting on the coals giving drink to poor damned souls" when the members of the Navy's Officer Corps arrive for their just deserts. They were remarkable people who served this country, in spite of itself and it's incapacity to perceive them as men, men, who, to this day, have never received from their country either the laurels or recognition so justly deserved. The US Navy Officers even after the return to "liberalism", and a greater sense of fairness to its enlisted men, has not seen fit to redress this grievous wrong. A wrong calculated, perpetuated and promulgated upon its officers' servants for 81 years (1893-1974)

The effect of Roosevelt's Executive Order #8802 on the welfare of us Messmen was zero. We were frozen in our Ratings. We had caught all of the hell during the era of exclusion but were denied the fruits of Randolph's victory. We stood by impatiently while "new Negro dudes" swaggered by with "right arm" rating badges (worn by Line Petty Officers only (Boatswains mates, Gunners mates, etc.). We were re-designated the Steward's Branch but were not allowed to wear an eagle on our rating badges until the latter part of WWII. Executive order #8802 got Negroes jobs in the war industries only. It did enhance the effort to get a better deal for Black sailors and soldiers, but the war was nearly over before the servants only rule was overturned by the Navy.

Instead we were quasi-members of the Navy and wore a quasi-military badge. As such, we were objects of ridicule, even by our own ignorant fellow Negroes, who failed to understand our victimization, and by white shipmates as well. We punched it out with Negro Seamen in the streets of Washington, Baltimore, San Francisco and San Diego, fought our own "red-neck' shipmates on the docks and fought the enemy at sea. This writer, as a Navy Steward, was contemptuously treated and assaulted by Negroes out of ignorance, and by whites, due to racial animosity. To merely stay alive he gave as good as he got and paid by breaking his hand in two places. To be a Steward in this era required that one be tough mentally and formidable in the use of bricks, knives, bottles, switchblades and his hands, as they were always outnumbered.

The Randolph victory did not win for the Negro "integration," rather it merely tempered the "discrimination." To train Negroes, a part of the Great Lakes Naval Training Center was set aside. Negro seamen and firemen were trained in this rigidly segregated base area, as were the sprinkling of Negro officers (none went to Annapolis), until much later. Negro Petty Officers were sent to Hampton Institute in Virginia for technical training. 'After training they had no place to go. By "gentlemen's agreement", white unit commanders refused to take them aboard ship. This had the unspoken approval of Secretary Knox.

There was massive resistance to allowing Negro Petty Officers to supervise white seamen. Consequently, most of these "over-trained Petty Officers", as well as the seamen and firemen, ended up in "labor battalions." Most worked as stevedores. As the draft or higher wages from war industry ammunition depots bled off civilians, Negro sailors were sent in as laborers. This constituted a breach of promise, angered these Negroes and caused their morale to plummet. These sailors often worked 12 to 16 hours a day. The white officers who commanded them felt they had been denied their chances, on grounds that there was "no glory in bossing Niggers", so morale plummeted to near zero.

The U. S. Navy unlike the British, German and Russian navies had never had a large-scale mutiny. This mismanagement of Negro sailors caused the first recognized mutiny since the USS Somers incident of 1842, in which Captain Slidell MacKenzie summarily hanged the Secretary of War's son. In 1938 Negro Messmen aboard the Light Cruiser USS Philadelphia at Pearl Harbor, allegedly mutinied. The Navy threw a cloak of secrecy around this incident and quietly discharged the dissidents, thus quieting the public outcry. This incident, in the prelude to WWII, was the first rumbling of Negro discontent. Instead of analyzing for causation all energy went into covering up the incident. The Negro seamen should not have been charged with mutiny, which required intent to take over command. A charge of "refusing duty" was the only proven act.

Though Negro leaders kept their word in marshaling the massive manpower, in the Negro community after Executive Order #8802, white officers in insidious defiance, retarded the total effort and frustrated and angered the Negro servicemen. According to John Hope Franklin, "3,000,000 registered for selective service, 1,000,000 actually served (500,000 overseas), 701, 678 served in the Army, 165,000 served in the Navy, 17,000 served in the Marines and 5,000 in the Coast Guard."[180] Entrenched racism did not allow for even salutary appreciation of this mass Negro effort. This failure in Human Resources Management resulted in what came to be known as the "Port Chicago Mutiny," the first such upheaval to be adjudged a mutiny in the Navy since 1842.

Unlike the comparatively small USS Philadelphia incident, the one at Port Chicago Munitions Depot, California, one of the largest such facilities in the world, could not be shielded from the merciless glare of the news media. Mismanagement of Negro human resources bore bitter fruit and gave the Navy a bad image in the Negro community, that still retards present day recruitment in that sector. It is believed that low morale of officers and enlisted men, backed by a deep sense of <u>unfair treatment</u> and <u>betrayal on part</u> of the Negro labor battalion, caused the Port Chicago blast in that these conditions encouraged "careless handling of ammunition." This assessment proved incorrect. Later investigations proved that <u>poor training</u> was probably the greatest contributor. This writer was at Port Chicago when the Korean War started. He talked to many reserve officers who were there in WWII and assisted CDR A. G. Beckman and Captain F. J. Eckhoff with race relations, during base mobilization for Korea.

On July 17, 1944 an explosion occurred at the magazine that destroyed one ship and its crew, leveled the seaward side of the base and crippled, seriously, the Pacific Fleet ammunitions supply effort. Of an estimated 265 killed at Port Chicago, 250 turned out to be Negroes. This was headlined in West Coast newspapers. This negative "social visibility" was heightened by two factors. First, the Negro press and leadership vociferously demanded to know why such disparity existed, in the number of Negroes to whites, employed in this extremely dangerous work. An unobtrusive measure revealed the "why" of so many Negro deaths.

Secondly, one group of Negro survivors of the magazine blast refused to resume working at ammunition loading and was tried for mutiny. This writer feels that charges of conspiracy and refusing duty would have sufficed. Mutiny rests on solid ground when an attempt to take over or seize command of the unit is involved. Failure to take this tack cost, and continues to cost, the Navy dearly, image-wise, in the Black community as it caused the Navy to be perceived as a racist institution and an uncompassionate one, as well. There were many very young and many poorly educated sailors, sandwiched between the regular seamen and the over trained Negro Petty Officers.

The trial dragged on for months, with the Negro press having a field day, and the NAACP, which fought the case with the brilliance and tenacity that characterized their defense of the soldiers of the 24th Infantry in WW1 at Houston, Texas. In World War I the organization fought this case over a period of years, until the last man was freed. Their fight with the Navy was always news worthy in the foremost Negro newspapers, the Pittsburgh Courier and the Chicago Defender. The Navy's image was damaged badly.

Negro seamen, where human resources management was concerned in WWII, were wasted. Roosevelt's 8802 order never bore the fruit that it should have. Richard J. Stillman said:

> "The civilian leadership placed first emphasis upon winning the war and gave in to the views of Admirals and Generals on racial treatment. Secretary of the Navy, Frank Knox, in a formal letter reflecting the feelings of his senior Naval officers, said that 'the policy of not enlisting men of the colored race for any branch of the Naval service but the Messmen branch was adopted to meet the best interest of general ship efficiency."[181]

Negro seamen were not allowed on fighting ships except for one PCE and one Destroyer Escort (U.S.S. Mason). They earned no awards or medals, to my knowledge. Medals were hard to come by for any person of color and they were simply not passed out for hard labor and not even for Black gallantry and valor after the Spanish American War.

> "No Negroes had been awarded the Congressional Medal of Honor since the Spanish American War. There had been a change in policy of those responsible for awards rather than any change in the heroism and gallantry of the Negro soldier. In the Civil War, sixteen soldiers and five sailors won the coveted medal, while in the Spanish American War, seven Negro servicemen received it. Fifteen Negroes on other occasions had served their country in a manner that merited it."[182]

General George S. Patton, Commander of the Third Army, was one of the few top commanders who did not believe that Negroes were incapable of fighting in a modern war and told the all-Negro 761st Tank Battalion, first Negro tankers to serve: "I don't care what color you are. I would not have asked for you if you weren't good." Neither the 761st nor the Negroes who rolled in the "Red Ball Express," his front-line truckers, ever disappointed him.

This writer knew and talked to many members of the Red Ball truckers. They would have followed George S. Patton to hell, simply because he trusted them, a factor in short supply in WWII officers in policy and top command positions.

One Navy man who really believed in Negroes and their fighting capacities was not an officer. After the death of Frank Knox, a rare man named James Forestall assumed the job of Secretary of the Navy and suddenly Negro sailors started to see daylight at the end of the tunnel of frustration and discrimination. James Forestall was an intellectual and a hardheaded administrator. Knox's racist policy had caused human resources to be so badly mismanaged until units were actually short of personnel, while vast cadres of trained Negro personnel wallowed angrily in discriminatory "busy work." Forestall acquired the services of Lester Granger of the Urban League as an Aide. He immediately reformed the Navy's racial policy and in 1944 issued a "Guide to the Command of Negro Personnel. He flatly stated, "The Navy accepts no theories of racial differences in inborn ability. It is but expected that every man wearing its uniform be trained and used in accordance with his maximum individual abilities."[183] James Forrestal was an activist and soon translated his policy into programs and action:

"In July, 1944, the Navy abandoned its segregated advanced training facilities for Negroes. Early in 1945, basic training was integrated. In August 1944, the Navy organized 25 auxiliary ships (Oilers, Tankers, and Cargo vessels) manned by crews that were 10 percent Negro. In October 1944, the WAVES permitted Negroes to serve as officers and enlisted personnel. In March 1944, 12 Negro officers (two Chaplains, three medics, two dentists, three Supply Officers and two Civil engineers and one Warrant Officer) graduated from Great Lakes Training Station. They were the first of 58 Negro Naval officers to be commissioned during WWII. The Marines at last opened their ranks to 16,000 enlisted Negroes who served until the end of the war in segregated supply and ammunition units."[184]

In spite of Forrestal's gallant effort, V-J Day found the employment of Negro sailors in segregated support units. Stillman says that "85 percent (The Negro Reference Book estimates 95pct) of the 165,000 Navy Negroes were in the Steward's Branch." This mismanagement probably caused young white men to be called up and possibly to die, before their number should have been placed in the draft lottery basket. What price racism! It is certain that this fair treatment would have prevented the near total morale collapse of Negro sailors. It is also certain that better management of Negro personnel would have enhanced the Naval war effort, via the prevention of massive waste, morale damage to Negroes themselves and the consequent damage to the Navy's image. Since Negro seamen, firemen and ratings were not allowed to go to sea, or ride crack fighting ships, it was left to the Officer's servants, the Stewards, Cooks and Mess Attendants, to uphold the honor of Negro men. It is a historical fact that these, "the last of the brethren", did so. They gave the lie to the myth that the Negro was a child-like coward who would not fight.

CHAPTER 20. THE BATTLE RECORD OF THE NAVY'S STEWARDS IN WWII

And First Shall be Last and Last Shall be First.

Up from de swamps of Georgia, up from de muck and slime,
Where we swamps and picks cotton fo Mas Charlie an he kicks us
and calls us shine.

But out heah in dis Pacific Ocean where dem Japanese bullets whine,
Write yo goddamned name in Jurdan
Death draws no coloh-line.

We don come a long ways a fitting, spose we didn't come fo de ride,
Makes damn little diffunce whether de Jap or de man gits yo hide.

So out heah in de Pacific Ocean where dem Japanese bullets whine,
write yo Goddamned name in Jurdan, Black boy, Death draws no
coloh line.

> Tulagi Island, British Solomons, 1943
> by an illiterate poet remembered by the
> author as Wash.

Wash probably did not know what syntax or meter meant but he
most certainly captured the psychosocial juxtaposition of the Stewards

who fought. James Forrestal, the leader who started the Navy on a giant step forward and back to its historical roots of liberalism, died before he could finish his work. It is said that he committed suicide by jumping to his death. The Stewards and, indeed, the Negro people having been reduced to quasi-paranoids as a mode of survival, conjured up plots and dark deeds as the cause of this man's death. "He was pushed," was a general belief among Stewards. Although he had not gotten around to lightening our load, we sincerely believed that he would have if he had lived. There was not a dry eye in the group, that I drank beer with, the night after his death.

The Navy could absorb the inefficiencies of leaving their Negro seamen on the beach and in the backwaters of the war, but they could not very well leave their Stewards, Cooks or Messmen there for the simple reason that they had to eat.

Stewards, Cooks and Mess attendants rode steel ships to hell's very gates in WWII. While it took from April 1942 to August 1944 to get the Navy to lift the order, restricting Negro seamen to shore duty, the Negroes of the Steward's branch wrote their names in glory and produced the first recognized Negro heroes in the sea services since 1898. They drew some of the first blood at Pearl Harbor and went on to ride some of the most effective fighting ships in contemporary history. They not only rode these crack units, members of the Stewards branch gave an account of themselves that gradually earned for them the grudging admiration of even the most hard-core traditional racist.

Dorie Miller was the first authentic Negro hero to emerge in WWII. Otto Lindenmeyer in his book, <u>Black History, Lost, Stolen, or Strayed,</u> makes the same point that E. Franklin Frazier makes concerning the scarcity of recognition and decorations for even real-life Black heroes. Only determined persistence on part of Negro leaders caused Miller's exploits not to be lost to history. Gilbert Cant, an early chronicler of the Pacific War, who managed to learn of Miller amidst the "common heroism, valor and chaos" in the immediate aftermath of Pearl Harbor says:

> "One of the heroes of the West Virginia went for a long time unidentified. He was a 22-year-old Negro who enlisted in 1939 and had advanced one rating to mess attendant, 2nd Class (Matt 2/C). He had no chance, under the policies then in effect, of ever becoming anything but a mess attendant, and therefore had never been trained to fire a gun. His battle station was near Captain Bennion (lost in West Virginia) standing ready to pass him coffee. Twelve weeks after Pearl Harbor, in response to insistent pressure by Negro and racial tolerance groups (designation for early 'white liberals'), the Navy identified the sailor in question. He was awarded the Navy Cross and advanced to Mess Attendant 1st Class (equivalent to a seaman 1st Class)."[185]

Cant continues:

> "In company with two officers and several enlisted men, Dorie Miller... was on the Signal Bridge... when the commanding officer received a fatal abdominal wound. While others sought to construct a stretcher to lower the Captain to a safer location, a Naval Reserve Lieutenant and Miller manned a pair of machine guns and fired upon the attacking planes until fires started by bombs rendered the machine guns useless. Unable to lower their Captain on an improvised stretcher, four officers and men, including Miller carried him from the blazing bridge of the ship to the more sheltered deck under the port side anti—aircraft guns. The dying Captain ordered the officers and men to abandon ship. Finding other means of escape blocked because of flames, they made their way to shore hand over hand along lines strung to the deck from a boat crane."[186]

The Navy's account of Miller's exploits is revealing in that it is both grudging and diluted. It commits the sin of omission in leaving out exactly what Miller did, thus detracting from the extent of his action. They further imply that Miller never engaged in action as an individual, that he was under the direct supervision of whites or only acted in concert with them. Insidiously implicit is that Miller was incapable, as an individual, of the resolution, gallantry, bravery and intrepidity for which he was cited. This early, biased perception of Negro fighting capacity rapidly dissipated during the war. This change in white perceptions was due to probably two factors:

1. The reassertion on part of combat Naval commanders of practicality that brought information into sharp relief, the cost, stupidity and unfeasibility of not training steward's to fight, thus denying the ships and their tired gun crews this immense available and ready resource.

2. The positive and cool combat behavior of the steward's themselves. The truth of the matter was that Miller, an untrained mess attendant, amidst the chaos created by falling bombs, strafing planes and searing flames, had stayed at the machine gun and coolly shot down four Japanese aircraft that morning at Pearl Harbor.

As the war wore on it became clear that Dorie Miller was not a freak or possessed of uniqueness uncommon among Negro men. Biased, induced perception distortion did both the Navy and the Negro people great harm. Since Negro seamen were "beached" as a matter of policy, it fell to the Steward's branch to dispel the mythology surrounding the combat capability of the Black man. That the Steward's did so is a matter of history and is amply documented. An example, Captain Thomas Leigh Gatch, Commanding Officer of the USS *South Dakota*, then called "Old Nameless', for purposes of thwarting Japanese intelligence, gave this account of the combat behavior of the Steward's who fought at the battle of the Santa Cruz Islands:

"At 12:19 another mixed flight of 24 dive bombers and torpedo planes attacked. This time a dive-bomber got through. I saw its bomb released from not more than 100 feet above the forward part of the ship. I hoped it would strike a turret and not the deck. It might blow a hole in the deck and it certainly would kill many in gun crews on the deck itself. Automatic gun forward was manned by Mess Attendants, some Filipinos, and some Negroes. They never stopped firing for a second. Those men are good. The bomb did land on a turret. That was the only hit we took and it was the one that got me."[187]

What is not said is that this explosion knocked all of the mess attendants down and sprayed many with fine shrapnel. They "held their cool". They got rapidly to their feet and continued firing. The South Dakota is said to have knocked down 32 aircraft that day, out of 34 at Santa Cruz, October 26, 1942. The Negro Reference Book reestablished respect for this little understood branch in their fifth edition in 1967 by allotting a full page to "Fighting Mess Attendants as follows":

NEGRO SDS AND MESS ATTENDANTS DECORATED

1. Dorie Miller, Mess Attendant 2/C took the place of a dead gunner and turned a machine gun against enemy aircraft. For "distinguished devotion to duty, extreme courage and disregard of his personal safety during attack" he was awarded the Navy Cross.

2. Leonard Roy Harmon, Mess Attendant 1/C, while serving aboard the USS San Francisco in the Solomon Islands "deliberately exposed himself to hostile gunfire in order to protect a shipmate, and as a result of this courageous deed was killed in action. Awarded the Navy Cross.

3. William Pinckney, Cook 3/C, "When a bomb exploded aboard his ship, the USS Enterprise, he saved his comrade's life at great risk of his own." Awarded the Navy Cross.

4. <u>Elbert H. Oliver</u>, Steward's Mate 1/C, although wounded himself and bleeding profusely took over the station of a wounded gunner and maintained accurate fire against enemy torpedo planes. Awarded the Silver Star.

5. <u>Charles Jackson French</u>, Mess Attendant, 2/C. When his ship had been abandoned during the Battle of the Coral Sea, he tied a rope around his body and attaching it to a raft carrying fifteen men, swam for two hours without rest until the raft was beyond enemy fire."[188]

"On the Pearl Harbor honor roles, taken from the official releases after the raid, the following members of the Steward's branch were cited as receiving commendations for exhibiting exemplary conduct in face of hostile enemy fire:

1. Navy Cross Miller, Dorie, Matt 1/C, USN
2. Secretary of the Navy Letter of Commendation Brooks, W. N., Matt 1/C, USN
3. Letters of Commendation from the Commander in Chief of the U. S. Pacific Fleet and Lesser Commands:

> Aranas, Benito, Off. Std. 2/C
> Bacot, J. D., Matt. 1/C
> Celestine, B., Matt. 1/C
> Manibusan, Balajadia, Matt. 2/C
> Walker, Thomas Ellsworth, Matt. 2/C
> Wallace, H., Matt 2/C."[189]

The twenty-three pages of Navy Honor Roll members are indicative of a fact that after the first shock of the surprise attack "uncommon valor became common." To be a recipient of recognition, taking into consideration the racial climate of this era, and the general chaos at Pearl Harbor in the aftermath of the devastating raid is indicative of another fact. The Filipino, Guamanians and Negro stewards and mess attendants who fought and died there gave an account of themselves, worthy of the best traditions of the service.

Messmen and stewards were a tough and unique breed. There existed no branch of Naval service which produced a more colorful group of fighting men, men who served these United States often under trying conditions. I would leave a gap in the actual portrayal of this branch and be guilty of a gross act of omission if I failed to mention some of the more colorful members.

1. Big John Wise, Destroyer/Carrier sailor. John weighed 345 pounds when he rode with this writer on the USS Princeton. His pants had to be ordered from the Naval Clothing Center at Brooklyn, New York. John was reported dead two times in WWII. He had one Destroyer shot out from under him, and one washed out from under him when a typhoon sank four "cans" that ran out of fuel right after WWII. John was among the possible, eleven survivors of the USS Spence and floated four days in the typhoon before being picked up. When John was later ordered discharged for obesity, another sailor, Vice Admiral Daniel Roper, on grounds that John didn't lack buoyancy, ordered his retention in service. He went on to serve in Carriers in the Korean conflict.

2. Anderson P. Royal, SDC (later had rate changed to electronics), this writer's classmate (Class #15, Unit B—East, Norfolk, July 1940), rode the crack submarine, USS *Silversides,* under Captain Creed Burlingame in WWII. Royal learned so rapidly, the emergent electronic aspects of submarine operations, that he was sent to

electronics school and was asked to teach at the Naval Electronics School, Treasure Island, California. After military service he did graduate in electrical engineering and went into education upon retirement.

3.   Nelson, R. Ridley, SOC, rode a sea going mine layer in WWII, saw much action in the Pacific and led a charmed life. Ridley was taken out of an anti—aircraft gun tub and ordered to work in the ammunition handling room below decks; a day or so later the gun-tub was blown to hell, killing or injuring the crew. When the tub was repaired, Ridley was ordered back topside to work with the gun crew. In the next action, the handling room below decks, which he had just left, received a hit that killed or injured the entire group. Ridley went on to become one of the Navy's top recruiters and earned honors while on duty in his hometown of Nashville, Tennessee.

4.   Shirley Day rode the crack Pacific Fleet submarine, USS *Harder,* commanded by Captain "Mad Sam" Dealy, inventor of the tactic known as the "down-the-throat-shot." This tactic required that a submarine meet Destroyers head-on to fire its torpedoes and veer away out of the path of it before it exploded. If the submarine missed, it could depend upon the Destroyer dumping half its load of "ash—cans" on its head. Day was put off the "Harder" at Pearl Harbor, against his will. He had been on board during all of her classic cruises into the Bongo straits. He stood on the deck and yelled curses at Captain Dealy as the "Harder" slipped her mooring and headed west on her last cruise. Sam Dealy called back through cupped hands, "Go home to your woman, you old fool. You've done your share, and you may be glad I put you off one day." The "Harder" pointed her nose westward, rounded Diamond Head and

was never seen again. She was sunk off Australia by one of <u>our own new Destroyer escorts</u>, whose green crew didn't know that she was in the area. Her entire crew was lost. Of the original group, Day is one of the few survivors.

5. "Money" Matthews, SDC, peerless poker player of whom it was said he would "bet you five dollars that a pig's tail wasn't pork." "Money" started ashore one time at Pearl Harbor with a shoebox under his arm. The Officer of the Deck said, "Boy, what's that in that box?" "Money, replied Matthews. The OD said, "Don't get smart with me; open that box." To his surprise the shoebox was full of money. The OD immediately called the Disbursing Officer to ascertain if the safe had been robbed, to which the Disbursing Officer said, "Oh it's his money, I just released it to him." "Money" was on his way ashore to chastise and fleece a few of the local "yokels."

6. "Big Brown," SDC, one of the tough ones, and former "Head-Boy", who bossed the "Lost Battalion" at Annapolis. Boy is a misconstruction, only a man with military bearing and a hard fist could hold this position. Brown did it well.

7. Alphonso "Scarface Davis," Matt. 1/C, head boy and boss of the "Lost Battalion", who replaced Big Brown and subsequently led the Stewards group (300 plus stewards) at the U. S. Navy Academy, and who taught this writer the art of leadership. If one was afraid of a few scars he could never hold down this billet.

8. "Lying" Lyle, SDC and Master yarn spinner, dared to laugh at the human comedy, surrounding the Steward's existence, during their direst moments.

9.   A. D. Henderson, Matt 1/C, lost his life aboard the USS South Dakota in the bitter fighting around the British Solomons in 1942.

10. John Horry, Matt 1/C, also fought around the Solomons, and lost his life there.

11. The CO at Newport, to prod submarine officer students, used Dave Ball, SD1. Ball taught many WWII submarine officers the finer points of diving the WWII diesel boat. he probably still holds the all-time record for no-hit soft ball games pitched. When American forces went to Australia (Perth) they ran into a problem. There was an Australian boxer who had beaten every American who faced him. According to Shirley Day, Ball was asked if he would take this tough on. Ball had been on a patrol lasting over two months. He told the officer, "Give me one day to get drunk and two days to train." This was granted. Dave Ball knocked the Aussie cold and Americans walked with a new swagger in Perth.

This story of Navy Messboys and stewards could go on and on. It is a tragedy that this writer does not possess the literary skills to tell it properly. What he has tried to say to those commissary men who might feel that they are lowering their status by stepping into the shoes of former stewards is that, "You are walking in the tracks of giants who wore seven-league boots." They were unheralded, and too often, went unappreciated but performed their duties as a group of professionals who saw action in all oceans with the possible exception of the Antarctic. Commissary men, Black, Oriental, and Malaysian peoples whom I have found, do not to this day understand the qualifications of this branch. "It took more than being Black and ignorant, or short and stocky, with a capacity to giggle and eat rice in order to become a crack Steward." That branch of people could not be trained in a two-year college! Like the Boatswains Mates, only years of exacting apprenticeship could produce a competent steward, with the many and varied skills needed, to function at the diplomatic level or administer the mess on an aircraft carrier, or in the larger BOQ's ashore, many of which are larger than some hotels.

There was no room for "dunderheads" in the administrative levels of the catering services. A poorly trained steward could lose $600 in three days of mess administration, on a Kitty Hawk class aircraft carrier, and an audit board would be hard put to find it. Ignorant stewards went to jail for misappropriation of funds. An uneducated steward could embarrass the United States and retard the Navy's "fourth mission". After all, the first person the VIP's came in contact with, in the Navy, were the stewards. Their (foreign and domestic VIP's) perceptions of the Navy and, indeed, the United States were basically formed in the first few hours of contact. Up until the recent amalgamation of the commissary and steward's branches, these perceptions were largely determined by the quality with which stewards catered to their (VIP's) needs.

The quality chief steward had to master international protocol, and to cater at the diplomatic level. He had to know double entry bookkeeping, post and ante mortem meat inspection, purchasing and cookery at the chef's level; be a baker, salad man and Maitre de Hotel. He had to be able to teach all of these, as well as prepare his men to participate in ship's evolutions. This writer knew some of the best and in tribute to these, would like to mention a few:

1. Oliver Wesson, SDC, crack administrator, leader, disciplinarian and teacher, whom this writer relieved off Korea, on the USS Princeton (CVA—37), taught him the finer acts of mess administration

and accountability, and how to "box" the fluctuating mess on an aircraft carrier.

2. Clarence R. A. Wright, SDC, now supervising counselor of the Alameda County Juvenile Authority, rode the USS *West Point*. Crack administrator and leader. He modeled as CPO for two decades of stewards and changed to Storekeeper when SD's were allowed to change rates.

3. Other crack administrators: Jesus Sablan, Leon Guerrero, the Author's leading Petty Officer on (USS Princeton CVA—37), Stacy Benton, SDC, abandoned the first USS Yorktown at Midway, Joe Melton, SDC, rode the USS Essex, Yorktown and Saratoga. P. Paul Provost, SDC, rode the USS Brooklyn; he was in some of the bitterest fighting in the North African and Mediterranean campaigns.

4. SDC, Frank Waterman, or Johnny (Spider) Webb could have managed any mess ashore or afloat.

5. Billie Culbertson, Destroyer sailor, survived the sinking of U.S.S. O'Brien. Culbertson saw action in both the European and Pacific theaters.

At the U.S. Naval Academy at Annapolis prior to WWII midshipmen were served coffee by some of the cream of the Black race, most of who were driven into the Navy by the depression. There were college men, such as Clarence Wright from Blue Field

State and Orville Ferguson from Wilberforce. C. L. Green and Willie R. McCamie, as high school graduates, worked mathematics up to and including calculus, and used to work problems for the midshipmen they served in Bancroft Hall. Today the Navy's two top stewards, for that is what they always will be though wearing the new designation "Mess Management Specialist", probably two of the best and brightest Master Chief's in the Service.

The top steward in the Supply Corps is George A. Cohen, a skillful administrator and teacher. Cohen reorganized and upgraded the cooks and stewards school at San Diego and is now assisting the Bureau with the mess specialists rating. Master Chief Melvin Williams, the top steward in the Navy administers the Secretary of the Navy and Chief of Naval Operations mess in the Pentagon. Williams served four Secretaries of the Navy. Williams is not a mere administrator but a teacher and diplomat as well. It is upon these two men that the Bureau of Personnel, Supply and the CNO (Admiral Zumwalt) has relied upon for advice in conducting the amalgamation of the two branches of service in an equitable manner. The Navy and the stewards are indeed lucky to have the dedication and keen analytical minds of these two men. Both are dedicated and possess vast knowledge, resources, insight and experience oriented to bring to the problem of amalgamation.

This writer is indebted to many skillful Filipino and Guamanian stewards in learning his Craft prior to WWII. There were many Japanese and Chinese in the steward's branch. If one wanted to learn table decoration, a must for the diplomatic level of catering, the Filipinos and Chinese were a tremendous resource, for they excelled in that area of food preparation.

How these many leaders learned to deport themselves, as petty officers and chiefs is remarkable. Chief stewards were not allowed to sleep in the Chief's quarters and did not associate with other Chiefs until President Truman's general order of #8802, in1948. Instead most Chief Stewards had to sleep with their men. The only rational assessment is that they possessed a great deal of native intelligence, dedication and natural leadership of a type that enabled them to perform with the certain knowledge regardless of how well they deported themselves beyond the seas, they would be second class citizens when they got home. Yet during the Red Summer of 1919 to 1932, when the U.S. Navy attempted total exclusion of Blacks from the service, these men served. Up to and during WWII, despite discrimination and segregation by Whites and scorn and denigration by their own people, members of the steward's branch maintained the only substantial presence of the minority races in the sea services. They showed the toughness to stick it out during the most bitter and trying years.

It was the Stewards, Cooks and Mess Attendants who displayed the bravery, gallantry and intrepidity in WWII and Korea that reestablished minority peoples as producers of first-class fighting men in the sea services. There are many more steward's besides the minuscule group mentioned here who quietly and doggedly gave their all, often their lives, to buy recognition, respect and dignity for their people. It is past the time when the Black, Yellow, White and Brown people of this country should have given to the steward's the hard earned recognition which they earned at such an awesome price. The service itself has shown its gratitude and given it recognition by removing this last vestige of institutional bigotry by dissolution of the steward's branch and of these minority citizens' final inclusion as persons in the Navy.

USS Salmon Submarine

Medals as displayed, left to right:
1. World War II 2. American Defense 3. Asiatic Pacific Campaign
4. Second Award United States Navy (Fidelity*Zeal*Obedience)
5. Korea 6. Korean Service 7. China Service 8. National Defense
9. Dolphins (qualification of submarines)
(10) A collection of medals in bar form.

Medals of honor when worn on uniform are displayed on bars and worn on left breast. Rank and service years are displayed on left arm of uniform. The (2) stars represent Master Chief, the eagle is the symbol of a Petty Officer's authority, the crescent moon symbolizes the steward's branch, the stripes represent rank and the bars represent (4) four years of service each.

Shot of S-4Division Chester and his shipmates

S-4

First Row : T. Florendo, SD2; A. Abad, SD2; L. J. Guerrero, SD1; A. Pascual, SD3; J. Ungoco, SD2, H. Rivers, SD1 Second Sow A. Sebastian, SD2, S. Wiggins, SDC, C. A. Wright, SDC; 1st LT B. E. Lynch; G. McDowell, SDC, W. H. Perkins, SDC, J. Taitingfang, SD3. Third Row : R. H. Brooch, TN; L. A. Ignacio, SD3; C. Williams, TN, C. W. Bell, TN, J. J. Davis, TN; J. Love, TN; R. W. Smith, TN; J. C. Mung, TN. Fourth Row J. Broaden, SD2, G. Ray, SD2; A. Turner, SD2; W. E. Baykins, SD3; C. Brown, SD2; R. D. Mullin, SD1; W. Phillips, SD3; H. O. Bexx, SD2; S. Garner, SD1, B. W. Bond, SD3 Fdth Row. M. B. Balante, TN; S. C. Arpon, TN; J. V. Ponce, TN; J. M. Custodio, TN; A. J. Scott, TN; R. M. Garcia, TN; C. P. Trias, TN; J. E. Horn, TN; H. L. Dotson, TN; F. Bates, TN. R. J. Jones,

Picture taken from USS PRINCETON CVS-37 year book 1954-55
Cruise: The Far West Then The Far East

Tree planting and dedication National Cemetery Washington DC

Placing of stone in National cemetery dedicated September 18. 1998 by Unit K-West and B-East. USN Mess Attendants Association.

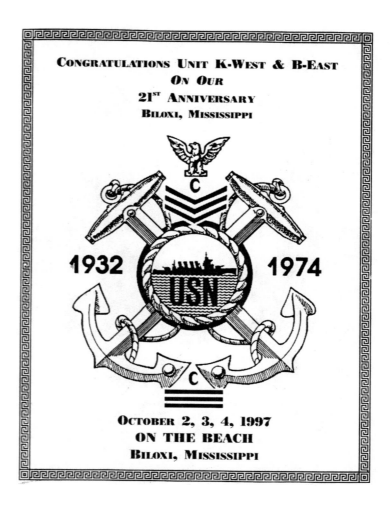

CONGRATULATIONS UNIT K-WEST & B-EAST
ON OUR
21ST ANNIVERSARY
BILOXI, MISSISSIPPI

1932   1974

OCTOBER 2, 3, 4, 1997
ON THE BEACH
BILOXI, MISSISSIPPI

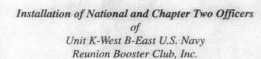

Installation of National and Chapter Two Officers
of
Unit K-West B-East U.S. Navy
Reunion Booster Club, Inc.

The installation of National and Chapter II Officer's Ceremony, conducted by Rev. Leslie Porter, (Ex-Navy) took place January 18, 2003 in Carson, California. National Officers not present consented to have stand-in shipmates. Chapter II Ladies' Auxiliary served a delicious lunch after the ceremony. Left to Right: James M. Lee (National President) Fountain Poole for (Rudolph Bryant-1st Vice-President) Curtis Fitzpatrick for (Allie Davis-National 2nd Vice-Pres.) Henry Cooper (National Secretary) Mack L. Harris (National Financial Secretary) Cyrus Napier (National Treasurer) John Green (President Chapter II) Albert Hinton for (Lloyd Pierce-Chapter II 1st Vice President) Golda Copeland (Chapter II Secretary).

CHAPTER 21. CHANGES IN U.S. NAVAL POLICY BETWEEN WWII AND THE "KOREAN CONFLICT"

The U.S. Armed Forces, on the eve of WWII, was one of the most segregated and most racist institutions in American life. It remained partially segregated until 1945, the end of that war. Secretary of the Navy Knox stood firmly against not only integration, but also Negro recruitment in general. He asserted that the Navy had always stood as a uniquely white institution, which was revealing of his racist induced blindness and /or ignorance. He argued that to open the door to higher numbers of blacks would necessitate integration, given the logistical difficulties of segregating a battleship, which would prove impossible.

The U.S. Navy, under intense political pressure, failed to yield to the demand for eradication of this most humiliating rule. That unspoken rule stipulated that Negroes be restricted to a <u>servants role</u>. The retreat from this rule was grudgingly and doggedly fought, by the Army, Marines, Coast Guard and U.S. Navy. In 1942, the Navy finally allowed Negroes to be enlisted in the general service ratings, but they did not allow integration or "sea duty". They did allow the first Negro to earn a commission as an officer. According to Peter M. Bergman:

> "Bernard W. Robinson became the first Negro to win a commission in the U.S. Navy when he became an Ensign in the Naval Reserve. Negroes were accepted for general service in the Navy, but only for service <u>ashore</u>."[190]

This <u>restriction relegated the Negroes to only the positions of</u> <u>"base companies"</u> <u>ashore, such as sub-units of labor battalions</u>. This policy caused a massive waste of manpower and money, work stoppages and severe political damage. For example, as previously mentioned, when the Naval Magazine at Port Chicago, California blew up, as a result on this vulnerable policy, the majority of those killed and injured were Negroes. In commenting on this grudging progress, Bergman says:

"The restriction of Negro Navy Men to shore duty was abandoned. Thereafter, steps were taken to end segregation in training, mess and recreation facilities. Exclusion of Negroes' enlistment in the Marines and Coast Guard was abandoned about the same time."[191]

However, there was no vigorous push for immediate application of this new liberal policy. Franklin Roosevelt was ever fearful of antagonizing the "Southern Bloc" of Southern Senators and Congressmen in Washington. The Navy was run by two successive Secretaries, <u>Josephus</u> <u>Daniels and Frank Knox</u>, both of whom were hard core segregationists. Both had fought any and all programs that sought to end discrimination and segregation. President Roosevelt had to, literally order Secretary Knox to cease and desist blocking the newly instituted race relations programs needed to effectively fight the War. Roosevelt needed the Negro Vote for his next run for the presidency. Knox still slyly dragged his feet, retarding the WWII Navy race relations' effort until his death in April of 1944.

Kai Wright says regarding the creation of black officers:

"The effort was lackluster, to say the least. Only fifty-two African Americans earned commissions in the program, out of a total of more than 70,000 graduates. As for the Navy "Golden Thirteen", they were all <u>commissioned into the reserves rather</u> <u>than the regular Navy</u>, which primarily drew its officers from the U.S Naval Academy in the period between WWI and the Korean Conflict (1945-1950)."[192]

There were always reserve ROTC student, University graduates, trained as Naval and Marine Officers to buttress the Navy in wartime emergencies, but people chosen to run the Naval Service were Naval Academy graduates. Needless to say, there were no Negroes prior to 1949.

The earlier discussion of the "restriction to shore duty" could lead one to believe that all Negro Navy men were so restricted. It must be pointed out, again, that the <u>men of the Stewards Branch were never restricted to shore duty, nor those of the Coast Guard, for</u> <u>obvious</u> <u>reasons</u>. The Officers of the Navy and Coast Guard were not about to shine their own shoes, peel their own potatoes or make their own coffee!

So this group of Negroes went to sea as they had always done. It took until 1944, nearly a year before the war was over, for the U.S. Navy to announce that it would allow Negroes to go to sea and man its ships in other capacities, besides that of servants. "In the same year, the Navy announced that it had allowed 500 Negro Seamen to go to sea on auxiliary ships."[193] The result was that two small vessels became a part of an experiment. They were the DE (Destroyer Escort) *U.S.S. Mason* and the PCE (Patrol Escort) *1264*. The war ended before this experiment could serve enough time to provide a full evaluation, as the fighting capacity of Black men. It is shameful and racist to test that capacity since Blacks fought with distinction for 100 years prior to this foolishness.

According to Mort Bergman, "There were 165,000 Negro seamen in the navy and 53 officers...by the end of the war. 95% of the Negroes were still serving as (Messmen). One of the lines that Secretary Knox had drawn in cement was that no <u>black women</u> would serve in the Corp of women Navy volunteers; women were intended to help maintain the stateside shore duties because due to sea duties, sufficient numbers of sailors would no longer be available. Knox asserted that since he didn't plan to allow black men on board ships as fighters, there was "no need" to replace them ashore with women. When Forrestal replaced Knox, after his death, this was negated when Phyllis Mae Daily became the first Negro nurse to serve in the Navy Nurse Corps."[194]

The Navy man who believed in Negroes and their fighting capacities was not an officer. After the death of Frank Knox, as previously stated, a rare man named James Forrestal assumed the job of Secretary of the Navy and suddenly Negro sailors started to see daylight at the end of the tunnel of frustration and discrimination. James Forrestal was an intellectual and a hardheaded administrator. Knox's racist policy had caused human resources to be so badly mismanaged until units were actually short of personnel, while vast cadres of trained Negro personnel wallowed angrily in discriminatory "busy work." Forrestal acquired the services of Lester Granger of the Urban League as an Aide. He immediately reformed the Navy's racial policy and in 1944 issued a "Guide to the Command of Negro Personnel." He flatly stated, "The Navy accepts no theories of racial differences in inborn ability, but expected that every man wearing its uniform to be trained and used in accordance with his maximum Individual abilities."[195] James Forrestal was an activist and soon translated his policy into programs and action:

> "In July, 1944, the Navy abandoned its segregated advanced training facilities for Negroes. Early in 1945, basic training was integrated. In August 1944, the Navy organized 25 auxiliary ships (Oilers, Tankers, and Cargo vessels) manned by crews that were 10 percent Negro. In October 1944, the WAVES permitted Negroes to serve as officers and enlisted personnel. In March 1944, 12 Negro officers (two Chaplains, three medics,

two dentists, three Supply Officers and two Civil engineers and one Warrant Officer) graduated from Great Lakes Training Station. They were the first of 58 Negro Naval officers to be commissioned during WWII. The Marines at last opened their ranks to 16,000 enlisted Negroes who served until the end of the war in segregated supply and ammunition Units."[196]

In spite of Forrestal's gallant effort, V-J Day found the role of Negro sailors that of segregated support units. Stillman says that "85 percent (The Negro Reference Book estimates 95%) of the 165,000 Navy Negroes were in the Steward's Branch."[197] Possibly this mismanagement caused young whites to be called up in the draft earlier than otherwise and possibly to die before their time. This was one of the prices of racism. James Forrestal, the leader who started the Navy on a giant step forward, back to its historical roots of liberalism, died before he could finish his work. It is said that he committed suicide by jumping to his death. The Stewards and, indeed, the Negro people, having been reduced to "quasi-paranoids", as a mode of survival, conjured up plots and dark deeds as the cause of this man's death. "He was pushed," was a general belief among Stewards. Though he had not gotten around to" lightening our load", we sincerely believed that he would have if he had lived. There was not a dry eye in the group that I drank beer with the night after his death.

What really gave the Navy the impetus to recruit black females for the WAVES was the fact that in the 1944 Presidential Election, Thomas E. Dewey, Roosevelt's Republican opponent, had made it a campaign issue. Despite this pressure, the Navy ended the war with only two black WAVE officers, Lieutenant Harriet E. Pickens and Ensign Francis Wills.

The above numbers provide an accurate assessment of the U.S. Navy's race relations program. Franklin also points out that 12,500 Negroes served in the Sea Bees, a construction and common laborer unit. The positive aspect of the Sea Bees was that one could emerge as a skilled craftsman. These policy changes regarding race relations seemed mind-boggling to the Messmen, given the point from which the Navy started! But in a real world assessment, progress appears to have been meager and grudging. Only few seamen were allowed to go to sea, in capacities other than Messmen, servants. However slow, some progress was made in allowing Negro Petty Officers and Officers to ride crack combat units rather than restricting them to barge auxiliaries, tug boats, labor battalions and Base Companies.

There was one small anomaly. There were still some Negroes, from WWI, serving in the Navy in 1940, who were not servants. They were "Chief Petty Officers", a rating a cook or steward could not aspire to. These pre-1919 blacks were machinists and chief commissary stewards, still serving out their time before retirement. These non-servant blacks usually had a relationship with some powerful Admiral. The Admiral would quietly get them assigned to some position where they would not have to direct the activities of white men. Consequently, they were allowed to serve out their time until retirement. This is reiterated here in order to remind the reader that there is always "over-lap". Social change is never instantaneous.

The Army recruited far more and commissioned more officers. The Army Air Corp brought in a black officers' program with the creation of the "Tuskegee Airmen" Program. They already had Negro officers in other areas. The U.S. Navy did not get a black Naval Officer graduate, from the Naval Academy, until 1949, four years after the end of WWII. He was "Ensign Wesley A. Brown". The Navy Nurses Corp had succeeded in getting black women officers before the War ended. The U.S. Marine Corp got their first black officer, Frederick C. Branch, after the War ended. Of the fifty plus black officers commissioned in the Navy, only two were assigned to sea duty. They were Ensign Samuel

Gravely, who later became the first black Admiral. <u>He reported aboard the PCE 1264 in May of 1945.</u> <u>The second was "James Hair", reporting aboard the U.S.S Mason in June.</u> These two vessels were an experiment with all-black crews, carried out in the later stages of WWII. The most dogged resistance was carried out by the U.S. Army. This is validated by the fact that the Army, years later, faced racial turmoil, in the ranks in Korea (1950), and much later in Vietnam.

<u>Morale</u> among black soldiers, however, was quite low on the eve of the Korean Conflict. The main reason was probably the fact that the civilian authorities seemed to be asleep at the wheel. They had no James Forrestal, who gave the navy a hard shove and clear direction. However, some attempts were made. According to <u>The Black American Reference Book:</u>

> "Shortly after WWII, the Army Chief of Staff Dwight D. Eisenhower established a board of senior military officers headed by Alvar C. Gillen, a civilian and former Solicitor General, to examine how Negro troops should be utilized in the peace time army. <u>The Gillen board report</u> was entitled <u>"The Utilization of Negro Manpower in the Post War Army"</u> and was published March 4, 1946.

The report emphasized the following points:

1. Maintenance of a 10% quota for black enlistment.

2. Future employment of black soldiers in segregated regiment sized units or smaller.

3. The necessity of encouraging an increase in the number of black officers.

4. The utilization of black NCOs' in white overhead and special units, thus permitting a limited amount of integration in the non-combat units.

5. The assignment of black units to <u>geographical areas</u> where local <u>sentiments</u> were favorable to black troops.

6. The integration on bases of busses, recreational facilities and officers messes, but, only where this policy <u>would not infringe on local</u> <u>customs</u>."[198]

Numbers 5 and 6 above are revealing, in that they indicate that the U.S. Army had made little progress in race relations, independent of the greater society during WWII and thereafter despite the negative impact on service efficiency.

As previously stated, Negro leadership was becoming increasingly sophisticated and politically active during this time. They refused to back off of their quest for the elimination of segregation and discrimination in the greater society as well as the Armed Forces. The issue was raised at the 1948 Democratic National Convention. When the progress stalled, due to pressure from the Southern politicians and delegations, Hubert H. Humphrey, the fiery young mayor of Minneapolis seized the ball and ran with it. He succeeded in getting the demands for action, in regards to Negro equality, placed as a plank in the Democratic Platform.

According to the <u>Black American Reference Book</u>: "President Truman returned to the White House, after the Democratic Convention, and signed Executive Order 9981, on July 26, 1948. It stated in the first paragraph: "It is hereby declared to be the policy of the President that there shall be equal treatment and opportunity for all persons in the Armed Services without regard to race, color, religion or national origin. This policy shall be put into effect as rapidly as possible, having due regard to time required to effectuate any necessary changes without impairing efficiency or morale."[199]

The reference goes on to point out that official Government policy, for the first time, stood squarely behind an integrated defense establishment. However, <u>it was to take six years to implement the</u>

<u>President's order</u>! This was the most important order in U.S. history, affecting positively, the welfare of black men in the armed forces.

Harry Truman was not a man to be played with. He tended to mean exactly what he said, once his mind was made up. The Fahy Committee, designated The Committee on Equality of Treatment and Opportunity in the Armed Forces, was formed to carry out Executive Order 9981. This committee demanded, and got, from each of the armed services in 1949, detailed plans for ending racial segregation and established deadlines for launching their integration programs. The Navy, Marines and Air Force complied and made good progress. Only the U.S. Army lagged behind in its effort. These actions occurred on the eve of the Korean Conflict of June 1950. Given the Army's historical record, their lack of progress in desegregating and integration comes as no surprise. This lack of urgency led to the collapse of morale of the all black 24th Infantry Regiment, later in Korea.

In 1950, the Army had "…22,672 Second Lieutenants, of which 818 were Negroes; of 5,220 Colonels, 7 were Negro; of the 776 Generals, 1 was a Negro."[200] The U.S. Army lagged far behind the other services, in the Armed Forces, at the start of the Korean Conflict in 1950. The U.S. Air Forces completed its desegregation program in twelve months. Although it had been the first service to support an official policy of integration, under James Forrestal in 1945, four years later, the U.S. Navy had too many black Stewards and too few black officers. Its report to the Fahy Committee on June 7, 1949, called for: "1) The issuance of a clear policy statement on racial equality for minorities. 2) A better publicized effort to attract black officers and skilled recruits; 3) Encourage more black applicants for ROTC; 4) Permission for men to transfer easily from the Messmen Branch; 5) Changing the rank of "Chief Steward" to the rank of Chief Petty Officer; 6) Elimination of segregated Marine Corps and Navy basic training units."[201] When the

Fayh Committee had completed its work a year later (May 1950), 52% of the black sailors were serving outside the Messmen Branch and the number of black officers had quadrupled from four to seventeen.

The author was very personally involved in the results of these actions. In 1949, computers were used for the first time in the grading of written examinations, possibly removing bias from the grading process. That year, for the first time, Chief Stewards were allowed to become Chief Petty Officers. Two promotions were granted service-wide! The author received one of the two promotions!

The U.S. Navy tried to remove some of the vestiges of discrimination by making superficial changes in some of the overt symbols. For example, shortly after he arrived at Kodiak, Alaska, in 1948, orders were received in early 1949 to prepare to change uniforms. Stewards and Cooks, prior to this, wore a mock emulation of the Chief Petty Officer's uniform. Another very unusual regulation allowed newly promoted cooks to wear the mock Chief's uniform upon becoming *3rd Class* cooks or stewards. White sailors could not dress like this until they made Chief Petty Officers. There was one humiliating drawback. The military aspects, as well as military authority, were not allowed.

Although a 3rd Class cook could wear a white shirt and bow tie, (instead of the regular tie worn by chiefs) he was not allowed to wear brass buttons, chevrons or eagles on his rating badge! Only real chiefs were allowed to do so. Although some cooks and stewards performed Petty Officer duties, they were not given Petty Officer authority. During WWII, they wore plastic buttons. With the new orders, issued in WWII, they could buy brass buttons, but they had to be hidden under a coat of dark varnish. Now cooks and stewards had been allowed to wear chevrons and eagles since 1943; however, the Navy did not grant them the authority that went along with the Eagle on the chevron until 1949. This was four years after WWII.

Upon reporting to Kodiak, the author was chosen as Division Instructor. His role was to teach cooks, stewards and Messboys (non-rated members of the Stewards Branch) the Military Requirements' section of the new naval promotion examination. This action was in preparation for granting cooks and stewards the opportunity to become real Petty Officers with the same authority as white Petty Officers. Stewards and cooks were stripped of their mock Chief Petty Officer uniforms and put into bell-bottom pants and regular stripe collar Navy tops, like the rest of the Navy's non-rated men. They were given a cash allowance with which to replace the mock Chief uniforms.

The 1949 examination was of historical importance. It put, for the first time in naval history, members of the Stewards Branch on equal footing with other specialist ratings, formally restricted to whites. Hereafter, members of this branch were to wear the same uniform and enjoy the same authority and privileges as whites. This occurred one year before the Korean Conflict. It was this plodding, but steady progress in addressing the race-relations problems that produced a higher overall morale in the U.S. Navy than in the Army, going into the Korean Conflict. The Navy acted just in time, but still suffered from its past racist image.

The U.S. Navy entered the Korean Conflict with a lousy race relation's record and public image. Incidents dating back to before, during and subsequent to WWII, drawing widespread publicity had served to tarnish the Navy's image. For example, as the 1940 presidential election neared, a group of African American Navy enlistees had spoken out publicly about their situation. In an open letter to the influential black newspaper, *The Pittsburgh Courier*, fifteen black Messmen encouraged blacks not to enlist as all they could achieve was to become bellhops, chambermaids and waiters. Eleanor Roosevelt and several civil Rights leaders intervened on the Navy's behalf, to counter this attack on the

Navy's image. The Explosion at Port Chicago, California did the worst damage, as detailed in an earlier chapter.

During the late stages of the Korean War, the author was assigned to the aircraft carrier U.S.S. Princeton, which was providing support off the coast of the theatre of operations. Reporting aboard as a newly promoted Chief Petty Officer, he found a Negro Lieutenant and several Chiefs, 1ˢᵗ Class Petty Officers, Stewards, Cooks and Steward Mates. This assignment provided an excellent first hand view of the results of the Navy's post-WWII race relations' efforts. The Princeton was an Essex-Class carrier fully loaded with an air group and a ships company numbering 3,350 sailors. The ships' crew was a microcosm of the diversity of the United States, containing all races, ethnic groups and creeds and colors. Consequently, from a human relation's standpoint, a carrier is probably the most difficult command in the Navy. It requires a high level of teamwork for successful completion of its mission. There is little or no room for narrow-minded bigotry or racist actions on the bridge of an U.S. Aircraft Carrier!

During the authors duty tour, while on the Princeton, he served under three Captains and four Executive Officers. Prior to reporting on board, he had assisted in preventing three race riots. The first had been in 1943 at Tulagi Island near Guadalcanal that had been set in motion by a visiting USO group. The audience at an outdoor theatre was all having fun until the cowboy actor, Randolph Scott, cracked a disrespectful joke about Eleanor Roosevelt. This was a real no-no in the minds of the Negro Messboys. Due to her efforts to integrate the military and obtain fair treatment for Negroes, Eleanor Roosevelt was held in almost "queen-like" status. When Scott's joke denigrated Mrs. Roosevelt, the Negro Messboys, who sat in a segregated section, became totally silent. One of them finally stood and said in a loud voice, "Who the hell do that cracker think he is insulting Mrs. Roosevelt?" Then, as if by command, the Negro sailors began grabbing dried coconuts, rocks or whatever they could get their hands on and bombarded the stage. Scott had to run off the stage in order to not get "brained". The Messboys ran up the hill and began to arm themselves. The intelligence of the commanding officer prevented a tragedy by listening to his Stewards. He prevented the all-white shore patrol from gong up the hill. It took all night for the author and two other bright Stewards to talk the Messboys, who were armed to the teeth, out of going down the hill, engaging whites and escalating the situation into a full scale race-riot.

The second race riot he helped prevent was at Guian, on Samar, in the Philippine Islands, in 1944. Guian was a staging area for outfits awaiting the invasion of Japan. There were many "packaged outfits", including ship repair, aviation radio, ordnance and P.T Boat repair units there. He had come from the Solomon Islands and was acquainted with Lieutenant Commander Frank Lemon. There were 400 Messboys, Cooks and Stewards attached to the packaged outfits. Mr. Lemon put him in charge of them. There was a pressing need to secure the base for the typhoon season. He had eight platoons numbering 50 men each. They were organized and put to work to ensure that the base would not be blown away by the coming typhoons. Racism reared its ugly head incident to our close proximity to, and competition for, the attention of the numerous Philippino women. Some of the white redneck types denigrated Negroes and told the Philippino population that Negroes were really part monkey and that they all had tails. Some Negro sailors were returning from the local village when they met a group of drunken whites. The whites told them, " You niggers need to stay out of the village cause we done told all the girls that you monkeys have tails." Then they committed a fatal error by picking the wrong Negro to lavish special abuse upon. He was, literally, a "time bomb" of anger and hatred, hating whites probably more than they hated him.

He was from rural Texas and the son of a sharecropper. He grew up witnessing his father humiliated, cheated and abused. The white sailors singled him out and told him, "As for you, nigger, you look like one of them uppity niggers and we gonna kick ya black ass." As they moved toward him, the leader was told to stop but failed to do so. This Negro pulled a 45 automatic and shot the leader in the head. As he turned to shoot more of the scattering whites, one of the author's stronger men was near enough to deflect his arm upward, and proceeded to disarm him. Without this action, more of the whites would probably have been killed. Two of the whites were from this Negro's unit. They recognized and reported him.

When the author arrived on the scene, most of the Negroes were armed and the rest in the process of becoming so. Luckily, he enjoyed the respect of his platoon leaders. They were able to get these sailors to put away their weapons and exacted a promise that none of them would leave the camp. His boss, Mr. Lemon, was approachable. He understood the potential for a race riot. Mr. Lemon persuaded the CO and the Provost to accept three suggestions: (1.) Declare the Philippino village off limits. (2) Restrict all personnel to quarters until they could be talked to and promises exacted. (3), move the courts-martial from the area. The court-martial was moved across the bay to Tacloban on Leyte Island. It took about two weeks to remove all of the tension, but the incident died without further violence. They only heard that the angry Texan was convicted and got a long prison term. They never saw him again. His name was Maurice Israel.

The third race riot prevention incident occurred at Kodiak, Alaska in 1949. It was initiated by white men's resentment over white women dancing with Negro men, at the enlisted men's club on the base. Often some white woman would ask one of the Stewards or Messboys to teach them the latest, hottest dance steps. This had gone on for some time with no one getting upset about it. The problems began when an air squadron arrived for a six-month tour of duty.

There was a hard-core redneck type in this unit. This group intervened during a black/white dancing session. The magic word, "nigger", was used and a fight broke out. It ended with the Negroes being told, "We're going to get you niggers". The Negroes went to the barracks and armed themselves with switchblades, bats and rifles. The author had worked for the CO for a while, so being the division instructor, he knew all of the participants. That year, 1949, all Stewards and Cooks who carried out the duties of petty officers, but denied the title, were scheduled to become full-fledged petty officers. His job was to teach them how to pass the Military Requirements component of the promotion exam. This was four years after the end of WWII and was the result of continued pressure on the navy. He had good standing with these men. With the help of Chief Steward Wesson, whom he later relieved on the U.S.S. Princeton, was able to prevent the hotheads from further exacerbating the problem. He exacted a promise from them to stay away from the Enlisted Men's Club. Through the CO, we got the redneck element cooled down. The pressure of Negro leaders, in the general population, intensified after the tragedy at Port Chicago. Otherwise, the Navy might have gone back to business as usual, looked the other way, and gone back to policies based on racial inferiority.

The author was well seasoned in the field of race relations prior to taking over as leading Chief aboard the U.S.S. Princeton. During his years on board, the Cold War intensified. The Russians would have been very pleased if the Princeton had had a stupid race riot while deployed in the Far East. Most of the U.S. Navy's high command never realized that the advent of national Negro civil rights leadership was not a problem, but a blessing. Such leadership, on part of the N.A.A.C.P. and Urban League, forced the services into keeping its race relations programs instead of shelving them between WWII and the Korean conflict. For example, of the officers that commanded the Princeton, two were well versed in race relations. They understood the political damage that could be caused by a race riot. The Captains were Otis C. Greg and Henry G. Sanchez, one of the few Hispanics to command an aircraft carrier. Credit should also be given to Vice Admiral Lester K. Rice, commander of Carrier Division #17, and Admiral Thurston B. Clark, Commander of Division 15, who supported and backed their captains in their efforts. Due to their savvy leadership, an atmosphere was created in which I was able to assist in the prevention of two race riots on the U.S.S. Princeton. One situation was between blacks and whites; the other was a Hispanic (Mexican and Puerto Rican) versus white confrontation. Either one would have provided a propaganda bonus for the Russians, embarrassing both the Navy and our country.

As stated earlier, on June 25, 1950, the United States was at war with North Korea. "Despite the efforts of the Fahy Committee and President Truman's Executive Order 9981, in May of 1950 when the committee completed its work, the 60,000 black Army personnel were still, for the most part, in segregated units. Several of the Fahy Committee members despaired of ever being able to alter the Army's segregationist position. With the advent of the Korean War, the situation changed quickly."[202]

The accelerated change in the Army's desegregation effort was not prompted by any lengthy deliberations, changes in morality or sense of fairness on the part of the top generals. Again, necessity was the impetus and driver of action! Little is written about the all-black 24th Infantry Regiment. At the end of WWII, they were not a part of the massive "bring the boys home" effort. They were left in Japan as garrison troops, while other units were hurried home aboard the troopships. The 24th was literally forgotten, out of sight and out of mind. They were guards for General Douglas McArthur, who had been given the role of reconstructing the Japanese Government.

Black troops had rarely been used in invasions or first assaults. These events produced the glory, the heroes and medals. Instead, they were most often used in the follow-up, mop-up operations, policing actions and garrison support. These mop-up operations were often more hazardous than the preceding battles. The role involved rooting out remaining enemy troops who had not surrendered, evaded capture or hidden out in the area jungles or towns. The fact that these enemy soldiers had not surrendered speaks to their level of commitment and fanaticism. Sniper techniques, booby traps and ambush were their methods of operations. Consequently, the troops involved in mop-ups were in constant danger in their search for the enemy; many were killed.

A black soldier of the 24th, who had been wounded in mop-up action on Bougainville Island, and ended up in the naval hospital on Tulagi Island during WWII, vividly described his experience to the author. "Man, imagine being landed on a strange island while the others are pulling out. You know little or nothing about the geography. You receive a half-assed briefing from the departing force guys. You don't know how many, what caliber or where the enemy forces are. Then imagine pouring rain, mud up over your boot tops and heat in the 80's and 90's! Between the sweat and the rain, you think that you will never be dry again. I would have given a month of paydays for a dry pair of drawers! You are surrounded by a green hell of jungle where you cannot see six yards ahead. You go out in this muck with half a platoon. You return with half of them wounded or dead. This goes on week in after week out!" The newspaper reporters and other media personnel depart with the glorious "invading" forces, so the hell of mop-up is not spotlighted in the headlines, nor televised.

Since no one had heard anything about them back home, the 24th vanished from the minds of both blacks and whites. This is probably the primary contributing factor to the Army giving this unit priority 10 for desegregation. They remained a segregated unit going into the Korean War in 1950.

When the Korean War began, the 24th Infantry Regiment was ready and still available in the theatre of operations. They were in Japan. Unlike stateside units, they had not had to sweat whether congress would allot the money for practice maneuvers or the firing range to sharpen their marksmanship. There was, as told to the author by one Master Sergeant, enough munitions left in Japan for them to practice, "whenever they got ready". MacArthur encouraged them to stay sharp. Further, many black soldiers found a home in Japan, got married and stayed in the Army when their enlistment was up, rather than return to the United States. Many, whom the author met in Yokohoma, while on liberty, expressed the view that they were treated better by the Japanese than they were in their racist hometowns stateside.

In Japan, as in most other countries, whites competing for the attention of local women did their usual thing. They told Japanese girls that Black men had tails like their monkey cousins and were part animal. A young lady who had attended Tokyo University told the author the following: "Even though most ordinary Japanese people had never seen black men before, we knew what they really were. Prior to the War, American Christian missionaries had been in Japan, teaching English language and literature. They had used the story of "Little Black Sambo" in their classes. Further, we observed that white servicemen were arrogant and looked down on our people. They often, when drunk, became vicious and mean. You very seldom saw a drunken black man abuse Japanese people. Rather, these black men brought candy and treats from the PX for Japanese children. When they found that some old people in my village had lost their sons in the war and were having difficulty, they brought food from the base for them. Further, this behavior extended to Japanese men who were really down and afraid after their defeat. Even when drunk, the black men did not call them dirty Japs and "squinch eyes" as the white men often did.

The Little Black Sambo doll was one of the most popular dolls sold around holidays. The author had a difficult time explaining to the young lady why black men hated the Little Black Sambo story. The story was used by whites in the United States, to demean and denigrate black people. One black soldier expressed the view that he had not been called "nigger" in so long that he probably wouldn't know how to get mad! They, the 24th, were among the first allied soldiers to enter the war.

So the forgotten 24th, on the eve of Korea, was literally a regiment of Sergeants. This is probably why the 24th stood fast while the entire South Korean Army, including U.S. Units, was in retreat and in wild disarray in first clashes with the North Korean Army. Consequently, it is not surprising that the 24th Infantry achieved the first U.S. victory of the war. This occurred on July 21, 1950, at the battle of Yechon Korea. Walton H. Walker commanded the 24th Infantry Regiment. As the war proceeded, the 24th was used in ways that ultimately led to the total collapse of morale of the unit.

Because of their tenacity and fighting ability, they were more and more often given the task of filling the breech when some section of the South Korean or Allied Forces line collapsed. They would be unceremoniously pulled out of their position and rushed miles away to plug holes in the battle line. These soldiers soon realized that they were being used in ways that brought on higher than necessary casualty rates. There was talk among the troops about being "cannon fodder". They lost trust in their field generals. The troops gradually stopped fighting. They would simply "fade away" in the face of the enemy. A song was made up by the troops that they named the "bug out boogie"! (When them mortar shells begin to thud, ole duece-four begins to bug) Their leader, Walton H. Walker, was killed in a vehicle accident. Maxwell D. Taylor replaced him. Taylor quickly recognized what was wrong with this previously strong fighting force. He advised his superiors of this situation and recommended that the unit be disbanded and integrated with white units. His recommendation was accepted. Thus ended the segregation of the U.S. Army! The remaining troops were spread among other units in the theatre. The 24th Infantry Regiment, formed in 1866, served in the Indian wars on the frontier, in the Spanish American and in WWI and WWII, was no more.

However, "necessity" worked in other ways, and venues to drive integration of the Armed Forces. For example, at the start of the Korean War, black enlistment shot up to 25 percent of the total enlistment's for July 1950 compared to only 8.2 percent, four months earlier in March. *The Black American Reference Book* tells us:

> "This rapid influx meant that the only way to maintain segregation was to place blacks in their own units, which were already over-manned, while white units were desperate for men. This hardly seemed logical. Thus one by one, local commanders-frequently at their own initiative and without decisive Pentagon guidance on the matter-integrated their units out of practical necessity to equalize the strength of their units."[203]

Korea was no exception. Removal of racial quotas brought a flood of new black soldiers. At the same time, black units were overstaffed, while white units were suffering proportionately higher combat fatalities. This fact increased the pressure at the front and back home to equalize the fighting effort. The Eighth Army Headquarters in Korea had adopted an unofficial policy of Integration by January 1951.

While the U.S.S Princeton was docked at Yokosuka, Japan, in the late stages of the Korean War, the author went to the adjacent ship to visit some friends. He was shocked and surprised to see *white Messboys* serving coffee! The first thought that came to him was, "Do they shine shoes, too?" As a former Messboy, it was beyond his imagination that a white sailor would ever serve coffee. This meant that the Navy had come full circle from total inequality, restricting minorities to the Messboy/ Stewards Branch, then to totally barring enlistment of Negroes to actual equality for Negroes. The author had heard rumors of the existence of white Messboys, but had written them off as the wishful thinking or wild imagination of Negro sailors. Given the fact that there is little to no mention of the black Messboys/Stewards Branch in the U.S. Navy history books, it is not surprising that this author could find only a single mention of white Messboys, and that was in a newspaper article!

The histories talk about the merger of the Stewards and Commissary "ratings" some years later, but if one is not familiar with Navy jargon, the fact that the black/brown/yellow Stewards were integrated with the white Commissary sailors might be missed! A United Press International (UPI) press release on the subject of Navy Stewards treated the subject as follows:

UP-104 (NAVY STEWARDS)

WASHINGTON (UPI) – LOWER AND MIDDLE RANKING NAVAL OFFICERS WILL NO LONGER HAVE FILIPINO STEWARDS TO MAKE THEIR BEDS ON SHIPBOARD, THE NAVY DECLARED TODAY.

THE ORDER, ANOTHER STEP IN THE NAVY'S EFFORT TO LOWER THE CASTE BARRIERS BETWEEN OFFICERS AND ENLISTED MEN, SAID THAT ENSIGNS, LIEUTENANTS AND LIEUTENANT COMMANDERS NOW WILL MAKE THEIR OWN BEDS ABOARD SHIP EXCEPT IN CASES WHERE THEY SERVE AS THE SKIPPER OR EXECUTIVE OFFICER.

FOR YEARS, STEWARDS ASSIGNED TO "OFFICER COUNTRY" ABOARD SHIP HAVE CLEANED THE QUARTERS, MADE THE BEDS AND SERVED THE FOOD OF ALL OFFICERS. NOW THE NAVY HAS SAID THAT ENSIGNS, LIEUTENANTS AND LIEUTENANT COMMANDERS WILL HAVE TO MAKE THEIR OWN BEDS EXCEPT WHERE THEY ARE THE SKIPPER OF EXECUTIVE OFFICER.

THE CHANGE CAME AS THE NAVY ANNOUNCED IT WAS MERGING TWO OF ITS "RATINGS" OR JOB CATEGORIES. BEGINNING JANUARY 1, STEWARDS, * WHO ARE LARGELY FILIPINO, AND COMMISSARYMEN, WHO ARE LARGELY BLACK AND WHITE, WILL BE COMBINED INTO THE SINGLE RATING OF "MESS MANAGEMENT SPECIALISTS".

NAVY OFFICIALS SAID THE STEWARDS HAVE BEEN VIRTUAL SERVANTS IN "OFFICER COUNTRY", A FACT THAT HAS SPURRED CONSIDERABLE CRITICISM, THE COMMISSARYMEN HAVE RUN THE ENLISTED MESSES ON BOARD SHIP.

NAVY OFFICIALS SAID THE STEWARDS REENLIST IN GREAT NUMBERS WHICH ALLOWS LITTLE OPORTUNITY FOR PROMOTION AND PACKS THE NAVY WITH MORE STEWARDS THAN IT KNOWS WHAT TO DO WITH. ON THE OTHER HAND, REENLISTMENTS WERE LOWER FOR COMMISSARYMEN AND THAT JOB CATEGORY WAS OFTEN UNDERSTAFFED. COMBINING THE TWO RATINGS SOLVES THE PROBLEMS OF EACH.

UPI 11-18 03:59 PES

* NOTE: Error= Officers. Stewards, EOORS and Stewards Mates were composed of mostly Filipinos and Blacks.

The level of publicity was so low that it is no wonder that the creation of white Messboys got very little attention in the general public. The single general publication on the subject, this author found, was a newspaper article by the nationally known satirist, Art Buchwald written years later (1971) and published in the Los Angeles Times. Under the headline of "WASP's in the Navy Mess Halls", he wrote:

> There was so much publicity attached to the announcement last week when the U.S. Navy promoted its first black officer to rear admiral that little attention was paid to another breakthrough in rigid Naval tradition. With no fuss the Navy announced that it had appointed its first white Anglo-Saxon Protestant waiter to serve in the U.S Navy officer's mess.
>
> The lucky seaman was John Paul Jones VII of Akron, Ohio. Up until Seaman Jones' appointment as mess boy, only Filipino and black sailors were permitted to serve naval officers. But after a secret Defense Department race relations' report, it was decided that if the Navy were going to have black admirals, it would have to have white mess boys to even things out.
>
> Although the U.S. Army and the Marines all used WASP attendants, the Navy, according to the report, couldn't find any qualified WASP seamen to wait on officers' tables. But the report found that mess boys in the Navy were not being selected according to qualifications, but according to race.
>
> There are many white sailors who are as good at serving officers as blacks and Filipinos," the report stated. "They have just not been given the opportunity to prove it. It is our opinion that if the U.S. Navy hopes to recruit more members of the Anglo-Saxon race, It had better open up its kitchens and pantries to Caucasian servicemen.
>
> Stung by the report, the Navy denied that John Paul Jones VII had been appointed to serve in the officers' mess because he was

white. "Jones, " a Navy spokesperson said, "was selected because he was the most qualified waiter we could find".

The public information officer was questioned about the fact that Jones's appointment came only one week after the Defense Department report was leaked to the press. "I'll admit," he said, "it sounds like a coincidence, but the U.S. Navy, and you are going to have to take my word for this, has been looking for qualified WASP mess boys for the last 192 years...

Unlike the Army in the Korean Conflict, who suffered serious race relations' problems in the field and some image damage at home, the Navy managed to leave this war without negative media grabbing headline incidents. In fairness, it must be pointed out that all of the Armed Forces, Navy, Marines, Army and Air Force did in varying degrees, accelerate their race relations efforts between the Korean Conflict and the Viet Nam War. This was done, primarily under the impetus of President Harry Truman.

When President Truman left office in 1952, President Dwight D. Eisenhower, a Republican and a war hero replaced him. Three factors shaped the race relations efforts of both the Armed Forces and the general population. First, using the "Dixiecrat" movement of 1948, more Southern Democrats switched to the Republican Party. They were in position to influence the White House regarding this issue. Secondly, two years into Eisenhower's presidential term, the Supreme Court decided Brown vs. Board of Education ordering the desegregation of all schools. And thirdly, Eisenhower, being new to politics, moved slowly and reluctantly in regards to race relations.

From WWII through the Korean War, the Negro leadership did not let up on its efforts to attain social justice. They, in fact, intensified the fight for Civil Rights and Civil Liberties. The Brown decision, followed by the Montgomery Bus Boycott in 1955 gave the movement such impetus that it was labeled "The Negro Revolt".

Additionally, that old leveler, necessity, worked in other ways to drive integration.

CHAPTER 22. RACISM RETARDS NAVY'S VIETNAM EFFORT

The eve of the Vietnam War found the U.S. Navy continuing to reflect the social norms of the greater American society, found itself still vulnerable to that old nemesis, Racism. The many lessons of World War II and the Korean Conflict regarding appropriate human and more specifically, racial relations were being ignored. As for African Americans, the Civil rights movement, while still pursuing the American Dream for Blacks, had spawned new levels of activism embracing "Black Awareness" and Black Power" movements.

According to Jack D. Foner, in a section of his book entitled "The Vietnam War and Black Servicemen", "Once in the service, Blacks were assigned to low-skill combat units. As of December 1965 almost 27 percent of Black soldiers were assigned to the infantry, compared to 18 percent of Whites... .In 1967, 20 percent of all Army fatalities were Black. Nonetheless, during the mid-1960s most Black military personnel and civilians had a decidedly favorable opinion of the armed forces."[204]

They considered the military establishment the most completely integrated segment of American society and the one that provided the best career opportunity for Black men. Reporters for newspapers, magazines and television alike sent back glowing accounts of the harmonious race-relations that existed in the integrated fighting forces.

As late as 1967 the New York Times reported, "The American ground forces are almost free of racial tension, and most soldiers, Negro and White, appear proud of this."

And then came the thunder! External to the armed forces the "Negro Revolt increased in fury."

Actually, the United States was engaged in three, then later four wars as we moved toward and into the Vietnam War. The first was the lingering Cold War engagement with Russia, internationally. The second was the growing Civil Rights Movement at home. The third was the growing "hot" war in Vietnam. And lastly, the divisive Anti-War Movement in protest of our involvement in Vietnam! As the Vietnam War dragged on, the Armed Forces were subjected to forces beyond their control. Although an ex-General and Chief of Staff of the JCS, President Eisenhower was not the decisive, hardheaded political leader that Harry S. Truman had been. He was compelled to move in the areas of desegregation and race relations, but did so reluctantly. Sending the National Guard to Central High School at Little Rock is an example.

Maybe not unnoticed but certainly unevaluated properly by the military, a coalition (the Peace and Freedom and Civil Rights movements) was made that was to prove devastating for both the Kennedy and Johnson Administrations and the morale of U.S. armies in far away Vietnam. White mothers, fathers and college students hit the streets in massive Peace Marches and Anti-war Protest Rallies. Many young people of means moved to Canada to avoid the draft.

The terrible forces unleashed proved to be beyond the control of the Government and most certainly any countermeasures available to the armed forces. Given the level of coverage by the media, it became impossible for the Generals and Admirals to prevent news of what was raging back home from entering the consciousness of Sailors and soldiers in the field. Initial lack of awareness may have caused the armed forces to fail to evaluate the import of this domestic sociopolitical turbulence as this phenomena was to subsequently affect the maintenance of discipline and morale in the field. Jack D. Foner says:

> "In 1966 the Student Non-violent Coordinating Committee (SNCC), the Congress of Racial Equality (CORE) and Dr. Martin Luther King's Southern Christian Leadership Conference (SCLC) joined the anti-war movement. Up until his assassination in April 1968, Dr. King spoke out against the war with increasing sharpness. ."We are taking the young black men who have been crippled by our society and sending them 8,000 miles away to guarantee the liberties of Southeast Asia which they have not found in Southwest Georgia and East Harlem". So we have been repeatedly faced with the cruel irony of watching Negro and White boys on TV screens as they kill and die together for a nation that has been unable to seat them in the same school. So we watch them in brutal solidarity burning huts of a poor village, but we realize that they could not live on the same block in Detroit."[205]

The downward slide of black morale started here and reached the crisis stage in the early part of 1967. The emergence of the "Black Militant" movement, toward Black self-segregation and the near total immersion of Black troops in "Black awareness", seriously weakened unit solidarity. This was accompanied by overt, "revolutionary symbolism", (dapping, Afro-hair, Black-power salute, etc.). The reaction of Whites to this phenomenon was one of fear and anger, as few really understood this abrupt shift, in the behavior of Blacks whom they once trusted and knew that they could depend upon in a fight.

Meanwhile, at home black critics of the war seized upon the angry cutting rhetoric, and loudly voiced two contentions exemplified by these two quotes:

(1) "We have to put an end to that war because that war is blowing up our future. The Reverend Andrew Young, then an executive Vice

President of SCLC and one of King's most able young lieutenants made this statement. It was based upon the Black perception that the war was draining off massive resources, resources disparately needed to counter the deteriorating situation of Blacks here at home. Further, that young Black manhood was being sapped in a fruitless war that even White people thought was stupid. This latter element was probably due to the rising rhetoric of White anti-war advocates.

(2) "War opponents used it (the war) as an indictment of American society that many Blacks had nowhere but to military service to look for economic security or career and status fulfillment." Finally they argued that "America, not Vietnam was the Black man's battleground."[206]

The messages from the Peace Movement, the Civil rights Movement and the Black Awareness Campaign affected the attitudes of both black and white members of the Armed Forces. This was intensified when Martin Luther King brought the Negro Revolt into alliance with the Anti-war Movement. The effect was a devastating blow to morale in Vietnam. Initially, there was a rift in the SCLC leadership. Others in the organization thought that inclusion of the Peace Movement under the SCLC umbrella would cause it to lose focus on the many problems of Civil Rights. It was further argued that the Anti-war Movement was a "white mans problem". King argued that important morality issues existed in both.

However, southern racist continued to fight doggedly against school integration, public accommodations and the right to vote. New leaders joined the fight via CORE, SNCC and The Black Panther Party overriding the gradualism propounded by staid organizations like the NAACP, National Urban League and SCLC. The strongest impetus for ending the debate and joining the Peace and Civil Rights Movements was the increasing number of black casualties in Vietnam. It was learned that the number of black draftees far exceeded their percentage of the pool; all white draft boards were routinely granting student and other types of deferments to whites, while drafting blacks to fill quotas. It was further learned that the number of blacks killed and wounded far exceeded their percentage of the population.

Whereas blacks had to fight draft boards twenty years earlier to get into the military in our popular wars, they were being enlisted en masse for this unpopular one. By 1967, African American percentages of battlefield deaths had declined from over twenty percent to the low teens, but still above the eleven percent of the total U.S. population figure.

What really drove a wedge between white and black soldiers beyond the seas was the concept of "Black Power" versus the relentless defense of white supremacy at home.

At the time of the foregoing events, the U.S. Military Services were considering possible de-emphasis of race-relations content in the Human Resources efforts. This action was being contemplated in complete disregard for the speed and awesome power of external phenomena to negatively alter the military environment and thus pose almost insurmountable problems for military commanders.

The assassination of Dr. King in April, 1968 catalyzed negative behavior on the part of Whites which validated even the wildest assertions of Black Militants, at home in the minds of most Blacks in combat arms in Vietnam. Foner's book is a major source of information here. It appears to be the most up to date and carefully researched book. Also, it corroborates eyewitness accounts, from many students in classes taught by the author.

The death of King caused sorrow and a sense of loss to most Blacks and Whites alike. But for White racists, the affect was to unleash the pent-up rage, probably intensified by Black militants and accompanying symbolization and rhetoric, long nurtured against the civil-rights advocates in the broader community. These, again, according to Foner, acted out their rage in a manner that made control of Black combat contingents all but impossible. It is a tribute to Vietnam combat commanders that any semblance of group cohesion was kept intact, as broader community drug abuse, along with anti-war sentiment and Black alienation all spilled over into the military institutions. For the first time in U.S. history, parents demonstrated against their government while their sons gave their lives 7,000 miles from home.

> In the spring of 1968 incidents of racial turmoil and discontent increased at military installations throughout the world. The assassination of Dr. King in April accentuated racial tensions and controversy, particularly in Vietnam. At Que Viet, a Navy Installation, Whites wore makeshift Klan costumes to celebrate the Black leader's death, and at Da Nang Confederate flags were raised. On the day of national mourning for Dr. King, Whites burned a cross and hoisted a Confederate flag in front of Navy Headquarters at Cam Rahn Bay."[207]

The author has been told by a ranking officer, whom he met when he was a mess boy at Annapolis and he was a Lieutenant (jg) in 1941, a person of immense integrity, and Retired as a flag officer, that a tragedy was narrowly averted in the aftermath of these incidents. According to several of my students who served ashore as fire control and liaison people, the demonstration previously described, came within a "hairs breath" of causing combat arms personnel to fire on these "Coast dwellers" (American staff and support personnel). Students told me that the Staff and support people, who lived in relative comfort in the coastal towns, contemptuously referred to the combat arms personnel who came in from the jungles covered with filth and grime, as "gravel crunchers, grunts and bush bunnies".

These non-combat troops and sailors, who usually had most of the women staked out, went around in clean uniforms, knew the MP's by first name and were the pimps and dope-pushers. These "Saigon commandos" treated combat troopers like dirt, according to the Fort Ord Drill Instructors who assisted me in the Phase I Human Resources Management class effort, at the Naval Postgraduate school. All were minority Vietnam veterans. These men told me that a "false-emergency" was declared in order to get the combat troops out of the coastal towns in the aftermath of King's death and the subsequent White-racist reaction.

They told me that the contempt and hatred between combat and staff/support people was mutual. One other item that probably few people even in the fighting forces there knew was that if this fight had started, there would not have been the usual Whites on one side and Blacks on the other. There were White, Black, Mexican, Puerto-Ricans, etc. who had, through combat experience, grown as close as brothers who bitterly resented the few racists who displayed behavior that tended to divide their units. Consequently this fight could have produced the spectacle of sizeable White contingents siding with their minority buddies against other Whites.

In order to prevent this already dangerous situation from escalating, the Commander of forces in Vietnam acted:

> "Because of the growing tension, an order was issued for the removal of all flags with the Confederate symbol. The reason given was that the Confederate flag was viewed as a "symbol of racism."[208]

But the "political reality" prevented this hard-pressed Area Commander from carrying out a decision supported by all of his experienced Field Commanders. This is one of the potent negative external forces over which the military commander exercised little or no control. According to Foner:

> "'When Representative William S. Stuckey of Georgia informed the house on May 6 that he was upset, angry and indignant because one of his constituents in Vietnam had been ordered to remove the Georgia flag from his bunk, the Pentagon assured him and other Southern Congressmen that servicemen would be allowed to fly their home state flags in Vietnam even if they carried the symbols of The Confederacy."[209]

Here, the immoral aspects of civilian politics intervened as a countervailing force in a manner that prevented an area commander and his subordinates from dealing effectively with a critical control problem that threatened the destruction of morale and esprit de corps of his combat units, thousands of miles from home.

The Department of Defense and the Military Services have been the leaders in many areas of scientific and technological advancement in our society. However, they continued to lag and follow the greater society in the areas of social change and race relations. On occasion and out of necessity, they have gotten out in front of the greater society in these areas. The pre-Revolutionary War and War of 1812 are examples; they are, however, exceptions to the rule to the point of being anomalies.

The American system of government is a strong contributor to this condition. America is a Federal Democratic system under which the Military is controlled and managed by a civilian authority. It is this civilian authority that has the greatest influence and impact on the social rules and regulations employed by the military. The civilian leadership has been more than willing to let the military professionals select and develop war machine technology and set battle strategies. It has rarely given up the power to set the social norms.

It has been only in times of war and threat that pragmatic necessity has caused the Military leadership to overrule the civilian norms. Of special note has been the role of Southern Legislators in the Congress and appointed Southern Administrators in the Executive Branch of the Government. They represent the strongest forces opposing and retarding the advancement in human and racial relations in the U.S. Navy and other branches of the military.

CHAPTER 23. FAILURE OF NAVY ADVANCEMENT IN HUMAN RESOURCES IN THE POST-VIETNAM ERA

The U. S. Navy seems to have had a head start on the other services in the area of human resources management, as its current program probably comes nearer to meeting the criteria of the organizational development process than other services. The foregoing chapter attempted to bring the persons up-to-date who may not have been familiar with the historical and socio-political events underlying the present HRM effort. This is based upon the very real assertion, "If an organization doesn't know where it came from, it will probably experience problems in ascertaining where it is going."

Two factors contributed to the Navy's human resources failure in the post Vietnam era. The first was the social climate, discussed in the last chapter. The Civil Rights/Black Power movements, combined with the Anti-War movement, impacted the morale and attitudes of its personnel. Unlike previous wars, Sailors suffered abuse and ridicule when they returned home, rather than the public adulation and glory of past wars. A major second contributor was "Project 100,000", a program implemented by then Secretary of Defense, Robert McNamara.

The launching of "Project 100,000" was extremely unpopular with the Civil Rights movement. This Project ordered Draft Boards to cease and desist from turning away young blacks that scored low on the Education/Intelligence tests. Instead, they were to lower the bar and recruit them. McNamara ordered the Armed Forces to set up education programs to enhance the literacy and education levels of these young men. This would have been a lofty and positive endeavor except the Civil Rights Movement saw it as being done for the wrong reasons. Civil Rights leaders questioned the overrepresentation of blacks among the returning dead and wounded (20% of the casualties, 11% of the population). Further, in 1967, less than 2% of the nations 17,000 Draft Board members were black. They were more likely to grant exemptions and deferments to young white men than to blacks.

"Secretary McNamara, despite his clear support of Civil Rights and the expansion of President Truman's order, had created a system that funneled poor blacks into the front lines while weeding out upper middle class whites. The easiest way to gain a deferment was to go to college or join the National Guard. Most of these blacks could not afford college; the National Guard, in many states, restricted blacks or outright banned them! These circumstances enraged the Negro leadership, causing a large and voiceferous outcry. It must be pointed out that McNamara had few options. A war cannot be fought without soldiers. The Human Resources failure, however, cannot be blamed on McNamara."[210]

The Armed Services, including the Navy, failed to follow through on the commitment to provide education as stipulated in the "Project 100,000" plan. Consequently, there was a large influx of blacks that could only perform the infantry role or more menial tasks. They often came from the cities, emboldened by the black power rhetoric, and unwilling to just go along to get along. Unlike the deferential Stewards and Messmen of old, when they felt that they were being treated unjustly, they would speak up, and out their frustrations, if insulted, fight back. The "glad to be heah" type darkie was history by this period.

During the latter stages of the Vietnam War, a race riot occurred aboard the U.S.S. *Kitty Hawk*, off the coast of Vietnam. After several extended periods of combat activity, the ship put into the U.S. Naval Base at Subic Bay, the Philippines, for replenishment of war material and a week of rest and recreation for the crew.

On the tenth of October, a fight occurred at the enlisted men's club at Subic Bay. While it cannot be unequivocally established that *Kitty Hawk* personnel participated in this fight, circumstantial evidence tends to support the conclusion of investigators, that some of the ship's black sailors were involved. Fifteen young blacks returned to the ship, on the run, and in a very disheveled condition at about the time the fight at the club was brought under control. The following morning the ship returned to combat, conducting operations from 1 to 6 p.m. There were 348 officers and 4,135 enlisted men on board. Of these, five officers and two hundred and ninety-seven enlisted men were black.

On October 12, 1972, the ship's investigator called a black sailor to his office for questioning about the activities at Subic Bay. Nine other black men accompanied the young man. They were belligerent, loud and used abusive language. They were not allowed to sit in on the investigation. The sailor was appraised of his rights. He refused to make a statement and was allowed to leave. Shortly after he left, a young white messcook was assaulted on the after messdeck. Within a few minutes after that, another young messcook was assaulted on the forward messdeck. The first indication of widespread trouble occurred when a large number of blacks congregated on the after messdeck. A messcook alerted the Marine Detachment Reaction Force. During the ensuing confrontation between the Marines and black sailors, the corporal of the guard, the only person with a firearm, attempted, or appeared to attempt to draw his weapon. This incident appears to have been one of the more inflammatory events. Events escalated from there with marauding bands, confrontations and blacks arming themselves. The actions of several black Chief Petty Officers and a black Executive Officer on board the *Kitty Hawk* quelled the uprising.

The Black Commander, Ben Cloud, XO, followed one group of 150 or so to the forecastle. They were armed and extremely hostile. He later stated he believed that had he not been black he probably would have been killed on the spot. He addressed the group for about two hours, reluctantly ignoring his status as the XO and instead appealing to the men as one black man to another. After some time he acquired control over the group, calmed them down and had them put their weapons at his feet or over the side, and then ordered them to return to their compartments. The meeting broke up at 2:30 in the morning and for all intents and purposes, the violence aboard the *Kitty Hawk* was over.

The ship fulfilled its combat mission schedule that morning and for the remainder of her time on station. During this period *Kitty Hawk* established a record 177 days on the line in a single deployment. The 21 men who were charged with offenses, under the Uniform Military Code of Justice and who requested civilian counsel, were put ashore at Subic Bay, to be later flown to San Diego to meet the ship on its return. The remaining 5 charged were brought to trial aboard the ship during its transit back to the United States.

A similar incident occurred aboard the U.S.S. Constellation, sister ship to the Kitty Hawk, while berthed at San Diego. Late one night, a group of blacks held a clandestine meeting in the ship's barbershop. The next day, an open meeting was held. At the suggestion of the commanding officer, the Executive Officer attended this meeting. He entered into the discussion, which turned out to be a general gripe session, as no specific complaints were aired, and no indications of possible trouble noted. The CO decided that, in order to prevent these meetings from becoming covert, no action would be taken to prevent further meetings but surveillance of all future meetings would be closely maintained.

During subsequent meetings, the blacks organized, elected representatives and assigned specific functions to members of the group. One of these functions, as so-called "legal Counsel", entailed an examination of the ship's records of Non-Judicial Punishment (NJP), also known as Captain's Mast, to determine where racial discrimination had occurred.

On November 1st, 1972, the CO directed the XO to personally attend that day's meeting. There the formalization of grievances occurred but, still, no specific complaints were aired which could have been resolved by command action. While dispersing from this meeting, an unidentified group of blacks assaulted a white messcook, fracturing his jaw. The next day, the CO identified 15 sailors as "agitators" and directed the XO to examine their personnel records to determine if any were eligible for command-initiated administrative discharge. Six apparently qualified, although further action eliminated one of them. The personnel concerned were notified of the pending action.

At the same time it was general knowledge that the ship's company would have to be reduced by 250 men in order to accommodate the air wing personnel who would embark prior to the ship's forthcoming combat deployment. Rumors circulated throughout the ship that all 250 would be administratively discharged with less than honorable discharges and all 250 would be black. Both rumors were false.

On November 3rd, the XO met with two members of the group and was asked to announce, over the PA system, that he would stop the administrative discharge proceedings. The XO agreed, in part, to the request, circulating a "flyer" announcing the halt of administrative discharges and announced over the PA, an open meeting of the Human Resources Council that evening.

At about noon the CO and XO were notified of a "sit-in" on the forward messdecks. The CO directed officers and senior petty officers to order their men to return to work as air evolutions were about to start. The "sit-in" broke up, but the participants regrouped on the after messdecks.

At the evening HRC meeting, the group fluctuated between 50 and 150, with all but a few participants being black. From 9 P.M. until midnight the HRC officers and men and the personnel officer attempted to respond to the group's complaints. However, the group's complaints were too broad to be answered. No specific cases of racial discrimination, which was the group's general complaint, were definitely identified. The tenor of the meeting rapidly changed so that by midnight the HRC members were being subjected to considerable verbal abuse. The HRC withdrew leaving the after messdeck to a crowd of about 100 sailors.

The group continued to meet, formulating a demand for the CO's presence, warning that if he did not appear, members of the group might "tear up his ship". The CO refused to accede to this demand and directed that the ship be "awakened" and that senior personnel patrol berthing compartments and passageways to preclude incidents such as happened aboard the *Kitty Hawk*.

The CO then informed his seniors by message that he was going to North Island and would place the dissident group ashore as a "beach detachment". This concept is normally applied to a liaison group placed ashore overseas while the ship conducts operations at sea. In this case, it was composed of the dissident group, senior advisory personnel and members of HRC. At about 4 a.m. the CO called for an all hands muster on the flight deck in an attempt to break up the sit-in. The group refused to move from the messdeck in response to that order.

The ship put in at North Island and the CO directed that "all those who wished to join this group" would be put ashore. Personnel from the naval air station and Commander Naval Air Operations met with the CO. At the advice of staff personnel, the CO met with the dissident sailors. At this point in time the dissident group had not yet formalized its demands; contrary to the advice of the staff, however, the CO refused to keep the men aboard his ship. The beach detachment was put ashore and, early the next morning, the ship put back to sea.

Over the next several days the beach detachment and various staff personnel met to resolve grievances. After returning to port to offload damaged aircraft and returning to sea again, the ship was directed to return to port so that the CO could become directly involved in the discussions. During this period, a series of telephone calls were placed between the Chief of Naval Operations, the Commander-in-Chief Pacific Fleet and the Commander of Naval Air Forces Pacific during which information, advice and decisions regarding the situation were passed. On November 8th, the CO met the group and received their demands. First, that a review of non-judicial punishment be conducted to determine whether he had discriminated against blacks. Secondly, that a review of administrative discharges be conducted for the same purpose. And thirdly, that all personnel involved in the incident aboard the Constellation be received back aboard and not prosecuted for their actions.

The CO agreed to the three demands with one exception; all personnel who were involved in prior offenses or who might have committed assault during the night of 3-4 November would not be immune to prosecution. He then ordered the men to return to the Constellation at the conclusion of overnight liberty.

The following morning, the group refused to board the ship. Instead, they mustered on the pier. They were allegedly acting on advice from an unidentified high-level source in the Pentagon that such muster would preclude their being charged with unauthorized absence. If such advice was given, it was erroneous. The ship then advised the men of their unauthorized absentee status and, at 9 a.m., they were transported back to the barracks. At 2 p.m., the men were informed that they had been transferred to North Island, in a disciplinary status, and that the charge against them would be 6 hours unauthorized absence. A total of 122 men transferred.

Contrary to press reports and subsequent hearings implying neglect and permissiveness in this area, the Navy possessed a myriad of programs whose focus was on equal opportunity and race relations long before the shipboard blow-ups that caused the nation to focus on these problems. As an example, the *Kitty Hawk* incident did not occur until 12 October 1972 and the *Constellation* incident, did not come to public notice, until November of that year.

Secretary of Defense Melvin Laird held meetings based upon the Civil Rights Act of 1964 and the subsequent additions to that act implied in the Civil Rights Act of 1968. He asked for and got the approval and signatures, of all of the Secretaries of branches of service, on the document entitled HUMAN GOALS CREDO 18 August 1969, three years *before* the *Kitty Hawk/Constellation* incidents. Secretary of the Navy John Chaffee issued through his Assistant Secretary for Manpower and Reserve Affairs, James D. Hittle, SECNAVINST 5350.6A, superceding SECNAVINSTS 5350.1, 5350.2A and 5350.6. He thus consolidated the myriad of fragmentary directives and issued a codified set of guidelines for the Navy Equal Opportunity effort at the policy level. In this document the Secretary delineated policy, objectives, goals and the responsibilities of commanding officers and methods of processing complaints. In reminding commanding officers of the fact that, directives, as such, were incapable of insuring equal treatment. The Secretary cited the fact that President Truman had issued Executive Order 9981 in July 1948. His implication was clear as the problem of inequality was still around.

Though Chaffee placed the awesome responsibility for equal treatment of service personnel squarely upon the shoulders of commanding officers, he also gave them the clout needed to deal decisively with external countervailing forces (such as housing and public places who discriminated against Navy men) that were formerly beyond their authority. He gave them the power to act against other institutions in the broader social environment beyond the borders of naval installations! Chapter two of SECNAVINST 5350.6A, dealing with off limits sanctions implied that a commanding officer required "Secretarial Approval" in order to exercise off-limits powers as sanction in cases of racial discrimination. This had, previously, effectively tied a commanding officer's hands. On 27 May 1971 the Secretary issued ALNAV 27/71 which stated:

1. Cancel that portion of paragraph #207 reference A, which implies a requirement for secretarial approval for use of off-limits sanctions in cases of racial discrimination. Local commanders both overseas and in the United States are hereby delegated authority and responsibility to impose off-limits sanctions in appropriate cases of racial discrimination as they do in cases of vice, brawling, unsanitary conditions and the like after all other reasonable efforts have proved unavailing.

2. Local procedures for imposition of off-limits sanctions in such cases should parallel those used for other off-limits declarations.

It is a fact that contrary to adverse press reports those officials charged with the formulation of Naval policy had, long before the

Kittyhawk and Constellation incidents, moved positively in their efforts to secure for each member of the Navy Equal Opportunity as pertains to fair treatment, assignment and promotion.

On the military side the same applies if we look closely at Admiral Elmo R. Zumwalt's tour of duty as Chief of Naval Operations. Here we find intense civil strife in the broader society, but no lack of action aimed at countering the adverse effects upon the Navy. Elmo R. Zumwalt, as CNO, was a stern, but fair, officer, in a traditionally conservative position. This probably intensified his "newsworthy appeal". Though he was, possibly, the most controversial Admiral to ever head the Sea Services, he did exhibit the daring and courage needed for the times. In moving on the race relations area of Human Goals he tackled a problem that had been carefully avoided, by CNO's, since 1919. Admiral Zumwalt, in a speech at the Naval Postgraduate School in 1974, after his retirement, admitted that some mistakes were made in trying to implement the Human Goals programs. To a question posed by a student "If you had to do it again would you still have proceeded as you did?" Zumwalt replied, "Yes, one must start somewhere. I would, however, do a better job of tooling up (training people and testing program impact) before actually implementing programs." "In issuing Z-Gram #66 in December 1970, all commanding officers were so informed of the CNO's aims and goals--the eradication of discrimination in Navy life. This was followed in August by Z-Gram #14 and in September Z-Gram #24. (Note: Fiscal rather than regular calendar dates probably accounts for 66 appearing before 14 and 24.) In January 1971 he established a Multi-Racial Advisory Council for Race Relations and Minority Affairs to develop and monitor policies and programs." [211]

"Prior to the Kittyhawk/Constellation incidents there were more than two hundred programs aimed at eradicating racism, improving

Navy life for all personnel and upgrading performance."[212] It is pertinent to again point out that most of these programs were formulated and in various stages of implementation long before the adverse incidents of 12 October 1972 (Kittyhawk) and November 1972 (Constellation). It would appear that the press made gross errors by inferring that top policy makers had dragged their feet in attempting to deal with the race-relations problem. Did Line Commanders drag their feet? Were they incapacitated by negative racial feelings? Were they incapacitated by lack of skills in this area of leadership or did they suffer a "functional fixity", and tremble before the massiveness of the problem? These questions and a myriad of others must await analysis by Naval historians.

After the Kittyhawk and Constellation hit the news media in October, it is a matter of record that all ranking Admirals in the Washington area, charged with executing policy, were assembled by Admiral Zumwalt and "raked over the coals." Zumwalt, in so many words, told them that programs did not fail, men did. He told this group that equal meant just that, equal. At this dressing down, the CNO said:

> "The time has come for me to speak very plainly, to speak without the usual cushions of jargon and without the exquisite politeness we sometimes use to mask the impact of our thoughts... The Navy has made unacceptable progress in the equal opportunity area, and the failure was not the programs but the fact that they were not being used. Some of the very things I feared 28 months ago, did, in fact, take place (he had assembled minority officers and wives at Washington months before)... The most destructive influence on the resolution of racial problems is self-deception. It is self-deception to think that you can legislate attitudes, you cannot. It is self-deception to feel a program is a reality, it is not. It is self-deception to think that the Navy is made up of some separate species of man-—that Navy personnel come to us fresh from some other place than our world——that they come untainted by the prejudices of the society that produced

them, they do not. It is self-deception to consider that all issues involving Blacks and Whites are solely racial in motivation, they are not. And, finally, it is self deception to consider the Navy or any other military organization as free wheeling--to each his own way."[213]

After this roasting the message was fired as a NAVOPS message to all subordinate commands and released to the Press. The act of releasing the speech to the press got Zumwalt into trouble with Congress. This reeked of public admonishment of high level staff. Admiral Zumwalt, on learning of the bad press and political ramifications, caused by his remarks, did some clarifying via the immediate release of Z-Gram #117. The House Sub-Committee notes this on page 17669-17670 of its report of Kitty Hawk/Constellation incidents.

This writer was in Mexico at the time the foregoing was in progress and got his information from the New York Times and the English language daily published for The New York Herald Tribune worldwide. He became alarmed when the speech became political. It is a fact of history that no officer has ever survived causing the Navy adverse publicity since the Somers mutiny of 1842. His alarm was exacerbated by the fact that two Presidents had paid with their lives for tampering with America's Black/White thing.

Could a Chief of Naval Operations do so and survive. This writer witnessed, as a Navy Steward, an invisible man in a white coat, the severe racist feelings unleashed by the Roosevelt (1942) and Truman (1948) attempts to integrate the Navy. He also knew what these feelings contributed to their failures to do so.

Mystery deepens when one asks ones self, "Why did Zumwalt proceed in Phase I of the Navy's Human Goals program by choosing the "awareness process" when safer, more polite tools were available?" The reason seems to rest in the text of his speech to the Washington area Flag Officers, especially his emphasis on "self-deception". It would appear that he did not back down. Rather, he ordered all Navy men and officers to receive racial awareness training by the end of fiscal year June 1973. This racial awareness effort was designed for 20 hours and was called UPWARD which means Understanding Personal Worth and Racial Dignity. The feelings surfaced, by UPWARD, reached an intensity that often precluded Navy men even addressing the other components of Phase I, such as the (1) Survey, and (2) Command Action plan formulation.

In the late 1970's, the U.S. Navy's commitment and zeal, as exhibited by Elmo Zumwalt, for using its Human Resources educational and operational assets to promote equal opportunity and racial understanding began to decline. The mandatory requirements for training, surveys for awareness and action planning by officers were gradually relaxed, after Admiral Zumwalt paid the price and left.

Since the early 1980's, the U.S. Navy has started a gradual return to a benign, "businesses as usual" posture. Although publicly espousing a pursuit of diversity, formal programs to achieve diversity are not in effect as yet. One can only hope that the residual effect of the earlier Human Resources training guides the way. The one area of visible change has been in gender equality and the utilization of women since the "Tail Hook" scandal.

In the recent War with Iraq (March 2003), women fighter and bomber pilots, operating from aircraft carriers, were highly visible, as were women in fighting roles in the U.S. Army. A Black female in the Army was taken prisoner by the enemy and rescued in a daring raid, along with her comrades. A Black General (Vincent Brooks) is the face of that war, as the chief spokesperson from the theatre of operations, on daily worldwide television. Just maybe some things have changed positively.

EPILOGUE

This story or history was written to correct one of the many wrongs in the recording of American History. It is a fact that the victors in battle or those in power in peace write the history of past events to support their views of what should have happened versus the cold hard facts. More often than not, the recording glorifies their own while ignoring or denigrating the enemy and those of lesser regard in their own societies. This has been true regarding the Negro in American society and, in particular, the Stewards/Messmen Branch of the U.S. Navy.

As I complete this story, black men and women are fighting and dying in Iraq, a Middle Eastern Nation, for the freedom of its people from the brutal, dictatorial Baathist Party regime led by Saddam Hussein. For three hundred years now, black sailors and soldiers have fought and died for American freedom causes all over the world, while enjoying limited equality and freedom at home.

Although progress has been made in race relations, freedom, equality and justice, the American dream is still a long ways from being realized by its African American citizens. African Americans are still at or near the bottom of the economic ladder. They experience the highest unemployment rate among United States ethnic and religious groups with the exception of immigrant Latinos. Poorly funded and administered schools, and a lack of wealth for college education, limit educational opportunities. Life expectancy and health care is far below that of the majority population. Although only 12% of the population, African Americans experience the highest incarceration rate, representing nearly 50% of the prison population.

Still, blacks fight on in foreign wars and for freedom and equality at home. The story of the Steward/Messmen Branch of the U.S. Navy is indicative of the courage and tenacity of African Americans in the face of bigotry, discrimination and race-based hatred in America. The instinct for survival and the hope for future justice, freedom and prosperity drive us on.

Today, there is a movement among historians of integrity, such as Howard Zinn, Jack D. Foner and Peter Bergman to revise these erroneous and incomplete stories with true accounts of past events. I hope that, this account of the struggles in the U.S. Navy and other Services to overcome the negative racial mores of the greater American society, will add to that truth seeking.

As for my 21 years of active duty service, catching hell as a servant, not allowed to do anything else regardless of intelligence, I can speak with truth and some authority as a functioning player regarding it's positive changes. I was either in the Navy or working on it's programs for forty years (1940-1980). When I entered the U.S. Navy, it was at a time of it's most Racist Personnel Policy. It is a fact of history that for its first 100 years, the enlisted men's division of the U.S. Navy was the most liberal of all of the U.S. Armed Forces.

It's Officer Corp, however, was possibly the most racist from its birth up to 1944. It had reduced Negro men to a "servants role" by its creation of the Messmen Branch in 1893, placing Negroes on the bottom of its hierarchical ladder, forcing them into a servants role, regardless of individual intelligence, skill or ability. This was their condition from 1893 until 1942. They even barred Negroes, from enlistment as servants, in 1919, for a period of 13 years. The Navy kept this demeaning, humiliating branch in place for a period of 81 years!

The Vietnam War brought the final demise of this humiliating "minorities only" branch. That war also caused the Navy to use blacks in all capacities, not just as Base Companies and labor battalions. It made the recruitment of blacks as officers and blacks as midshipmen acceptable at the Academy at Annapolis. And, finally, it forced the creation of black Admirals. I, a former Messboy, had the pleasure of entertaining three Black Admirals for dinner at my home…Rear Admirals Robert Toney, Walter Davis and Paul Reason, who later became commander in Chief of the Atlantic Fleet! Vietnam forced all of the Armed Services to come to grips with Racism as a countervailing factor in the retardation of America becoming a true Democracy. Many ask, "Was Vietnam worth it?" I say, yes, if measured via progress of Race-Relations.

As I was retiring in 1980, the Human Resources and Race Relations training programs were under assault by the service technocrats. An effort was underway to kill these education programs. Perhaps the long Vietnam War forced those education efforts to last long enough, to become a part of the Military culture of Enlisted men and Admirals leading the U.S. Navy today. Proof might lie in the fact that, despite two Gulf Wars and long stints at sea, no racial incidents have surfaced to damage the U.S. Navy's image.

Perhaps the most positive proof that the U.S. Navy and the U.S. Marine Corps' Human Resources Management and Race Relation Programs have been well done, over a long enough period to have become "positively institutionalized", rests on the fact that, in recent history, neither service has suffered severe image damage, incident to racial and sexist incidents. Both the Army Academy, West Point, and the Air Force unit in Colorado, have suffered incidents that caused their services to be dragged through the muck of the news media. The Air Force was recently hit over sexism. It was revealed that female cadets were badly treated. Several officers suffered irreparable career damage and a General Officer was relieved of command. The Army seems to have learned a hard lesson. So far, in its two latest mobilizations, neither the ugly head of racism or sexism has reared it's morale destroying presence. It's hoped that the U.S. Navy will remain so lucky or blessed.

The presence of Black Messmen did more to keep the heat on the U.S. Navy than any other factor in American life. Their very presence denied the Navy the ability to claim that its policies were not racist. The legacy of this group of officer's servants is one that any people should be proud of. Looking back, I can be doubly proud, as I know better than most historians and scholars, how far this group climbed. For example, during the twenty-one years of service, as an officer's servant, I can remember when, for mere existence, Stewards, Cooks, Mess Boys/Mess Attendants or today's Stewards Mates—we had many names—had to fight the Germans and the Japanese at sea, as well as Rednecks on the docks. Often, our fellow Blacks, who in competition for dances with the local damsels, told girls that we were nothing but "flunkies and boot licking Uncle Toms who shined Naval Officers' shoes." Luckily for us, many Stewards, Cooks and Mess Attendants were on the Ship and Naval Station's boxing teams. Many a group of Redneck type received boxing lessons that they never forgot, for thinking that, since we were usually outnumbered, they could take Alabama type liberties with us. Older Rednecks knew better. They also knew that many of us carried candy-striped, "East Dallas Specials" (switchblades), and straight razors as equalizers. Their advice to newly recruited Rednecks was, 'You had better leave them niggers alone!' It was never that we were gallant but because "They don't fight fair." A "fair fight", for those Rednecks, was one where Mess Boys were outnumbered, ten to one. We were very familiar with Black Mess Boys being beaten-up on the docks, by drunk Rednecks, ex-Ku Klux Klansmen. But, in most instances, these bullies ran into the Mess Boys' " hollow square" and got a "boxing lesson". I need to explain: We would form a square, place two or three boxers on each end and form lines on both sides of six or seven men, back-to-back, so that we couldn't be separated.

I've seen, on several occasions, a "square" with groups of Rednecks, with black eyes, broken noses and cracked jaws, sitting or lying on the ground around the entire square. Naturally, when the Shore Patrol or the Marine Guards came, if they were in overwhelming force, the men in the square were arrested. If they arrived in not overwhelming force, we were told simply to "clear the dock".

So, over the years, this group of men, often ill-educated, Southern Negroes (Southern Negroes being a requirement until WWII), took the heat, ran the race and kept the faith that there would be a better way.

I read the phrase, "And first shall be last and last shall be first" so long ago, I have forgotten the source, however, this is coming to pass, for the Cooks, Stewards and Stewards Mates of the U.S. Navy. Those Stewards who, by their steadfastness, stubbornness, valor and gallantry in action, probably, are responsible for today's Black Admirals. For example:

1. The only medals for gallantry in action earned by Blacks, in World War II, were by Cooks, Stewards and Mess Attendants.

2. The only ships named for Black men in U.S. Naval history— there are three—are named for Cooks, Stewards or Mess Attendants.

The first ship was named for Dorrie Miller, a Black Mess Attendant aboard the U.S.S. West Virginia at Pearl Harbor. Miller, who was untrained in ordinance, took over a 50 caliber machine gun and shot-down Japanese airplanes. How many remains is dispute.

Miller received the Navy Cross.

The second ship was named for Leonard Roy Harmon, a Mess Attendant aboard the U.S.S. San Francisco at Guadalcanal, in 1943. Harmon was top side on the San Francisco when he observed a major caliber shell. It was glowing and headed into the Frisco. The White Mate with him froze. Harmon had the chance to enter the hatch and save his own life. Instead, he took the split second remaining and shoved his friend down the hatch. He died as a result of his actions. He received the Navy Cross. The U.S.S. Harmon is named for him.

Very recently a third ship was named for an officer's Cook, William Pinckney, who was decorated for uncommon valor, in action aboard the U.S.S. Enterprise in the British Solomon Islands, during the battle of Santa Cruz Island.

There you have my account of, Black Men and Blue Water.

ENDNOTES

1. Bryant, Samuel W. The Sea and the States: Maritime History of the American People, New York, 1947, P. 40
2. Ibid., P. 31
3. Ibid., P. 31
4. Ibid., P. 31
5. Stivers, Reuben E. Privateers and Volunteers: The Men & Women of our Reserve Naval Forces: 1766-1866, Annapolis Md. 1973, Naval Institute Press, P.3
6. Ibid., P.3
7. Ibid., P.4
8. Ibid., P.4-5
9. Stamp, Kenneth M., The Peculiar Institution, New York, 1956, P.25. (Published under "Vintage Books" by Alfred A. Knopf, Inc. & Random House, Inc.
10. Bryant, Samuel W. , The Sea and the States, New York, 1947, P.21
11. Ibid., P.21
12. Ibid., P.21
13. Ibid., P.21
14. Ibid., P.50
15. Jordan, Winthrop, White Over Black: American Attitudes Toward the Negro, 1550-1812, 1968, Univ. of North Carolina Press, P. 23,32,47 & 53
16. Ibid., P. 53
17. Bryant, Samuel W., The Sea and the States, New York, 1947, P. 10-11
18. Ibid., P. 11
19. Myrdal, Gunnar, An American Dilemma

20 Aptheker, Herbert, <u>A Documentary History of the Negro People in the United States,</u> New York 6th Edition), 1968, Citadel Press (see preface)

21 Ibid.,

22 Franklin, J. H., From Slavery to Freedom: A History of Negro Americans, New York, 1956 (Revised 1967) see Vantage Books Edition 1969, P. 128. Also see Alfred Knopf and Random House Editions.

23 Ibid., (Aptheker, P. 1 of the Introduction) of feudalism from the European Mainland, the concept of "indenture" was easily grasped

24 Franklin, J. H., <u>From Slavery to Freedom</u> (See "Servitude and Slavery In the Southern Colonies") P.71

25 Crane, jay David and Elaine, <u>The Black Soldier: From the American Revolution to Vietnam</u>, William Morrow & Co., 1971, New York, Introduction P. 1

27 Stivers, Reuben E., <u>Privateers and Volunteers/The Men and Women of the Reserve Forces: 1766 to 1866</u>, Annapolis, Maryland (Naval Institute Press) 1975, P.30

28 Ibid., P. 30

29 Bergman, Peter M. & Mort, N, <u>The Chronological History of the Negro In America</u>, New York, Evanston & London, 1968, Harper & Row Pubs. P. 51

30 Ibid. P.50

31 Bennett, Lerone, <u>Before The Mayflower</u>, P.66

32 Ibid. Bergman, P. 50

33 Ibid., Bergman, P.51

34 Ibid., Franklin, John H., <u>From Slavery to Freedom: A History of Negro Americans</u>, New York, 1967, Alfred A. Knopf, PP.134-139

35 Ibid., Stivers, Elmo, P.31

36 Ibid., P. 31

37 Harrod, Frederick S., <u>The Development of the Modern Enlisted Force (1899-1940),</u> Naval Institute Proceedings, Sept.1979, Annapolis, Maryland P.47

38 Sweetman, Jack, <u>American Naval History: An Illustrated Naval Chronology, US Navy & Marine Corps, 1775 to the Present</u>, 1984, Naval Institute, Annapolis, Maryland, P. 15

39   Ibid., P 15

40   Bryant, Samuel W., The Sea and the States, New York, 1947, Thomas Y. Crowell Co., New York, P.105

41   Morrison, Samuel E. & Commager, Henry S., P. 425

42   Bryant, Samuel W., P. 108

43   Ibid., P. 108

44   Knox, Dudley W., A History of The United States Navy   P. 45

45   Harrod, Frederick S., Naval Institute Proceeding, Sept.1979, Annapolis, Maryland P. 47

46   Southard, Samuel, Naval Institute Proceeding, Sept.1979, Annapolis, Maryland P. 47

47   Ibid., P. 47

48   Sweetman, Jack, American Naval History, P. 25

49   Ibid., P.28

50   Ibid., Knox, Dudley W., A History of the United States, 1936, Van Rees Press, 1936, Page 81.

51   Ibid., P. 81-82

52   Ibid., Bergman, P.96

53   Ibid., Bergman, P. 80

54   Ibid., Bergman, P. 80

55   Foner, Jack D, Blacks in the Military: A New Perspective, New York, 1974, Praeger Pubs. Inc., P. 20

56   Ibid., P. 20

57   Schlesinger, Arthur M., The Almanac of American History, New York, 1983, G. P. Putnam & Sons, P. 195

58   Ibid., P. 195

59   Ibid., P. 193

60   Franklin, John H., From Slavery to Freedom: A History of Negro Americans, New York, 1967, Alfred, A. Knopf, Pubs., P. 169

61   Ibid., P.169

62   Ibid., P. 169

63   Foner, Jack D., Blacks in the Military: A New Perspective, New York, 1974, Praeger Pub. Inc., P.16

64   Ibid., Foner, Jack, P. 16

65   Franklin, John Hope, From Slavery to Freedom: A History of Negro Americans (3rd Ed.), Alfred A. Knopf; New York, P. 171

66   Ibid., P. 171

67 Franklin, John Hope, P. 172
68 Foner, Jack D., <u>Blacks in the Military in American History</u>, New York, 1974. Praeger Pubs., Inc. P.28-29
69 Ibid., Foner, P.29-30
70 Ibid., P. 30
71 Foner, Jack D., <u>Blacks in the Military: A New Perspective</u>, New York, 1974, Praeger Pub. Inc. P. 27
72 Schlesinger, Arthur M., <u>The Almanac of American History</u>, New York, 1983, Bison Brooks, G. P. Putnam & Sons, P. 273
73 Ibid., P. 275
74 Franklin, John Hope, <u>From Slavery to Freedom: A History of Negro Americans</u> (3rd Ed.) Alfred A. Knopf, New York, P. 271
75 Ibid., (Franklin), P.269
76 Harrod, Frederick S., <u>Manning the New Navy: The Development of the Modern Enlisted Force</u>, U.S. Naval Institute Proceedings, Sept., 1979, Annapolis, Maryland, P. 269
77 Ibid., Bennett, Lerone, <u>Before the Mayflower</u>, P. 374
78 Ibid., Schlessinger, P. 287
79 Ibid., Bennett, P.373-374
80 Ibid., Bergman, P. 236-237
81 Stivers, Reuben Elmo, <u>Privateers and Volunteers: The Men and Women of the Reserve Forces</u>, Annapolis, Md., 1975, Naval Institute, P. 221
82 Ibid., Stivers, Reuben Elmo, P.233
83 Ibid., P.233
84 Ibid., P. 350
85 Bryant, Samuel W., <u>The Sea and the States: A Maritime History of the American</u>
86 Ibid., Foner P. 39
87 Ibid., P. 45
88 McPherson, James, M., The Negroes Civil War, New York, 1967, Vintage Books, P. 153-154
89 Ibid., Bryant, S.W., P. 299
90 Ibid., Stivers, P. 394
91 Ibid., Bergman, P. 245-246
92 Ibid., Franklin, P. 305

93 Shapiro, Herbert, <u>White Violence and Black Response: From Reconstruction to Montgomery.</u>, Univ. of Mass. Press, 1988 P.7

94 Ibid., Shapiro, P.7

95 Ibid., Shapiro, P. 7

96 Ibid., P. 7

97 Smith, Carney, <u>Black Firsts: 2000 Years of Extraordinary Achievement</u>, Detroit MI., 1994, Invisible Ink Press, (flyleaf)

98 Ibid., Bergman, P.279-280

99 Ibid., Franklin, P.330

100 Ibid., Franklin, P.330-331

101 Ibid., Bergman, Peter M., P. 282

102 Bergman, Peter M., <u>The Chronological History of the Negro in America</u>, New York, 1969, Harper and Row Pubs., P. 241

103 Harrod, Frederick S<u>., Manning the New Navy: The Development of the Modern Enlisted Force</u>, U.S. Naval Institute Proceedings, Sept., 1979, Annapolis, Maryland, P.48

104 Ibid., P. 48

105 Ibid., Harrod, P. 48

106 Bergman, Peter M., <u>The Chronological History of the Negro in America</u>, P. 282,

107 Newby, I.A. The Development of Segregationist Thought, Homewood Ill./Nobelton Ontario, 1968, P.21

108 Newby, I.A., <u>The Development of Segregationist Thought</u>, Homewood, Ill./Nobelton Ontario, 1968, P. 21

109 Ibid., P. 21

110 Bean, Robert Bennett

111 Newby, I. A<u>., The Development of Segregationist Thought</u>, Homewood Ill./Nobelton Ontario, 1968, P.46

112 Montague, Ashley, <u>The Concept of Race</u>, New York, 1964, The Free Press, P.93

113 Ibid., Montague, P. 93

114 Ginzburg, Ralph, 100 Years of Lynching, New York, 1962, Lancer Books, (see back cover)

115 Ibid., Ginzburg, P.9

116 Ibid., P. 124

117 Ibid., P.114

118 Ibid., P. 21

[119] Ibid., Foner, P.87
[120] Foner, Jack 0., <u>Blacks and The Military in American History: A New Perspective</u>, New York, 1974, Praeger Publishers, Inc., p. 104.
[121] Ibid., P. 104
[122] Ibid., p.105.
[123] Maskow, Arthur, I., <u>From Race Riot to Sit—In: 1919 and the 1960's</u>, Garden ', New York, Double Day and Co., Inc., 1966, p. 22
[124] Ibid., P. 23
[125] Foner, Jack 0., Blacks and the Military in American History: A New Perspective, Praeger Pubs., New York, 1974, p. 107.
[126] Ibid., P. 107
[127] Ibid., P. 28
[128] Davis, John P., The American Negro Reference Book, Englewood Cliffs, N.J., 1966 Prentice Hall, Inc. P. 597-598.
[129] Ibid., P. 599.
[130] Foner, Jack D., <u>Blacks and The Military in American History</u>, P. 129
[131] Foner, Jack D., <u>Blacks and the Military in American History: A New Perspective</u>, New York, 1974, Praeger Publishers, Inc. P. 123
[132] <u>The American Negro Reference Book</u>, 1966 , Prentice Hall, Inc. P. 621-622
[133] Foner, Jack D., <u>Blacks and Military In American History</u>, New York-Washington, Praeger Pubs., P.81
[134] Ibid., P. 81
[135] Franklin, John Hope, From Slavery to Freedom, New York, 1967, Alfred A. Knopf, P. P. 423
[136] Franklin, John Hope, From Slavery to Freedom, New York, 1967, Alfred A. Knopf, P. 422
[137] Ibid., P.423
[138] Blatcher, Charles III, <u>Of Thee I Sing: Minority Military History</u>, National Minority Military History Museum Foundation, P.O. Box 14188, Oakland, CA 94614
[139] Foner, Jack D., Blacks in the Military in American History, New York, Washington, D.D., Praeger Pubs., Inc. 1974, P. 88

140 Bennett, Lerone, Jr., <u>Before the Mayflower</u>, Johnson Publishing Co., 1962, (Penguin Books, 1962, Baltimore, Maryland), P. 386
141 Bennett, Lerone, Jr., <u>Before the Mayflower</u>, Baltimore, Maryland, 1966, Penguin Books, P. 304-305
142 Ibid., Bennett, P.306
143 Bennett, Lerone, Jr., <u>Before the Mayflower</u>, P. 389
144 Foner, Jack, D., P. 114
145 Ibid., Foner, P.115
146 Ibid., Foner, P. 115
147 Ibid., Foner, P. 108
148 Ibid., Foner, P. 108
149 Ibid., Franklin, P.457
150 Ibid., Foner, P. 111
151 Ibid., Foner, P. 111
152 Ibid., Foner, P. 112
153 Ibid., Foner, P. 116
154 Ibid., Foner, P. 117
155 Ibid., Franklin, P.458
156 Ibid., Franklin, P.459
157 Foner, Jack, D., <u>Blacks and the Military in American History</u>, Praeger Publishers, Inc., P.126
158 Ibid., Franklin, John Hope, P. 460
159 Smyth, Mabel M., <u>The Black American Reference Book</u>, Englewood Cliffs, NJ, 1976, Prentice Hall, Inc. P.895
160 Bennett, Lerone,Jr., <u>Before the Mayflower</u>, P. 304
161 Ibid., Bergman, P. 490
162 Ibid., Bergman. P. 489
163 Ibid., Bergman, P. 490
164 Ibid., Bennett, P.305-306
165 Ibid., Bennett, P.305-306
166 Ibid., Knox (Negro Ref. Bk.) P. 897
167 Ibid., Franklin, P.587
168 Ibid., Franklin, P. 535
169 Ibid., Bergman, P. 309
170 Foner, Jack D., Blacks and the Military in American History, New York, 1974, Praeger Publishers, P. 135

171 Sweetman, Jack, American Naval History: An Illustrated Chronology of U.S. Naval and Marine Corps 1775-Present, Annapolis, Maryland, 1984, U.S. Naval Institute, P.172

172 Alden, C.S., Ph.D., and Wescott, A., Ph.D., The United States Navy: A History, New York, 1943, J.B. Lippincott Company, P. 428.

173 Cant, G., The American Navy in the Pacific. This book is out of print and could not be found, hence the quote may not be exact and is dependant upon the memory of this author, resultant to Can't vivid description.

174 Ibid., Miller, N., P. 328

175 Ibid., Miller, N., P. 328

176 Ibid., Alden and Wescott, The United States Navy A History , P.430

177 The Chronological History of the Negro In America, P. 501-502

178 Smyth, Mabel M., The Black American Reference Book, Englewood Cliffs, New Jersey, 19976 Prentice Hall, Inc. P. 896

179 Streb, Richard W., Life and Death Aboard the U.S.S. Essex, 1999, Dorrance Publishing Co., P.7

180 Franklin, John Hope, From Slavery to Freedom, Random House, New York, 1969, P.529

181 Stillman, Richard J., Integration of the Negro in the U.S. armed Forces, Fredrick A. Praeger, Pub., New York, 1968, P. 28

182 Franklin, J.H., From Slavery to Freedom, Vintage Books (Random House), New York, 1967, P.590-591.

183 Stillman, Richard J., Integration of the Negro in the U.S. Armed Forces, Frederick A. Praeger, Pub., New York, 1958, p.30.

184 Ibid., p. 30.

185 Cant, Gilbert, America's Navy in WWII, John Day Company, New York, 1943, P.369. (This is the first acknowledgement of the revised policy after Pearl Harbor.)

186 Ibid., p. 369

187 Ibid., Cant, Gilbert p.62-63 (written under severe censorship due to war needs). Explanation in parenthesis by author is inserted for clarity.

188 Davis, John P., The Negro Reference Book, Prentice Hall, Inc., Englewood Cliffs, New Jersey, 1967, P. 632-634.

189 Black, C., <u>Remember Pearl Harbor</u>, Harper Bros. Pub., New York, 1942, P. 277-300 (Army and Marine Corps Honor Rolls may also be found here.) (See pp. 85-86 for more complete account of Miller during attack on the IJSS West Virginia.)

190 Bergman, Peter M., <u>The Chronological History of the Negro in America</u>: New York, 1969, P. 498; Harper and Row Publishers.

191 Ibid., P.504

192 Wright, Kai, <u>Soldiers of Freedom: An Illustrated History of African Americans in the Armed Forces</u>, New York, 2002; Black Dog and Leventhal Pubs., Inc., P. 160

193 Franklin, John Hope, <u>From Slavery to Freedom: History of Negro Americans</u>, New York, 1967, Alfred A. Knopf, P. 588

194 Bergman, Ibid., p. 508

195 (See the preface to the U.S. Navy Department Publication titled, <u>A Guide To The Command of Negro Personnel</u> , Published in 1944.

196 Ibid., (A Guide to the Command of Negro Personnel)

197 Stillman, Richard J., <u>Integration of the Negro in the U.S. Armed Forces</u>, Frederick A. Praeger, Pub. New York, 1968 P. 30

198 Ibid., Smyth, p. 898 <u>The Black American Reference Book</u>

199 Ibid., Smyth, p. 899 <u>The Black American Reference Book</u>

200 Ibid., Bergman p. 510

201 Ibid., p. 525

202 Smyth, Mabel M., <u>Black American Reference Book</u>, 1976, Prentice-Hall, Inc. Englewood Cliffs, NJ, p.900

203 Smythe, Mabel M., <u>The Black American Reference Book</u>, 1976, Prentice-Hall, Inc. Englewood Cliffs, NJ, p.900

204 Foner, Jack D., The Negro and the Military in American History, New York, 1974, Praeger Publishers, Inc., P.204-205

205 Ibid., p.206

206 Foner P.206

207 Foner P.213

208 Ibid., p. 213

209 Foner, <u>Blacks and the Military in American History</u> p. 213

210 Wright, Kai, <u>Soldiers of Freedom</u>, p. 237

211 See NAVOP-R31221/040 July 72 (Paragraph 3)

[212] See NAVAOP-R101704Z/19Z Nov. 72 ZEO ZOC (underlining for emphasis by author)

[213] For full text of this speech, see message designate R-101704Z-19Z Nov. 72-ZEO-ZOC.

Printed in the United States
146994LV00004B/4/P